S. G. MACLEAN

The Bookseller of Inverness

QUERCUS

First published in Great Britain in 2022 by Quercus
This paperback edition published in 2023 by

QUERCUS

Quercus Editions Ltd
Carmelite House
50 Victoria Embankment
London EC4Y 0DZ

An Hachette UK company

A CIP catalogue record for this book is available
from the British Library

PB ISBN 978 1 52941 421 9
EB ISBN 978 1 52941 419 6

10 9 8 7 6 5

Typeset by CC Book Production
Printed and bound in Great Britain by Clays Ltd, Elcograf S.p.A.

Papers used by Quercus are from well-managed forests and other responsible sources.

Praise for *The Bookseller of Inverness*

'Delivers everything you could possibly want from a historical crime novel, and then gives you a bit more . . . Her best yet'
Andrew Taylor

'This tender, well-researched novel is an excellent work of historical fiction . . . with the imagined characters and situations seamlessly stitched into recorded reality'   *Literary Review*

'A twisting, absorbing plot'   *Sunday Times*

'Well-written and well-plotted, MacLean is gifted with a writing style that blends literary storytelling with a fast-paced mystery'
Scottish Field

'A brilliant tapestry of a novel . . . an intensely character-driven plot of betrayal, revenge, guilt and loss . . . the world it conjures up leaps off the page with a vivid authenticity'   *Historia*

'This is an expertly plotted crime thriller built around the complexities of Jacobite histories: Walter Scott meets tartan noir'
The Times

'A great read, with tragedy, betrayal, heroism and all the usual complications of family, magnified by war, espionage and the ever-present threat of arrest, and execution'   *Living Edge*

'Everything you could ask for from a historical thriller – gripping, immersive and filled with intriguing characters. S. G. MacLean can make any period sing with life'   **Antonia Hodgson**

'An intricately wrought, compulsively page-turning tale . . . so perfectly conjured and so convincing that you can smell the heather and taste the blood'   **Craig Russell**

Shona (S. G.) MacLean has a PhD in history from Aberdeen University, specializing in sixteenth- and seventeenth-century Scottish history. She has written four highly acclaimed historical thrillers set in Scotland, *The Redemption of Alexander Seaton* (shortlisted for the CWA Historical Dagger), *A Game of Sorrows*, *Crucible of Secrets* and *The Devil's Recruit*, and a series of historical thrillers set in Oliver Cromwell's London. The first and third books in the series, *The Seeker* and *Destroying Angel*, have won the CWA Historical Dagger and the second and fourth, *The Black Friar* and *The Bear Pit*, were longlisted for the same award. S. G. MacLean is married with four children and lives in Conon Bridge, Scotland.

To Ailie and Steven

Introductory Note

The Battle of Culloden, which took place on 16 April, 1746 on Drummossie Moor near Inverness, brought to an end the last great Jacobite rising in support of the House of Stuart. Over six decades, a series of serious attempts had been made by their supporters to restore to the Stuarts, the throne lost to them by the flight of James II in 1688. Taking their name from James – *Jacobus* – supporters of the House of Stuart became known as Jacobites.

While there remains a perception that Jacobitism was a Highland phenomenon, Jacobites hailed from all over Britain and Ireland, and Highland clans were, in fact, active on both sides from the early battles of the 'Glorious Revolution', and throughout various false starts and risings (1708, 1715, 1719, 1745) until the aftermath of Culloden itself. Some clans stayed on the same side throughout – the Argyll Campbells, for instance, were the greatest supporters of the Whig/Hanoverian lines, in which they were joined by the Mackays and, in the two major risings of the '15 and the '45, by the Munros, whereas others – the Farquharsons,

MacPhersons, MacLeans, Camerons and Lochaber Mac-Donalds, amongst others, were consistently Jacobite. Other clans – most notoriously the Frasers under Lord Lovat, 'The Old Fox', changed allegiances, and some, such as the Grants, the MacLeods, and the Mackintoshes, were divided.

Although the Jacobite cause drew support from all over the British Isles, a series of key facts underline its strong association with Scotland and the Highland clans. Firstly, several leading clan figures were forced into exile at each unsuccessful attempt of the Stuarts to regain their throne. However, whilst a chief might have been away in Italy, France, Germany or the Low Countries, his power base – including financial support and a ready supply of trained fighting men – in the geographic region dominated by his clan remained available to be called up by him. For this reason, the risings tended to start in the Highlands, and also to garner greater active support there than they did further south. Secondly, a distinct 'Scottish' dimension was added following the Treaty of Union of 1707, when some leading Scots felt they had not benefitted from the Union as they had expected to, and consequently adopted the Jacobite cause. Finally, whilst individuals from all over Britain and Ireland suffered for their support of the Stuarts, it was the Highlands that paid the heaviest price. The determination of the Duke of Cumberland after the Battle of Culloden to break the clans so that they could never again rise to threaten his family's hold on the British throne manifested in a scorched-earth policy in the summer of

1746, and a hunting down of Jacobites by military parties led by men so consumed with the desire for revenge as to have been described by one leading historian as 'psychotic'. The atrocities perpetrated on men, women and children by government troops following the Battle of Culloden have filled many pages and resulted in Cumberland's nickname of 'The Butcher'. But Cumberland's squads never caught the prey they were most assiduously hunting – Charles Edward Stuart, the Bonnie Prince Charlie of legend, evaded them for five months as he skulked in the west Highlands and Hebrides before escaping by ship to France.

Amongst measures to break the clans and prevent future risings, the wearing of tartan and the playing of bagpipes were proscribed, Highlanders were forbidden to carry weapons, a commission was set up to value and sell off the estates forfeited by the leading Jacobite chiefs and a programme of road building and fortification was intensified, the map-making work of the latter forming the basis of the Ordnance Survey. The heritable jurisdictions of the chiefs were abolished.

In the aftermath of the '45 rising, as had happened after the '15, the provisions of the Treaty of Union were subverted to allow trial in England for acts committed in Scotland, and large numbers of prisoners were shipped south under dreadful conditions to stand trial where they were less likely to provoke riots. Many died a traitor's terrible death. Many more, women and young boys as well as men, were transported to the Caribbean and North America to be sold into indentured servitude from which most never returned, following routes that had already begun to be traced, and setting a pattern for the full involvement of Highlanders and the Highlands in the Caribbean trade and the British Empire.

In the early years following Culloden, though, Jacobites continued to hope and to plan, as their charismatic, mercurial, flawed prince travelled incognito through Europe, trying to drum up support for just one more throw of the dice, while his Hanoverian enemies continued to pour huge resources into stopping him.

Main Character List

JACOBITES

Iain MacGillivray	Bookseller of Inverness
Hector MacGillivray	Iain's father
Mairi Farquharson	Iain's grandmother
Aeneas Farquharson	Mairi's kinsman and servant
Catriona Lamont, Janet Grant, Eilidh Cameron	The Grandes Dames. Mairi's lifelong friends
Donald Mòr	Bookbinder
Richard Dempster	Bookseller's Assistant
Bailie John Steuart	Merchant

HANOVERIANS

Major Philip Thornlie	Engineer with the Military Survey
Captain Edward Dunne	British Army officer
James Munro	Sheriff-Depute of Ross
Major Calum Mackay	British Army officer

Gavin Bremner	Doorkeeper at Castle Leod
Mrs Elizabeth Rose	of local landed gentry
Julia Rose	Elizabeth's daughter

OTHER INHABITANTS OF INVERNESS

Ishbel MacLeod	Confectioner
Tormod MacLeod	Ishbel's son
Barbara Sinclair	Milliner
Hugh Sinclair	Barbara's father
Arch MacPhee	Town Constable

Prologue

Mairi Farquharson handed her friend a cup of warmed brandy. 'You must have courage, Janet. Only a little longer and all will be well.'

But Janet Grant's hands were shaking so that she could hardly take hold of the cup, never mind raise it to her lips. Her face was white as a winding sheet and her eyes huge with terror. 'But what if I cannot do it, Mairi?' She indicated her swollen stomach, the miraculous pregnancy after so many that had been lost. 'What if I should give myself away and fail him? What if Colin should never see his child?'

Mairi took back the cup, placed it on the sideboard and took hold of Janet's hands in hers.

'Listen, if you do not do this, he will never see the child anyway.' Janet's husband faced trial for his part in the late, failed Jacobite rising under the Earl of Mar. If he was not got out of the Tower tonight, he would face a traitor's dreadful death. Mairi should not be having to spell this out to her friend. 'There will *be* no mercy, there will *be* no eleventh-hour reprieve. We must do as we planned, Janet, and pray to God that Colin has greater courage than you have.'

The barb hit home. Janet straightened herself, a little rankled. 'If Colin had not courage, I would have no cause to carry out the plan.' Janet was to smuggle skeleton keys and a bottle of good brandy to her husband in the gaol, in the hopes that he would get his gaoler drunk enough that the fellow might not see him use them.

'No,' said Mairi, 'you would not. Do this thing, Janet, and in a few hours we will all be on a boat bound for France, and the mob on Tower Hill disappointed of their entertainment.'

Janet's resolve seemed to recover a little. 'And you will be at the place you told me of?'

'We will be exactly there,' said Mairi, 'and then we need never see this benighted town again, until the king's return.'

After Janet had left, the skeleton keys secreted under her stays and the bottle of brandy in her basket, Mairi moved quickly. She pulled from under the straw mattress the bundle of brown woollen clothing she had picked up several weeks before and hurriedly removed her own. She did not regret the fine French silk gown or good Flemish lace petticoat she must set aside in place of a housemaid's plain attire. She had grown up on the Braes of Glenlivet in simpler dress than

even a London housemaid and had thought herself none
the worse of it, until one day Neil Farquharson's eye had
fallen on her, and soon after raised her to a different life.
Her silk-braided kid leather shoes she parted with without
hardship for a pair of modest workaday items. Then she
brushed loose her hair and tousled it. 'It was these tresses
of yours that bewitched me,' Neil would sometimes say,
turning his hand softly in the smooth auburn folds. 'You're
a vain minx,' he would laugh when he found her sitting at
her glass, before encircling her waist in his arm and pulling
her round to him. An hour, less, and she would have those
arms around her again.

She was sorry to have to tie a handkerchief over her hair,
and set a hat atop it, but for tonight she must pass for an
Englishwoman. She put away the brush and bundled her
own clothes under the thin bedcover in what might amount
to her own recumbent shape. Then she threw some soot
onto the dying fire and snuffed out the one candle in this
small room at the top of a London draper's house. They
had lodged here, she and Janet, since they had followed
their captured husbands south. The whole household was
at this moment at its family worship. Mairi blessed the
Providence that had put her in a Puritan house and went
swiftly through the kitchen and out at the back door into
a city swarming with soldiers.

It was a murky night, a disgusting smog rising from
the river to cloak the town. She was glad of it. To think
she had thought Inverness dirty when first she had seen it!

Inverness, a town of barely four streets and a handful of wynds and closes. This London of theirs, that King James had so set his heart on, was a lowering monster, a many-toothed beast waiting to consume the unwary.

They had been terrified of this town, herself and Janet, when first they had disembarked at Tilbury. They had found friends though, persons of the lower orders that they knew they could trust. The merchant, Bailie John Steuart in Inverness, was in constant correspondence with their people in London and the continent. He had found an acquaintance who had got them in at the draper's and arranged for a boy to guide them to those parts of town where they needed to be: Newgate, the Marshalsea, Tower Hill. Through the dirt and noise of the city they had traipsed after their guide, and soon found themselves in the train of other women, other Jacobite wives fearful they would soon be made widows by the Elector of Hanover's British government.

Mairi had been a child, seven years old, when their clan had rallied to Dundee's call in 1689 in the cause of the late King James. She remembered watching the men marching away from the Braes of Glenlivet to their wasted triumph at Killiekrankie. And then, twenty-six years later, a married woman with children of her own, she had seen her own husband, a captain on horseback, ride away from Braemar with their son William, in the cause of another King James. It had not entered her head nor Neil's either that they should not go out for the king. If they should die on a London

4

scaffold, so be it; better that than live the rest of their lives in shame and disgrace.

It had been Neil and William's good fortune to be consigned to Newgate with others of Clan Chattan, that great confederation of MacGillivrays, Mackintoshes, Farquharsons, MacPhersons and others. Neil had told her, when she'd been allowed in to visit, that it was a shameful thing for so many Highland men to be kept prisoner by such specimens as guarded them at Newgate, and that those fellows would never have lasted half a day out on the hills. If it hadn't been for the manacles that held them, the Highlanders would have taught their gaolers a swift lesson.

'Then do so,' Mairi had said.

'What, how?'

'They will take off your manacles before you go to trial. I have heard it. That will be the moment.'

And that was exactly how it had happened. The guards, not understanding that the privations of their gaol were as nothing to what their prisoners had been inured to from birth, let off their manacles on the night before they were to go to trial. It was in the exercise yard, it being thought desirable that the half-starved men might have some practice in walking and standing upright before they must stand at the bar and hear their fate pronounced. They thought there was nothing to fear from these miserable captives.

There was no piper, but one of the youngest lads had given the battle cry, '*Creag Dubh Chlann Chatain!*' – the Black Rock of Clan Chattan. Before the guards had had the first idea of what was happening, they had been over-whelmed, and fourteen Highland savages, gentlemen every one of them, had disappeared into the London night.

A message had been got to Mairi at her lodging of where Neil, their son William and two others were hiding out, the fourteen having gone their different ways in their confused flight through the unfamiliar city. Mairi had already paid handsomely for a boatman to take them down the river, to meet with the sloop that would take them to France. All that remained was for Janet to do her part, that Colin Grant might also escape that night, because Neil had made it plain that he would not go without him.

From her lodging at the top of Do Little Lane, Mairi went directly towards the river, pausing to glance down Knight Rider Street before crossing to St Bennet's Hill. Her heart was in her mouth as she went along Thames Street, before turning down to Broken Wharf, all the while her hand firmly gripping the small knife she had secreted in her apron. She ignored the lewd calls of shore-porters and watermen as she hurried past, and only just managed not to scream as a rat ran over her foot. There had been no rats in Glenlivet, and she had never yet learned to abide the creatures that so teemed in the streets and about the walls of Inverness, but she would pick up the first one she saw and kiss it full on the face should they get back there safe.

The streets were in darkness, but she would not trust herself even to a link-boy to light her way tonight. Mairi's eyes were good and her sense of direction sure, and it was

not long before she felt herself enveloped by the damp air
rising from the river. She kept to the darkness of the walls
towards the narrow alleyway and the old rope store where
Neil and the others had taken shelter. She was about to
round the top of the alleyway when a figure emerged from
it, almost colliding with her.

Mairi's small knife, her *sgian-dubh*, was out and an inch
from the man's breast when her wrist was caught in a firm
grip. 'Not tonight, Mistress Farquharson, for the love of
God. I would live a while yet.'

Her terror subsided. 'Hector MacGillivray! It's your good
fortune I didn't kill you.'

The man loosened his grip and she lowered her knife.
'What are you doing walking abroad?' she said. 'It's not
time yet. Janet Grant has not long gone to the Tower.'

'I know,' he said. 'But the boatman swears he will only
carry six, as he claims is agreed and paid for, and Colin
Grant and his wife make seven.'

'He lies in his teeth!' said Mairi, ready to go and intro-
duce the swindling boatman to some Highland manners.

'I know, but he has the upper hand on us and he knows
it. We cannot risk being informed upon.' Hector swallowed.
'I will shift for myself.'

'But there is nothing arranged,' said Mairi. She had no
liking for the swaggering young man, so pleased with his
elegance and his French manners that had turned her own
feckless daughter's head, but she didn't wish him into need-
less danger either.

'I will find something. They won't be looking for one of us alone, and even should they spot me, I can outrun them.'

That much was true, she knew. Hector MacGillivray could outrun every man in Strathnairn. The redcoats with their clunking guns and heavy shoes would come nowhere near him.

'What does my husband say to this?' she asked.

'Neil doesn't know. It is only myself that has spoken with the boatman. I am younger than most of the men in that hut, Mistress Farquharson, and faster than any of them and I carry no injury. I will be halfway to France by the time any of them notice I'm gone.'

Still Mairi could not like him, but it was a courageous thing he did, and she let him go.

Thirty Years Later: Drummossie Moor, 16 April, 1746

The music was different, and Iain MacGillivray could not understand it. He tried to turn his head towards it but a searing pain down one side of his face almost overwhelmed him. He sank his head again into the wet heather and the moss until the surge of it passed. What was he doing on the heather though? The hail was still hurling itself down as it had done the whole day, biting into his face, but the other elements were all wrong. He should not be smelling the earth like this. He should not be tasting blood. And the howling he could hear was not the battle-cry that had last roared in his ears, it was a wounded, animal howling.

He had heard it before, at Prestonpans, at Falkirk, but it had never been as bad as this. How long had he been here? He didn't know. One moment he had been charging across the moor, the pipes of Clan Chattan driving him forward, with his cousin Lachlan ahead of him, and now he was here, lying on the cold wet earth.

But where was Lachlan? He shifted and heard a low grumble beside him. Lachlan. Thank God. His cousin had somehow managed to pull some of his own plaid out from underneath himself to drape over Iain. When had he done that? It was impossible even to tell what time it was. The sky above them was going from one depth of grey to the next, and beneath them was black earth, brown heather and the rust of blood. A thousand miles they had marched, far to the south and back home again, to this, Culloden. He managed to turn enough to look Lachlan in the eye and what he saw there portended nothing good.

With some effort, his cousin asked, 'Who's it for?'

'What?'

'The lament. Who's it for?'

Iain forced himself now to look towards the sound. The battle tunes were no more to be heard, and it was indeed a lament, coming from one piper and getting further away. He followed the notes as they faded from the battlefield.

'Who's it for?' Lachlan asked again.

Who was it for? Who was it not for? But through the hail, past the bodies, Iain could see them, the Chisholm piper playing his chief's youngest son off the carnage that was

Drummossie Moor. His tongue felt as if it were turned to lead. 'Roderick Òg,' he said. 'Going home to Strathglass.' Young Roderick, who had led out a hundred of his father's men in the Jacobite cause. Walking behind his bier, stricken with shock and grief, were his two older brothers, in the red coats of the British government army, Cumberland's army. Old MacIan, chief of the Chisholms, had played a dangerous double-hand, and he had lost.

A curse came from somewhere deep within Lachlan. Iain made some move to get up, but Lachlan put an arm on him to keep him down and obscure the sight of him from any curious redcoat. All around them were men of their clan, dead and dying.

A new coldness passed through Iain. 'Where's my father?'

'Hector? Who knows?'

Iain had last seen his father with broadsword aloft and head thrown back, yelling a mortal intent upon his enemies. Hector MacGillivray, who had spent more than half a lifetime a gentleman in France. He'd been charging towards the government lines and their bayonets as if his life had no other purpose. Iain could see him, in his mind's eye, disappearing into the smoke of the government guns. And then nothing. 'But where . . .?'

'Wheesht,' said Lachlan. 'The lines went awry. He'll be among the MacLeans, or the MacPhersons, maybe.'

Maybe. Perhaps God knew where the MacPhersons were now, but Iain didn't. Not here, at any rate, on this patch of the moor, with the MacGillivrays, lying dead and half-dead in a pile, blasted to pieces by grapeshot, waiting for Cumberland's men to pick over their bodies. Iain saw Lachlan's eyes drift over to meet those of James MacGillivray, his neighbour. James owed Lachlan money, the price of a pair of shoes in Perth, and a drink or two. Lachlan would never have that money. James's hands had been blown to kingdom come and his eyes were staring open into an eternity where he would never pay his debt. That was the chance you took: lend a man a few shillings for the sake of a pair of shoes and a dram, and watch him die across your legs, in the cause of a foreign prince.

'The prince?' asked Iain.

'Prince Charlie's away,' said Lachlan, his voice bitter. 'Long gone, hauled off the field by his Irish devils. They can haul him off to Hell with them, for all I care.' All that Lachlan had fought for was lying dead in the heather around them. All but Iain himself. Iain was living yet, but whatever had splintered and torn down through half his own face from eye to mouth had put a crater in Lachlan's knee so that his cousin couldn't get up even if he'd attempted to.

Lachlan, in his turn, was appraising the damage done to Iain. He made a show of screwing up his face. 'Well, it's not the end of the world – for all your success with the women you were never that bonny in the first place.' He coughed, his lungs convulsing. Lachlan's humour couldn't mask his discomfort. He would lose his leg from the knee down for certain. Their raillery seemed to take his mind off the pain, and Iain was glad of it.

'Bonnier than you,' retorted Iain, 'even with half of Cumberland's grapeshot in my cheek.'

'What?' Lachlan winced as he fished out his retort. 'Who would know, behind that curtain of hair that you're always flicking back like a lassie? Look at it! Falling over your face, as if a barber or a periwig-maker were things unheard of in the town of Inverness, or even a ribbon, for God's sake.'

Ribbons! Were they talking of ribbons when all around them, where there weren't groans, there were screams? Shattered men calling for mothers who had never seen Drummossie Moor.

Iain would not call for his mother though. He never had, from long before he had first been deposited by his grandmother's servant at Lachlan's father's door in Strathnairn, with the instruction that her grandson was to be trained in the ways befitting a Highlander. It had been made clear, Lachlan's father had once told him, that Mairi Farquharson and her servant were as one in thinking the child would have been better off amongst her own relations in Glenlivet, but the boy's father, it seemed, had insisted he should be brought up amongst his people, the MacGillivrays. Hector himself had been in Paris, or Rome, or St Petersburg or some such place – it had not been specified, and it hadn't mattered. Lachlan's father had taken it as an honour that the grey-eyed, almost white-haired boy from France had been given into his care.

The hair had darkened over the years, but from that moment Iain had been Iain Bàn. Fair Iain. And almost

from that moment, he had attached himself to Lachlan. A
foster-child brought from elsewhere to be raised in the clan
had been nothing new, but everyone had known Iain's story,
and been keen to tell it back to him – the absent father, the
wanton mother that had run off – and so the boy arrived
from France had learned he must either turn his back on
his adversaries or stand and answer them. The boys of
Strathnairn had soon learned that Iain Bàn MacGillivray
was his father's son.

Iain was drifting off into the memories. He forced himself
back out of them. To give into them here and now would
be the end. All over the moor, Cumberland's soldiers were
picking their way through the scattered or piled up bodies
of slain Jacobites. Officers on horseback gave the yay or
nay as their men called to one another, rifling corpses and
plundering the dead. At their officer's say-so, they rammed
bayonets into the bodies of stricken men who could not
defend themselves. A party of them was prodding its way
over to where Iain and Lachlan lay amongst the slaughtered
of Clan Chattan – Mackintoshes, MacGillivrays, Farquharsons and others.

Iain uttered an oath.

'Wheesht,' repeated Lachlan, pressing down on his arm.
'Play dead.'

Iain could feel the warmth going out of him, feel his eyes
flickering. The party crossing the moor towards them had
stopped where a half-dozen MacDonalds lay, limbs entangled, blood staining through their plaids into the moor,

their living essence going back into the earth. A soldier stepped amongst the bodies, poking each with the edge of his bayonet until he came to the last, that lay a little apart from the others. He poked and the man let out a cry. Someone playing dead, as they were. The soldier smiled and reached for his pistol as he looked towards his officer. 'I've a squealer here, Major.'

Iain looked towards the man on the horse. Hawley, who'd had his arse whipped for him at Falkirk. A cruel man, loathed by his own soldiers. There would be another dead MacDonald on Culloden field in a moment. Iain closed his eyes, but instead of pistol shot he heard Hawley's drawl, 'Not that one,' then the sound of the spared man getting himself away as quickly as whatever injury he had would let him and the sound of the scavengers moving on.

'Close your eyes, Iain,' Lachlan whispered, 'play dead.' Two redcoats had broken away from the others and were coming in their direction. They were about to pass by when one told the other to wait.

An impatient, 'What?'

'That one – the shoes. You'd get money for them.'

Barely conscious or not, it was all Iain could do not to rise up and plunge his dirk into the neck of the one and then the other as they pulled the Perth shoes from James MacGillivray's feet. They passed, eventually, with their booty.

*

Iain woke with the cold, and the searing pain of the left side of his face. Darkness was falling, but there were pockets of light, warmth even, dotted around the horizon, like bonfires in the night. He couldn't see the redcoats now, nor the dragoons – they must have had their pickings, and the Highland companies that fought for Cumberland would be long gone into the clanlands, in pursuit of their spoil. The figures moving around the moor now were moving more slowly, their searching amongst the fallen not for plunder but for husbands, brothers, sons. Somewhere, coming closer, was the sound of drums, Cumberland's drums, playing the dead beat. There was a party moving onto the moor from the south and a prisoner was being led across the battle-field – not dragged along on foot, but on horseback. Iain would have known her anywhere, just from the way she sat that horse. Lady Anne Mackintosh, 'Colonel Anne', as they called her, that had called out her clan for Prince Charles in defiance of her husband's service in the Hanoverians' army. They must have gone to Moy and got her, and now they had taken her here to view the carnage, look on the broken bodies of the men who had rallied to her standard. And they called the prince's army savages.

Once the party was out of sight, Iain tugged at Lachlan's plaid. 'Come on, Lachie, we'd better get off this field or we'll be dead of the cold.' It was difficult to speak for the wound in his face so he tried again. 'Come on, I'll help you up. You can lean on me and we'll get into the town and down to my grandmother's house. We'll get a surgeon to look at that leg of yours.' Iain heaved himself up on one arm. Felt the cold rush into his face, broken heather and bits of rusted shot clinging to the blood. 'Lachie, will you wake? We'll starve up here if we don't freeze first. Lachie!'

Lachlan made no response. Iain raised his fist and thumped his cousin's chest. Nothing. Damn the fellow, he could fall asleep anywhere. He raised his hand again to strike a second time, and a strong arm grabbed him by the wrist and held his fist where it was. 'He's gone, Iain.' Duncan Fraser from Farr.

'Let go my arm, Duncan, or I'll tear it off you! A night on the moor with his leg like that would kill him.' Iain tried to wrest his arm from the fool's grip, but Fraser held it firm.

'He's gone, Iain. He's gone.'

ONE

The Bookseller

Six Years Later: August, 1752, Inverness

Ishbel MacLeod watched her boy Tormod scamper down the close past Bow Court and out onto the street. He was desperate to get out every day at this time to watch the children spill out from the school at Dunbar's Hospital. Tormod spoke constantly of going to school and all he would do once he got there. Ishbel went after him, admonishing him to keep to the agreed streets, not to wander, and not to think of going down to the river or up to the Foul Pool or to the old burial ground of the Greyfriars. Tormod could not stay to listen. The school bell would be rung soon, the children released into the summer's evening.

Ishbel looked up and down Church Street – there was nothing to alarm her, no unaccounted presence. The red-coated soldiers were going about their own business and taking no interest in the small boy. The inns and taverns were quiet as yet, the worst of them at outlying parts of the town in any case. Down the road a little, on the other side of the street, the door to the bookshop was still ajar. Tormod was rarely away from the place, oblivious, it seemed, to the bookseller's dark moods and forbidding demeanour. She knew the bookseller's habits almost as well as her own. The place would not shut until the tolbooth bell tolled six, and then the man himself would not emerge till eight, when he would lock the door carefully behind him. Those forced to remake their lives rarely deviated from the patterns by which they ordered their days. Ishbel knew this.

She saw two women, Mrs Rose and her daughter, go into the bookshop. They had not had to make their lives anew. They walked in the street in freedom and good clothes. Ishbel was rarely out of her apron, tendrils of hair escaping from the linen wrap around her head, her pale face often flushed from the heat of the cookhouse where she spent her days making her confections. The Roses did not have burns on their hands and arms where they had been careless. Neither did they have tiny, silver scars on their wrists, remarked by no one, where manacles had chafed, because they had not been able to run fast enough.

Julia Rose was startled by what sounded like a murmur of amusement from the bookseller's desk. Turning her head as far as she dared, she risked a glance in that direction. Never before had she heard such a sound amongst the shelves and cabinets of this bookshop. It was rare, in fact, to hear any sound at all in here, save the *sotto voce* murmuring of customers, fearful of unnecessarily disturbing the man behind the desk, or the occasional furious Gaelic outburst from the fellow who was said to work in the backroom bindery, and whom she had never seen.

'Julia!' her mother breathed, but the warning came too late – the bookseller had noticed her look at him. As he pushed back the curtain of pale blond hair that swung habitually across the left side of his face, she saw the scarring. The right side was unmarked, a flawless reminder, but the left . . . she had never before seen it so clearly, hatched the full breadth of his cheek and from the corner of his mouth upwards, stopping just short of his eye. For a moment she was frozen, could not turn away, but then some commotion from the upper gallery took his attention and released her from his gaze.

'What's your problem?' Iain MacGillivray demanded.

The stranger had been scanning the shelves for some twenty minutes, taking books out, opening them, cursing, shoving them back in. From the state of his clothing, the smell and dirt of him, Iain thought it hardly likely he would be able to afford any of the volumes he was so intent upon.

'You are sure these are the books from Castle Dounie?'

'As I told you when you first asked.'

'From the Old Fox's own library, you are sure? These are not others that have come in since?'

'Since what?' asked Iain. 'The place has been ashes a good six years.'

'They're Lovat's books?'

'Aye, they're Lovat's books.' Simon Fraser, Lord Lovat, the Old Fox. Beheaded five years ago, after a lifetime of duplicity, intrigue, espionage, violence, abused friendships, ill-judgement and ultimately, pathos. Lovat had called out his men for the Hanoverian cause in the '15 and he had called them out again for the Jacobites in the '45. In the end, it had to be said, the Old Fox had cared nothing for princes or kings, he had cared only for the clan, and for that he had lost his head, and the Frasers had been forced to watch their livelihood driven off and their homes burned in front of them. Within two weeks of the battle of Culloden, Castle Dounie on the banks of the Beauly river had been reduced to blackened rubble. But the officers and men of the government's burning party had been no fools: they'd stripped what there was to strip of the place first and taken the books of his library to the marketplace of Inverness to be turned into money. Iain's grandmother, who was no fool either, had sent her servants out into the marketplace to buy them. In time, the books had come here, to his shop.

'What are you looking for?' Iain asked.

The man didn't look at him as he carried on taking books off the shelf and opening them to examine the inside of the boards before shutting them again and putting them back.

'I'll know it when I find it,' he said.

Iain's impatience grew. 'If you tell me what you're looking for, I can tell you whether it has already been sold. It's been six years.'

The man continued to ignore him.

Iain looked to the pendulum clock hanging on the gallery wall. 'Well, you'd better find it in the next quarter hour or you can come back tomorrow.'

'Tomorrow?' The fellow turned to him with a wild eye. 'I'll be gone from Inverness tomorrow.'

Iain shrugged. 'That's none of my concern.' He descended the short flight of wooden steps to the lower floor. 'I'll be locking the door of this shop at six o'clock, and you'll not still be in it.'

This last comment he directed not only to the dirty man in the gallery, but also to the two women who'd been at the library shelves nearly half an hour. Iain went back behind his desk, picked up the Smollett he'd set down there, and resumed reading. It was the younger woman who came across with the books, as it always was. Her mother remained in the library recess, clearly fearful that he might eat her. He was tempted to growl, but the townsfolk thought him odd enough without Elizabeth Rose running screaming from his shop.

Julia Rose set the books down in front of him. He finished his paragraph before looking up. 'And the returns?' he asked.

'There.' She indicated the two volumes she had set on the table in front of his desk when she and her mother had come in. Iain took the register of the Circulating Library from its drawer and turned the pages until he came to the one with the Roses' names at the top. Everything was written in the neat italic of his assistant, Richard Dempster, whose project the library was. But Richard was away in Perth, and not expected back for two days. The Roses, as Iain might have expected, were model patrons: their subscription was always paid, their books never late, they had yet to incur a penalty or fine. After a moment he nodded and marked 'returned' against their previous choices, before putting out his hand to receive the first of this week's books. Ramsay's *Tea Table Miscellany*. The mother. The daughter's choice was Charlotte Lennox, *The Female Quixote*.

'That one's just in,' he said.

The young woman looked mildly surprised to be addressed like this, which was fair enough, thought Iain, as it was more than he had ever said to her before.

'I know,' she said, emboldened.

'Julia! The books. We cannot be here the whole day. I have ordered our supper for six.'

Julia Rose lifted the two books and went out behind her mother. The shop door had hardly shut behind them when it was opened again by someone coming in off the street.

Aeneas.

Aeneas's nose wrinkled in distaste as it always did when he was obliged to come into the shop. 'Your grandmother sent me,' he said.

The most unnecessary arrangement of words in the man's whole lexicon, thought Iain. The idea that Aeneas should take it upon himself to do something that was not at Mairi Farquharson's behest was almost as ludicrous as the behaviour of the characters in the book he was reading.

Aeneas lifted the volume of Hume's essays just returned by Julia Rose, before putting it down with a dismissive 'pfft'. He was not a man to indulge in uncertainties or questions of perception. 'The mistress bids me remind you that you are to play for the ladies this evening, after they've had their supper. She bids you not be late.'

The *Grandes Dames*. Iain had forgotten. 'I'll not be late. Am I expected to eat with them?'

Aeneas regarded him sourly. 'I would hardly think so,' he said. 'Nine o'clock. Sharp.' With a last look around the shop lest he had missed something requiring his disapproval, he left.

The man in the gallery had never stopped his rifling of the books and Iain was not inclined to stay open any longer on his behalf. He called up the steps. 'We are closing.'

'But it wants five minutes of the hour!'

Iain sighed. Five minutes. What would he do with the extra five minutes in any case? But then came the familiar shout from the bindery, a stream of Gaelic invective rounded off with, '*A-mach a seo!* Get out of here!' and then, 'Son of Damnation, Iain Bàn, there's a man here will die of thirst.'

Iain left his desk and went through to the back. Donald Mòr had his back to him and was folding away his needle cloth on the worktable beneath the window. His brass tooling instruments were already shut away in their leather case, and the gold leaf securely locked in a cabinet with the precious Dutch gilt paper that he used for the most expensive end-leaves. Beeswax, vinegar and the concoction

Donald mixed for the final leather treatment were all stoppered and on a high shelf. Cuts of hide were stacked neatly and ranged according to their quality – calf, sheepskin and goat hide of Morocco. Printed sheets, arrived from presses in Glasgow and Edinburgh and awaiting folding into folio, quarto or octavo for stitching and binding into books, were stored in an orderly manner in a deep dresser. The last thing to be locked away was always Donald's own stamp, engraved in the '45 by an Edinburgh silversmith and his most treasured possession. It showed an oak tree, symbol of the Stuarts, surrounded by Prince Charlie's motto, 'Look, Love and Follow'. The authorities had long since given up trying to get Donald to surrender it, and indeed had probably by now forgotten that almost every book that went out from the bindery of MacGillivray's Bookseller's was imprinted with the symbols of loyalty to the Stuart cause. Almost every book, but not those commissioned by the officers of the town's British garrison. Donald might be a devoted adherent of the King over the Water, but he was not an idiot.

The bindery extended deep into the back yard and all was immaculate. It was Donald Mòr's kingdom, and in it, he would brook no interference other than, to Iain's bewilderment, the frequent attendance of the confectioner Ishbel MacLeod's child. Iain himself put up with the boy's presence only to keep the peace with Donald, on the strict understanding that the child would cause no disturbance in the bookshop itself.

The domestic, as well as the industrial, area of the room was a picture of discipline. Set into one wall was a box bed. Donald's clothing – the old tartan plaid that he refused to give up but knew not to be seen in outside and a few linen shifts – was kept in the long press on the other wall, which also housed his broadsword and a pistol. The redcoats quartered in the town would have been surprised to learn of their presence there.

Donald would speak only in Gaelic. 'Is that cursed fellow not gone yet?'

'I'll have him out in a minute.'

'It's Friday night, by God!'

Iain opened the pouch he had brought through from behind his desk and with exaggerated precision laid out a number of coins on Donald's supper-table. It was the agreement that had been reached between themselves, the kirk session and the town council, as the price of him being allowed to retain Donald in his employment. Without it, Donald would have been shipped off somewhere where his riotous drunkenness could not disturb the good burgesses of Inverness. Donald would have his wages on a Friday night. Little could be done about the outrages he would perpetrate between then and when he at last stumbled senseless to his bed at some point on the Saturday, but he could thereafter be relied upon not to be seen about the streets of Inverness until the Monday morning. He would then be a model of sobriety until the next Friday night. At all costs, there would be no disturbance on the Sabbath.

Iain felt the malevolent eye of Morag upon him as Donald counted out the coins. With the binder gone, she might come and go as she pleased with none to answer to, although it was a question which of the pair answered to the other. No one knew where she had come from, this vicious feline that had appeared at the back door to the bindery one morning and padded in to claim dominion. Half wildcat at least, she and Donald spat and hissed at each other throughout the day but were seldom to be parted.

His coins counted, Donald nodded briskly to Iain and went out to the barrel in the yard to begin his ablutions.

Iain went back through the door of the bindery into the bookshop proper and locked it behind him. He had learned within a week of taking Donald into his employ that whilst even in drink Donald regarded his own workplace and habitation as sacrosanct, the bookshop itself was a different matter. Iain had opened the door to the premises on the morning after one of Donald's rampages to find a scene of utter chaos. Maps and other prints had been defaced and more books littered the floor than remained on the shelves. Worse, volumes whose binding had alerted Donald to the work of one of the many publishing houses with whom he was at feud were piled into the hearth, showing signs of attempted, but defective, incineration. That very day, Iain had had a lock and new bolts put on the inner bookshop door, and Donald had never set foot in the place unsupervised since.

The last of the locks to the bindery bolted, Iain went up

again to the gallery. The man was still working his way intensively through the remains of Lord Lovat's library.

'We're closing.'

'An hour more,' said the man. 'I'll pay.'

Iain took the book from his hand. 'You've been told. We're closing. Now.'

As he was reaching up to return the book to its place on the shelf, he saw a movement of the man's hand to beneath his jacket. An old move that he'd been well schooled in by his cousin Lachlan many years ago, on long summer afternoons in Strathnairn. He had the man slammed up against the shelves, his arm twisted up behind his back before the fingers ever touched the dirk they had gone for. 'Out. Now,' he repeated.

Iain could hear the pain in the man's voice as he breathed the words out, 'All right, all right.' As soon as the grip was loosed, the fellow was down the stairs and out, throwing one last, aggrieved look behind him as he left the shop.

The place emptied, and the door bolted, it took Iain the best part of an hour to finish tallying his ledgers, putting the shelves to rights and returning books to their allotted place in the library section. The last thing he did before snuffing out the candles was to go round the floors with his broom. It was the most satisfying task of his day – sweeping out all the dirt, all the traces of themselves his customers had brought into the shop. Even when his assistant Richard was here, Iain always performed this job himself. Then he extinguished the candles, all but one, and took the flask of whisky from the pocket of his coat where it hung on a nail on the wall behind his chair. From the cabinet beside him he took out a glass – one of six of Italian crystal sent many years ago by his mother, in one of her fitful remembrances. He caught his own reflection in the glass of the cabinet. Better in the dark. He poured himself a good measure of what Aeneas procured from the illicit distillers of Ord and took up his book.

It was after eight when he set it down again. He put on his coat, snuffed out the last candle and went out into the street, making sure to lock the door behind him. The air of the August night was warmer outside than it was inside his shop. He took off his coat again and slung it over his arm.

Darkness would soon fall on the town. Church Street was coming alive in ways different from its daytime incarnation. The industrious, polite, respectable Church Street had closed up its counters, lit its lamps, and turned its back. Schoolboys had long since swarmed from the confines of the grammar school at Dunbar's Hospital, back to their mothers or their lodgings, whilst the bedesmen and women on the upper floor had had their supper and gone to their slumbers to the sound of the scriptures. The books of the Kirk Session library would be safely locked away. The shadows cast by the stones of the High Kirk bled now into a deeper darkness, awaiting the trysting and concealments of the night-time hours. It wanted two hours still of the summer curfew, and the town constables had not begun their peregrinations. The soldiers of the garrison were heading for their favoured taverns. Decent women lost no time in getting home, more desperate women, not yet banished to the desolation of the Haugh, pinched their cheeks and agreed their territories.

A little way up from the bookshop, and at the other side of the street, was the close running down past Bow Court and the establishment where Donald Mòr was wont to commence his night's drinking. Nearly two hours the bookbinder would have been at it by now – the trouble wouldn't be long in starting. And indeed, at that moment, there came an explosion of noise from the close, a smashing of glass and splintering of wood. Cursing to himself, Iain went over the street, ready to extract his binder from whatever trouble he had got himself into, but he had only just reached the mouth of the close when the form of a man came barrelling backwards out of the bottle shop, knocking him sideways. Iain's feet slipped in the mud of the causey and went out from under him. Before he could make purchase on anything to steady himself, the right side of his face connected with the ground. It was not long before grit was mixed with iron as the blood trickled from his lower lip. He made an attempt to lift his head and saw his coat lying in a heap a few feet away. There was a sound of tinkling metal somewhere and a fine silver button rolled past him, to disappear into the gutters.

He lowered his head back to the ground and shut his eyes for a moment. When he opened them again it was to find a small set of brown toes level with his vision. He raised his gaze to meet a pair of brown eyes, bright against their dark skin. Tormod. The boy brought back with her from Virginia by the confectioner, Ishbel MacLeod. The child that was rarely out of his shop. For a moment, Iain stared back, but suddenly the boy jerked sideways and Iain saw that Ishbel had taken hold of his arm and was directing him back up the forestair of their small house. He began to heave himself back up on his feet. The man who'd bowled into him had disappeared back up the close into the tavern, pursued by a ward constable and a further five enthusiastic townsmen. A couple of jeering lads made a great show of taking off as Iain finally got himself upright. A party of infantrymen passing up from the harbour to the castle looked over and laughed about drunken Highlanders. Brushing himself down, Iain made no response other than to curse their mothers and grandmothers for them to the tenth generation, quietly and in his native tongue.

When he had finished, he saw that Ishbel was still standing there, long tendrils of dark red hair escaping her cap, her mouth pursed a little at his profanities. He puffed out his lips and glanced away a moment. 'Sorry,' he said.

She held out his jacket, which she had picked up. 'Thank you,' he muttered, wishing nothing more than to escape his humiliation, although she was only the town's confectioner and no one to him.

'It is nothing,' she said, something drawn out in the words, then she went up the stairs after the boy. Iain watched as she disappeared through the door and closed it behind her.

They were the first words they had ever exchanged. He'd seen her come and go sometimes from the kitchen of his grandmother's house, fine boned and delicate as the confections she spun, but he'd never before had cause to converse with her. He stood there a moment and heard the door lock above him.

His whole body was weary as he began to trudge homewards. If any on the street noticed his disarray, they didn't say. But then, ahead of him, a figure emerged from a wynd coming up from the river. Iain cursed softly. It was the milliner, Barbara Sinclair. He was in no humour for Barbara tonight. He had just lighted on a doorway to step into to avoid her notice when he heard her light laugh.

'Iain Bàn MacGillivray. So you've been in the wars again. Who have you left lying in the gutter tonight?'

Iain grunted. 'I was at the end of someone else's accident, that's all. Where are you going?'

Barbara's small shop on the High Street would have been long closed, and she herself lived with her elderly father, across the bridge on the other side of the river. Most traders lived over their premises, but Barbara's father disliked the town, she said, and didn't want to be bothered with half the silly women of the Highlands traipsing over their threshold, talking of hats. 'Besides,' she had said when he'd asked her about it, 'it would make our arrangement a little difficult, wouldn't it?'

'Arrangement'. It was hardly that. They'd spent the occasional night together, or hours of a night, in the workroom behind her shop. Barbara was a widow – how often a widow was a matter of speculation in the town, but she certainly had no desire for another husband. Iain had no desire for any attachment to her either, but there were nights when he was drunk, and felt alone, and Barbara Sinclair seemed to possess the ability to manifest herself when he was at his lowest. Like now.

'Look at the state of you,' she said, taking his jacket and brushing at the dirt on it with a handkerchief. 'If you come up to the shop, I can put on another button for you, and mend that cuff.'

He shook his head. 'I'm late as it is. But perhaps later . . .'

'Not tonight, Iain Bàn. I have other things to see to.'

They parted near his grandmother's house. Iain went by the back courtyard, as he always did. Before entering the house, he took a moment to survey himself. His stockings were muddy, but not torn. The ministrations of Barbara's handkerchief had improved the look of his jacket a little, but the button was definitely gone. The Grandes Dames would have a field day if he turned up like this. He leaned his head back against the outer wall of the house a moment and looked to the night sky. One day, after another. But to what end? To get through a day in order to endure the night so that he might make it to the next morning and so begin again. One day after another. He was managing. Almost.

TWO

The Grandes Dames

In the kitchen of Mairi Farquharson's house on Church Street, Aeneas regarded Iain with the same look he'd been giving him for over thirty years. As far as Aeneas was concerned, Iain was not enough Farquharson and too much MacGillivray. Aeneas had never forgiven Iain's father for seducing Iain's mother in the heady days of the '15 rising, and he had never forgiven Iain for being the result.

Iain couldn't say for certain that he truly remembered the first time he had encountered Aeneas, or if it was just the remembering that he remembered. He knew the facts of the matter: it had been in 1720, in Brittany, thirty-two years ago. He had been almost four years old, playing out in the street with his companions, when his nurse had swept out, and in her flurry of Breton French, gathered him up and set him down at the pump in the backyard of the Vannes townhouse. She'd brushed furiously at the dust of his apron, at last giving up and removing it, thrusting him through the parlour door and closing it behind him. In his mind, Iain turned his gaze to the chair by the hearth, and the strange man sitting there. Dusty from travel, the man had been dressed in the manner sometimes favoured by his father. His father, Hector MacGillivray, had been standing at the window, dressed not in the plaid and kilt of his visiting countryman, but in a manner befitting a gentleman in France, employed on the business of his king, James Stuart, eighth of Scotland and third of England.

Even as he was being propelled by his nurse through the kitchen towards the parlour of that French town house, Iain had heard raised voices in the Gaelic tongue. Four years old or not, he'd known this was not right. Gaelic was the language of the night, with doors closed and shutters pulled to, and strangers come from afar.

The man in the chair had turned a cropped head and black eyes towards Iain, assessing him. There had been disappointment, succeeded by displeasure signalled by a slight tightening of the mouth. Hector on the other hand had been looking not at Iain but at the visitor, clenching and unclenching his fist as he did so.

Hector had bent down and picked Iain up, bringing him close to his own face. Iain had seen the trace of dark red stubble on the strong jaw, smelled the mix of aromas that was his father. He'd reached a hand up to the velvet ribbon that tied his father's hair and rubbed it between his fingers. Hector had begun to speak, looking all the while not at Iain but at the stranger. 'This gentleman is Aeneas Farquharson, Iain. He is a kinsman of your late grandfather,

your mother's father, and employed in your grandmother's
service. He has come to take you to her.'

'To my mother?' Iain had asked.

There had been a short silence before Hector had said,
'No. To your grandmother. In Scotland.'

And the next day, Iain had left Vannes, sitting up in
front on the stranger's saddle. He'd been taken aboard a
boat set for the open sea. Days of sickness, tears and bewilderment later, he'd been put ashore at the port of Leith
to be set down on his feet in Scotland. A respite of two
days followed and another boat, this time to Inverness, and
this, his grandmother's house. Thereafter, he had spent the
dark winter months in the town and the months of light
in Strathnairn, fostered in the traditional way amongst his
father's people, the MacGillivrays. It had been twenty-five
years before he'd seen his father again.

Aeneas's cropped head was grey now, the eyes still black,
and tonight in this kitchen, the mouth was still pursed.
'There's a tear in those stockings and a button gone from
that coat.'

Iain fingered the silk thread hanging loose. 'There was
an . . . incident.'

'A relative to the one that scraped your face, no doubt.'

Iain heaved a sigh. 'A close relative. Are they here?'

At Aeneas's nod he set his foot on the stair leading up to
his grandmother's bedchamber.

'There's no time to change your stockings but you'll not
go up amongst the ladies in that coat!' insisted Aeneas.

Iain glanced down at the coat with its smears of dirt and its missing button. He shrugged. 'Between the candlelight and the punchbowl, they'll hardly notice.'

Aeneas rose from the hard-backed Orkney chair he favoured. He held his stick in his hand the way Iain had seen him ready his claymore. 'You'll respect your grandmother and her guests, Iain Bàn MacGillivray or you'll not take a step further on those stairs. Coat!'

Iain conceded. 'All right.' And as an afterthought, 'Sorry.' He shrugged off the coat and handed it to Aeneas in exchange for the clean, deep green velvet one the housemaid had been clutching to her as she watched the confrontation play out. There was no point in Iain asking how Eppy had known he'd be needing a clean coat. News travelled from the bottom of Church Street to the top faster than the Ness in spate went the other way.

Once satisfied, Aeneas handed him his fiddle and motioned for him to lead the way up the stairs.

He knocked and opened the door into his grandmother's room. And there they were, suspended in the candlelight against the background of dark wood, heavy velvet and damask, as if captured in oils by Allan Ramsay himself: the Grandes Dames. His grandmother Mairi Farquharson and her three lifelong friends: Catriona Lamont, Janet Grant and Eilidh Cameron. Swathed in silk and lace, their jewels glittering, flickering light from fire and candelabra turning the amber in their crystal punch cups to liquid gold. The silver strands in their hair, the lines on their brows, the veins on the backs of their hands carried in them the whole story of the Jacobite cause. For over six decades, fathers, brothers, husbands, sons and grandsons had given their all for the House of Stuart and, through it all, these women had not wavered.

Eilidh Cameron was the first to greet him, her eyes dancing like a girl arrived at a ball. 'It's yourself, Iain Bàn. You've never been working this late in the shop?'

Before he could answer, Catriona Lamont was leaning in across the table. 'Well, I commend him for it. Many a shilling is lost by the trader who shuts up shop too early, and—'

'Catriona!' scolded Iain's grandmother. 'Would you keep an eye on your cards! You're waving them about for all to see, and there's Janet Grant taking note of every one of them.'

'I am not looking at her cards!' protested Janet, raking in her reticule. 'I can hardly see my own.'

Iain rose from making his bow and began to circle the card table, dipping to kiss the papery cheek of each woman in turn. It seemed to him they had been like this for all of his life, but the portrait hanging to the left of the great fireplace, a companion to that of his grandfather on the right, told a different story.

Iain's grandmother was not so greatly changed from the young married woman of the portrait, painted by some French master at the time of her marriage, over fifty years ago. The dark chestnut hair was now white, the blue eyes a little paler, the mouth a little thinner, but anyone who knew her would know that to be a portrait of Mairi Farquharson. And whilst Mairi had been young, in her prime, so too had the others. They had ridden out, each one of them, behind the men of the '15 rising in the name of King James. And not one of them had been much mellowed by the time Iain himself had gone out thirty years later when Charles Edward Stuart, Prince of Wales, had rallied the clans to the cause in the '45. Catriona and Eilidh, indeed, had followed the prince's army to Edinburgh and Holyrood, and shown their younger compatriots what it was to comport themselves in the court of the Royal Stuarts. And the wages of their devotion had been to see homes rendered to ashes and rubble, loved ones lost to the carnage of battle, the brutality of its aftermath, to gaol fever, transportation or the scaffold. Had Cumberland been in the habit of hanging high-born Highland women, they would have lost their lives too. Iain was ashamed to think he had considered playing before them in a dirty coat that was missing its button.

He took up his bow. 'What would you have, tonight, ladies?'

The question was not necessary – he could have reeled them off before they answered him – 'Derwentwater's Farewell', 'The King Shall Enjoy His Own Again', 'Lord Lovat's Lament'. Any Hanoverian officer from the garrison strolling below the open window might make of these loyal tunes of the Jacobites what he would. Iain drew the bow across his fiddle and the room slipped back in time. Beyond the pools of light cast by candle and fire, he could almost see the ghosts as they passed amongst the women. There was his grandfather, Neil Farquharson that he had never met, placing a hand on Mairi's shoulder; there was Catriona Lamont's father, mourned over fifty years; there was Eilidh's husband with her brother, arguing and laughing at her side, and there Alasdair Grant, Iain's own childhood friend, looking over Janet's shoulder and shaking his head at his mother's hand of cards.

As the last strains of 'Lord Lovat's Lament' faded, and she'd finished wiping a tear from her cheek, 'even though, God knows, the old rogue was asking for the axe his whole life,' Eilidh Cameron examined her cup. 'Where has that fellow Aeneas got to, Mairi? Is there a drop of punch left in that bowl at all? I'll swear, that man begrudges me every mouthful.'

Iain was about to go round with the ladle himself when Aeneas reappeared and after exchanging a nod with Mairi Farquharson proceeded to fill the crystal punch cups to the top of the rose engraved upon them.

A cup or two of punch himself, on top of the whisky he'd had from his flask in the shop, and Iain began to forget the hurt in his shoulder where he had fallen. The old stories were told again, the favourite poems recited and the loyal toasts openly drunk to the health of King James VIII, far away in the Palazzo del Re in Rome, and of his son Charles, Prince of Wales, wherever in Europe he might be.

As the evening drew to its natural end, Iain's grandmother rang the bell for Aeneas to come and escort her guests home. Eilidh Cameron was woken from the settle on which she had fallen asleep and persuaded to put on her shawl, and Janet Grant took charge of the small, greatly indulged dog belonging to Catriona Lamont, with whom she always resided when she came into town from her home in Corrimony. Before going out into the night, the women looked to their brooches and pendants, snapped them shut or arranged their lace to cover the miniatures secreted beneath. Images of the prince, the cardinal duke of York, and the king were obscured from potential viewing by hostile eyes. Iain was kissed again, his proficiency on the fiddle outrageously praised, the old promises made that a pretty girl of good family would soon be found for him, and then they left into the August night.

Their guests gone, Iain and his grandmother drank one last toast, raising their cups as they did every night to the portrait hanging across the mantelpiece from hers. Neil Farquharson, her husband, his grandfather, executed one bright May morning on Tower Hill in London in the year 1716, after a failed attempt at escape, six months before Iain had been born.

THREE

Saturday Morning

The air in the room was chill, despite the sun streaming in at the window and over the breakfast table. His grandmother would have no fire lit in here on a summer's day and much of the warmth of the previous evening was gone with the old friends who had brought it. The days leading up to a gathering of the Grandes Dames were filled with an energy and anticipation that permeated the whole house; the day after with the knowledge that another of their nights was over, and the days of their glory slipped further away.

Iain's chair scraped on the bare wooden floor as he pulled it out. His grandmother turned her head from her observation of the doings on the street below. 'Lift it, Iain. A hundred times, I have said it. Lift it. You mark the boards.'

'Sorry. So,' he said, inclining his head towards the turret window, 'what does Inverness have to say for itself today?'

'It says that its bookseller was sent rolling down onto the street from Bessie Stewart's tavern last night, like a common vagrant.'

'Ah. So Aeneas has . . .'

Now she did turn around. 'Aeneas? Aeneas nothing. I have eyes in my own head, Iain. It was evident from the moment you walked in here last night that you had been in some form of altercation, and poor Eppy was up half the night cleaning and stitching your coat.'

'Half the night? A few streaks of dirt and one button. I'd have done it quicker myself. Anyhow, I wasn't in the tavern, nor any altercation either, but only caught at the wrong end of someone else's tussle as I passed the end of the wynd.'

Mairi Farquharson wrinkled her nose, as if the smell of last night's gutters had just reached it. 'Bessie Stewart's is a low place. It's long past time you were married.'

'Ach, who would have me?'

'Plenty,' she said, putting down the spoon with which she'd been scraping out the last of her breakfast from her china cup.

'Do you think it?' He took a ladle from the bowl himself, although he had not the stomach this morning for the concoction of cream, sugar, brandy and beaten egg with which they began each day. 'At thirty-six, with a crumbling bookshop, a face that looks like a plough's gone over it and a family that would scare a stableful of Hanoverian horses?'

Mairi pointed her spoon at him. 'That bookshop, as well you know, may be of great use to our cause one day. Bailie Steuart will hardly live for ever.' The business of the town merchant Bailie John Steuart had served for years as the chief conduit for communications between Jacobites abroad and the loyal Highland clans. It was understood that when the good bailie was no longer able to fulfil this role, Iain and his bookshop would take his place. 'As to your face . . .'

Iain took a deep breath and turned away.

'You will look at me while I'm talking to you, I hope?' He did as she asked.

'The scars on your face are a mark of honour. You should carry them with pride, considering in whose cause you got them.'

'No. Of course. I'm sorry,' he said.

She nodded, as far as she would go towards accepting his apology. His grandmother moved on to another well-rehearsed topic.

'I should not have left you in France so long. I should have had you back here the minute the news came you were born, but your uncle persuaded me against it, said you should be left with your mother. William was always too soft.'

Too soft. William Farquharson, Willie. Her only son and the pride of his family, more beautiful even than his sister, some said. Iain had never met him. Willie had been felled by a redcoat's bullet at Glen Shiel in 1719, days before his twentieth birthday. By that time, his sister Charlotte, Iain's mother, had already lost interest in motherhood and Hector MacGillivray both, and abandoned man and child in France, in pursuit of more elegant adventures. Despite Hector's best efforts, the news had reached Mairi in Inverness soon enough, and she had lost no time in sending Aeneas to bring home from France the last of her line, to be raised as a Highlander should be.

Iain reached for an oat bannock and spread it with butter and quince marmalade. Food was all one to him, who as a prisoner and on the transportation ship had known real hunger. But the taste of the marmalade took him by surprise. 'This is very good,' he said. 'Flossie never made this.'

'No indeed. Flossie cannot be persuaded to meddle with the boiling of sugar. I had some at Eilidh Cameron's and conceived a great liking for it. It's the confectioner, Ishbel MacLeod, who makes it. She brought it here early this morning. I will have her bring more if you like it.'

'Oh? Well . . . I could always ask her myself.'

Mairi treated this unwonted interest in domestic affairs with a look of astonishment, but the arrival of Aeneas, a note in his hand, brought to an end all talk of jams and sugar.

'It's come from Jenny Campbell.'

There was a stillness in the room. A note sent from the tiny, wooden, turf-roofed cottage on the banks of the Ness where the washerwoman Jenny Campbell lived with her son was a thing of significance. Jenny was one of a small number of people in the town by means of whom Jacobites in exile circumvented the authorities' interest in the posts. For a year or so after Culloden, the military authorities had taken a great interest in correspondence coming into the town, but for the last four or five years they had switched their attentions to the tearing open of the country by the building of new roads, bridges and forts and had grown somewhat lax in the matter of the posts. If they had ever wondered at a washerwoman being in receipt of letters off boats in the harbour, or from Edinburgh or London, they had never taken the trouble to look into it. Which was just as well. The letter Aeneas had just brought in, however, had not come from Edinburgh, nor London, nor anywhere like them.

'It's from the tolbooth.' Mairi read over the short note once, and then again. She said nothing but glanced at Iain before handing the note to Aeneas.

The steward read it, and evidently found the contents troubling. He also darted an involuntary glance towards Iain. 'I suppose it must be answered. I'll go.'

'I'll go myself,' she said, 'but you will accompany me. Send Eppy up to help me dress.'

Iain didn't need to ask about the nature of the note, whatever its details. Notes that arrived via the medium of the washerwoman all related to one thing – the cause. If the Hanoverians thought the atrocities perpetrated upon the Highlands by Cumberland after Culloden had put an end to the hopes of the defeated, they were quite thoroughly mistaken. There were still Jacobites enough who, despite what it had cost them, would give up the Stuart cause only with their last breath. Whatever was in the note had put a light in his grandmother's eye that he had not seen for some time. Seventy-three years old she might be, but she looked a deal younger, and made no concession to those years, even when it would be in her better interests to do so. 'Whatever it is,' he said, 'surely Aeneas can see to it.'

For the first time Iain could remember, Aeneas took his part. 'He's right. The tolbooth is not a place for you.'

His grandmother stood up and pushed back her chair, scraping it more loudly on the floorboards than ever Iain had done. 'I would remind you both that I have spent longer in the tolbooth of Inverness than either of you.'

There would be no arguing with her. When the redcoats had raided this house after Culloden and found her grandson there, the women desperately trying to treat his wounds, they had hauled Iain off with countless others to the Gaelic kirk, and sent Mairi to the tolbooth gaol for a fortnight. Iain drained his cup and stood up. He spoke to Aeneas. 'I'll be at the bookshop. You'll send for me if you need me.'

He collected his mended coat from the housemaid and shrugged it on as he walked through the courtyard before stepping out of the gate into the street. A breeze from the river carried with it a whiff of the tannery, and Iain felt the old longing to be in Strathnairn, with his cousin Lachlan. But Lachlan's lifeblood had seeped long ago into the soil of Drummossie Moor, where he lay still with half of their clan at the Well of the Dead. Iain set his shoulders and walked more quickly, ignoring housewives and kitchen maids coming from small lanes and back courtyards with baskets over their arms or bundles of laundry on their backs. He ignored the dogs wandering down the street, and they ignored him, set as they were on making for the town middens to see what pickings might be had before the scaffy men got at them. They were lean, hungry things, not like the two terriers Aeneas kept to see to the rats that were so hated by Iain's grandmother.

Some officers of the government's Military Survey were passing by on the other side of the street. Major Thornlie, who occasionally came into the shop in search of mathematics books, or for drawing materials or to have some old, damaged volume rebound, gave Iain a brief nod, which he returned. There were not many redcoats, officer or otherwise, whom he would even acknowledge, but Thornlie was one of them. Donald Mòr too took extra care when preparing materials for him. 'An honourable man, and damned few amongst them,' Donald would say, whenever Iain brought in a commission from the major.

There was little activity yet outside Catriona Lamont's house and Iain's grandmother had often voiced the opinion that the servants were near as fond of their beds as their mistress. The tolbooth, just beyond the Lamont house, gave no clue as to who within it might have summoned his grandmother at so early an hour of the morning.

Iain went in the other direction. To the north, the massif of Ben Wyvis stood immovable against a clear sky, not even a suggestion of a cloud troubling its long, level top. The bookshop was almost at the bottom of the street, a last bastion before commerce gave way to the relentless business of answering to God. Beyond his shop stood the graveyard of the High Kirk, where on Cumberland's orders Jacobite prisoners had been shot dead in cold blood. Then there was the kirk itself, whose ministers had in vain pleaded for mercy for those same prisoners, and at last was the Gaelic church where the captured of Culloden had been thrown one upon the other like rubbish into a pit. Iain's stomach turned every time he thought of it. He would gladly have clambered over the bodies of dying men to be amongst those shot outside, but Cumberland had wanted a goodly number of prisoners to display to the people of London, and he had found himself instead herded onto one of the prison hulks in Inverness harbour and taken south. Six years ago. His hand trembled as he searched in his coat pocket for the key to his shop.

Nothing. He cursed and tried again. Still nothing. He tried his other pockets – they too were empty. He stood there a moment, his eyes closed and his teeth clenched in frustration, cursing Donald Mòr that he couldn't trust him with a key in the bindery, cursing his assistant Richard Dempster for not yet being returned from Perth, and cursing Eppy for taking the key from his pocket while she cleaned and stitched the coat. There was nothing for it but to go home and retrieve it.

But the flustered Eppy, called away from her duties getting her mistress ready for the unexpected morning venture to the tolbooth, denied all knowledge of the missing key. Her tirade, in Gaelic, was addressed entirely to Aeneas, who was waiting in the kitchen to escort Mairi on her outing.

'Did I not check both the pockets, on the chance that him-self might have had the sense to put the loosed button into one of them? And it is hardly for me to say where he might have dropped the key *on his way home!*' Iain's occasional dalliance with the milliner Barbara Sinclair was known and thoroughly disapproved of by the young maidservant.

He gave up on his own house and retraced his steps of the previous evening, paying particular attention to the ground in the vicinity of Bow Court, near to where he had fallen. There was nothing. He glanced up to the window where the confectioner lived with her boy, and half-thought he saw a movement at it, but when he looked more carefully, there was nothing. A smell of scorched sugar was drifting to him from the stone bakehouse that formed the ground floor of her small home. The bakers of the town guarded their privileges closely but were prepared to concede the baking of cakes and the like to a handful of women. Ishbel, who spun her confections only for private patrons and did not seek to sell her wares openly in the town, was permitted to operate her small venture from the lower room of her house. Iain went to the open doorway and found her pouring an oozing mass onto a polished stone slab where it instantly began to cool. She must have heard him, but only looked up once she had finished. She watched him, a long curl of auburn hair falling over her forehead, from green eyes that seemed to suspect everything.

He cleared his throat. 'Did you find a key?'
'What?'

He had almost forgotten how to talk to a woman, but then, it was hardly a difficult question. 'I was wondering if you'd found a key. In the alley last night. I think it dropped from my pocket when I fell.'

Her eyes were unmoving. 'I found nothing but your coat, which I gave to you.'

He wondered what she had to be so wary of. She was a MacLeod. With one or two honoured exceptions, the MacLeods in general had not gone out for the prince in the '45, although their chief had long-promised they would. She should have little to fear from the authorities. But then, he reflected, Cumberland's soldiers after Culloden had not stopped to distinguish compliant Highlanders from those who had rebelled against them, and many a woman had suffered for a cause she'd had no part in. Perhaps it was to do with Virginia, where the young widow claimed to have returned from, or perhaps it was the boy. Whatever it was, Ishbel MacLeod was forever distrusting, forever watching for something, and at this moment she appeared most particularly distrusting of him.

'Well, if you do find it when you're . . .' he indicated the alleyway with a vague wave of his hand, 'sweeping, or something, will you send your boy over with it?'

As he left, he made one last search of the ground at the end of the vennel, but it proved futile. He gave up the key as lost and went up to the castle yard in search of a locksmith. It was a good hour after his habitual time of opening that he finally crossed the threshold of his shop.

He knew, the moment he closed the door behind him, that something was not right. He wasn't alone in the shop. His desk was on a small dais a few feet in from the door, elevated in such a way as to allow him a good view of all parts of the ground floor and gallery. On that dais, on his Swedish desk chair that he had had Bailie Steuart ship for him from Gothenburg, a man was sitting. The man had his back to him, but the battered brown hat he wore told Iain that it was the customer he'd had to remove from the gallery the night before. The intruder made no effort to turn, or to answer when challenged as to 'what in Hell's name are you doing here?'

A different kind of apprehension began to creep through Iain. He reached for the old shepherd's crook that he kept by the door and advanced slowly to the dais. Still there was no movement. He spoke again, but again received no response. Extending the crook to hook the arm of the revolving chair, he began to pull the intruder around to face him.

It was, as he had guessed, the man who had been searching with such determination the day before through the books of Lord Lovat's collection. He was dressed as he had been then, other than that the kerchief at his neck and the front of his waistcoat were no longer simply grubby, but now stained a deep, rusted brown from the blood that had come from the slash across his neck. His eyes were wide open, but they saw neither Iain nor anything else any more.

Iain looked around the ground floor area and cast a glance up to the gallery. There appeared to be no one else in the shop and no sign of further disturbance. On his desk lay a dirk like the one he had once habitually carried, before the bearing of arms or the wearing of tartan had been forbidden to Highlanders. Tied to the hilt of this knife, though, was a white silk rosette. Iain's heart began to quicken. It was the white cockade, as worn in his own blue bonnet and in that of practically every other soldier of the prince's army in the '45. The white cockade, the most recognisable of all the Jacobite symbols, on the hilt of the knife that had been used to cut the throat of the man sitting dead in his locked bookshop.

'Well, he sure as death didn't do it himself.'

Arch MacPhee had never been a man for unnecessary subtlety. One of the four burgesses currently serving his turn as constable for the Church Street ward, he was also one of Iain's few friends.

'He wasn't here when I shut the place last night, Arch, I swear to you, and I haven't been back till this morning.'

'Oh, I know all that well enough,' said Arch, a shoemaker by trade, as he circled the dais as if confronted with a knotty philosophical problem rather than a dead body. 'The fellow was nursing his twopenny of ale at Bessie Stewart's long after you picked yourself up off the street and limped away up the road.'

'You saw him?'

Arch nodded. 'He didn't look like he particularly wanted to be seen, but it does a man no harm to be on the lookout.'

'Do you know him?'

Arch screwed up his face. 'I don't think so. I'd have come to give you a hand up, but, ach, I knew you could handle yourself.'

'Thanks very much,' said Iain. 'But if you saw me, at least I can't be accused of having stayed in the shop to murder customers.'

'Though you hardly go out of your way to welcome folk in,' replied Arch with a small, quick grin. 'But there were plenty more than me saw you knocked down while he was still huddled over that ale in Bessie's. And the garrison would have had people keeping a good eye on your grandmother's house last night, with the ladies in conclave.'

Iain gave an uneasy laugh.

'It's true,' said Arch. 'Did you not know? It was Lord Bury himself that decreed it. When your grandmother and her cronies gather together that house is to be watched, dusk till dawn. He said he didn't trust them an inch. If anyone left that house last night, they'd have been seen.'

Iain had to appreciate the irony. The return earlier in the year of Bury as regiment commander in Inverness had brought with it a hardening of attitudes towards known Jacobites, but on this occasion it might just have saved his skin.

Other town officers came, and it was a long morning of questions about the dead man, his visit of the day before, and most especially about the keys to the shop. That Iain had somehow lost them in the incident with the man – now in the tolbooth – hurled from Bessie Stewart's tavern was accepted as likely enough, and it was already known that his assistant Richard Dempster, who possessed the only other key, had been away on business in Perth and not yet expected back.

Heads were shaken, the perplexity of the thing acknowledged, and arrangements made for the mortcloth to be fetched and the body carried, with as much discretion as possible, the length of the street to the tolbooth.

The constables had insisted on viewing the bindery, which he acceded to on their understanding that should any damage be done to the materials and equipment of Donald Mòr, he would have no hesitation in naming names. It was a relief to find that Morag was nowhere in sight when he opened the door. Donald himself, according to one of them, had last been seen the previous evening, while it was yet light, heading for the Kessock ferry and roaring about a Munro who owed him money. It was agreed that he was like as not in Dingwall gaol by now and could be questioned when the good burgesses of that town saw fit to return him.

Only once he had closed the door after the town's officers and finished sweeping the floor and scrubbing the boards of the dais did Iain sit down at his desk and consider the questions he'd been asked and the answers he'd given. He'd told no lies, but neither had he volunteered answers to the questions the officers could have asked. They hadn't asked him which books the dead man had been looking through, so he hadn't told them the man had been interested only in the books once belonging to the executed arch Jacobite and occasional turncoat, Lord Lovat. They hadn't asked him who else had been in the shop yesterday afternoon, so he hadn't felt the need to tell them. They hadn't asked him if the dirk was, when they arrived, exactly as he had found it, so he hadn't told them he had removed from its hilt a bloodstained white cockade.

He put his hand in his pocket and removed the unravelled strip of ribbon, then laid it at the bottom of the stove beneath some logs, to be burned the next time it was lit. Whatever tunes he might play to honour his grandmother and his own dead friends, he was done with the Jacobite cause and he was damned if the death of this stranger was going to somehow entangle him in it again.

FOUR

The King's Agent

The looks that greeted him when he entered his grandmother's kitchen confirmed for Iain that the whole tale of
the morning's events at the bookshop were already known
at the other end of Church Street. Eppy clearly did not
know what to say, and Flossie the cook was looking at him
as though he had brought the corpse of his unfortunate
customer in on his back.

'Will you bring up some warm water, Eppy, I need to
wash.'

'I . . .' The girl opened her mouth and looked at the cook.
Flossie straightened herself. 'Aeneas wishes to see you. In
his cellar.'

Iain's head was thumping after the events of the morning,
and he was damned if he was going down to the cellar for
another inquisition over God alone knew what. 'Aeneas
can find me for himself,' he said, as he turned towards the
door. 'Eppy, the water!'

But the cook stepped forward and took hold of his arm
as she had not done since he had been a boy. 'You must go,

Iain Bàn.' The use of his by-name, *Bàn*, and the anxiety in her eyes, dissuaded him from any further resistance.

'What is it, Flossie?'

But Flossie only shook her head and shut tight her lips as she handed him a candle to light his way down the stone steps to the cellar.

Iain rarely ventured down to the cellar. He hadn't been a fearful child, but of all the tales of ghosts and selkies and other malevolent spirits he'd been told to while away the long winter nights, it was those of the cellar of his grandmother's house that had truly scared him. Flossie had told him that that was where the water wraiths gathered at night, to consider whose soul they would next lure to a watery damnation. He had once questioned why Aeneas went down there, and Flossie had told him it was because Aeneas had already agreed his bargain with the Devil.

The cellar now, as then, was the province of Aeneas, who managed the household stores and kept an eye on the brandy, port and wines his grandmother had the merchant, John Steuart, import for her. The whisky was got closer to hand, from her native Speyside, or over in Ross, from the men of Ord. The steward did not encourage interference and Iain had never had any desire to take over these responsibilities from him. On the few times he had had cause to go down those steps, the memory of the darkness and horrors of the Gaelic chapel had engulfed him.

At the bottom of the steps Iain felt a shiver go through

him. It was as if the chill of the nearby river pervaded the walls. He lifted his candle. Aeneas was there, waiting, and as the glow of light revealed him in full, Iain realised that his hand was extended and in it was a pistol, and that the pistol was cocked. Stupidly, all he could think of in that moment was the intricacy of the engravings as the candlelight played on the steel weapon, but then Aeneas said, 'Ah, it's you,' and lowered his arm. Instinctively, Iain looked around him. From the shadows behind the steward a figure stepped into the light and Iain's heart almost stopped. Instead of being tucked tidily under the preferred white periwig, the long, reddish-brown hair was bound together in a dishevelled plait. No Highland plaid or philabeg, no blue velvet coat or red waistcoat of an officer of the Royal Eccosais, no pristine lace cuffs and white gloves, but the tattered short jacket, grubby shirt and canvas slop breeches of an English sailor. This was no sailor though. The image Iain had tried to banish for over six years, of his father charging ahead of him on Drummossie Moor into a blur of British army cannon fire and bayonets, flashed again through his head. Yet here he stood before him, in the cellar of his grandmother's house: Hector MacGillivray. His father.

Aeneas put away his pistol and cleared his throat. 'Your grandmother will expect you within the half-hour, at most. You will not keep her waiting: there is much to discuss.' Aeneas's face was more set with displeasure than ever as he mounted the stair, bearing his candle away with him. Iain was only vaguely aware of the clunk of the cellar door as he closed it behind him.

Iain felt as if the floor might go from under him. Hector took a step closer, into the circle of light from their remaining candle. He tilted his head a little to the side and gave the smile that would creep along his jaw to infiltrate his whole face. 'Have you nothing more for me then, than to stand and gape like one of Esther MacGillivray's heifers?'

'I thought you were dead.'

His father gave a gentle laugh. 'What? It would take more than a fat German butcher on a horse to kill me.'

Iain could not laugh. 'He killed plenty others.'

His father's smile faded. 'Aye, I know that, and many of them better men than me. But the Devil had a few ploys in mind for me yet and saw me off the field unscathed.'

'I thought you were dead,' Iain repeated. 'Where did you go? How did you get away? Searches were made . . .'

Hector took a step towards him, his hand outstretched. 'Have you not a hand to give your father?'

'A hand . . .?' Iain's voice was hoarse, disbelieving. 'There was never a word.'

Hector dropped his hand. 'I couldn't. For your own safety. And the nature of my work for the king has often required a great deal of secrecy. I could not – but you must believe, Iain, that I thought of you often.'

He had come further into the light and under its glow he seemed little changed. Sixty-three years old now, and the handsome face was almost as firm, the stomach as flat as Iain remembered. There were more lines about the deep blue eyes and the mouth than there had been, and the stubble on the jaw showed much paler now, but the look in the eyes was that of a man not ready to relinquish his prime, and the back was straight as a ramrod. Hector put out his hand and carefully lifted the hair away from the left side of Iain's face. He could not prevent a small 'oh' of sorrow from escaping his lips. 'Is if painful?' he asked.

'Not any more,' said Iain, forcing himself not to turn away.

'Thank God it missed your eye. Grapeshot, was it?'

'Aye.' He shrugged his shoulders. 'Flossie up the stairs there was a good long time picking it out. I'm not sure she wasn't enjoying it.'

Hector gave a gentle laugh. And then, seeming to have difficulty finding the words said, 'I – was heart sorry, when I heard about Lachlan.'

'I left him dead,' said Iain. 'My cousin, my foster-brother, closer than blood, and I left him on that moor, dead.'

'There is no more honoured ground than where he lies, Iain, and those with him. They are in *Tìr nan Òg* now.' *Tìr nan*, the Land of the Ever Young.

Iain went past his father and sat down on a pile of sacking, rubbing his face with his hands. What point in saying to Hector that it was harder for the living? Everyone knew that. In any case, his mind was filled with questions. Where had he been? How had he survived the charge on that day?

How had he ever got away? Too many questions, shouting for attention in his head. Eyes screwed shut, he pushed them back. What mattered was what Hector was doing here now. Yet he shouldn't be here now.

Iain stood up again. 'But what are you thinking of, showing your face here? Surely you know that you were excepted from the indemnity?' It had been five years since the British government, having executed or transported as many as they could get away with, and tired of their bulging prisons, had issued a general pardon for those involved in the rising. But there had been exceptions to that pardon. Iain might have believed his father was dead, but the government had not, and they were not going to permit a man who had been out for the Stuarts in every rising since he could hold a sword, and was known to have been an agent of the king in exile, to walk free and wait for the next time. Moreover, there had been rumours that after the battle, Hector had skulked in the Highlands in the wake of the fugitive prince, taking messages from one group of supporters to another. An 'Excepted Skulker' who had aided Charles Edward Stuart in his escape from their justice, Hector remained beyond the pale of their forgiveness. Iain had believed none of it, for surely if his father had still been alive, he would have communicated that to him? But here in front of him was the evidence to the contrary. 'There is still a price on your head,' he said. 'Tell me at least you didn't walk in broad daylight down Inverness High Street.'

Hector indicated his clothing. 'I came by sea, Iain. Well-forged papers in my pocket, and I never made it as far as the High Street. I was in a fight in the first tavern I came to and thrown out on the street by the second. The good bailies of the town had me lifted and taken to the tolbooth as I was on the point of entering the third.'

Iain was astonished. He himself had had many a scrape in his other life, before the rising, but his father? 'Since when did you fight in taverns?'

Hector laughed. 'Since I landed in Inverness and found myself drinking in between a Mackintosh and a Macdonell. Of course, they came to blows over some incident at Keppoch sixty years ago and I ended up in the middle of it. When the constables arrived the whole establishment swore that the two were as amicable as could be imagined, and that it was the English sailor who started it. So, as you can see, it was the English sailor who was hauled off to the tolbooth.'

Iain was not yet ready to laugh with his father. 'And then you exposed my grandmother by having her come to bail you out and bring you to her house?'

'God, Iain, we've had our moments, Mairi and I, but I'd no more want to see her in the tolbooth than she would me out of it. But she and I have always understood the king's cause requires us to rise above our personal animosities. Certain arrangements have been agreed upon for some time, should they need to be brought into play. I am on His Majesty's business. When I found myself . . . inconvenienced,

I sent a coded message to your grandmother by means of the washerwoman. Aeneas then this morning escorted your grandmother to the tolbooth, on the pretext that she had an objection to her share of the latest stent that the good magistrates have imposed on the householders of the town. Whilst there, just to alleviate the tedium, Aeneas took the opportunity to pass the time by viewing the prisoners. All a performance for the benefit of the tolbooth attendants, but the point of the viewing was to establish that the note had, indeed, come from me. The good Aeneas then went to the harbour, where my ship's master was handsomely paid to take himself up to the tolbooth and effect my bail, on the understanding that I would no longer be permitted to go into the taverns of the town. The master was more than happy to oblige.'

Iain was not reassured. 'And what? You just walked in here in broad daylight? Half the garrison will be here before dinnertime.'

His father looked at him carefully. 'Perhaps, but it will not be on my account. Nobody saw me enter this house. The ship's master paid my bail, took me back to the ship, and from there, by means which it is better you don't know, I came here.'

'But what . . .?'

His father held up a hand. 'We have much to talk about, Iain, but I think we should go up to your grandmother now.'

Iain could not once recall his father and his grandmother

having been in the same room together. He knew that they must have been, at the time of the '15 rising, before he was born, when Hector MacGillivray had met and then seduced Mairi and Neil Farquharson's young daughter. Iain's grandmother's subsequent dislike of Hector was surpassed only by that which simmered like lava in Aeneas's heart. Taking a heavy breath Iain lifted the candle and went to the bottom of the cellar steps, 'You have more courage than I thought,' he said, leading the way.

And yet, when they reached her inner sanctum, Iain saw that Mairi Farquharson had seated herself in state, arrayed in her finest gown and lace, Aeneas standing behind her chair, as if ready to receive an ambassador. But then he recalled that Hector, even in the shabby garb of an English mariner, was 'on the king's business'.

It was Aeneas who spoke first. 'Iain, your father has come here on a matter of great importance to His Majesty's cause.'

There was a tightening of Iain's stomach. 'What matter?'

Hector looked from Aeneas to Mairi. 'I am not at liberty to say, but you should know that it is something of the greatest consequence.'

'Surely, if it is something my grandmother is to be instrumental in, she should be told what it is.'

'Your grandmother, as you know, has played her part on very many occasions.'

'And am ready to again,' interjected the lady from her seat. 'I have done whatever has been asked of me for over sixty years. Your father will tell me precisely what I need to know, and it is not my place to ask any more. Nor yours, Iain.'

Hector accorded her a nod of thanks then turned to Iain. 'On this occasion I had not intended to involve her beyond the business of getting me out of the town gaol.'

'Which she has done,' said Iain, his eyes flitting from one to another in the room, trying to gauge where this might be leading.

Hector was standing with his back turned, looking up at the portrait of Neil Farquharson, painted over forty years ago, when Neil had been in his prime and the executioner's block on Tower Hill a thing of the future. He turned around and conceded Iain's point. 'Yes, and I would have troubled her no further but for a *complication* that has arisen.'

Iain felt a deadening inside. It was evident his father had not intended to spend even one evening with him. But he put it aside – he was no longer a child. He had come to the understanding many years ago that in his father's life there was one thing that would always matter more than he did. 'What complication?'

'This morning, as I was being released from the tolbooth, my skipper and I had to wait a moment while four men, attended by the bailies and others, came into the building carrying a bier. The gaoler lifted the mortcloth to see who was being brought in and was informed that the unfortunate was a stranger who had been found murdered in your bookshop.'

Iain poured himself a glass of brandy. 'That need not delay nor inconvenience you,' he said, betraying a bitterness he had not intended. 'The thing will be cleared up in its own time. I don't even know who he is.'

Hector furrowed his brow. 'But that's just it, Iain. I do.'

FIVE

The Book of Forbidden Names

It was well on in the afternoon that Iain again entered his shop. He made sure to lock the door behind him, but only after his companion, Hector, now a soberly dressed clergyman, had also stepped inside. Whatever Eppy's tardiness in the repairing of Iain's jacket the night before, over the last two hours she and her needle had been a whirlwind of industry under the expert direction of his grandmother. Iain's second-best Sabbath coat and breeches had seen their mother-of pearl buttons exchanged for plain pewter. A dull black waistcoat belonging to Aeneas had been let out across the back to accommodate the taller, more broad-shouldered man. Shoes Iain had never liked had had pewter buckles attached to them, and good, unworn stockings been found. A hat was called into service that had been left behind after a soirée several months before by a somewhat tipsy Episcopal minister from the Black Isle.

There had been one moment of awkwardness as they'd walked down Church Street together. Barbara Sinclair, her old father on her arm, had emerged from the end of Baron Taylor's lane. Barbara was the kind of woman who drew attention to herself without seeming to make the slightest effort to do so. She was dressed in a green velvet jacket and russet gown which served to set off her long dark curls. She glanced at them very briefly, her eyes like those of a cat, and bestowed on them a small smile and slight raise of the chin as she passed.

When they were a little way further down the street Hector said, 'Who was that?'

'Her name's Barbara Sinclair,' said Iain. 'She's a milliner.'

'I didn't mean the courtesan,' said his father, 'but the old fellow that was with her.'

'She's not a courtesan,' said Iain.

'She would be, in Paris, I can tell you that. Well, whatever she is, it's the old fellow she's with that I'm wondering about.'

'That's her father, Hugh Sinclair. He kept an inn in Perth or somewhere before he was taken prisoner to London after the '15. I don't know where they went after that – she doesn't talk of it, for I think it affected the old man badly. They came here two or three years ago, for his health, but he rarely stirs from their home. She has built up a good trade amongst the ladies of quality.'

'I may well know him from those times then,' said Hector. If he was going to say any more, it was lost in the approach of a keen-eyed spinster who was ever on the lookout to put an end to that situation. Hector summoned an abundance of ministerial charm and sent her on her way blushing like a sixteen-year old.

Iain was anxious, even after they had arrived safely at the shop. There were army officers enough in Inverness whose careers and indeed pockets would suffer no harm at all, should they be the one to finally put a rope around the neck of the excepted skulker, Hector MacGillivray. 'You might still be recognised.'

His father raised his eyebrows. 'What? Under all this? If the prince can outwit the best intelligence of half of Europe whenever he pleases, I'm sure I can pass muster for a few more hours in the town of Inverness. Besides, there are these.' He reached in his pocket to take out an item. Aeneas, with the help of a set of tools usually reserved for the maintenance of the household clocks, had made the necessary adjustments to a pair of Janet Grant's spectacles, found only that morning down a cushion of the sofa where she'd dropped them the night before.

Hector put on the glasses again and made a point of peering at his reflection in the glass of one of the shop's long bookcases. 'Now,' he said, 'look at that. I hardly recognise myself.'

It was nevertheless with evident relief that he removed the spectacles once more and stashed them in his pocket, muttering, 'It's a wonder the woman can see a thing.'

'That would explain her misfortunes at the card table,' answered Iain, 'but they certainly seem to have done the trick in transforming you. Hettie Peden will be telling everyone about the charming English clergyman she met going up Church Street with Iain MacGillivray.'

Hector's eyes twinkled. 'I may have sent a gallant flutter the old bird's way, I'll admit.' And then he was at the desk, dealing with the business that had brought them here. 'This is where you found him?'

'Yes.'

Davie Campbell, the dead man's name was. Hector had told them earlier, in Mairi Farquharson's bedchamber.

'A scoundrel. A thief and assassin for hire who is not particular who pays him, as long as someone does. He usually plies his trade around Glasgow and in Ulster. He served in Loudoun's regiment for a time, but he cared no more for the Hanoverian cause than you or I do. He was taking a chance though, showing his face in Inverness. He was in the tavern I got barrelled out of last night. Clearly, I wasn't the only one in this town to recognise him, and I'll tell you something else for nothing: Davie Campbell never read a book in his life.'

Hector walked slowly around the desk and chair where Davie Campbell had died. He paused and reached out a hand to lift the book now lying on the desk. '*Peregrine Pickle*,' he said. 'This'll be Smollett's latest nonsense, I suppose?'

Iain glanced at the book. 'It was Young Glengarry, when last he was here. He said I should read it – said it might cheer me up.' He shrugged. 'It's amusing enough.'

'I daresay,' said Hector, setting down the volume and

returning his attention to the business in hand. 'And the dirk was left how?'

Iain took a quill pen from the stand on his desk and improvised the placing of the knife.

Hector nodded. 'So it had been placed, rather than having fallen. And the cockade was definitely attached?'

'Yes.'

'You did well to remove it before calling in the authorities.'

'Open display of support for the cause has not been much encouraged in these parts of late years.'

'No.' His father was still walking slowly around the area of the desk and chair. 'I didn't mean that. The cockade was a message. Davie Campbell was killed by one of us, and whoever killed him wanted that to be known.'

'Why? Surely it could just as easily have been someone on the other side, casting the blame our way?'

'If that were the case, they'd just have left his body here in your shop.' Hector straightened and stood up, only now appearing to take in the rest of his surroundings. He took off the wig that formed part of his disguise and rubbed his head. 'What on earth was he looking for?'

'Well, whatever it was,' said Iain, 'he thought he would find it among Lord Lovat's books.'

'Young Simon Fraser?'

'No. His father – the Old Fox.'

'The Old Fox?' Hector gave a grim laugh. 'Will that Devil never die?'

'He died quite comprehensively more than five years ago, as I recall,' said Iain. 'Unless the papers and the engravers and the printmakers had it wrong, of course.'

Hector smiled in spite of himself. 'No, there were enough there on Tower Hill to see it, after all. So many the scaffolding collapsed. But the Old Fox wouldn't need collapsed scaffolding nor his head nor innards nor anything else to cause trouble. But . . . you have his books?'

'Yes.'

'Then it may be . . .' He paused. 'There is something I heard, when I was last in Paris, a rumour only. I paid it scant attention because it was a rumour of an old rumour that I thought could have little bearing on the business I'm employed on. But – where are the books?'

Once, Iain would have been desperate to know what his father's business was, but no more. Whatever had brought Hector to Inverness was unlikely to bode well for a bookseller who wished just to be left alone to get through his days without trouble. 'Lord Lovat's books are up here.' He led the way up to the gallery. He indicated the rows of shelving along the wall above the shop's window. 'My grandmother bought them from the government soldiers that looted Castle Dounie before they burned it. As I told Davie Campbell yesterday, I've sold a good few of them over time. Whatever he was looking for might well have gone.'

'And yet he came back to the shop. He must have believed it was here. Do you keep a catalogue of your books?'

'In the desk.' Iain went downstairs to retrieve the bulging

folio. He laid it before his father and opened it at the first page of the Lovat Collection. 'The books that came from Castle Dounie are all noted here. Those sold are marked thus,' he indicated a symbol in the second last column of each entry, 'and the name of the buyer noted here, in the last column.'

His father nodded then looked from the ledger to the bookcase. 'So every book not marked there as sold or set aside for the library should be on these shelves.'

'Yes.'

Hector removed his coat and rolled up the sleeves of his shirt. 'Well then, we had better make a start.'

As they worked systematically through the volumes, the occasional customer would try the door, a few rapping with the knocker when they found it to be shut. Even the most persistent gave up in the end. All but one of them. Muttering as a sharp tattoo of iron on wood began to play out a fifth time, Iain left his father to the search and went downstairs.

'We're closed,' he shouted.

The knocking came again.

Now he swore and angrily pulled the new key from his pocket. 'We're closed!' he started to say again as he wrenched the door open but stopped short when he saw that it was Barbara Sinclair standing there. Her father wasn't with her.

'Barbara.' He pushed his hand through his hair. 'This isn't a good time.'

She tried to step into the shop but he stood in her way. 'I can't talk to you just now, Barbara.'

'I only wanted to know that you were all right. I heard of a man being found dead in here this morning, and then when I saw you going down the street with that stranger . . .' She was trying to see past him, further into the shop that she had never set foot in before.

He put his hand on the edge of the door and began, very gently, to close it. 'There's nothing to concern yourself about. I don't even know who that dead man was.'

'But the stranger,' she persisted.

'An English minister looking for books. I don't know his name either.' He put his hands on her shoulders and turned her towards the street. 'I have things to be getting on with. Go back to your shop.' He locked the door again behind her.

Upstairs, Hector was still engaged in his search. A sly, untrustworthy, self-seeking man Lovat might have been, sometimes a brute, but he had been a well-educated brute and a great lover of literature. His studies at the King's College of Aberdeen and his various travels on the continent had nurtured in him marked tastes for classical authors which had been enhanced by an interest in the new French philosophy. Lovat's had been a library of substance. Iain's father was distracted more than once, relating witticisms of Montesquieu, in whose company in the *salons* of Paris he had often been, or Voltaire, who he affirmed to be a great admirer of the prince. They found themselves tracking along one or two false trails. One book from Lord Lovat's collection, a slim edition of Blair's 'The Grave', was in the bindery for repair; another, a fine copy of Thomson's 'The Seasons', Iain had recently moved to the library. The sun was almost set by the time they had it, but at last they did have it – the name of the one book from Lord Lovat's collection which should still have been on the shelves but was not. Hamilton of Gilbertfield's English version of Blind Hary's *Wallace*.

Iain sat down on the floor and stretched wide his shoulders. 'Two hours. For that.'

'Two hours well spent,' said his father, wiping the dust from his hands on the sober black breeches and sliding down beside him.

'How?' retorted Iain. 'The book is a cheap edition, and to be found practically anywhere. There is no great secret in it – half the country will have read it long ago.' There was not a schoolboy the length of the country who did not know the story of Scotland's greatest hero. 'What's more,' he continued, 'as I recall, that copy was not in the best of condition. Little wonder it never sold.'

'By design, perhaps. It seems the Old Fox was as clever as ever.'

Iain raised his head from the slump in which he had been sitting. 'Father, I am weary to my bones, I haven't made a shilling all day over this business and I have missed my dinner. I would be very glad if you might enlighten me.'

Hector held up a finger. 'One indulgence more.'

Iain slumped back again. 'If I must.'

'Think – how did Davie Campbell search through these books? Did he consult only the spines, or did he look inside them?'

Iain cast his mind back to the previous afternoon. The prevailing image was of Davie Campbell taking books off the shelves, one after the other, with no regard to any title or author's name embossed on the spines. 'He never looked at the spines or the fronts, it was inside – the boards, not the pages themselves that he seemed interested in.'

'Was it, now? What can you remember of the boards of this book?'

'Well, as I said, it was not in the best of conditions. The spine was somewhat faded and there was some foxing on the pages.'

His father drew a breath in a manner Iain recalled from childhood, when Hector was trying to be patient with him. 'The boards, Iain. What do you recall of the boards?'

Iain thought. The book had been in such common circulation, and this one in such tired-looking condition that he had almost thrown it out at his last check of stock, but something about this particular copy had caught his eye enough to make him hold onto it. And his father was right – it had been on the end leaves, pasted to the boards at the front of the book.

'They were marked,' he said. 'It was what made me hang on to the book in the end. I thought it interesting.' He recalled it quite clearly now, it had been on the inside of the front cover as he'd opened it – what might be expected to have been a blank board was instead embossed with six black marks – rosettes. He had thought them rosettes, at least. Two of them had had a line scored through them. Even as he described the markings to his father, he understood what they had actually been.

'Cockades,' said Hector. 'Black cockades.' As worn by their Hanoverian enemies in the late rising. 'What Davie Campbell was in here looking for was *The Book of Forbidden Names.*'

The title found an echo somewhere in Iain's head. Words, bandied with other curious tales to pass the time as they'd awaited their fate in that prison hulk at Tilbury fort. He looked at his father. 'I thought that was just a story.'

Hector sucked air through his teeth and gave a slight shake of his head. Iain felt a sudden shiver, as if all the warmth had gone out of the day. 'I'll light the stove downstairs and you can tell me about it.'

The stove lit, Iain found his father a chair, but Hector preferred to stand. Iain remembered that now – Hector was always moving or ready to move, never comfortable, never settled anywhere. Before he started to speak, Hector took a careful sip of the whisky Iain had poured for him.

He began, 'You know I am in His Majesty's service.'

Iain laughed. 'Father, that has been the fundamental fact of my life.'

Hector took a breath, as if to say something in response, but let it go. 'I spend much of my time travelling between

Paris, Boulogne and Rome, communicating between our people and the king in the Palazzo del Re. Increasingly, I have been – shall we say – *shadowing* the prince on his father's behalf.'

Iain stared at his father. 'You've been spying on Prince Charlie?'

'I wouldn't wish to see it in that way, and nor would His Majesty. I'd lay down my life for the prince, as so many others have done already.' Hector waved a hand as if dismissing his own life as a thing without value. 'We know he's headstrong, and that quality took him very far, but increasingly he refuses advice, takes dangerous decisions.' He indicated the amber liquid in his glass. 'Keeps dissolute company. It's my task to keep an eye on him for his father without him knowing I'm doing so. I'm sometimes in his company – the *patronnes* of those same Parisian salons graced by the *philosophes* will always find a place for a gallant Highland gentleman who can recite a ballad or pay a compliment. When I'm not in his company, I move amongst others of our people, keeping an eye on who can be trusted and who cannot. That's what has brought me here. I can tell you no more for now.'

'But what has this to do with this *Book of Forbidden Names*, or my shop?'

Hector held up a hand. 'I'm coming to that. When I'm in Paris, there's a lodging house I use, in the Faubourg St Germain. It's on the Rue St Dominique, very close to the convent of St Joseph.'

Iain might have told his father that those places were only names to him, that he was just a bookseller now, with no interest in the quarters, streets and convents of foreign cities, but he didn't want to interrupt Hector's flow.

Hector continued. 'Shortly before I left Paris, a tale came to me that I only half-listened to – my mind was all on the business that has brought me here, and so I paid it less attention than I should have done. The tale was a curious one of the ramblings of an old Highland gentleman who had just breathed his last in the convent. The place is a residence of some ladies of very high rank who are sympathetic to the prince's cause – in fact, Prince Charles himself has often found sanctuary there. But to the point: it seems the old fellow, in his dying hours, mumbled about the Old Fox, and Castle Dounie, and the *Book of Forbidden Names*.'

Iain watched his father carefully.

'There have been rumours,' said Hector, 'since the aftermath of the '15 rising, not long before you were born, in fact, of a book listing the names of the traitors to the cause. The names are said to be marked, encoded somehow within the pages, the very text, of a particular copy of some ordinary book. The title of the book they've been marked into – the host book, if you like - I don't know, but that particular, special copy is referred to by those of our people who have heard of it as *The Book of Forbidden Names*. The names are of Jacobites who took government bribes – either of money, or the promise of their own liberty – to betray plans, sabotage communications, inform on their comrades. Many good men lost their liberty, their lands and even their lives because of the activities of these traitors. It was believed that the copy of the book with the names encoded within its pages was in the possession of one who had found them out, but nobody could ever discover who that was or where the book was kept. Until an old man died in a Paris convent, after rambling a while in his sleep of the Old Fox and the *Book of Forbidden Names*.'

Iain understood now. 'Lord Lovat had this book?'

His father spread wide his hands. 'Who else, when you think of it? Who else could have found out such knowledge in the first place? Who else would devise a code, make a written record, allow hints of its existence to be dropped, and keep it hidden away for years, to make use of when it suited him most?'

Hector had a point. From his youth, long before Iain had been born, before even Hector had been born, Simon Fraser, the old Lord Lovat, had played a double game, at times keeping his cards so close to his chest that even he himself must hardly have been able to see them. It was fitting, somehow, that he had made such a secret of this book of secrets that it had outlived him.

'And do you think there are any names in it from the '45 rising as well?'

Hector shrugged. 'There were messengers going back and forth from the army to Castle Dounie and his other hiding places the whole time. I doubt there was an insect crawled under a rock the length of Scotland that Lovat didn't know about first. Whatever the truth of it, the corridors of that convent in Paris were echoing to it not so long ago, and someone with great interest in its contents must have got wind of what the old fellow was saying; that'll be the person who was paying Davie Campbell to find the book.'

'To find out the names of the traitors?'

'That's certainly one possibility.'

'And the other?' asked Iain.

Hector picked up his glass, untouched since that first sip, and held it up to examine its tones in the light. 'Because they're in it,' he said.

SIX

At the Horns Hotel

'You might at least smile, Julia,' said Elizabeth Rose to her daughter.

'A person cannot always be smiling, Mother.'

'You might at least make a start. There will be no officers at home.'

Julia studiously avoided following her mother's gaze through the short passageway connecting their small private dining area to the rest of the parlour of the Horns, and as far as to the window table where three officers were taking a late supper. Captain Dunne was holding forth to a bleary-eyed lieutenant and a young subaltern who contributed little to his senior officers' conversation. Julia had felt Dunne's eyes on her since she'd come into the room. She could still, in fact, almost feel his hand on her shoulder, in the small of her back, feel his breath on her cheek as they'd danced together at the assembly in the town house less than two weeks ago. She had loathed every minute of it.

'I have no interest in officers.'

Elizabeth Rose leaned forward. 'Then what, Julia? You are twenty-seven years old. You cannot wish to be an old maid for ever. Your aunt was asking if I had considered the colonies.'

Julia stared at her mother, utterly lost for a response.

'Oh,' her mother brushed crumbs from the table, 'I told her I could not do without you, at such a distance. But it is a pity, you know, for many of the best men have gone to make their fortunes overseas, and young women who don't keep an eye open to their opportunities are left with such as . . . well.'

She glanced across the room and this time Julia did look too. The street door to the main parlour had opened and Iain Bàn MacGillivray had walked into the room. There was a moment's hesitation and then his eye took in the English officers; Julia could feel the resentment radiating from him. The place seemed to hold its breath, but the officers did little more than sneer and the bookseller passed on, making for the far end of the room.

'Unbelievable,' said her mother.

'What?' said Julia.

'That he should walk in here with such a demeanour, when he is lucky to be free to walk the streets at all. But they are all the same.'

'Mother,' Julia said under her breath.

'Well, you *know* he is a Jacobite and his grandmother practically chief amongst the rebel women here, as bad as Anne Mackintosh.'

'Mother!' Julia leaned forward across the table, her teeth gritted. 'He will hear you. And think of the soldiers . . .'

'Whom he would have butchered at half the chance.'

'And they him. He is a bookseller, Mother.'

It was her mother's turn to talk through gritted teeth. 'And was not always so, as well you know.'

'That is all done with now, Mother.'

'Julia, you must understand – for them it is never done with.'

Just as her mother said this, the bookseller passed by the opening to their dining apartment. Julia could not recall having seen him anywhere other than in his bookshop. His clothing was not ostentatious, and yet she could see the cloth was a little finer, the cut a little better than that of anyone else in the parlour of the Horns. She'd heard the stories – of wild times and ungoverned escapades in the days before the '45, of courage and endurance during the late rebellion, of privation and transportation in its aftermath. He seemed somehow to carry them all within him, shut off to those, like herself, who were on the outside. His hands, she had noticed before, were fine, left unscathed by the shot that had so ravaged the hidden side of his face. Tonight she saw that the long, slim fingers were a little ink-stained. He passed on and took up his position with his back to the far wall, his eyes fixed on the street door. The landlord, who appeared perturbed that Iain Bàn MacGillivray should be in his establishment at all, quickly sent his boy over to ask what the newcomer would have.

'Whisky,' said the bookseller.

The officers by the window were getting louder all the time. The air in the room felt dangerous. Julia wanted nothing more than to be gone but it seemed as if her mother would never be done picking at the plate of veal collops in front of her. They should not have been here at all, in the Horns, but the aunt with whom they'd been meant to stay while in town was tending a child with scarlet fever. Julia had wanted to go home, back to Cantray Braes, but her mother had insisted they stay to have their fittings and make their purchases for the winter. It was also understood that they would remain in town until after the next assembly.

The thought of it almost turned Julia's stomach. She felt Captain Dunne's eyes on her and then saw him lean in and say something to his lieutenant. Both men laughed. The subaltern joined in too, but a little too late. It was intolerable. The bookseller's attention had also been taken by their laugh. She couldn't read his face as he stared over at them, but as he turned away, he caught her watching him. She was so startled she couldn't move from his gaze. After a moment he returned to his whisky and to staring at the door.

As time went on the officers were joined by others and the talk was becoming rowdier. Her mother at last pushed aside her plate and swallowed the dregs of her burgundy, and the landlord warned the soldiers of their language, but it was not on the women's account. Coming in off the street and removing his hat as he did so was a tall and, aside from the spectacles which made him squint at everything, somewhat handsome minister, who looked to be some years older than her mother. As the minister offered the room a benign smile, the bookseller, looking at him, drained his whisky.

The minister was now casting around the parlour of the Horns, exhibiting confusion as to where he might sit. He approached the entrance to their alcove.

'Please,' offered Julia's mother, 'my daughter and I are going up for the night. Take our table.'

The English clergyman – for it was clear as soon as he spoke that he was not a Scotsman – accepted the offer with a smile. 'If you are sure, madam. But I have no wish to drive you away. I would happily join you, if you had no objection?'

Julia could have wept. All she wanted to do was to get to her bed.

'You're most welcome, Reverend—'

'Ingolby,' he said, making a somewhat too gallant bow for a clergyman. 'The Reverend Daniel Ingolby.'

'Mrs Elizabeth Rose, and this is my daughter Julia.'

Julia could see the look flash across his eyes, though he tried to hide it. She could have told him she'd seen it a hundred times before. 'Daughter,' the look said. 'How could a woman as beautiful as Elizabeth Rose have such a plain daughter?' An elderly aunt had remarked upon it once, within her hearing. 'It is as if so much beauty has been taken up by the mother there is none left for the child.' A cousin had tried to cheer her by assuring her that she was not actually ugly, she was simply not remarkable enough to attract notice. The clergyman essayed a smile. His teeth were good and even beyond his disconcerting spectacles the smile seemed to inhabit his eyes. Somewhat to her surprise, Julia smiled back.

Elizabeth Rose had her head tilted slightly. 'Do I detect Yorkshire in your accent, sir?'

The man beamed. 'Indeed. And you, madam, you are native to this locality?'

'My husband is kin to the family of Kilravock. Our home is at Cantray Braes.'

The English vicar gave every intimation of never having heard of the place or the family, which Julia knew would not please her mother. She decided to intervene.

'I wonder what brings a Yorkshire clergyman to Inverness?'

'Oh, many things,' he said, removing the spectacles. 'But principally I have come on behalf of my brother, a merchant in Leeds, who has had advice that there is soon to be a great deal of land to be acquired in these parts, for a song.'

Julia felt her indignation rise. 'For a song sir? What manner of song?'

He laughed. 'Oh, a good loyal song, that King George might himself tap a toe to. The late rebels are to have much of their land made forfeit, if I am not mistaken. When the commissioners of the Forfeited Estates have finished their reckonings, it will be there for the taking for those with the money to spend who might better manage it.'

Elizabeth Rose gave her a warning look, but Julia ignored it. 'The land is to be managed? And the people who live on it?'

'Oh, they will be managed too, my dear, never fear it. They will have the virtues of *labour* explained to them. Efficiency. Where there is money to be made, men of talent aplenty can be found with the wherewithal to make it.'

'And your brother came by *his* wherewithal in the town of Leeds?'

The clergyman gave her a look suggesting that he was considering reassessing her. 'He has a cotton manufactory and does very well out of the American trade. He has a mind to invest it in the civilising of these parts.'

'How very fitting.'

He examined her more closely. 'How so?'

'It is all something of a neat equation . . .'

'Julia.' Her mother's voice carried a hint of weariness, as if she had heard this before and had no interest in hearing it again.

The clergyman held up a hand in a placating gesture. 'No, madam, I assure you. I am interested in what the young lady has to say.'

'The lands you speak of were forfeit by the chiefs who went out in rebellion for the Young Pretender.'

The Reverend Ingolby acknowledged this.

'Many of those who followed their chiefs out in rebellion found themselves transported across the ocean to work on those same plantations from which your brother draws such profit. The sweat of their brows will be invested back into the soil from which they grew.'

'You are indeed a mathematician,' said the clergyman.

But her mother, who had been scanning the street door and not at all given the impression of listening said, 'Your equation lacks one element, Julia – the negroes who have not seen and could not care about Scottish soil. And besides, some of those transported from here do well enough out of their bargain, I am told.'

'How so, madam?' asked the vicar.

'Well, would you rather be hanged or transported?'

'A life of slavery—' he began.

'Slavery? The transported rebels are not slaves, sir. They can buy their freedom, if they have the money, and some have made their way very well.'

'More have died in the meantime,' said Julia, feeling her cheeks begin to burn.

'It is the chance they took,' replied her mother, implacable as ever on the subject, 'when they rebelled against their lawful king. Time and again. It is the chance they took.'

The vicar reapplied his spectacles, as if to take refuge from the disagreement he had unwittingly set on foot between mother and daughter. He looked over to where the officers sat.

'That is Captain Dunne, is it not?'

'It is,' said her mother. 'Are you acquainted?'

'No, not at all. It is simply that I know of some of his exploits, and I thought I had heard someone point him out in the street.'

'My daughter might effect an introduction. Captain Dunne is a particular friend of hers.'

Julia studied to keep her temper. 'He is not, Mother. I danced with him once.'

'And might again if you would show him the slightest encouragement.'

'The captain finds himself encouragement enough. He needs no further stimulus from me.'

'You are twenty-seven years of age, Julia.'

This last was hissed *sotto voce* as the clergyman turned to hail the cellar boy for a glass of port, but Julia was sure he had heard every word.

'Please don't trouble your daughter, madam. I'm sure the captain and I will make each other's acquaintance in time enough.'

The bookseller had ordered another whisky. His attention was no longer on the door but on the officers at the other side of the room. It was a wonder they didn't feel his eyes boring into them – he did nothing to hide his hostility.

'There,' said her mother. 'There is one of your transportees who is somehow come back and walks the streets as free as any honest man.'

The minister looked about him.

Julia's mother moved her head slightly to indicate where Iain MacGillivray was seated.

'Surely,' said the minister, leaning closer and lowering his voice, 'that's the bookseller. I was in his shop only today.

He sold me a collection of Rutherford's sermons, and a very fine edition of *The Pilgrim's Progress*.'

'I have no doubt he did,' replied Elizabeth Rose. 'I would have to concede that he knows his business, but I am not comfortable even a minute in his company.'

'He is quiet, Mother, that is all.'

'Quiet? As a sleeping mastiff. He simmers with hostility.'

'He has suffered, Mother. You know that.'

'Suffered? You refer to his face? Some scarring is a small price to pay for one who should have faced justice at the end of a rope.'

'He was out for the pri— for the Pretender, I take it?' said the minister.

'He and his entire family,' said Elizabeth Rose. 'The most disloyal parcel of rebels to be found in all His Majesty's dominions, I'd warrant, but he is the last of them. His grandmother keeps a nest of vipers in her house on Church Street that has been at the heart of every piece of trouble for the government since before I was born.'

Julia thought she glimpsed a spark of amusement behind the small, round glasses. She followed her mother from the table as they bid the clergyman a good night. They had to pass by the bookseller to reach the stairs. Elizabeth ignored him, but as Julia went by, he suddenly looked her way. Startled, she heard herself stutter, 'Good night.'

'Good night,' he said.

*

Hector watched the women leave the parlour and retook his seat. Rose, she had said. The Roses of Kilravock. Staunch Hanoverians through every rising. The captain by the window, Dunne, made no effort to conceal his appraising of the daughter as she disappeared up the stairs.

'Pity she wasn't more like her mother,' said his lieutenant, when the women were completely gone from view.

'Not a bit of it,' said Dunne. 'She'll be all the more grateful.'

Hector heard the scrape of a stool as Iain moved past him, murmuring, 'Queen Mary's House.' He somehow contrived to jog Dunne's elbow as he went by the officers' table, and the captain cursed as the deep red wine spilt down the white stock of his shirt. Hector quietly sipped his brandy, called for another, drank that too and then, at last, went out onto the street.

Hector affected nonchalance as he walked the short distance from the hotel to the large house on the corner of Bridge Street and the riverbank where Mary Stuart, Queen of Scots had stayed when she'd visited the town almost two centuries ago. The unfortunate queen had been denied entry to her own castle of Inverness by its Gordon keeper. Four generations past, and the Stuarts still could not walk free in their own kingdom. But that would not be the case for much longer, God willing. Few lights showed in the windows of the large house, and Hector could hear little noise coming from it. Just as he was wondering if he was expected to knock at one of the doors, he heard a light humming from the courtyard close to the side. Cautiously he paused at the opening and looked down into the close. It was ill-lit and stank of things the town scavengers had disdained to meddle in. Hector's eyes were not what they had been and he kept his hand over the place his dirk was hidden. He paused as he registered a form further into the close, sloped against the wall. The form stirred. It was Iain, his hat down over his brow, his silhouette almost indiscernible in the murk.

Hector scanned the rest of the short passageway before he spoke. 'What is it?'

'There were two copies,' said Iain.

'Two . . .'

'Two copies of Blind Hary's *Wallace*, same imprint, same edition, that were marked with black cockades. Something was bothering me, and then I remembered. I checked through the catalogue again – my eye must have slipped over it the first time – and there were two almost identical copies of that book in Lord Lovat's collection.'

Hector shook his head. 'There was only ever one spoken of. That was what gave it its power.'

'There were two,' said Iain. 'The other one was in better condition, but the markings inside more crudely done – as if someone inexpert had been trying to copy it. Also, two of the cockades had been crossed off.'

Hector scanned his son's coat. 'Do you have it?'

Iain shook his head. 'I sold it, about a year ago, in a

job lot to an officer who was stationed at Castle Leod. He expected his regiment to be sent overseas and wanted volumes of little value because he would be leaving most of them behind.'

Castle Leod. Principal stronghold of the Mackenzies, seat of the attainted Jacobite Earl of Cromartie. The earl had only been saved from the executioner's axe by his pregnant wife, who'd gone on her knees to beg the Hanoverian king for mercy. He'd got away with his neck, but he'd never see his home or his lands again. 'And is he still there, this officer?'

'No,' said Iain. 'His regiment shipped some months ago.'

'And the castle?'

Iain shrugged. 'Possibly a factor, trying to collect the rents.'

Despite the danger of their situation, Hector let out a laugh. 'Good luck to the Devil then.' Forfeit or not, much of what income could be got from the decimated Jacobite clan lands evaded the government's collectors altogether, finding its way instead to the exiled chiefs.

Hector leaned against the wall opposite to Iain and took a minute to think. Complication upon complication. He had precious little time for complications. Yet there might be things in that book that would throw light on present concerns as well as past wrongs. 'We'll need to get hold of it.'

Iain nodded. 'Tomorrow morning, I will set out first thing. I'll go by the Kessock ferry and I'll be at Castle Leod in time for my dinner. I'll tell the factor I'm there to buy back some of the books. He'll hardly care which as long as he gets the money.'

Hector considered. There was something of the old light in Iain's eye, that he'd begun to think he wouldn't see again. 'If you wait a few hours I'll be able to come with you. I have someone to see first thing, out at Petty.'

Iain was already turning away. 'I don't need a bodyguard to go into Ross and buy a few books. I'll set out at dawn, do the business, and stop the night in Dingwall. I'll be back here before dinnertime the next day.'

'Easter Ross is crawling with Munros, Iain.'

Iain stopped and looked round in disbelief. 'Munros? Look about you, Father. How do you think we have all managed to live together while you have been courting kings and supping with Messieurs Voltaire and Montesquieu? We lost and it is *here* that we have had to live with it.'

Hector waited for his son's anger to subside, then said, very quietly, 'We lost, Iain, but it isn't over. I would not be here, if it was over.'

SEVEN

The Merchant

Hector had had to rise at a truly ungodly hour in order to be out of town and on the road to his rendezvous. He'd told the landlord of the Horns that he was making for the new fortress being built out at Ardersier. He was seeking advice, he had explained, on some land he was to have surveyed on behalf of his brother, the cotton manufacturer. The landlord advised him to seek out a Major Thornlie. 'The major's been here five years on the Military Survey and knows every last cairn and bog in the country.'

But Hector had no intention of going as far as the fort, or of making himself known to any officers there.

The road heading eastwards out of town had been much improved of late due to the requirements of the new fortress, a Leviathan in the making that was intended to crush any future rising from the Highlands before it could begin. Three sides would face the sea, ready to blast from the water any foreign assistance intended for the Stuarts, and to the landward a ditch had already been dug that was three hundred yards long and fifty wide. Let them dig their ditches and throw up their bastions, Hector thought. Long before their Leviathan was complete there would be a Stuart on the throne once more.

Hector recalled his last journey eastwards from Inverness, on that unseasonably wintry April night in 1746. The retreat from England at last complete, Prince Charlie's depleted, bedraggled and half-starved army had somehow taken Inverness. Many of the clansmen had peeled away to their own countries in search of rest and provisions. But then word had come that Cumberland, marching westwards from Aberdeen at the head of the government's forces, had managed to ford the Spey. No amount of telling the prince to melt into the hills and wage guerrilla war until the clans were refreshed would do it. He had been adamant – his Highlanders had never yet been beaten by the government's army in the field. They would fight.

It had been madness.

But then had come the flash of genius, the idea that might have been the saving of them. The report came to the Jacobite high command, stationed at Culloden House, that Cumberland's army was encamped outside the town of Nairn. It was the duke's birthday – the men would be given drink. A twelve-mile night march would take the prince's army to the very tent-ropes of his cousin's sleeping forces. The government soldiers would be killed where they lay, before ever they could take hold of their weapons.

Charles had been enraptured. Seven months after landing

with half a dozen men on a tiny Hebridean island, seven months of rallying, marching, fighting and retreating, complete victory was, astonishingly, in his grasp. The desolation enveloping him since the chiefs had forced him to turn back from Derby was gone. By dawn, his Hanoverian cousin's army would be in tatters and he would have won back his father's throne.

Somehow, they had managed to stir; somehow, that exhausted, depleted, starving army had been got to its feet and told the final push had come. Somehow, they had been formed into two columns and started out on that march towards Nairn. And somehow, somewhere in those twelve miles of riverbank, moor, bog and hillside, the columns had become separated from each other. The van of one had wandered, inexplicably, off course, its rear left stumbling about lost in the dark between Kilravock and Cawdor. When finally the leading column had come within sight of Cumberland's camp, the prince's column was too far behind and the first fingers of light had already begun creeping across from the east. The government's army was already waking, the most advanced of the Jacobite soldiers so close they could hear them calling to one another. It was too late – their moment was gone.

Clansmen, Irishmen, French piquets and English Jacobites far from home had trudged the desperate miles back along the Nairn to Culloden, some of them sleeping as they marched – Hector himself had seen it. Twenty-four miles through the cold night and the cruel dawn on empty stomachs – such had been the preparation for the battle of Culloden of Prince Charles Edward Stuart's army.

Hector shook his head. What was done was done, and it was the now that required his attention. Ahead of him was Alturlie Point, a place notorious for smugglers, and just beyond it, his destination – the turfed roof stone warehouse belonging to the merchant, Bailie John Steuart.

Hector approached the place carefully, noting that the door was still bolted and the window shutters closed. He edged his way round, but there was no sign of life save for the oystercatchers parading the water line. Suddenly, a sound from amongst the whins put the birds to flight. 'Hands above your head and turn around.' Hector stood stock-still. His knife was secreted in a pocket of Aeneas's waistcoat; pistols had he none. The command was repeated, this time with greater insistence. Hector did as he was bid and turned around. An elderly man, his head tilted to the side as if for better aim, was holding a musket level with Hector's chest, and gave every impression of being prepared to discharge it.

'Hector MacGillivray,' he said.

'Bailie,' said Hector carefully. 'Are you intending to use that?'

'That would depend,' said the bailie, 'on what you are doing here.'

'I have come in response to your letter.'

'On whose behalf?'

'On whose . . .?' Hector was beginning to wonder

whether the bailie was in fact grown senile. 'On King James's.'

The bailie observed him for a moment longer, then at last lowered his gun. He sniffed before extracting a heavy iron key from a pocket in the folds of his long, shabby coat. 'Well, come in then.'

It was dark inside the storehouse, and colder than it had been out on the shore. A scattering of vermin at their entry provoked an irritated mutter from the bailie. It was a minute or two and some more muttering before he had lit two candles. He then poured a measure of oil into a lamp which he also lit.

The spreading light revealed a cavern of barrels, crates, sacks, earthenware bottles and glass jars. Beneath those dun and dull coverings, Hector knew, were the riches of the world. Some of the barrels would contain brandy brought ashore here off French boats in defiance of the customs at Inverness; others whisky from the Speyside glens, destined to be taken on those same boats as they headed the other way. From the good bailie, the citizens of Inverness might also obtain oil and olives shipped from Ligorno along with the oranges, raisins and lemons so prized in the making of their punch. Spices, muslins, tea and sugar come from the ends of the earth by way of London or Rotterdam; almonds, walnuts, coffee were stored along with soap, rope and window glass from the Baltic. Flint stones from the Channel Islands were stacked next to paper that Iain sold in his shop. There was nothing to be had that the bailie could not get for you. Yet for all the treasures the warehouse contained, the only furnishing in the place appeared to be an old, tall writing desk behind which the bailie was now shuffling. Any other means of comfort being notable by its absence, Hector set a wad of sacking on a handy crate and sat himself down.

The old man wore no periwig, and his lank hair lay in ragged grey strands on the shoulders of his heavy coat. By interludes of lamplight as he moved, Hector could see that the elbows of his coat were shiny and its hem frayed. The bailie's woollen stockings had been darned more than once, and the boots repaired many times. His hands and face were of the thin, sharp-boned sort that looked as if they had never been warm. A man whom the world had already begun to leave behind. Hector was not fooled for a minute.

'Your message took some time to reach me.'

The bailie sniffed. The tip of his nose was red. Hector imagined he was perpetually cold. 'I had fears it had gone astray, although I doubt that any interceptor would find much in it to excite themselves about.' The bailie's family life and business interests allowed his intelligence to be transmitted in the most plausible of coded letters.

'Perhaps not,' said Hector, 'but the information encoded in its lines may be vital to us. Your service is much valued, Bailie Steuart.'

The bailie gave a dismissive clear of his throat. 'If it were a little less valued, I might have been living at my ease in France by now.'

The old merchant, ever pleading indigence, had travelled to Boulogne the previous year, in hopes of obtaining a pension from the Court of France, as one who had been of service in the last rising. But it had served King James's interest better to have him here, in the heart of the Highlands, with his ear to the ground and his pen in his hand. The bailie's numerous family and friends were dispersed to the four winds: Edinburgh, London, Newfoundland, Carolina, Jamaica, Bombay. There was not a corner of the globe to which he might not innocently send a letter, not a ship going out from or calling at Inverness or Cromarty in which he might not have some legitimate cargo. His domestic trade and the incessant chasing of debtors and mollifying of creditors had him in correspondence with every nook and cranny in the Highland hinterland and almost every settlement of any note in Scotland. As Aeneas had observed to Hector in the cellar of Mairi Farquharson's house the previous day, 'If Bailie John Steuart does not know of something, you may be certain it hasn't happened.'

'You would have grown listless in France, Bailie – it's a country full of disappointed men living on the scraps from others' tables. You're your own master here. But to the point: your late letter hints that the prince might be about to expose himself to some great danger.'

The bailie gave a long sniff. 'You will be aware of the plans mooted by Alexander Murray, Lord Elibank's brother.'

Hector nodded. 'To kidnap the Elector of Hanover and his whole family on their way to the theatre? The man is surely mad.' The individual known to Jacobites as the Elector of Hanover was, to almost all the rest of the world, King George II of Great Britain and Ireland.

'You might think so,' said the bailie. 'But the plan was to involve Young Glengarry, whom Elibank had met in London. Young Glengarry, as you know, is much in the prince's company.'

'And one as charming as the other,' said Hector. Charles Edward Stuart and Alastair Ruadh Macdonell, Young Glengarry, were two handsome young men of impeccable lineage that should have the world at their feet but instead wandered Europe, fugitives in disguise, denied their patrimony or their destined place in society.

'The short of it is,' continued the bailie, 'Glengarry has three hundred good men in and around the city of London that he can call upon. The elector and his family are to be kidnapped on their way to the theatre. With the Hanoverians removed from the heart of the kingdom, the English Jacobites will then rise and prepare the way for the homecoming of the rightful king. The prince will be waiting on the French coast, ready to sail at a moment's notice.'

The English Jacobites. There was nothing more dear to Charles's heart nor to the success of any plan than that the English Jacobites should rise. He had even lately turned Protestant, to reassure them. 'They won't rise unless there is hard evidence of support from abroad,' said Hector.

'There is word of the King of Sweden,' said the bailie.

That much was true, Hector knew. The King of Sweden

stood ready to send forces to land on the Yorkshire coast. All depended though on the assistance of Prussia, and Hector had told Charles to his face that any promise of help given to him by Frederick would merely be a ploy to annoy his uncle, King George, the Elector of Hanover, and would come to nothing in the end. He had thought the prince had listened to him.

The bailie muttered that the games played amongst the courts of Europe were of less concern to him than a spoiled consignment of salt pork. 'All Europe might dance whatever jig it likes, but I can tell you, Young Glengarry was here and taking numbers of clansmen ready to rise again as long as two years ago, to take back to the prince. Whatever plan was afoot then came to nothing, but he was here again in April, as you may have from Bishop Forbes in Edinburgh, who dined with him. He has had much ado looking into the financing of the thing. I have already sent out orders for guns and ammunition to be landed here in a matter of weeks.'

'Weeks?' Hector was stunned.

The bailie continued. 'The date of the attempt on the Hanoverians is set for November. The clans will need to be ready to march by then. I have written time and again to the prince that some of those on whom he will most rely are ill-provisioned, but I doubt he has any more sense now than he had before.'

Hector could hardly argue with the bailie, and who could argue with Charles Stuart? He had arrived seven years ago on a scrap of an island in the Hebrides with seven men and hardly a gun between them: within weeks they had taken Scotland and been in a fair way to take England too, before the gods of war had awoken and seen what the Young Chevalier had done whilst they slumbered. To tell the prince to abandon his new plan because the Highlanders were ill-provisioned, when he believed he had the might of Prussia and Sweden behind him, were as much use as whistling on the breeze.

'Frederick will never send the Prussian army out in support of King James.'

The bailie shrugged. 'Does it matter? All that matters is that our people in England believe he will. Then they will rise. What was not accomplished the last time might very soon be accomplished if more of them are persuaded to come out this time.'

Hector's mind was spinning. How was it that this shabby merchant of Inverness had intelligence that was not known at the king's court in Rome? The answer was not really so difficult to find: because even King James had as good as given up on his eldest son, but the Highlanders never would.

The bailie bent down beneath his desk a moment to re-emerge with a thick folio volume which he thumped down onto the desktop but didn't open. 'I keep copies of my letters in here. Should anyone come across it, they would think this only a bundle of business or family correspondence. It is occasionally of use to me, however, should I need to remind myself of some detail.'

He leaned forward on the desk. Hector asked to see the letter book, and to have it explained to him. And so the old man began to turn over the pages. Some missives he dismissed as being indeed family concerns or private matters of no consequence, but more were quite other than what they at first appeared. First, he would draw attention to the date, and let Hector himself call to mind what had been the prevailing movements and incidents of the time. Then he would show how the name of one of his many children would correspond instead to a person of consequence in the Jacobite interest. He gave Hector to understand that amongst letters addressed to his eldest son, John, were several which had in fact been for the eyes of Prince Charlie himself. His widowed daughter, Mrs Wedderburn, domiciled in London, was oftentimes a front for one of the prince's own chief agents in that city. His other daughter, 'my daughter Newton', cover for another, who roamed England and the continent as required. Many were the requests to the prince under the guise of 'John' to let his mother (the clans), know when he would return to the Highlands, or at the very least details of the place and time at which they should meet. 'Daughter Wedderburn' was often given very specific instructions of goods to be acquired and sent home – calico, coats, oranges, sugar – that only the recipient would realise meant cannon, powder, rifles and swords. The boats by which they were to be sent, the means landed, were similarly coded. Daughter Wedderburn was indeed a force to be reckoned with, poor widow that she was. Almost nothing had passed in the Highlands but the bailie knew and had tried to inform the prince of it.

'You wrote with a warning against a person whose activities threatened the prince. Is this related to Elibank's plot?'

The bailie swallowed. 'I fear someone who does not have the Stuarts' best interests at heart has at least got wind of it. My daughter Wedderburn informs me that one of my letters to her had been tampered with before it reached her. It was around the same time that one of our people, employed in some insignificant post at Whitehall, reported rumours of a new informant in Pelham's pay.'

'There's nothing new in that,' said Hector. 'Prime Minister Pelham has agents all over Europe, attempting to track the prince's movements. I've spotted a good few of them myself. He'd be as well setting fire to his money, for all the good it does them.'

'That may well be,' said the bailie. 'His Highness's ability to make himself disappear is much to be admired. But there are fears that this person is trusted. One of our own.'

Hector felt a chill grip his stomach. 'And this letter your daughter fears was intercepted . . .'

The bailie's mouth was pursed, and for the first time, he could not meet Hector's eye.

'The name of my son-in-law's ship was on it. The "calico" she was to arrange for sending four three-pounder artillery pieces got at Antwerp. My son-in-law was warned just in time. His ship was raided less than an hour after he had got the guns off and hidden elsewhere. All that was lost were a few casks of whisky he had taken down from Ferintosh for a client in the city. The customs men were greatly pleased, and he much out of pocket.' The old man's chest sank in a sigh. 'I fear it is coming a little close to home, but if this plan of Elibank's finds its way to government ears, the prince will be walking into a trap the minute he lands in England.'

'The clans would already have to be on the move by then,' said Hector, 'if they were to take Edinburgh and cross into England again.'

The bailie nodded. 'Exactly so. There is not much time. As I say, the arms will begin to arrive in a matter of weeks. There are preparations under way in Yorkshire too. Should the government come to know the detail of these plans, the names of the men and women involved, and catch them in the very act, King James's cause will be finished. Those caught will be butchered as were so many before them, and the prince himself might well be taken.'

'And this informer?'

'All I know is that he goes by the name of "Pickle".'

'Pickle? All right. Thank you, Bailie. You did well to send your warning. I will uncover whatever I can, but I can spare no more than a few days before I must travel back to France to tell the prince, one way or the other.'

It was arranged that a berth would be found on the bailie's son-in-law's ship due to depart Cromarty in a week's time, and then they toasted Elibank's enterprise with a dram of

Old Ferintosh. As he savoured the last drop of his dram, Hector said, 'Talk of new traitors brings rumours of old to mind.'

The bailie said nothing, only watched him.

'You acted as agent for Lord Lovat and his estates.'

'The Old Fox?' asked the merchant. 'Of course. The Frasers had a good trade in salmon, timber and grain – all gone to the government now, of course. And Lovat knew a good bottle of wine and who could get it for him.'

'Did he ever speak to you of *The Book of Forbidden Names*?'

'No, he did not,' said the bailie.

'But you know of it? You have an idea what's in it?'

Steuart regarded him with an old man's eye. 'What I know is that *The Book of Forbidden Names* deals in long-past wrongs, and should it ever be found, its pages were better burned and the ashes buried deep than its contents be meddled with.'

Julia Rose had risen early and taken a solitary breakfast in the parlour at the Horns. There was no sign, this morning, of the English clergyman whose attentions the previous evening had briefly animated her mother. But she had seen him again last night, after she and her mother had retired to their room. She had chanced to look out of her window and her eye had been taken by the sight of someone she was sure was Iain MacGillivray disappearing into the close at the end of Queen Mary's house. Being assured that her mother was asleep, she had remained at the window, transfixed, waiting for him to re-emerge, only to see the Reverend Ingolby disappearing down the end of the same close. The clergyman had reappeared a very few minutes later, but although she had stood there at the window until her fingers grew numb with the cold, there had been no further sign of the bookseller.

So now, by dint of some casual questioning of the Horns' parlourmaid as her breakfast was brought, Julia learned that the English minister had left early, on his way to some business at the new fort, and it was not known when he might return. The ensuing morning involved a tiresome round of visits to tradespeople and merchants as her mother ordered up the wherewithal that would be needed to see their household out by Kilravock through the coming winter. It was only by declaring that her mother might choose any headdress for her that she wished for the forthcoming assembly that Julia was able to miss the trip to the milliner's shop. The woman made her ill-at-ease, and Julia had more than once seen Captain Dunne or some other officer exit Barbara Sinclair's shop. On the pretence that she was not, after all, enjoying *The Female Quixote*, she said she wanted to go down to the bookshop to exchange it for another. Her mother was more than happy to let her go down there alone.

Julia was still some way from the shop when she noticed that a small boy, the child the confectioner Ishbel MacLeod had brought back across the Atlantic with her, was sitting on the step at the shop's front door. As she drew closer, she saw that the door was closed. She tried to look in at one of the windows, but could see nothing of the inside, for the shutters had not yet been opened.

'It's closed,' said the boy, who was holding what looked to be a silver button, apparently examining it.

'But where is the bookseller?' she asked. The image again came to her mind of the strange English clergyman emerging alone from the wynd in which she was sure he had gone to meet Iain MacGillivray.

'Iain Bàn's not there,' he said, engrossed in the button.

'And the binder?'

The child shook his head. 'Donald Mòr's not there either.'

Julia looked around her, but there was no one else anywhere near them. 'But what has happened to them?' she asked, her voice rising in anxiety.

The child tossed the button in the air and caught it, quickly stashing it away in a pocket of his waistcoat. He was a good deal better dressed than many of the urchins of the town, although, like most of them, he went barefoot. 'Donald Mòr will be in the gaol somewhere,' he said.

'But the bookseller?'

'I don't know. When Richard gets back from Perth, I'll ask him.' And in a moment he was up and gone.

Julia called after him but he had already disappeared into Bow Court. She had completely forgotten about Richard Dempster, the bookseller's assistant, so shadowy a figure did he make himself. She tried the door to the bookshop, but to no avail. She even went down the little alley at the side and through the back courtyard to look in at the bindery window, but there was no sign of life there other than a large, feral-looking cat which arched its back and hissed at her when she came too close. She backed away out of the gate, frightened of she knew not what.

EIGHT

Castle Leod

Sitting with his back to the ferryman as the boat pulled across the firth towards the Black Isle, Iain watched the town of Inverness gradually recede. In truth, the place was a scrap of a thing, a jagged ribbon, tumbled down from its castle hill to trail along the riverbank and stop just short of the sea. To the west, it had crept across the seven stone arches of its bridge until, amongst the homes and lanes of the not-quite-town, it petered out and was lost on the shore road to Clachnaharry and the Aird of the Frasers. But what caught Iain's eye now were the two prominences of Tomnahurich and Craig Phadrig. Tomnahurich, the Hill of the Yews, was where the fairy folk were said to reside. In his childhood, he had believed this without question and had thrilled to tales of fiddlers who'd gone inside the hill to play for the fairies, and not come out again for a hundred years. His tutor had warned him gravely never to play his fiddle at Tomnahurich, and Iain had sworn never even to think of it. Sometimes he wondered whether, if only he could play the right tune, the hillside might open up to admit him and not release him until all the horror of these past few years was gone.

But then, Craig Phadrig a little further along his eyeline, mightier than the hump of Tomnahurich, reminded him that there would always be new wars to replace the old. An ancient people had had their fortress on the top of Craig Phadrig, and watched out over the firth, commanding all approaches, before even the word of Christ had come to the Highlands. That people was forgotten now, their fortress gone, their names unknown. Further still to the west lurked Loch Ness, and the fastnesses of the Great Glen.

To the east of the town, past the earthworks for that new monstrous fort, Fort George, were the broad, rich plains of Moray. There, agriculture was practised and Scots spoken. There, were other towns and trade, going all round the coast to Aberdeen. To the south were the mountains that held back the world.

Iain had always known, of course, that there were other things, other places, far on the other side of those mountains. He'd been born and lived his first years in France, after all, and had studied and learned his trade in Edinburgh, long before the '45 rising. But Edinburgh had been as nothing to the London he'd seen after the rising, when he'd finally been dragged up from the hold of *The Jane of Leith* at Tilbury fort to be paraded through the streets. When he'd been able to lift his eyes, it had been to discover a city that was like some whole chaotic library whose catalogue had long since been lost. It was a miracle he'd ever got out of it. But Inverness? What was the town of Inverness? Not even a story, but a paragraph perhaps, an aside in some intrepid traveller's letter or in a few pages from an English officer's journal, scribbled down before he moved on to better things.

The wind changed and he changed his seat, occasioning much grumbling from the ferryman. With his back turned to the town, he saw now that amongst his fellow passengers was James Munro, sheriff-depute of Ross. Munro sometimes came into his shop, always keen to see any new treatise from the great minds of Edinburgh or Glasgow, or their brother *philosophes* of France. He was a man who knew his books, and one of the few patrons whose company Iain did not mind.

Munro shifted along on the bench to make more room for him. 'Have you business on the Black Isle today?'

'No. Castle Leod. I'm looking to expand my library stock.'

Munro raised his eyebrows. 'From Castle Leod? I believe there's just a caretaker in the place now, while the commissioners for the Forfeited Estates complete their work. From time to time there'll be a detachment of soldiers moving from one cantonment to the next. I wish you good luck of it.'

Iain was keen that Munro might not enquire too closely as to the nature of the books he was going to the castle in search of. 'And yourself? Are you headed for Foulis?'

The sheriff shook his head. 'I have court this afternoon

in Dingwall, where I will no doubt be presented with the usual assortment of vagrants and delinquents, and then I must make for Tain.'

'Where the delinquents will be different, I'm sure.'

Munro laughed. 'They'll have different surnames, at any rate.'

As the ferryman negotiated a sudden swell of the tide, Iain thought of Donald Mòr. He cleared his throat. 'It's possible my binder may come before you in Dingwall today. He was last seen on Friday, heading in that general direction.'

The sheriff-depute showed little surprise. 'Well, it wouldn't be the first time. How you manage to get work of such quality out of him is beyond me.'

Iain shrugged. 'Donald is a perpetual storm. He's a hurricane, when in drink. But in his workshop, at his workbench, he is the eye of the storm.' That same binder had not long ago done some very fine work on the sheriff-depute's treasured copy of Mackenzie's *Criminals*. Iain pressed his advantage. 'If you were inclined to set bail at all . . .'

Munro sighed in resignation before naming the likely sum, which Iain duly produced.

'I'll see to it that it's handed over to the clerk. I'll try to get him done early and he should be back over your side of the water by tonight, as long as he doesn't land himself in hot water the minute he gets out. The Presbytery of Ross is after his blood – the blasphemies he has in his vocabulary . . . Quite astonishing.'

Iain promised to do what he could to keep his binder to the southern shore of the firth in future.

Disembarked, James Munro mounted his horse. He looked at Iain. 'You're walking to Castle Leod? It's a good twenty miles at least. But,' his voice dropped, 'you're no doubt able for it.'

Iain merely nodded. It was the closest they had ever come, the sheriff-depute and the bookseller, to referencing the conflict in which they had fought on separate sides, Munro as a cavalry officer in Cumberland's army, Iain as an infantryman in Prince Charlie's. The government forces had, for a long time, been astonished by the speed at which the Highlanders could cross the country. Those in the government's own Highland regiments though, had well understood what they had to deal with. As the wind coming down the firth whipped his hair over his face, Iain recalled standing side by side with James Munro, seeing Munro's kinsmen buried at Falkirk after that battle, before they and others had parted again to join their respective armies. Each of the two men knew that he might well have been called upon to kill the other, and would have done, if it had come to it.

Iain watched the sheriff-depute ride away, before setting off himself at a good pace along the shore towards Redcastle and the Mackenzie hinterland beyond. He began to think about what might await him at Castle Leod.

He had only been to the castle once before, long ago, in the company of his grandmother. It had been a great thing to be allowed to accompany her, although he had been somewhat terrified by the old earl, who had survived a variety of what Mairi Farquharson referred to as 'scrapes', but what others had let slip had included trial for murder. Most of Iain's memories of that early visit were impressions, fleeting images. He recalled having been permitted to go with the Mackenzie herdsmen to an ancient hill fort from which views might be had for miles down the firth. The men had told him stories of Norsemen sailing up that firth to make their capital at Dingwall and of a powerful seer who had thrown his stone of prophesy into the loch below them. They had assured him that many of the seer's prophesises had already come to pass. That night there had been a ceilidh in the great hall of the castle. Iain had been encouraged to scrape his inexpert bow across his fiddle with some of the best players amongst the Mackenzies, and story after story had been told. He had been well-warned though not to ask at the castle about the prophesies, for one of the earl's kinswomen had had Coinneach Odhar, the Brahan Seer, burned to death in a barrel of oil at Chanonry Point. Iain had hardly been able to wait to get back to Inverness to terrify his schoolfellows with tales of Norsemen and horseless chariots and seers' curses.

At last cresting Knockfarrell, the hill overlooking Castle Leod, Iain stopped at the site of that same hillfort to eat the bread and cold mutton Flossie had sent him away with. There were no Norsemen sailing down the firth now, only government patrol boats and further up, in the Bay of

Cromarty, the trading ships loading produce and people for Leith, London, Carolina and the Caribbean. The world was getting on with its business and he had somehow fallen out of time. He put away the remains of his meal and set off down towards the seat of the Mackenzies and their chief, the now forfeit Earl of Cromartie.

Castle Leod, at a distance, was a fantasy from some tale of Charles Perrault, but grew solid and substantial at Iain's approach – a seat of power. The closer he got, the more imposing the keep became, towering five storeys above him. The castle, pink-washed that it might be known to have been the home of a notorious Jacobite, was still here, but the Cromartie family was not. The third earl, son of the reputed murderer, was somewhere in England now, perhaps rubbing his neck where the axe had been ordained to strike, checking in the looking glass that his head was still upon it. Cromartie had paid very dear for his support for the Stuarts, but his life at least had been saved by the imprecations of his pregnant wife. As to those fiddlers whose skills had transfixed Iain, they would be slashing at sugar cane in the Caribbean now, or tobacco in Virginia, if not dead.

All around the outside of the keep was strangely quiet and almost empty. There were no horses in the stable and other than the few hens pecking around him, there appeared to be little activity of any sort. Iain peered up at the high, narrow windows of the tower house, but had no sense of being watched. He might have wandered on to the set of a play after the players had left it. He went up to the sturdy, iron-studded door that had seemed so huge to him as a boy, but under whose lintel he now wondered if he might have to stoop to pass beneath. Above him, a sculpted limestone frieze over the door showed the skulls and antlers that had loomed over him on that first visit. It was a marriage stone, put there long ago by an earlier chief, but it had frightened him then, and even now it struck him as being utterly imbued with the sense of death.

He was just about to lift the heavy iron ring and knock when he heard the sound of a key turning and the door opened out to him. He addressed the servant woman in Gaelic but she responded in English, her accent from Cumberland or perhaps somewhere further south. He had heard it before, at any rate, on their march into England.

'What do you want?'

He explained his wish to examine the castle library, with a view to making an offer on some of the books. He took pains to emphasise that the presence or otherwise of a resident factor need not be an impediment to the handing over of money. The woman looked to be considering the proposition, but her deliberation was cut short by the appearance of a man behind her. A Highlander, he was short and unkempt in appearance, scrawny brown hair sticking out from beneath a dirty bonnet. Before he spoke, Iain had a strong sensation of having seen him somewhere before. The man told him in Gaelic that there was a detachment from the regiment in Inverness coming for the night, and that he should return at some other time. When Iain asked when the soldiers were expected, the porter responded that it was not his business to know, before shutting the door on him.

There was nothing for it but to wait. He went down the slope of the castle mound and sat beneath the branches of a sturdy Spanish chestnut tree, planted in the days of Mary Stuart. With his back against the two-hundred-year-old trunk, he closed his eyes and listened to the buzzing of the black bees amongst the flowers in the grass at his feet. He could hope that it was Major Thornlie of the Military Survey, or someone of that sort coming out from Inverness, in which case there would be no difficulty in him going through the castle library. Even if it wasn't Thornlie, he was certain he could get at the books on the promise of money to be made. He opened his eyes to the sound of horses coming along the Achterneed road, red jackets standing out harsh against the greys and purples and pale greens of the landscape. His heart sank. Not Thornlie, but Dunne, Captain Edward Dunne, whose glass of wine Iain had contrived to knock down the man's front in the Horns only the night before.

Iain knew Dunne for one of the most loathsome men in the entire army of occupation. He'd learned his trade in the weeks and months after the battle of Culloden. An ensign in Cholmondeley's 34th Foot in the summer of 1746, he had served under the barbaric James Lockhart, a Scot whose forces had burnt, shot and raped their way through the country in search of escaped Jacobite soldiers and any who had helped them. Lockhart's forces had perpetrated especial atrocities around Glenmoriston, near where Iain's grand-mother's great friend Janet Grant had her family home. It was just a matter of weeks, in fact, since Iain had escorted his grandmother on a visit to Janet's house in Corrimony, only to find Dunne there, en route to Glen Cannich and demanding his dinner and feed for his horse. Janet had looked more terrified than he had ever seen her when they'd arrived, and it had taken every ounce of restraint Iain possessed not to throw the Englishman out of the house. He had, nonetheless, left the captain in no doubt as to his opinion of him, and his disdain had been reciprocated. Of all the officers he might have seen riding along the road to Castle Leod, this was the worst.

As he watched Dunne's approach at the head of the party, Iain experienced some of the old feeling of when the enemy came in sight. He had thought those feelings buried under the weight of the last six years, the depredations, the loss, but at this moment, what would he not have given to have had his claymore in his hand? What would he not have given to experience once again the madness of the charge? For all the anger his father's years of silence still kindled in him, Iain knew that should whatever had brought Hector from France come to fruition, nothing would stop him from fighting for it at his father's side. With renewed purpose, he walked back up to the front of the keep.

Dunne appeared not even to notice him. He dismounted and handed his horse to a stable boy who suddenly appeared, before turning to the men behind him to give orders for the storing of the 'rents'. The pack horses and carts behind the soldiers were laden with chests of grain, hides and cheeses, and beyond them cattle were being driven onto the castle park. It was only as he was about to pass beneath the doorway of the castle that Dunne finally noticed Iain.

His face registered his displeasure, and he looked about him as if suspecting an ambush. 'The Jacobite bookseller,' he said, his mouth curling in contempt.

'Captain Dunne,' replied Iain, summoning all his reserves of civility.

'Hawkers to the kitchen.' Dunne's eyes swiftly took in the distance between himself and his men.

Iain went straight to his story of the books he had sold to Lieutenant Archer and that he hoped to buy back.

'What sort of books? How many?'

'A dozen or so of general interest, that might make a useful addition to my circulating library.'

Dunne snorted as he passed beneath the lintel. Iain was taken with a strong desire to see it fall down on his head. 'It always amuses me to see you savages attempt to ape a gentleman,' said the officer. 'You can look at the books, and if I decide I don't need them to kindle my fire you can make me an offer.' Once into the castle, he roared for brandy before disappearing up the stairs, swearing about this damned hellish country.

Left alone in the lower hall, Iain looked about him, at a past familiar and a present hostile and alien. It was one thing to deal with the redcoats in his own shop, to encounter them upon the streets or in the taverns and coffee houses of Inverness. It was quite another to take himself into the heart of their occupation. He needed to master the anger he felt in Dunne's presence if he was to find the book he'd come for and get it safely out of Castle Leod. To his right, the crest of the Mackenzie chief, *cabar-feidh*, was still carved on the stone wall. Iain took heart. 'All right then, Cabar-feidh,' he said to himself, 'let us do this.'

Glancing down the passage ahead of him for any sign of the unwelcoming doorman, Iain turned to his left towards the wide stone steps of the main stair of the castle. Emerging onto the first floor, he listened, but there were no sounds suggestive of the English captain. Castle Leod, Iain remembered from that childhood visit, was a warren of doors concealing cupboards or spiralling stairs in corners that led from room to room and floor to floor through the thickness of the walls. He would start with the great hall.

He had expected to find devastation here, evidence of wanton destruction, but though the tapestries, paintings, glass and silverware that had once graced the room were gone, the essentials of the place were as he remembered them, down to the trailing flowers painted on the lintel of the fireplace. It was the people who were absent – the earl, in exile somewhere in England, his young heir another of the dispossessed who after his release from the Tower had made his way across the North Sea to enter Swedish service. Iain wondered if the Mackenzies would ever set foot in Castle Leod again.

There was no sign of any books, nor of Captain Dunne either, in the great hall. Iain crossed to the dining room but Dunne was not there either. He supposed the officer had taken himself to some private chamber on one of the upper floors. He stood a moment in the dining room, and thought if he closed his eyes he might still hear his grand-mother's voice ringing round the room as she gave forth on a chieftain's duties and responsibilities. The old earl's protestations about his debts to the government's coffers she had dismissed as merely another reason to be avenged on them. The results were to be seen now, in this all-but-empty, echoing castle. There was a rumour, though, that the old Mackenzie factor and the countess's family, even some of the local clansmen, had managed to spirit away much of what was valuable, for safe-keeping, before the redcoats had been able to get their hands on it.

But the book Iain was looking for had been brought into the castle with a British army officer after the place had already been cleared, so there was a chance that it was still here, somewhere. He was on the point of leaving the dining hall and heading up to the next floor, when a door in the anteroom to the dining hall took his eye. If it was a cupboard, any old books might well be stored there. The door opened without protest and he found himself looking into not a cupboard but a small room, akin to the 'cabinet' in some houses he knew, where letters were written and papers kept. There was indeed a desk, and writing materials, and, what made his heart beat the faster, two bookcases against the facing wall. All was lit by a small window to the south, looking out over the castle lawns. Iain entered the room, closing the door from the dining room as softly as he could behind him. An investigation of yet another door in the far corner revealed an exit back out onto the main castle stairs.

The room hardly merited the name of library, and he doubted very much it would have been used as such in the earl's time, but Iain was certain that if the *Book of Forbidden Names* was indeed still in Castle Leod, this was where he would find it. He crossed over to the bookcases. One of those contained nothing but an old account book, and the other was almost a third empty, but Iain could see straight away that many of the books in it were those he had sold to Lieutenant Archer.

Listening again for any sound of Dunne nearby, he set to work. A book on the top shelf caught his eye immediately. *The Gentle Shepherd*, by his old bookselling mentor, Allan Ramsay. Iain became lost for a while in recollection of his Edinburgh days, and of the nights playing his fiddle as his friends sang the ballads from that play. Nights from a different time, a different world. He was snapped back to the present by the sound of more horses coming up the castle drive. He crossed quickly to the window and looked out. Two more soldiers.

The new arrivals focused his thoughts and he turned his full attention to the other volumes in the bookcase. He had no candle, but the afternoon light was strong enough to illuminate the collection. It had been a decent assortment of works, he remembered, although the condition of the books had not been the best and Donald Mòr would have been very dismissive about some of the binding.

Noises from outside told him the horsemen were now dismounting. Iain crouched lower over the shelves to run his eye over the spines. He checked them again. He couldn't see the copy of Blind Hary he had come for, that contained Lovat's *Book of Forbidden Names*. His heart started beating faster and he felt his stomach clench. It must be there. Surely Archer had not taken it away with him? He stopped. He was sweeping the shelves too quickly, without method. He took a deep breath and began again, slowly this time.

If Archer had ever used a system in the placing of his books, it was gone now. Old volumes of *The Spectator* and *The Scots Magazine* jostled for space with works by Cervantes and Milton, Thomas Gordon's translation of *Tacitus* sat cheek by jowl with *Moll Flanders* and Rutherford's *Letters* thundered impotently alongside Hume's *Essays Moral and Political*. The sun moved behind a cloud and the light in the library became murky. Puffs of dust rose in the air as he disturbed the books on their shelves, pulling out possible candidates for the volume he was looking for.

There were only the bottom two shelves left to search when he heard a clamour of competing voices come from outside into the hall below, bringing with them spurred boots on the stone floor. Amongst the voices was one he recognised – Calum Mackay from Sutherland, an officer of the Black Watch. Iain had gone through the grammar school of Inverness with Calum Mackay. They had even been at the college in Edinburgh together for a time, before their lives had taken them along different paths.

They had had some wild escapades together in their time, he and Calum, but Iain had no desire to linger here a moment longer than necessary. It soon became clear though that the new arrivals were ascending the stairs and would soon be in the great hall. His heart sank as he heard Dunne's voice, issuing from above.

'Major Mackay. I thought we might conduct our business in the dining room.'

Quickly, Iain crossed to ensure the door to the dining room was firmly closed, then went back to continue his search. He'd hardly got back to the shelves when he heard the voices louder, the men having arrived in the room next door. His fingers flew on, and suddenly, there it was. How easily he might have missed it, wedged as it was between a copy of Ramsay's *The Ever Green* and one of Ruddiman's editions of Douglas's *Aeneid*. He had his finger on the spine of Lord Lovat's old copy of what to anyone else in the castle would be nothing more than Blind Hary's *Wallace*, but which he knew contained in its encoded pages *The Book of Forbidden Names* for which he had come. Suddenly the door from the dining room swung open and Captain Dunne's voice rumbled into the room.

'MacGillivray. You're not finished yet?'

'Almost,' said Iain. 'I just have to finalise my list.'

'Well, you'll have to leave off. I have business to discuss that's none of yours. Take yourself down to the offices and make up your list, and your offer.'

But then there was a cry of, 'Iain Bàn MacGillivray!' Calum Mackay had appeared in the doorway behind the captain. 'By God it is!' Beaming broadly and speaking in Gaelic, Mackay shouldered his way past his subordinate and strode over to take Iain by the hand. 'Fifteen years, man, it must be fifteen years.'

Despite his situation, Iain could not help smiling back. 'Near enough, Calum. It's good to see you.'

Mackay took him by the arm and turned to call out to his sergeant, whom Iain also vaguely recognised, to come and see who he had found. As he did so, his leg caught the corner of the Blind Hary's *Wallace* from where Iain had left it sticking out on the shelf and accidentally knocked it to the floor. Iain went to pick it up but Mackay was there before him. He lifted the book, whose front board was now hanging off, and, switching back to English, apologised to Dunne.

'I'm sorry, Captain. I seem to have damaged your book.'

'Not mine, sir,' replied Dunne. 'Just some old rubbish Archer left behind. MacGillivray here was about to make me an offer for them.'

'Oh well, Iain Bàn,' said Mackay, 'I doubt you'll be wanting this one now.'

Iain, holding out his hand, attempted to appear indifferent. 'No doubt my binder could do something with it, make it saleable.'

But the major didn't hand over the book. He was looking instead at the title page, a broad grin spreading over his face. 'Blind Hary. Oh, do you remember how we used to act out the parts? Poor Lachie always played Wallace.'

Iain nodded. 'And you were always Andrew Murray.'

'But who were you?'

'I think it was settled that I should stick to my fiddle.'

Mackay roared with laughter, then stopped, his face momentarily grave. 'We'd have done better to stick to play-acting though, would we not? Damn your Charlie Stuart.' They'd started moving through to the dining room now, and Mackay still had the book in his hand. 'We've some matters to discuss, as the captain says, Iain. But I'm sure he won't object to you joining us here for supper afterwards, will you, Captain Dunne?'

The captain's mouth betrayed him with an involuntary curl and Iain intervened.

'I've to get back to the town tonight, Calum.'

'Tonight? Nonsense. It'd be dark long before you got there and our patrols can be none too nice about sleekit big fellows like yourself skulking about in the dead of night, terrorising decent folk. The town of Inverness will hardly fall down if it can't get its hands on your books for a morning.'

There was nothing to be done. Promising to join them when they were ready, Iain left the dining room to take himself down to the castle's offices and make up a list of books that he had no intention of buying. The last thing he saw before he closed the door behind him was Calum Mackay absently laying the copy of Blind Hary's *Wallace* down on the dining table in front of him.

NINE

Old Stories

In Inverness, Julia found her mother's round of visits near interminable and was weary to her bones by the time they arrived for supper at the salon of Lady Ross. Lady Ross had acquired many of her ideas from a girlhood in France, courtesy of a long-dead Jacobite father. Lady Ross's husband had kept his head down in the late rebellion and she had quickly learned to shed her own family's questionable allegiances, if not their cultural habits.

The salon was the best that could be made of it, under the circumstances. Lady Ross had brought in Ishbel MacLeod the confectioner to serve them chocolate and sweetmeats of her own preparation. There was a hopeful music teacher lately hired by the town, as well as two young men of good family about to depart for the second year of their course at the college in Edinburgh and full of half-digested ideas of Hume and Voltaire. One of them at least had a facility for reciting poetry. The other did not but insisted on doing so all the same. The question of proper reading material for young ladies was raised, young Abigail Ross again threatening to weep over *Clarissa*. A lately published volume of the poems of Alasdair Mac Mhaighstir Alasdair was discussed with much enthusiasm, until one of the ladies present opined that it was a pity he was a Jacobite.

Julia had attended such gatherings so many times before, she might have predicted exactly the pattern this one took. Her heart sank when one of the young students suggested they act out a scene from Ramsay's *Gentle Shepherd*. Parts were being cast when, to Julia's immense relief, Lady Ross's sister, late as ever, swept into the room, her eyes burning with a secret she could not wait to tell.

'Marjorie, what on earth is it?'

Marjorie Ross carelessly divested herself of her outer garments, sending a housemaid scuttling about the floor to pick them up.

'A skulker,' she said, as she sat down between her sister and the music master, who had hastily jumped aside at her approach.

'What?'

'In the town. I heard it at the pewterer's, from Lachlan Dallas. He'd been in the Horns last night and was sure he saw there an excepted skulker.'

'One that had been out with the prince?' asked her sister, forgetting herself, it being more politic in certain company to refer to Charles Edward Stuart as 'The Pretender'.

'And with his father too.'

Guesses were made, of high-ranking gentlemen and low-ranking thieves, and each time, her eyes shining, Marjorie

Ross shook her head, until her sister said, 'Not Hector MacGillivray?'

Marjorie looked towards her sister. 'The very one.'

'Who is Hector MacGillivray?' asked Julia as the younger men looked nonplussed and her mother and her friends drew their heads together, remembering. No one answered her, so she repeated her question.

It was Lady Ross herself who answered her, waiting until she had helped herself to another sweetmeat from a tray proffered by the confectioner. 'Hector MacGillivray was the most handsome man in the Old Pretender's army in '15 and he still cut a fine figure following the Young Pretender out in the '45. Half the women in Inverness were throwing themselves at him – Jacobite or no – when they took the town from the government army in the September of 1715. Of course, it was Charlotte Farquharson that got him.'

'Charlotte . . .?'

'Mairi Farquharson's daughter. Bonniest girl in the town, but wayward, oh!'

'An Italian courtesan now, they say.'

'What? She'll be well past fifty!'

Marjorie Ross shrugged. 'Still. It's what they say.'

'So does that mean Hector MacGillivray . . .' began Julia, seeing it at last.

'Is the bookseller's father,' Lady Ross finished for her. 'Ian Bàn was quite the young blade himself, you know, before the rebellion and his transportation.'

They carried on talking, and the conversation moved

to more general reminiscence of that earlier rising, when the Old Pretender, a young man himself then, had also come to Scotland, and when they too had been young, and hopeful. And eventually, as she had known it must do, to reminiscence of Arthur Rose, killed in a valiant, foolhardy attempt to take back the town for the Hanoverians. Julia knew though that her mother would be thinking of another of her father's kinsmen, Henry, cut down in his prime far away in fighting at Preston at the same time. Henry, whom the young Elizabeth had loved. Elizabeth had grieved nine long years before eventually agreeing to marry Julia's father, but Julia thought her mother's life had never really moved beyond the day of Henry's death.

The salon and the supper had gone on a lot longer than usual on account of the news of the skulker. Once they had got back up to their room at the Horns Julia started lighting the candles. She stared at her own reflection in the window and wondered if she would tell her mother what she had seen from that window only the night before. She was still trying to find the best opening when her mother's voice broke into her thoughts.

'It was the clergyman.'

Julia turned around. 'What?'

'Last night, in the parlour downstairs. The man who called himself the Reverend Ingolby. He was Hector MacGillivray.'

'You recognised him?'

'Not then, no, although when I saw him, I experienced

that sensation of already knowing him. It was only when Marjorie Ross came in and told us about it that I realised why.'

The listing of the books was the work of half an hour, but it was after almost two hours of being left to it in a boot room with nothing but a wooden meal-chest or the floor to sit on, that Iain was finally told he might go up and rejoin the officers. The manservant mumbled it to him before turning away back to the kitchens. Still, there was something in his glimpse of the man's face that made Iain think he had definitely seen him somewhere before. Taking his book list in his hand, he went upstairs. Shafts of pink and golden light fell to touch the stone steps from the window, beyond which the sun was slowly sinking down behind Ben Wyvis. Iain abandoned any last hope of getting back to Inverness tonight.

It was clear from the sounds reaching him from the dining room that whatever the army officers' business had been, it had not been conducted dry. Their voices were at such a pitch that they didn't hear him when he knocked at the door. He tried again.

'Come in!' shouted Mackay.

Iain went in and was almost overwhelmed by heat and pipe smoke and the reek of male sweat. The soldiers had clearly already taken their supper, the remains of which lay scattered on platters on the sideboard – bread, cheese, salmon and cold beef and pickles. What was left of the food was drying in the heat and the punchbowl had already been brought into play, the whisky in it so strong that it must have seared their throats. Cheeks that had been flushed from the ride of the afternoon now approached vermilion, and eyes were becoming glassy. Iain's sense of apprehension rose: Calum Mackay was a good drunk, he remembered that from their student days – the best of company, up to a point. But he was only a good drunk up to that point, and after that he became a dangerous liability. Iain assessed what was before him and saw to his relief that Calum was as yet at the genial stage.

'Well,' said Dunne, 'here's one of them if I'm not mistaken.' He turned to the young ensign who was doing everything he could to remain in an upright position. 'You will not yet have learned, Warren, that there are as many breeds of Jacobite as there are vermin. You think, no doubt, that this fellow is the bookseller he claims to be, but you will note the scarring on his face, the sullen look in his eye, the contempt he can hardly keep from his mouth. The major will tell you, I have no doubt, that this is one of the fabled Clan Chattan, a MacGillivray who—'

There was amusement in Calum's eye as he turned over a cherry stone between his fingers, examining it minutely before breaking in with, 'Oh, indeed, an inveterate MacGillivray.'

Dunne swallowed down his punch and slopped some more into his cup. As much spilled onto the tablecloth as went into the drinking vessel. He was very drunk, and fixed Iain with an unpleasant smile. 'Well, they won't be much good the next time their beloved Teàrlach lands in this festering country, will they? Feeding the worms on Drummossie Moor, most of them, and good riddance to the vermin.'

The room went very quiet, very quickly. All that could be heard was the crackling of the fire and the sound of Dunne's wet, heavy breathing. Iain felt the anger surge in him and had actually taken a step towards Dunne when the sergeant, who had not been drinking as the officers had, placed a cautionary hand on his chest, and, with the smallest of nods, directed his gaze towards Calum Mackay.

The major was white with anger and Iain could see the veins in his forehead stand out as they had always done when he was at his most dangerous. The tension emanating from him suffused the room. At last he started to speak.

'You think my country "festering", Captain?'

Dunne made a noise as if he would laugh but then at last registered Calum Mackay's mood and began to sober. 'No, Major. No, not your country, this . . . his.'

Mackay's fist slammed down on the table so hard that more of Captain Dunne's punch spilled from its glass and a candle almost went out.

'His country is *my* country, you cretin. And,' his lip curled in disgust and he turned his head from Dunne as if he could hardly bear to look at him, 'you are not worthy to lick the boots of the men who died fighting for that Italian fop on Drummossie Moor.'

The look on Dunne's face suggested he might willingly have risked court martial if only he could have thought of a suitable riposte to the major. Instead he settled for glaring ahead of him like a chastised schoolboy.

Calum gave a snort of derision before turning to Iain and talking in Gaelic. He asked of old acquaintances in common and spoke of those in the army and others in the Americas, whether by their own volition or King George's. He talked of his family in Strathnaver. Dunne, clearly thinking himself and his misdemeanour forgotten, reached again for the ladle, but before he could approach it to the punchbowl, Mackay had pinioned his wrist to the table.

'I think you've had enough, Captain, don't you? Besides, I would have some entertainment.'

'Entertainment?' queried Dunne.

'I would have a story.'

'Story, sir?' said Dunne, getting more sober by the minute.

'Even you must know what a story is, Captain.'

'I . . . yes,' the man protested. 'But . . .'

'You are not a storyteller?'

Dunne said nothing.

Calum turned to Iain, grinning. 'We'll make a *seanchaidh* of him yet, what say you Iain Bàn?'

'I daresay it could be done,' said Iain, watching the English officer all the time.

He was still watching the English officer when he realised Calum had stretched across the table and picked up the copy of Blind Hary's *Wallace*, its front board still dangling by threads. The major muttered in annoyance as the corner of the hanging board trailed into his food. He ripped the board off and threw it into the fire behind him, the black cockades stamped on it curling and burning before Iain's eyes. Fortunately, none of the five red-coated officers in the room could take their eyes off Calum Mackay, whose fingers were now swiftly turning the pages of the book. 'Here,' he said at last. 'This bit. Read this bit, Captain Dunne.'

Dunne hesitated then took hold of the torn book.

'That bit,' said Mackay.

The captain began to run his eyes across the lines as the rest of the men in the room watched him. All Iain could look at were the ashes of the burned board as they turned white.

'Aloud!' roared Mackay. 'Read it aloud!'

'Sir . . .' began Dunne.

Calum Mackay's eyes were like flint and his voice dropped very low. 'Read it aloud.'

Looking around him as if expecting one of his countrymen to intervene, Dunne's face contorted and he began to read.

> *Promiscuous crowds one common ruin share.*
> *And death alone employs the wasteful war.*
> *They trembling fly by conquering Scots oppress'd,*
> *And the broad ranks of battle lie defac'd;*
> *A false . . .*

He stopped and looked up. 'Major, this is treason.'

'It's poetry, you unlettered oaf. Read it!'

The muscles working in the captain's jaw showed an impotent fury, but he read on.

> *A false usurper sinks in ev'ry foe,*
> *And liberty returns with every blow.*

Mackay continued to look at the captain but addressed Iain.

'A false usurper, eh?' He held up his glass. '*Slàinte*, Iain Bàn.'

'*Slàinte mhòr*, Calum,' replied Iain, giving the Jacobite toast in return as he raised the glass he had filled for himself from the punchbowl. Calum raised an eyebrow but smiled. Iain had often suspected that, left to his own devices and not having to adhere to the loyalties of his clan, his old school fellow would have gone out for the prince, Italian fop or not, rather than taking up his sword in the Hanoverian cause.

The sergeant was clearly concerned that tensions between the officers might escalate. He approached Calum and leaning down, said something into his ear.

Calum swivelled. 'What's that, Archie?'

'Culrain, sir. You are expected tonight at Culrain.'

Calum nodded and stood up, seemingly stone cold sober. 'Aye, I am. I'll take my leave, Dunne. See those orders are put into effect. You are to seek out any evidence of some new stirring amongst the clans, or whether anything is known of this matter concerning Elibank. But you will tell your scouting parties to conduct themselves as gentlemen or they will answer to *my* discipline. You are not under Lockhart's command now.' Then he put out his hand and gripped Iain's. 'It's been good to see you, Iain Bàn. Watch out for yourself.'

He picked up the book and for a moment it seemed he would take it away with him, but then, to Iain's relief, he set it back down. 'I prefer the old Charteris edition,' he said, 'in the Scots.' Without saying anything else, accompanied by his sergeant, he left. As the sound of Calum Mackay's boots on the stairs receded, Iain resolved to have Donald Mòr bind for his old friend the best copy of the Charteris that he could get hold of.

The officers remained on their feet until it was clear that Calum Mackay had reached the ground floor. Dunne then crossed to the window and watched the major and his sergeant collect their mounts. Only then did he speak.

'You can leave us now, MacGillivray. Bremner, the porter, will no doubt find you some suitable kennel.'

'The books . . .' began Iain.

'Damn the books! I've a mind to burn the lot of them. Leave your list and make your offer in the morning and I'll think about it.'

It was as good as he was going to get tonight. Iain was considering how he might take the book he had come for without them noticing when Dunne suddenly said, 'Wait,

MacGillivray. My pipe has gone out. Pass me that book, will you.'

Iain cast about the room for another book, any other book, but there was none. 'Your damned Wallace!' growled Dunne. 'Give it here.'

With Mackay gone, the power in the room had changed and Iain had little option but to do as the captain commanded. He picked up the book and walked around the table to hand it to the officer.

Dunne's smile as he took it was such that Iain would happily have wiped it from his face. Still looking at him, the captain took the book and passed it to the ensign. 'Light a spill for me, will you, Warren.'

The ensign quickly understood and, avoiding Iain's eye, he tore out the last page, which he then twisted into a spill. Iain could only watch as he put it to a candle flame and then Dunne's pipe. Dunne puffed, grimaced and said, 'It's not taken, Warren. Try again.'

The ensign did so, and again, and again, repeating the performance at least half a dozen times, until the end of the book was thoroughly mutilated and Dunne himself grown bored. He took it from the young officer and tossed it past Calum Mackay's empty chair towards the fire. So drunk was he now though that his aim was askew, and it landed not in the flames but on the sooty hearth. Another bowl of punch was called for, and Iain took the opportunity to leave the room.

He had half-expected to be directed to the castle dungeon, but the sleeping place accorded him was high up amongst the garrets. The place stank of bats and murmured with the sounds of the black bees that had also made their home there. His bed was a pallet, none too clean, on a stone floor in the turret and exhibiting the remnants of straw strewn long ago. Iain would have preferred to lie outside, where the fresh heather would provide him with better comfort, but he could not leave the castle without the book, and he could not get the book until the redcoat soldiers were either gone to their own beds, or passed out. The sounds carried up to him by stairways and passage-ways suggested the second might happen before the first. Iain lay down on the pallet in his coat and listened for any sound that the soldiers were giving in for the night. It was a good long time before he heard the sounds of the ensign valiantly hauling one officer after another to his feet, to assist them to stumble up flights of stairs on which they would otherwise surely break their necks. Finally, he came to the last object of his efforts – Captain Dunne himself. Iain could hear the ensign coax and plead, invoking Major Mackay's orders that they were to ride out early the next day. This provoked a stream of near-incoherent invective and eventually the sound of glass smashing against a wall. The captain would not be told, in his own castle, by God, when he would retire.

It was cold and dark as pitch when Iain suddenly awoke to silence. He had no idea how long he had been asleep. There was a crick in his neck and his candle had gone out.

He stretched out his shoulders and listened. Nothing. He peered through the darkness and then sat stock-still. At the top of the steps into his garret he wasn't sure if he truly saw or just imagined the merest hint of a movement of light emerging from below. He stood up as soundlessly as he could, his legs stiff, and continued to watch. There was definitely light, and it was definitely moving.

For a while he was aware of no noises to accompany the moving light, other than the usual sounds of a sleeping castle, but then he realised the circle of light was, by stages, spreading, and that someone carrying a lamp or candle was coming up the steps.

Iain retreated further into the darkness of the garret and waited, hardly daring to breathe. Now, the light was breaching the top of the steps and he could just hear the softest of padding. And then the light was snuffed out. For a moment, all was silence. He didn't move and neither, it seemed, did the night visitor. Something scuttled in a corner and Iain turned without thinking towards it. Suddenly a hand was clamped over his mouth, another over his left wrist and a voice was whispering in his ear, 'Not a word, Iain Bàn, or we're done for!'

TEN

The Return of Donald Mòr

'Donald! What in Hell's name . . .?'

The binder clamped his hand over Iain's mouth again. 'Wheesht! You'll have us strung up.' When he saw that his point was made, Donald released him once more.

'What in the name of all that's holy are you doing here?'

'Getting you out of the Devil's own claws! And indeed, I'd be asking what you're doing here yourself, but there's hardly a minute to be lost.'

'Donald—'

'Shh! Not a word. I'll tell you when we're safe away from Castle Leod.'

'But—'

Donald had already set off back down the stairs. 'Would you be back in the hold of one of their prison ships? Come on then!'

Iain lost no more time, but at the first landing they came to he took hold of Donald's arm and spoke into his ear. 'I need to get hold of something from the dining room before I leave.'

'Oh, no doubt,' said Donald with a degree of complacency that bore little relation to their situation. 'But be sure and keep your mouth shut when we're going through the hall, lest you wake that blackguard.'

'Dunne's still in there?'

'Well, there's one of them in there, that's for sure, snoring like a pig. I near enough tripped over his stinking carcass. Now hush!'

Iain said no more and followed Donald as the binder made his way expertly down turn after turn of the darkened stairway that was designed so that any attacking swordsman going up would have to fight left-handed, whilst any defender coming down could fight with his right. At last they stopped, and Donald turned the handle of a door in front of him. They stepped through it cautiously, and Iain found himself once more in the great hall. The logs in the fire-basket had fallen to ashes in the huge hearth, and a solitary candle spluttered on an oak dresser. His finger at his lips, Donald crossed to the dresser and lit his own again from it, then he proceeded to the dining room, whose door was ajar. Iain went after him, never taking his eyes from the slumbering English officer.

Once in the dining room he took the candle from Donald Mòr and went to the fireplace where, to his great relief, the remnant of Blind Hary's *Wallace* – encompassing *The Book of Forbidden Names* for which he had come – still lay amongst the soot and ashes of the hearth. He picked it up, conscious of Donald's close scrutiny, and stashed it beneath his waistcoat. A thought came to him and he pulled out the list of books he'd made up as pretence for his visit, with his offer price beside it, and set it on the table for Dunne to find. 'That's all I came for,' he said, about to step through to the main stairway, 'we can go now.'

'Not that way,' said the binder. 'The front door is locked.'

'You locked it?'

'For the love of God,' said the binder in exasperation, 'where would I be getting the key to Castle Leod? Have you seen the size of the thing?'

'How did you get in then?' asked Iain. 'Some way by the kitchen?'

'Indeed, I did not. Gavin Bremner the porter – that shiftless fellow from the Nairn march – is sleeping there.'

'The Nairn march? What are you . . .?' But Iain saw that questioning his binder was futile whilst they were in the middle of their current predicament. 'We'd break our necks trying to go out at these windows.'

Donald put on his most affronted face. 'You can jump out of all the windows that please you, Iain Bàn MacGillivray, but I'm going this way.' He pointed to the wall opposite the dining room door. Iain was beginning to wonder if Donald was gone mad, for there was nothing where he pointed but bare wood panelling. There was not even a window. Donald, though, curled his fine binder's fingers around the corner of the central panel and pulled hard. Iain could hardly believe what he was seeing as the panel came away and the binder, crouching somewhat to accommodate his wiry arms and legs,

disappeared into the darkness beyond. Iain followed, having
to crouch even more before pulling the panel shut again at
Donald Mòr's hissed instruction. Soon he was gripping on
to a rope on the wall as he negotiated a very narrow spiralling stairway that carried a decided reek of damp. Neither
he nor Donald uttered a word as they made their careful
progress down steps hardly broad enough for their feet. At
last the stairway ended and they came to level ground and
a vaulted tunnel in which neither could stand up straight.
Donald, still with his candle, bent forwards and began to
scurry at a great pace. Iain could do nothing but follow, his
back aching at having to stoop so low. Now Donald came
to a halt, lifted up a hand and bashed with his fist above his
head. There was a hollow sound, as if he were knocking at a
gate or wooden box. With a short expression of glee, Donald
snuffed out his candle and heaved upwards. A thud sounded
of trapdoor on earth and in a rush of cold air, Iain found
himself looking up through branches into the night sky. In
a moment, both he and Donald were sitting stretching their
shoulders against the trunk of an old Spanish chestnut tree.
A good way behind them, sleeping sound as if enchanted,
was Castle Leod.

'Right,' said Donald, 'we'd better get going.'

'Which way?' said Iain, still not understanding what was
going on. 'By Dingwall?'

'Dingwall?' A torrent of invective. 'I'm only out of their
damned gaol. Would I be here if the word was not already
at Dingwall? We'll go by Fairburn.'

'Fairburn . . . but what word?' Iain could make no sense at all of what Donald Mòr was saying, albeit his binder was stone cold sober. His question, though, was addressed to the man's disappearing back. Donald was on the move again.

Fairburn lay almost directly to the south, on a steep rise across Strathconon. The river could be a devil to cross, but Donald refused to go all the way back to the Sguideal ferry. As they ran, Iain's legs took a while to find their rhythm but soon he had it, and he opened up his chest to take in the night air. Less than an hour ago he had been sleeping, unable to keep his eyes open, but now he was wide awake, his whole body sparkling, powered on by that old, urgent thrill of the chase, that sense of being invincible.

Their ascent of Knockfarrell – 'the Cat's Back', as the Mackenzies called it – told him that he spent too long at his desk nowadays, in his shop, and that he needed to get back out amongst the hills. A couple of wrong turns up deer paths aside, their feet found the right tracks and they were soon on the ridge and beginning the descent towards Loch Ussie. Past the loch, they were greeted by the glowering land-bound cliffs looking down over Brahan and across Strathconon. Choosing their way carefully, only once or twice did their feet disturb scree that sent them scrambling on their way down.

The cliffs finally negotiated, they headed down towards the insinuating darkness of the river. Iain recalled that of all Donald Mòr's many attributes, swimming was not one. On the retreat back to Scotland from Derby, the binder had only been carried safe across the icy waters of the Esk by being bound to one of the packhorses. Fortunately, at Moy they found a small boat.

The old tale of the water wraith of the Conon came to Iain's mind, but the shadows cast by ash and silver birch concealed no enticing woman in green, waiting to lure them to their deaths. He pushed the boat, Donald and all, into the water and jumped in, taking an oar. On the far bank an otter slithered to its den.

On the steep ascent to Fairburn, Donald Mòr never flagged, and Iain's admiration for the skills and determination of the old skulker only grew. Only the occasional startled deer, or darting owl or fox moved past them in the darkness, until they at last came within view of the grim edifice of Fairburn Tower, from whose bartizans could be viewed territories for miles around. Little would pass between here and the Fraser country that the Mackenzies of Fairburn would not see. This was 'safe' territory, in so far as any was, but still they took precautions not to be seen, creeping by stone walls, going carefully between gorse bushes and trees, to take shelter by an old, disused outbuilding where they might stop and rest a short while.

After they had caught their breath, and keeping his voice low, Iain said, 'If it isn't too much to ask, Donald, you might tell me what possessed you to come in the middle of the night and drag me out of Castle Leod?'

'Well,' said Donald, as if he had only been waiting for the opportunity, 'it was yon Munro that's sheriff-depute – very good of you, by the way, the bail money, very gentle-man-like.'

'Get on with it, Donald.'

'I heard Munro tell the gaoler in Dingwall that he'd met you on the Kessock ferry. I took the liberty of enquiring what you might have been about, as you should surely have been seeing to your business today – and indeed, who is in the shop whilst you are here? Not Richard? He can hardly manage things himself. Is he even back from Perth?'

'Donald,' warned Iain.

'I'm getting to it, if you would not interrupt. Well, Munro told me you were away to Castle Leod to buy back some books you had sold last year. Now, I know for a fact that there was nothing but badly bound rubbish in that lot you sold to the Archer fellow. So, I says, "He has surely some other ploy on hand."'

'Not to Munro?'

'Munro? No! To myself. And then, when I went to take a bit of dinner to keep body and soul together – for de'il a crust of bread did they give me in that hole of a gaol in Dingwall – I heard tell that there was word of an *excepted* skulker landed at Inverness.'

In the moonlight beaming through the clouds, Iain could see that the binder's eyes had narrowed and were fixed, very securely, upon his own. 'There was a *name* being bandied about.'

Still Iain said nothing.

'A name being bandied,' pressed Donald, 'of one that

would be strung up and filleted in a minute, should Bury or Wolfe or some other of their ilk lay hands upon him, and one known to you very well. And now here you are taking off without a word to lie the night at Castle Leod, in the very heart of that nest of vipers.'

At last Iain relented. 'Has my father been named?'

Donald gave a brisk nod. 'Your father's name has been one of those swirling around the watering holes of Inverness and Dingwall, and there is word of search parties to be sent out at dawn. I wouldn't put it past that Captain Dunne to have clamped you in manacles in the dungeon of Castle Leod, should he have got word that Hector MacGillivray was returned, and you there right under his nose. Better you're back in Inverness with friends around you than on your way to a prison ship.'

Iain could not argue with the logic of this. 'But how did you know about that passageway out of the castle?'

Donald flung out his hands as if it were obvious. 'Was I not lying three months cheek-by-jowl with a Mackenzie in a hole in Carlisle, waiting to draw lots for the which of us they would shoot? There's damn little about any Mackenzie that I don't know, I'll tell you that.'

Iain's laughter was stopped short by the sight of a distinct bulge in each of Donald's coat pockets and one in his waistcoat. 'What have you there?'

In the darkness Donald's eyes gleamed. He slid his hand into his waistcoat. 'What do you think?' and he laid before Iain three volumes, tied together with string and in tattered bindings. 'There was a fellow in the shop only last week asking if you had this, and you did not, and it was custom lost, which you can ill afford.'

'What are they?' asked Iain, unable to make out the titles in the dark.

Donald worked himself up to a state of great disdain which always presaged his use of the English language, of which he was not fond. '*A Choice Collection of Scots Poems both Ancient and Modern*. A terrible state these volumes are in, but I will sort that, and you can make a pretty penny out of them.'

Iain was almost speechless. 'You took the time to get those? You might have been caught and hanged.'

Donald snorted. 'They've tried before. They'll never get a rope around the neck of Donald Mòr.'

Iain turned over the books. 'They'll think I stole them.'

'Them? There's not one of them in that castle would know one end of a book from another. But never mind that – what were *you* doing in Castle Leod under the same roof as such as those?'

Iain brought out his jacket and slowly unfolded it to reveal the copy of Blind Hary's *Wallace*.

Donald's face twisted in scorn. 'How drunk did they get you, that you took that and left this?' He indicated his own treasure.

'It was this I went for, Donald.'

Donald scrutinised him and Iain saw his mind working. 'This is why Hector has come back to Scotland.'

Iain shook his head. 'No, my father is here on some other business, and he will not tell me what that is. But it is because of him that I went to Castle Leod to find this.'

In as few words as possible, he told Donald Mòr of the discovery of Davie Campbell's body at his desk in the bookshop and of the black cockades that had been on the front board of the book. Before he could say anything else, Donald had said it for him. '*The Book of Forbidden Names.*'

'You know of it?'

'I've heard tell of it.' Donald was now looking at the book with a degree of apprehension, rather than the disdain with which he'd greeted its first appearance. 'How come it's in that state?'

'Whoever killed Davie Campbell has the original. This is a rough copy Lord Lovat must have made. It was in better condition when first I found it though.' Iain explained about the captain and his pipe. 'It's lucky he was so drunk he couldn't throw straight or it'd have gone into the fire.'

Donald's voice was very low, and he was now looking at the book as if it was a grenade. 'Better it had done.'

'Why?'

'It may be that not all the names in it are dead.'

'But that's the very point of getting hold of it! My father is certain Davie Campbell was sent by someone named in this book to prevent their treachery to King James being known.'

'And I've no doubt Hector is right.'

'But it could be someone seeking to know the names of the traitors for themselves.'

'Exactly. And you should just leave them to it. Let them do what they have to do. What's to be gained by you, or Hector for that matter, looking into it? The people who were meant to die because of it deserve to die, but your meddling can only bring to light things that are best left forgotten. Burn the thing. Nothing will be gained by your meddling in it.'

Iain picked up the book and tucked it inside his jacket before standing up. 'I have spent the last six years trying to forget things best left forgotten, Donald, but they find me all the same. My father is an agent of King James. He bade me go to Castle Leod to find this book and it'll be him I hand it to when I get home to Inverness, no matter the consequences.'

ELEVEN

Searches Are Made

Though her mind was filled with questions she hardly knew how to ask, Julia slept better after Lady Ross's salon than she had on the previous night, no longer convinced that the bookseller had come to some harm at the hands of the visiting English clergyman. When she awoke next morning, she took a moment to note that her mother was no longer there beside her. There was no sound of her moving around their rooms either. It took little time to establish that her mother's cloak and boots were also missing. Elizabeth had been prone to bouts of melancholy and solitary wandering for as long as Julia could remember, but usually she was much happier when in the town. Julia dressed hurriedly and ran down the stairs into the breakfasting parlour, where she was told that her mother had been up and out almost an hour ago. The pot-man, overhearing her conversation with the parlourmaid, said he had seen her turning up Castle Wynd.

'But where was she going?' asked Julia

'Well, it would be to the castle,' replied the man. 'Where else?'

Julia went out onto the street. The merchants on the Exchange were setting up their stalls and opening their booths, ready for the day's market. When she turned onto Castle Wynd she found herself face to face with her mother coming the other way. The look on Elizabeth's face told her everything she needed to know.

'You've been to the garrison.'

'Yes,' said Elizabeth. Despite having been reduced almost to rubble by the Jacobites as they left for Drummossie Moor in 1746, so that it might prove useless should Cumberland's forces reach it, the castle of Inverness retained some offices of use to the army of occupation.

'You were informing on the English preacher.'

'I was informing on Hector MacGillivray and his disguise.'

'And did you also . . .'

'What?' Her mother, who had continued walking back to the Horns, stopped now and looked her in the eye. 'Did I what, Julia? Did I tell them that when he had been in the Horns, disguised as a Yorkshire clergyman, his son had also been there? Did I tell them his son spoke to no one, watched his father arrive and was still there, watching him, when we left? Yes, Julia, I did. Whatever foolish notions may have begun to creep into your mind regarding the bookseller, I would counsel you to dispel them. God willing it will not be long before he is on a transport ship away from Scotland, for good this time, if not at the end of a rope.'

As Julia struggled for a reply, shouts of 'Make way!'

could be heard at the other side of the Exchange, followed
by flashes of red as a party of soldiers coming down from
the castle cut a swathe between the half-opened stalls and
booths. By the time the two women had reached the front
of the Horns, the soldiers had overtaken them and turned
onto Church Street. Seemingly oblivious to the military
party, Elizabeth went into the hotel, but Julia did not.
Regardless that she had no cloak or hood and was shod
only in her indoor slippers, she went after the soldiers. By
the time she too had reached the top of Church Street, they
were banging on Mairi Farquharson's door.

'They're coming,' said Aeneas, stepping back from the
window and preparing to go downstairs to receive the
search party.

It was no surprise to Mairi Farquharson that a detachment of armed troops was on its way to her house. Word
that Hector MacGillivray had been sighted about the town
had been circulating almost a full day. It was a wonder to
her that she hadn't had a visitation before now. She handed
Aeneas back the papers they had been going over. 'And you
think it's a coincidence that Hector MacGillivray should
reappear, hot on the heels of word of *The Book of Forbidden
Names?*'

Aeneas nodded. 'You know I have no liking for the man,
but I think were he *not* here on the king's business as he
claims, he would hardly have come to this house.'

Mairi nodded. 'You always were the cleverest of the

Farquharsons. I would have been lost many a time before now, had it not been for your counsel.'

'You know you can rely on me, Mistress.'

There came another, more insistent, hammering at the door.

Mairi sighed. 'I suppose we had better admit them.'

Aeneas went downstairs. After an appropriate delay in answering their forceful knock, and a few minutes more for the requisite ceremonial, he reappeared at the head of a party of half a dozen redcoats. Mairi recognised Major Thornlie. That was something – he, at least, had the reputation of being a gentleman.

'Mistress Farquharson.' He brought his heels together and gave a precise bow of the head. He must have cut a handsome figure as a young man. In fact, although he'd not see forty again he cut a handsome figure even now, the black eyepatch and slight halt as he walked notwithstanding. 'I trust you will forgive this intrusion into your home.'

'You trust much, Major. My forgiveness will depend on the nature of the intrusion. I see you've not arrived alone.'

The major had the good grace to look slightly abashed. He clearly had not arrived alone. The reputation of the government army's search parties was well known. She looked beyond his shoulder to the corporal and four infantrymen she had seen follow him down the street. 'No,' he said. 'I have not. I would ask your permission, madam, for my men to make a search of your house. Word has reached the garrison that your son-in-law, the excepted skulker Hector MacGillivray, has returned to Inverness.'

Mairi remained unmoved. 'I commend your delicacy, Major, but as I am sure you know, I have no son-in-law. Hector MacGillivray and my daughter Charlotte were never married, and I believe she is now – situated, shall we say? – with an Italian count of limited means but excellent pedigree. At any rate, she and the person you mention have been estranged more than thirty years.'

Thornlie's mouth moved slightly, not in embarrassment as she might have expected, but possibly in an effort to mask his amusement. '*The person I mention*, madam, is also your grandson's father, and indeed was known to have been under this roof on several occasions during the last rebellion. I have it on good authority that he was seen two nights ago in the Horns Hotel, and that only yesterday morning he claimed to the landlord that he was coming out to Ardersier to consult me. So, with all due respect to your daughter's honour, whether she and the person in question were married or not is of no interest to me. Is he here?'

Mairi also had to prevent herself from smiling. She had heard that Thornlie, an engineer with the Military Survey, was no fool.

'No, Major, he is not.'

'And your grandson?'

'Gone into Ross on business. To . . .' Here she feigned vagueness and Aeneas, now standing at her shoulder, came to her aid.

'Castle Leod, I believe, Mistress.'

'Thank you, Aeneas. Yes, Castle Leod. You might enquire there.'

Thornlie turned to the corporal. 'Is that not where Captain Dunne has gone?'

A look of apprehension flashed across Mairi's face. Dunne's name was known and reviled amongst them.

'He's expected back in town by the end of the week, sir,' said the corporal.

'Hmm,' said Thornlie. 'I'm puzzled as to what business your grandson might have at Castle Leod.'

Mairi and Aeneas both simply looked at him, offering nothing.

Thornlie changed his tack. 'And when is he expected home?'

'As soon as he completes his business, I would imagine. He is a grown man and I am not his keeper.'

'You will have no objection, then, to my men searching this house?'

Up to this point, Mairi had spoken only to Major Thornlie, but now she looked at the men behind him. 'On the contrary, Major Thornlie, I object in the strongest degree, but I am hardly in a position to stop you.'

Thornlie nodded and turned to his men. 'Corporal, you will ensure the men conduct themselves with the utmost propriety. Any damages will be paid from out of all your wages, and any indiscipline will be punished in the strongest terms.'

The corporal, more attuned to Captain Dunne's approach to the local inhabitants, showed by the look on his face his contempt for the house and its occupants. He had no option though but to say, 'Of course, Major.'

Aeneas followed the soldiers out of the room, with the clear intention of keeping a very close eye on everything they did. The major remained standing in the middle of Mairi Farquharson's chamber. 'Would you sit, Major?' she said.

'No, madam. Thank you.'

'As you will. You will have no objection in my continuing my employment?'

He looked momentarily confused as there was no book or needlework in front of her. 'None whatsoever, madam.'

'Good,' she said, and recommenced looking out of the window. She could feel a relaxation in the room, as if the major had allowed a lessening in the rigidity of his posture, perhaps even the makings of a smile.

He took up his position at the other edge of the bay window. 'You are a student of human nature, I see,' he said. 'I imagine there is little that passes in the town that doesn't come under your view, madam.'

'Oh, as you know, the town is full of alleyways and closes well beyond the scope of my vision.'

'If not your oversight.'

Mairi put down her lorgnette. 'Do you accuse me of something, Major?'

'I think you have knowledge of things that it is your duty to report to His Majesty's government.'

'Do not doubt, Major, that I ensure His Majesty hears of anything I consider to tend to his well-being.'

Thornlie laughed now and turned away from the window. 'I suspect we speak of different majesties, Mistress Farquharson.'

'For me, there is only one king.'

'Hmm,' he said, though not ill-humoredly. He appeared to wince as he did so.

'Will you not sit, Major?' she repeated.

He hesitated then pulled out a chair into which he lowered himself with care.

'An old wound?' she asked.

'Fontenoy,' he said.

'Ah yes, I believe the person you are now searching my house for also saw service in that engagement. Under Drummond's command, if I recall, the Royal Ecossais.'

'Fighting for the French,' he replied. 'Well, I hope he enjoyed his victory, for all it lasted.'

Cumberland had been called back from the disgrace of defeat at Fontenoy to lead his father's army against the growing Jacobite rising under Charles Edward Stuart. Hector MacGillivray, alongside many other exiled Scots and Irish Jacobites fighting in the armies of France, had returned to take their place in the prince's army and face Cumberland at home.

'Do you never get a hankering for home, Major?'

'My home is wherever I roll out my bed for the night.'

'No one was born a soldier.'

He turned his patched eye towards her. 'No. But many die soldiers.' After a moment's silence he said, 'I was born the second son of a physician. My brother showed a facility and willingness to follow in my father's footsteps, but I had none. All I ever wished for was to become an engineer. And so I have. I have been here five years now, but our work is almost at an end.'

'I will not pretend I've found your roads and bridges to be altogether an inconvenience, although I see no reason for the building of your monstrous fort. I understand from my grandson that you decamp to Edinburgh soon?'

'Indeed. This is to be the last year of the survey. Once I leave Inverness this time, I'll not be back.'

Usually, Mairi was glad to see the back of any redcoat, but she experienced a small sensation of disappointment on Iain's behalf, because she knew he liked this major, and the number of intelligent men with whom her grandson would consent to pass the time of day could be counted on the fingers of one hand.

The search of the house went on for almost an hour, passed between Mairi and the major in discussion of Greenwich, where he had trained and which she had only seen 'in passing' on her way from Tilbury, at the end of the '15 rising.

'Your husband was "out" on that occasion,' the major said, a little hesitantly.

'He and all our friends,' she said.

'I believe he did not come home.'

'No,' she said. 'He died on Tower Hill in May of 1716, betrayed. I watched him suffer.'

'I'm sorry,' he said.

She gave him the briefest nod of acknowledgement and after that very little of any import was said between them. They whiled away the time in commentary on the events playing out before them on the street below. There was her friend, Janet Grant, talking with the milliner Barbara Sinclair. 'Janet will not be happy about that,' she said. 'She doesn't like the milliner and won't as much as go into her shop, although the woman makes the finest hats between here and Edinburgh.'

All the time, the sound of Thornlie's men walking about her house, the opening of doors, cupboards, the moving aside of furniture, travelled in and out of their hearing. As feet were heard mounting another flight of stairs, crossing the threshold into another room, Thornlie would glance at Mairi Farquharson and she would afford him a tight smile, wondering what the soldiers of his occupying regime might find.

Mairi studied to hide her relief when the corporal, closely attended by Aeneas, returned to report to his senior officer that neither the fugitive nor his son had been found.

The major stood up. 'Again, Mistress Farquharson, I hope you will pardon our necessary intrusion.' Then he turned to the corporal. 'We'll proceed to the bookshop.'

Aeneas's face, already a study in displeasure, now took on a thunderous mien. 'Mistress Farquharson has already informed you that her grandson is not yet returned from his business in Ross. The shop is not open.'

Major Thornlie watched Aeneas for a moment before turning to Mairi.

'I assume you have a key to your grandson's premises?'

'No, I do not. He keeps the key about his person. His assistant has a key but he too has been away on business. The place cannot be unlocked before one of them is back.'

'On the contrary, madam,' said Thornlie. He gave a brisk bow and, commanding his men to follow him, left.

Mairi and Aeneas waited until they heard the sound of the front door closing. Then the old woman smiled at her steward. 'They came nowhere near, I take it?'

'They appeared somewhat put off by the aroma of a herring which that careless girl Eppy must have let slip from her basket when last she was down there. The soldiers didn't linger too long in their search of that part of the cellar.'

'Good.' She stood up, as if sitting for so long had forced a weariness into her bones. 'I am very pleased to hear it.'

TWELVE

A Raid on the Shop

Julia had been standing so long in the street outside Mairi Farquharson's house that people were starting to ask her what was wrong. The sight of the corporal who usually attended Captain Dunne banging on the door and demanding entry chilled her. The stories of Dunne's cruelties after Culloden, the pleasure he seemed to take in inflicting suffering, were well known. There had been great relief all over the Highlands when the regiment in which he served had left in '47, and apprehension when he had returned to the town last year. But Dunne was evidently elsewhere today, and Major Thornlie was in charge of the search party. The search seemed to take a long time, and it was only when the rain that had been threatening all morning began to penetrate the thin cotton of her summer gown that she started to make her way back to the hotel.

All was in darkness when she reached their rooms. The shutters she had opened earlier had been closed and no candle or lamp lit. Julia could hear her mother's breathing and a stirring from the bed.

'Have you finished making an exhibition of yourself?'

'I, an exhibition? I did not take myself to the castle at the crack of dawn to report upon rumour and gossip.' Julia felt her voice rising and tears threaten as she fumbled to undo the buttons and loops of her damp gown, before rifling their trunk for an alternative.

Her mother sat up. 'What are you doing? Don't tell me you're going out?'

'Well, I'm not staying in.'

'Julia! I forbid it.'

Julia was now furiously working with the fastenings of the floral sack-back gown that she was supposed to keep for visits. She ignored her mother until she had achieved an acceptable degree of neatness, then went to the dresser to attend to her hair, which had also suffered in the rain. As she glared at herself in the glass, she recalled her aunt's opinion that her natural curls were one of the few advantages God had given her. The procedure calmed her slightly and without turning around she said, 'As you never tire of reminding me, Mother, I am twenty-seven years old. I will do as I choose.'

Back out on the street she was at first at a loss. She could hardly present herself at Mairi Farquharson's door to ask whether the government soldiers had found the excepted skulker in her house or if they had arrested her grandson. She decided she would go to the bookshop. Iain MacGillivray would not be at his grandmother's house in any case, he would be at the bookshop.

For the second time in two days, Julia sensed something was wrong as she drew closer to the bookshop. A small crowd of people had gathered on the street outside. She quickened her pace, then came to an abrupt stop. The door was open, but its lock was splintered. It had been forced.

'What's happening?' she asked, trying to see past the onlookers. 'Where is Iain MacGillivray?'

A soft voice answered her from behind, so quiet she almost didn't hear it. 'Soldiers, looking for the skulker.' It was Ishbel MacLeod, the confectioner who had served them at Lady Ross's soirée. Julia felt a wave of shame wash over her, as if the woman must know it was her mother who had informed on Hector MacGillivray.

A small voice piped up from somewhere around her elbow. 'He's no' there.'

It was the confectioner's boy, still playing with his button, as if oblivious to everyone around him.

She bent down a little. 'The skulker is not there?'

The boy continued to concentrate on his button, his face very serious. 'I hope he's no' there, but Iain Bàn's definitely no' there. He's not back yet and neither is Donald Mòr. Richard's back from Perth though, he's in there, him and Morag and all the soldiers.'

'Who is Morag?'

The boy looked up at her as if she might be a simpleton. 'Donald Mòr's cat, of course. And she does *not* like soldiers.'

At that moment a shriek came from inside the shop. Ignoring their admonitions not to go in, Julia threaded her way quickly through the rest of the onlookers and pushed at the open door. She stepped over the threshold and then stopped. All around was chaos. The bookseller's desk had been upended, the drawers pulled out and the wall cabinet behind it smashed. What had been the library corner, in which she had spent so much time, was now a pile of upended bookcases and damaged books. Book-shelves affixed to the shop walls were in the process of being denuded of their contents by two red-coated soldiers. Broken glass from framed prints dashed to the ground lit-tered the floor. Another soldier was bashing at panels and grabbing at shelves as if testing for hidden passageways. Through the opened door to the bindery she could see a soldier with a hand to his face and blood seeping through his fingers from what was evidently a row of deep slashes from an animal's claws. High on the window sill, her back almost impossibly arched and spitting as if defending a litter of kittens from an eagle, was the bookbinder's cat.

Julia felt tears prick her eyes. The place was filled with soldiers but there was no sign anywhere of Major Thornlie. She bent down to pick up the large ledger lying open face down on the floor. It was the bookshop catalogue, dam-aged but apparently intact. Just at that moment, there was a clatter from above as another row of books was swept from a shelf in the gallery.

'No, please!'

Julia gathered up the hem of her skirt and ran up the stairs. Richard Dempster, the bookseller's assistant, was up in the gallery, attempting to stop one of the soldiers in his frenzy of destruction. The redcoat, not even turning from his work, flung out the butt of his rifle, hitting him in the face and sending him tumbling against the wall.

Behind Julia came a sudden shout. 'Rifleman! You will stop that right now!' She whipped round to see Major Thornlie making his halting way up the stairs.

Any time she had seen him before, it had been at a distance, whether around town or at the assemblies. He always seemed aloof, never dancing, only watching, with his one good eye, as if the other, covered by its black patch, might see things that pleased him better. Her mother said it was because he was lame that he did not dance. She stood in front of the bookseller's assistant, attempting to shield him from further assault.

'What is going on here, Major? This is an outrage.'

The major seemed momentarily confused to see her there. He surveyed the devastation in the gallery. 'I ordered my men to search this shop. The damage is unfortunate, and they have acted to excess in my absence, but we're looking for a traitor, an excepted skulker sighted in the town. We have received information suggesting he might be here.'

'Information from my mother.' Of course.

The major didn't deny it, only adding, 'What your mother told us merely confirmed what had been suggested from other sources.'

'Even so,' replied Julia, 'you can hardly think to find the man you're looking for skulking behind the books on these shelves. And for this man to be assaulted when he was merely trying to protect his employer's property . . .'

Thornlie looked behind her to where Richard Dempster sat on the floor, his arms gripping his knees, shaking.

'I just give him a slap sir, that would hardly make a dent.'

'Quiet!' said Thornlie to the soldier. He took a step forward, and looking first at Dempster said to Julia, 'If I may?'

She stepped aside and Thornlie stood over the trembling man. 'You are the bookseller's assistant?'

A nod.

'Your name is Dempster, is it not?'

Another nod.

'I knew your brother, Thomas.'

Richard Dempster slowly turned to face the major.

'This man will not hurt you again. Rifleman!'

'Yes, Major!' said the soldier who did not understand why but knew that in hitting the bookseller's assistant he had somehow crossed a line that should not have been crossed.

'Give off your search up here. Clearly neither Hector MacGillivray nor his son are to be found in this gallery and,' he surveyed the scene, 'I see nothing suggestive of any concealed apartment. Go and report to the corporal in the bindery.'

When the soldier had left, Thornlie squatted down to Richard Dempster's level. Julia could see that the action gave him some pain.

'I am Major Philip Thornlie; I also come from Manchester. I knew your brother Thomas many years ago, before he set off on his medical studies. He used to assist my father.'

'Dr Thornlie?'

'Yes. My father was greatly saddened to hear of Thomas's . . . death, and William's. So was I.'

The young man seemed to recover himself a little. He wiped a sleeve across his face. 'Thank you.'

The major straightened himself again. 'Could you take him somewhere, Miss Rose, until we are finished?'

She was so startled to be so addressed by him, that he even knew her name, so confused by the exchange she had just witnessed, that she could find nothing but a small 'Yes,' in response.

'Thank you.' He left to make his awkward way down the steps.

By the time Julia had also returned to the ground floor, having persuaded Richard Dempster to leave off the task of clearing up until the soldiers were finished, Thornlie had righted Iain MacGillivray's desk and appeared to be examining the shop's catalogue. Suddenly, she heard a small squeal, followed by the sight of the confectioner's boy running across the shop from the street door in the direction of the bindery. The child appeared oblivious to the major's presence in his rush to get to the bindery door. He finally brought himself to a halt in the doorway where he whistled and uttered a Gaelic profanity that should have been well beyond his years. 'Stone mad,' he then said, in English. 'Donald Mòr will go stone mad.'

At that same moment, Ishbel MacLeod appeared at the street door. She shouted across the shop in Gaelic. 'Tormod! Come away from there this very minute!'

The boy only grew more agitated. 'But Donald Mòr . . .' he persisted.

'Come *now*, Tormod!' The woman's face was a picture of terror, and the boy gave in and did as he was bid. Julia knew something of Ishbel MacLeod's story and supposed the boy she had brought back with her from Virginia to be the orphaned child of a slave whom she would train at little expense in her own craft. She placed her hand on Richard Dempster's arm and suggested they should go after them.

'I've behaved like a fool,' said Richard, some bitterness in his voice.

'I don't think the major thinks you a fool,' she answered as they entered Bow Court. They'd hardly reached the doorway of Ishbel MacLeod's kitchen when the child Tormod, spying them, ran to the bookseller's assistant and began to pull him by the hem of his waistcoat. 'Donald Mòr will go stone mad, won't he, Richard?'

'Undoubtedly,' said the Englishman, at last managing to raise a smile.

Assured that Richard Dempster would be taken care of, Julia crossed back over the street. The remaining crowd had stood back, and the soldiers were coming out. The corporal, his face still bleeding, was cursing and making oaths about what he would do when he finally got his hands on Iain MacGillivray and his blasted father.

Julia hung back as they passed, then stepped into the shop. Somehow the silence of the devastation was worse than when the soldiers had been in the heat of their destruction. She hardly knew where she should begin. All around there were books, broken glass, toppled cabinets. Then a sound, the creaking of a cabinet door, startled her. Major Thornlie had not gone back up to the castle with his men, but was sitting in the bookseller's revolving chair, near the desk which he had righted. In his hand he held a glass, of the most delicate-looking crystal, filled with some amber liquid.

He put the glass down and made to stand up. 'Miss Rose.'

'Please, don't put yourself to the trouble. This is hardly the place for civilities.'

He stood, nonetheless. 'If you will pardon me, it is exactly the place for civility. The barrier between ourselves and savagery is finer than gossamer. Once rent, we do not easily recover ourselves.'

Julia flung out her arm. 'You don't think this savagery?'

Thornlie drained his glass then set it down. 'No, I do not. I have seen savagery. I have seen what men will do to other men, to women, to children. This is not savagery, Miss Rose.' He looked around him and let out a sigh. 'I take no pleasure in the damage though. Believe me or not, but had I not had to make my report to my Lord Bury at the castle after our search of MacGillivray's grandmother's house, I wouldn't have permitted such . . .'

He seemed lost for the right word. Julia supplied it. 'Thuggery.'

He looked as if he might defend the charge but took a breath and instead laid down the book he had in his hand. 'I must go,' he said. He stopped when he reached the door and half-turned.

'Miss Rose, I . . .'

'Yes?' she said.

There was a pause, then, 'I . . . wish you good day.'

The cursing from the bindery was long and astonishing. Richard Dempster had stopped in his sweeping away of glass and stood, motionless with dread. Julia made an attempt to put her hands over the ears of Ishbel MacLeod's boy, but the child had jumped up with glee from his place stacking pages on the floor and run towards the bindery.

'Donald Mòr!'

At least the binder halted in his cursing to greet the boy. 'Tormod Beag!' he said. Little Tormod. 'And what howling pack of devils has done this to my bindery?'

'The devils in the red coats,' replied the child, without a moment's hesitation.

This was greeted with a further torrent of invective.

'But you will be avenged, Donald Mòr, will you not?' asked the boy, anxious.

'I will be avenged to the twentieth generation. There will not be a corner of their ill-gotten dominions will not tremble at the name of Donald Mòr.'

'What will you do, Donald?'

'Terrible things,' said Donald in a long, hoarse whisper

that almost made the child's eyes start from his head. 'But first, it will behove us to set the bindery to rights.'

Julia was so intent on watching the terrifying man and the child set to their task together, completely at ease in one another's company, that she didn't notice Iain MacGillivray come in behind her.

'What,' he breathed, 'what has happened here?'

Richard Dempster put his broom down and went towards him. 'I'm sorry, Iain, I tried to stop them.'

The bookseller stood up from where he'd crouched down, picking glass from a small book, then leaned towards his assistant, peering. 'Richard, what has happened to your eye? What did they do to you?'

Despite the ministrations of the confectioner, Richard Dempster's eye was now red and so swollen it was almost altogether closed. He turned his head away, as if embarrassed. 'It was nothing, just a rifle butt.'

'A rifle butt?' The bookseller's face was white with anger.

'It was the red soldiers.' Ishbel MacLeod had also come into the shop. 'They were looking for a skulker.'

'They were looking for your father,' interjected Julia.

Only now did the bookseller seem to see her. A look of confusion crossed his face as he looked from one woman to the other.

'My father?'

'Yes.' Julia was in so far now she could not go back. 'They heard that he had been in the Horns the other night and . . .'

The bookseller stared at her. 'They heard . . .?'

Julia's mouth had turned dry and she thought her tongue would hardly work. 'Yes. It was my mother. I'm sorry.'

He watched her a moment then turned away. 'I think you had better not be here then.'

She felt her cheeks flush and her other self would have fled to the door, but she somehow heard herself say, 'I want to stay and help.'

He didn't look at her. 'I think you have done enough.'

THIRTEEN

Another Cockade

Iain stood in the middle of his devastated shop and it was as if the last years of cobbling back a life for himself had never been. He had had to get rid of the Rose girl – in that moment all he could see was a Rose of Kilravock, Hanoverian to the core. Could they not let him live in peace? Had Ishbel MacLeod not taken her by the hand and persuaded her out, he wouldn't have trusted himself not to throw her out onto the street. He sank down amidst the broken glass and scattered books and put his head in his hands. No one spoke for a moment until Donald Mòr said, 'It could have been worse.'

Iain had had to restrain Donald when they'd arrived in the yard to find the back door to the bindery swinging open. It had been a good thing that the soldiers were gone, for when they'd surveyed the broken glass and scraps of leather strewn all over the floor, he was sure that Donald would have killed the first soldier he'd laid eyes on. And yet, they all knew it could have been worse. It had been worse, six years ago – much worse. While he'd been bound, prisoner, in the Gaelic kirk and then in the hold of *The Jane of Leith* down to London, atrocity after atrocity had been perpetrated on those left behind. Raiding parties from the government army had hunted through the Highlands in retribution on those clans that had gone out with Prince Charlie, or those suspected of giving him shelter. From the Cairngorms to the Hebrides and back, Cumberland's men had burned, murdered, destroyed. Men taken in the act of surrender had been hanged, women defiled – a pregnant woman raped and left for dead, a baby wrested from its mother's arms to be dashed to the ground. A boy of seventeen, on this very street, beaten so badly over the escape of a prisoner from the cellar of his mother's house that he died three days later.

All the while Iain had been helpless to do anything about it, chained in one stinking prison hole after another. But his grandmother had seen it. They had all seen it, the Grandes Dames. Janet Grant had perhaps had it the worst, if there could be degrees in such things, when the men of her clan in Glenmoriston and Glen Urquhart had been persuaded to surrender their arms. Her only son, born the same year as Iain, had been shot in cold blood after the battle as he tried to make his way home. Janet had been abused and insulted, forced to witness younger women, married women, raped in front of their husbands, see homes plundered, innocent men hanged. She hadn't been the same since. Why should the redcoats behave any differently now? It could all come back as surely as his father had come back.

A sudden thought took him, and he looked from Richard to Ishbel. 'Were they at the house?'

Richard shook his head. He didn't know, but Ishbel, her face like stone, said, 'Yes. This morning.' Iain was up, out from amongst the broken glass and the strewn books and running up the street.

As he burst through the gate into the back yard, he almost crashed into Eppy, who was holding an old wooden bucket as far away from herself as she could.

'Oh Mother Mary!' she said, pressing a hand to her breast. 'I thought it was the red soldiers back. If I'd dropped that bucket it would be yourself that would be cleaning it up.'

'Eppy, are you all right? Is my grandmother all right? And Aeneas? Did the soldiers take him?'

'Take Aeneas? No indeed. It would take more than those milksops to take Aeneas Farquharson! And the mistress is in a high good humour that the red soldiers were so out of sorts at not finding what they were looking for. She has called the ladies round for an afternoon tea that she might tell them all about it. But oh, it's Eppy that has to take this up to the Foul Pool and then clean up after all the red soldiers' dirty feet and . . .'

Iain slumped with relief against the wall, taking in long draughts of air to slow the pounding in his chest as the girl went past him, bearing her bucket of what his nose told him was virulently stinking fish.

On his way up the stairs, he was confused to hear laughter coming from his grandmother's room. Her laughter and, almost unheard of, Aeneas's. Without ceremony, he pushed the door open. He was not a foot into the room when an arm whipped round his neck and a dirk was put to his throat. Then, just as suddenly, the arm released its hold and he saw his father, to his right, sheathe his dirk.

'Iain Bàn MacGillivray! You'll get yourself killed bursting into rooms like that.'

'Bursting . . . Grandmother, have you any idea . . .?' Iain looked from one to the other of the trio, his eyes finally settling on his father. 'You are here?'

'I've been here since yesterday afternoon, when I got back from seeing Bailie Steuart at Petty.'

'But how can that be? Was the house not searched this morning?'

'Top to bottom,' said Aeneas, the unfamiliar ghost of a grin still troubling his lips.

Iain went over to the sideboard and poured himself a large whisky from the decanter there. He looked to his father. 'How is it they didn't find you?'

Hector looked to Mairi Farquharson, who nodded.

'You'll know the story of how the Old Fox escaped in December of '45?'

'Of course I know it!' said Iain. The story of how the octogenarian Lord Lovat, kept prisoner in a house on this very street, had been spirited away through a concealed doorway to the unguarded house next door and then down a dark lane and away on the river, was a favourite of the Grandes Dames and recounted at almost every gathering. 'I know it and all that crew up at the castle know it as well. There are no secret doors in this house.'

His grandmother cleared her throat. 'That's not quite so, Iain. You'll recall, when you were a small boy, not long arrived from France?'

'Yes,' he said.

'You used to enjoy hearing stories. All sorts of stories. You'll have forgotten many of them, I'm sure. But there was one you did not like, and I doubt that you'll have forgotten it.'

Iain thought for a moment. 'The cellar,' he said at last.

His grandmother looked at Aeneas and then back to him. 'We thought it best that you were discouraged from visiting the cellar. There is a false section of wall, about six feet or so from the corner closest to the river. It pushes outwards into a short tunnel coming out further down, where a person might enter or exit without calling attention upon themselves.'

'Surely they searched the cellar?' said Iain.

'Oh, they did,' said Aeneas. 'But this is a large house, and the cellar runs the full length of it. Only someone with a deal more patience than that corporal had would push at every brick. It's as well Major Thornlie, who I suspect might be less easily fooled, remained up here with your grandmother.'

'Keeping an eye on me,' she said, her face suffused with amusement.

'Indeed,' continued Aeneas. 'But as an extra precaution, we had arranged a disincentive for the soldiers.'

Iain looked again from one to another and saw his father wrinkle his nose.

'The fish.'

'High to the heavens,' said his grandmother. 'If there's one thing you can rely on Hughie Gollan to have for you, it's bad fish. We first got word last night of a rumour that Hector had been recognised.'

'Who from?' asked Iain.

'The confectioner,' said Aeneas. 'A smart lassie that. She'd heard it at Lady Ross's.'

Iain had no time to wonder at Ishbel MacLeod's allegiances as his grandmother had taken up her tale again. 'We knew it wouldn't be long before we had a visit from the garrison. Aeneas got a bucket of bad fish from Hughie and put it in between a barrel of ale and the false wall.'

Aeneas laughed. 'The delicate stomachs on those fine fellows – they wouldn't go within six feet of it.'

'I hope that Eppy's got rid of it by now,' said Mairi. 'Eilidh Cameron has a nose on her like a fox hound.'

'She's away up to the Foul Pool with it,' said Iain absently, his mind struggling to keep up with everything he was being told. He finished the last of the whisky and put down his tumbler. 'Right.' He went to the door.

'Iain,' his father said.

'My shop is in pieces, Father. I will see you tonight.'

'But Iain,' echoed his grandmother. 'The book.'

'The book?' he said.

'Yes. At Castle Leod. Did you find it, the *Book of Forbidden Names?*'

It was dark, and well past suppertime, by the time the shop had finally been set to rights, in as far as it could be. Replacing the glass in the cabinets would cost more money than Iain could well spare, and some of the damaged books were beyond the talents of even Donald Mòr to repair. It wouldn't be long though, till Willie Johnston the chapman would be back in town, and Willie had patrons aplenty willing to buy odd parts of a book and trust that one day they might come upon the rest.

At some point – he couldn't have said when – the Grandes Dames had appeared in the shop, or at least two of them had. Catriona Lamont had gone home to see to her dog, but Janet Grant and Eilidh Cameron, having been informed by his grandmother of the raid on his premises, had arrived bearing with them a basket of food and a determination that they would supervise the clear-up. Eilidh Cameron took herself into the bindery, where she and Donald harangued each other loud and long, as was their habit. Janet went up to help Ishbel MacLeod in the gallery where the remains of Lord Lovat's library lay scattered over the floor. It soon became clear that there was not room up there for them both and Janet sent the younger woman down to assist Iain and Richard Dempster below, where the damage was worst.

Ishbel set herself to clearing up, of more help than Richard, who could not settle on where to start, or how to finish anything, and Iain wished he had somehow retained at least the basics of conversation with a woman. She stayed to the end, after the Grandes Dames had finally gone, 'to bid farewell to Hector,' as Eilidh Cameron had whispered to him when they left. The boy Tormod had fallen asleep in the bindery and was laid on the bed by Donald Mòr, who had cautioned the rest of them to be quiet as he continued to tidy around him. After Eilidh and Janet had left, Richard was persuaded to take himself to his own small attic chamber at the top of the shop. 'We will need you fresh in the morning, Richard, so that we might open up again,' Iain had said.

As Ishbel moved around the shop, seeking out the last small shards of broken glass as they glinted in the candle-light, Iain recalled the facility, the easy charm he had once had at his fingertips in his dealings with women. It was like recalling another man, another life altogether. At ceilidhs in Glenlivet or Strathnairn, it had always been Lachlan who'd hung back and watched, his foot tapping to the music until he'd drunk sufficient whisky for Iain to haul him up onto the floor and propel him in the direction of a pretty girl. Now he had some inkling of the awkwardness Lachie had always felt.

When the last of the clearing was done, she said, 'I should go and get Tormod.'

'Yes,' he said, but then, before she'd reached the bindery door, he heard himself saying, 'Will you take a drink? I only have whisky.'

She looked to the bindery door, then he saw that her decision was made. 'All right,' she said.

He poured the measures into his Italian crystal glasses which had somehow survived the wreckage. She held the glass up, and he saw the light dance in its lines.

'These are very beautiful,' she said.

'My mother sent them to me some time ago, from Italy.'

'Ah.' She said no more, and he guessed she had already heard something of his mother's story.

He found himself at a loss again and then said, 'The girl Rose, was she all right?'

'I think so,' she said. 'But you should make amends. She stood up to the soldiers for you, you know.'

'She did?'

Ishbel nodded. 'Richard told me. When the fellow hit him with his gun, she tried to stop him. She tried to stop them destroying the place.'

Iain let out a long, 'Oh,' of regret and sank his head in his hands. 'I will do something. A book, or something.'

Ishbel took a sip of her drink. He could see her savour its subtleties and messages of other places. 'What happened to Richard?' she asked at last.

Iain looked away. 'Too much,' he said at last. 'Too much for one man.'

'Julia Rose said Major Thornlie spoke to him of his brother. I didn't know he had a brother.'

Iain swallowed more of his whisky and put the glass down in front of him. 'Richard was the youngest of three sons.

His father was a physician in Manchester who had always supported King James's cause. When, in the year 1745, we marched over the border into England, Richard and his two brothers all joined the prince's army at Manchester. On the retreat from Derby, all three were left behind with their regiment to hold Carlisle. When the Hanoverians retook the place, as any fool might have known they would, all three brothers were taken prisoner and thrown into Carlisle gaol. The authorities soon, in their wisdom, discovered they had too many prisoners in Carlisle, and so it was ordered that the best of them be taken to London for trial.'

He could see from her face that she had some idea of what was to come, but he couldn't stop. 'They were put on a prison hulk where there was hardly room for a man to turn around, little food or water, and scarcely a breath of air that did not carry in it fever and disease. I know whereof I speak.' He looked up and she nodded but said nothing and he carried on. 'Richard's middle brother was dead and thrown over the side before they ever docked at Tilbury. His eldest, Thomas, a physician like their father, was tried in London, condemned, and executed. A long, drawn-out and agonising death that Richard was forced to witness. Richard himself was spared execution because he was only seventeen years of age.'

Iain saw by her face that he might have stopped some while back, but there was no point now in not getting to the end. 'After his release from Newgate a year later, he couldn't face going home to his father, but instead set to wandering the country. I met him at a tavern in Glasgow when I returned from Virginia. I took him back here with me.' He drained the last of his drink and looked into his empty glass. 'That is what happened to Richard.'

They sat in silence for a few minutes. When Ishbel had finished her own drink she said, 'I had better get Tormod,' and Iain didn't know how to ask her to stay a bit longer. Fragments of phrases rushed through his mind before he could grip hold of them. And then, Donald Mòr was carrying the sleeping child through to go across the road, and he didn't know how to say that he would do it. As Ishbel MacLeod was going out of the door he finally said, 'I'll do something – about Julia Rose. I will make amends.'

He sat and had another dram, with Donald Mòr, and asked him about Ishbel's boy. When he finally returned to the house it was to find the Grandes Dames only just departing. Aeneas looked tired to the bone, his disconcerting good humour of earlier in the day was all but gone and his brow clouded with its habitual black look. His efforts to be rid of his mistress's guests were greatly hampered by the superlative fuss the women were making of bidding farewell to Hector MacGillivray.

'And you'll be certain to assure His Majesty of our continuing devotion . . .'

'It will be the first thing I tell him, Eilidh.'

'And that should he ever think to grace the town of Inverness . . .'

'Should King James ever disembark at the Citadel quay

he'll not be staying at your house, Catriona Lamont, that's for certain, with that wee brute of a dog . . .'

'Oh, Mairi, how can you . . .'

'And you leave on Friday night?' enquired Janet Grant.

Hector nodded. 'During the assembly. Aeneas thinks it the best time.'

'Any of the garrison not on duty out at Fort George will be too taken up with dancing and drinking. There'll be no better time for him to get away.'

Eilidh Cameron stopped in the process of putting on her cape. 'Oh, the dancing. I remember the very night you first walked into the assembly in Perth in 1715, and stood up with Charlotte. Hardly more than a girl herself then. Oh, but you lit up the room, the pair of you! Do you not remember it, Mairi?'

Iain's grandmother gave her friend Eilidh a sharp look. 'Remember it? Aye, do I. And have rued it every day since.'

It would be a cold day in Hell before she was ready to forgive Hector for the deflowering of the daughter that she'd had higher aspirations for. There followed much kissing of hands and blushing of cheeks that should have known better, and the ladies were at last gone out into the night.

It was very soon afterwards that Hector was ensconced in Iain's chamber, in Iain's favourite reading chair and surrounded by a blaze of candles. In his hands was the *Book of Forbidden Names*.

'What did you tell them of it?' Iain asked.

'Who? Mairi and Aeneas? Only as much as we know.

Mairi thought she had heard something of it once but had discounted it as nothing more than a story.'

'And did the rest of the ladies have anything to say about it?'

Hector shook his head. 'We didn't tell them.' He pointed to the book. 'Whoever the traitors in this book, whether great figures or people of little consequence, Lovat obviously thought he might employ them in some way to his own ends, should the need arise. There's danger for the people named in these pages, and danger for those who know of it, as Davie Campbell found out when he went looking for it in your shop. The fewer people exposed to it the better.'

'Can you make any sense of it?' asked Iain.

'A little. The text on the pages is Blind Hary's *Wallace*, as it should be. Every few pages, marked in the bottom corner, near the margin, is a small black cockade, and pairs of numbers written very faint down the side. I think the numbers are a code, and that they correspond to particular letters in each case. When I can work out which ones, I should be well on the way to having the names.'

Iain left him to it. Hector had shone at mathematics in his class at the university in Glasgow, so long ago. But, despite the best ministrations of the nimble-minded Aeneas and the efforts of the grammar school master of Inverness, Iain had failed to develop any interest whatsoever in the subject.

'I should have told Ramsay to bolt his door when he saw you coming,' Hector had said of the Edinburgh bookseller by whose trade Iain had been so entranced that he'd abandoned his own degree altogether.

Watching his father work, Iain felt the beginnings of a warm glow in his stomach. The resentment of realising that for six years Hector had let him believe he might be dead had begun to fade; its edges blurred into nothingness. The events of the day and the destruction wrought by the soldiers in his shop had reminded him that the cause his father had lived for all his life still mattered and that no good could come from trying to persuade himself that it didn't. It wasn't over. He drifted off to sleep, images flitting through his mind of his flight from Castle Leod, of a broom sweeping glass from the floor, and of Ishbel MacLeod passing quietly amongst the debris of his shop, a candle in her hand.

The hammering that woke him was loud and desperate. Iain shot from his bed. His father, who had slumbered in the chair as the candles spluttered out, was also on his feet.

'Good God, what is that? What hour of the night is it?'

Iain threw a plaid over his shoulders as he ran, barefoot, through the door. 'I don't know.'

All through the house, doors were opening, feet running. By the time Iain reached the front door, Hector was only a step behind him. 'Are you mad?' he said to his father, 'Get down to the cellar.'

'Not till I know who that is,' said Hector, positioning himself flat against the wall to one side of the door.

Aeneas, his bed cap askew and a pistol in his hand, told

Eppy and Flossie to get up the stairs to their mistress. Iain saw that the hand which did not hold the pistol held a dirk. He put out a hand, 'Give me the knife,' and Aeneas thrust it towards him before cocking the pistol and calling, 'Who's there?'

'Dod Fraser from Dochfour. Let me in, Aeneas, for any sake, before the watch comes after me.'

Hastily, Aeneas thrust his pistol into Iain's free hand and began to pull back the heavy bolts on the house door. A small, exhausted man almost fell through it.

Iain's grandmother's voice rang down from the top of the stairs. 'Dod Fraser! What in the world are you doing calling up my house in the middle of the night?'

Dod twisted his cap in his hand. 'Oh, Mistress Farquharson! The news I bring. It would break your heart to hear it.'

Iain's grandmother stopped where she was on her descent of the stairs. Her voice was almost hoarse. 'Is it my brother?'

Dod shook his head, the tears welling up. 'Dead, Mistress. Murdered.'

Hector stood out from behind the door and Dod nearly jumped out of his skin. 'Hector MacGillivray. Oh, the word is at Dochfour already that you are back in Inverness.'

'Never mind that,' said Hector. 'Kenneth Farquharson is dead?'

'Murdered,' repeated Dod. 'A knife to the throat and a white cockade on the hilt. He got word that he was to go to the castle – I don't know who from.'

'Here at Inverness?' asked Iain.

'No,' said Dod, impatient. 'Bona. He went out with the dogs. He never came back. When I heard them howling, I went across myself and found him there, dead amongst the ruins.'

Hector looked to Iain and then back at the distraught messenger. 'A white cockade? You are certain?'

'Certain as I'm standing here. A knife in the throat and dead, cold as a stone.'

A noise started up from the stairway. It was the keening. Eppy started it and within a breath Flossie had joined her. But not Mairi. Iain's grandmother had slumped down on to the stairs, her face as immobile as a headstone in the kirk-yard. Kenneth Farquharson, Kenny, had been her youngest brother and her favourite. Many a night Iain had spent with his friends in his inn at Dochfour, making fun of this very pot-man, Dod Fraser, in the days before the prince had come and the life they'd known had ended.

Iain turned to his grandmother and then to his father. 'How can it be?' How could it be that Iain's uncle had had been killed by a dirk with a white cockade in its hilt? How could it be, that Mairi Farquharson's own brother had suffered the death of one of those in the *Book of Forbidden Names*? Hector looked as astonished as Iain was himself, but Mairi's lips had started to move, and past the sound of the keening Iain heard her words.

'"For even thy brethren, and the house of thy father, even they have dealt treacherously with thee . . ."'

He went over and crouched down in front of her, took

her hands, but she paid him no heed, instead continuing to speak from the Book of Jeremiah.

'"I have forsaken mine house, I have left mine heritage; I have given the dearly beloved of my soul into the hand of her enemies."' She stood up and started to remount the stairs. Before she reached the top, she turned around and said to Aeneas, 'Tell my brother's servant to leave my house.'

They'd told Flossie and Eppy to stay with Mairi and see that she didn't get up again till morning, and then taken Dod Fraser down to the kitchen and made him drink brandy. Poor Dod was distraught. He had served his master forty years at that little inn by the Bona ferry where Loch Dochfour met Loch Ness. They'd seen roads blasted where before there had only been drovers, and bridges built. They'd watched General Wade's great boat arrive to transport the redcoats down the loch to their barracks of Fort Augustus at Kilchuimen. They'd given shelter to clansmen on the way to join risings in the name of King James and again when they returned, hungry and bedraggled at their end.

Hector was a long time in unpicking the threads of those forty years, going carefully with Dod, asking the right questions, all under the sharp black eyes of Aeneas Farquharson. 'Glen Shiel,' he said eventually. Aeneas leaned in closer as Dod looked down at his hands. 'Tell us again what happened in the year 1719.' And so Dod went through it again. There had been a messenger on his way to the clans in Strathspey, to tell them of the landing of the Jacobite exiles with three hundred Spanish troops. The plan had been to join with other chiefs and clans, Rob Roy MacGregor amongst them. After the messenger had left the invading forces' encampment at Eilean Donan, word had come of the government navy scouring the west coast. Down out of Ross the messenger had come, through the country of the Mackenzies and the Frasers, to cross the loch at the Bona ferry. It was the innkeeper himself, Mairi Farquharson's brother, that had the tack of the ferry, and Dod Fraser that manned the oars whenever a traveller should need to be transported across the narrows at Bona. And so it had been the day in 1719 that the messenger had come to rouse the Strathspey clans.

Iain knew the rest. Before the messenger ever got near the clans, Major General Wightman at Inverness had been informed of the Jacobites' landing and their location and was marching his forces westwards. The armies had met at Glen Shiel on the tenth of June, King James's birthday, and had fought it out hard. In the end, the Jacobite forces came off worse, over a hundred of them lying dead and many more wounded. The rising of 1719 had ended before it began.

Hector had it worked out before Iain did. 'Kenny Farquharson told the redcoats, didn't he?' said Hector. Dod started to shake his head, but Hector went on. 'There were rumours at the time, until Mairi threatened to cut out the next tongue she heard it from.'

Dod was looking terrified now. 'What could Kenny know of Glen Shiel? He never heard of it until after it happened.'

'Oh, did he not? He knew something was in the wind though, when you took that messenger across at Bona,' said Hector.

Dod put out his hands. 'Oh, Hector man, we all knew there was something in the wind.'

Aeneas, who had been becoming increasingly agitated, sprang from his stool and took a handful of Dod's neck-cloth, twisting it round so that the man's eyes boggled. 'I have outlived my patience, Dod Fraser. You'll give us the whole tale right now! Did Kenny Farquharson inform the British of the '19 rising or not?'

'All right, all right!' declared Dod, rubbing his neck as Aeneas loosened his grip. 'Now, the inn, you know, was a poor place in those days, though God knows there were plenty pleased enough to get to it. And Kenneth had lost everything in the '15, for there was surely never such a gentleman as Kenny Farquharson,' here Dod gave an anxious glance at the stair door, 'your good mistress's brother.'

A grumbling started in the back of Aeneas's throat, and Dod hurried on. 'The redcoats were up and down the loch, for the building of Fort Augustus at Kilchuimen. Good custom they gave, and Kenny with a family to feed – he could hardly turn them away. And so, a wee bit of this and that they would ask him about, now and again – just to help keep the law amongst the clans.'

'My grandmother's brother was a paid informant,' said Iain, the image of his favoured uncle dissolving in front of him.

'No, no,' assured Dod. 'Not inform them, for he'd nothing to inform – it was just he would tell them if there was a lot of coming and going from certain places. Kenny didn't really know anything.'

Hector stood up and pushed away his stool. 'He knew enough, and he knew what that information was worth, what it would cost. What it did cost.'

'But they gave him no choice, Hector . . .'

'By God,' said Aeneas, brandishing his pistol, 'but I'd have given him a choice.'

'He stopped, though,' said Dod, desperately. 'After that, when they changed the regiments. When General Wade was here and it was just the roads and the bridges building, and the private militias keeping the peace. Kenny Farquharson never told them a thing after 1719.'

On Hector's face was disgust, but in Aeneas's eyes was hatred beyond anything Iain had ever seen. He had such a grip on his pistol that Iain feared he might fire it. And indeed, Aeneas did raise the hand that held the gun, but it was only to point towards the stairs.

'Her son!' he rasped.

Dod looked baffled but Iain understood. William Farquharson. Willie. His mother's brother who had got away to France after the escape from Newgate in 1716, only to return three years later to try again. At Glen Shiel.

'Her son,' repeated Aeneas, once more waving his pistol in the direction of the stairs. 'Shot like a dog at Glen Shiel. Nineteen years old and left to die in the dirt! The hope of his family, the flower of his clan! Dead by his own uncle's treachery.'

Dod was now looking desperately from Hector to Iain, as if waiting for one of them to intervene.

'Get out,' said Iain, turning away from the pot-man he had known almost all his life. 'Get out and never come back again to this house.'

Aeneas, who looked drained beyond measure, as if he had travelled that night from Dochfour himself, was persuaded to go to his bed. Iain warmed milk over the embers of the kitchen fire, then, pouring it into two pewter mugs, put a good slug of whisky into each and carried them upstairs to his chamber. Hector was already settled back in his previous position, more candles lit and the *Book of Forbidden Names* out on the table in front of him. He barely took his eyes off the book as he reached for the drink.

'Is he in it?' said Iain. 'My grandmother's brother?'

'He must be – Dod Fraser was pretty clear about the white cockade on the hilt of the dirk. And if Kenny Farquharson's name is in here, it will give me the key to the code for working out the rest of the names.'

'I don't understand why he took the dogs though.'

'What?' said Hector, a little impatient at being interrupted in his study of the book.

'Dod said my great-uncle took the dogs with him to the castle at Bona.'

Hector was untroubled by this. 'Perhaps something in the

message bidding him go there had a threat in it? Besides, would you go over to Caisteal Spioradain on your own?'

Caisteal Spioradain. Castle of the Spirits, the ghosts of all the men murdered there over the centuries. Few would set foot there alone.

'But why didn't the dogs protect him?'

'Who knows? A haunch of venison, a rabbit or two – a dog is easily distracted,' said his father. He frowned as Iain pulled out a stool. 'You'll get in my light. Besides, you'll be more use after a night's sleep.'

Iain made no protest and where the four hours went between then and him waking, he could not have told. In the corner of his room, where the candles had burned very low, Hector was still awake, and writing.

Iain sat up. 'Have you got it?'

'Nearly. I'll have Kenny Farquharson's name soon, and once I have that, it won't take long for the rest to follow.'

'And then what?'

Hector at last looked up. His eyes were bleary and his skin grey. He gave a tight smile. 'That all depends on the names.'

FOURTEEN

Bisset's Close

Iain didn't lift his head as he went from his grandmother's house to the bookshop the next morning, but still he could see people approach with condolences in their mouths, then veer away, having thought better of it. News of his great-uncle's murder had flown into the town from Dochfour as if on Dod Fraser's heels.

Richard Dempster looked at him with some surprise when he entered the shop, but before he could ask Iain anything Donald Mòr was through from the bindery like a shot. He didn't mince his words.

'By God, MacGillivray, dark tales from Dochfour! How is the *cailleach*?' Donald always referred to Iain's grandmother as 'the old woman', one of the few people he spoke of with any degree of awe. 'Eilidh Cameron and all that crew will be round there already, I suppose, raising a great noise. You do well to leave them to it. But murdered! What are you going to do about it? He has no son.'

Iain had expected this. 'I'm not going to do anything, Donald.'

'Nothing?' Donald stepped forward, his face furious. 'When did I ever think to see the day a MacGillivray would have a kinsman unavenged! It's not long past the time that the whole of Clan Chattan would be out for him.' Donald took another step towards Iain, leaned in, conspiratorial though there were only the three of them in the place. 'They still would, you know. If Mairi Farquharson gives the word, the culprit will be dealt with in short order. There are plenty yet with arms that the redcoats don't know about.'

Iain unbuttoned his own coat and hung it up. 'My grandmother will be giving no such word.'

Donald opened his mouth, clearly about to argue, but then a glimmer of understanding crossed his face. He dropped his voice even lower. 'What is it, Iain? What happened between them?'

But Iain opened the desk drawer to take out the catalogue. 'There are . . . deep things, Donald, of long ago. My father is trying to get to the bottom of them, but the time is not yet.'

Donald nodded, apparently satisfied. 'Hector is the man that will do it. But you will let the *cailleach* know, when the time comes, that she can rely on me.' It had clearly not occurred to him that the death of Mairi Farquharson's brother could in any way be connected with the *Book of Forbidden Names* that he had so earnestly counselled Iain to destroy.

Iain touched the binder's shoulder. 'My grandmother has always known that, Donald, thank you.'

Everything being said, Donald returned to his workshop, his fingers still flexing. Richard Dempster, who had been watching them both, and trying to follow their conversation in Gaelic, went back to his tidying and making ready the bundle of loose chapters and parts of books to be offered to the chapman when he called. The glazier came, assessed the damage to the cabinets, gave his price and left again.

All through the morning, Iain tried to adjust his catalogue, strike out his losses, tally what was left, but nothing in front of him would take hold – his thoughts turned continually to the question of who had murdered his great-uncle. The list of those who would have a motive was a long one, for Kenneth Farquharson's treachery at the time of Glen Shiel had left the families of a hundred men bereaved.

At some point in the morning, the street door opened and a head of shiny black curls sped past his desk in the direction of the bindery. The boy was not followed by the confectioner. Tormod knocked on the bindery door, provoking a torrent of abuse in the process, along with the demand to know the son of which brindled hell-dweller disturbed him.

'It is I, Tormod MacLeod, Donald Mòr!' The child announced himself as if he were the representative of a visiting chief, and to Iain's bemusement was received accordingly. The door was opened and the boy told to enter. 'And leave that door open, that I might see if those red soldiers come back to the shop.'

Tormod did so before going to stand beside Donald at

his workbench. The binder nodded at him. 'Now, not a word till I'm finished this.' The boy watched mesmerised as Donald stamped out a pattern of gold leaf ornaments, '*fleurons*', into the blue morocco cover of the volume he was working on. As he worked, he began to tell the child a story purported to be from that very book. The tale was so outrageous, of witches and warlocks cavorting as they feasted on the organs of the innocent, that Richard, able to catch certain words that were recurring favourites of Donald's incendiary vocabulary, asked Iain whether he should not intervene.

'Leave them,' said Iain. 'The boy will come to no harm with Donald Mòr.'

The story ended, Donald began to sing a ditty, in Scots, a language he used only rarely and had not quite mastered. By the end of the first verse, Richard had again raised his eyebrows in Iain's direction. It was clear Donald was teaching the child Captain Robert Stewart's 'Epitaph on the Death of the Duke of Cumberland'. Not only was Cumberland not dead, but the poet's imagining of the duke's reception into Hell was unlikely to go down well with any passing government soldier who overheard it. Iain's attention was already on the binder and the boy though, or, more specifically, on the boy. As Donald ended each verse, Tormod would throw something high up in the air and watch it spin before catching it. The object caught the sun and glinted as it spun. Iain pushed his stool back from his desk and walked through to the bindery.

Donald looked up and kept singing, absent-mindedly now though, as he saw Iain looking at the child.

'Let me see that button.'

The chubby brown fingers closed around the object, and the boy's mouth was clamped shut. His eyes, amber in the sunlight, didn't move from Iain's.

'Let me see the button,' repeated Iain.

The child's lips parted slightly, a smile somewhere not far off. Iain saw him glance quickly at the door. Then Tormod sprang for it, dodging past him with the nimbleness of a mountain goat. Iain swung himself round, knocking over a pot of Donald's glue. The binder's fury followed Iain across the shop and out into the street, where a disappearing small brown foot told him that Tormod was running home.

An old cobbler seated on a bench outside Dunbar's hospital called out, 'A thief, is it?'

'No,' shouted Iain as he turned the corner after the child. He had almost caught him when the boy suddenly jumped onto the forestairs of his house. Iain started after him, just as the door at the top of the stairs opened, and there was Ishbel.

'What on earth is going on?'

'He's chasing me!' yelled Tormod, diving past her to take sanctuary in his own house.

'You are chasing him?' She looked at Iain, incredulous.

'He has my button,' said Iain.

'Your button?' Ishbel was even more astonished.

Iain took a moment to gather his patience. 'The silver

button your son has clenched in his fist belongs to me,' he said.

He might as well have said that the child had just murdered the provost. All trace of amusement disappeared from the confectioner's face. She went a ghostly white. 'Who told you that?'

'Told me? No one told me. He's been throwing it up in the air in my shop for a good ten minutes.'

Ishbel stared at him, then, seeming to recover herself, she spun around and demanded Tormod come back out. 'Show me what you have in your hand.'

'Haven't anything,' he said, a little sullen.

'Tormod, I will tan your hide and take it to Donald Mòr for the covering of books! Show me what is in your hand.'

The lower lip protruded once again, and the child held out his hand, slowly unclenching his fingers. Ishbel took what was in his palm and held it out towards Iain. 'Is that your button?'

He picked it from her fingers, his own brushing hers as he did so. There was no doubt. There was the wrought silverwork, the Clan Chattan crest with the motto, 'Touch Not the Cat'. His grandmother had presented them to him when he'd come home at last in '48 and told him how proud she was of him. The only time in his life. Eight silver buttons that had been on his coat the night he had tumbled at the end of this alley, the night Davie Campbell had been murdered in his shop. By the time he'd reached home there had only been seven.

Tormod was peeking from the back of his mother's skirts. Iain ascended the steps and bent down to the child's level. 'Where did you get it?' he asked.

'It was on the ground. When that man fell into you and you went over on your arse.'

'Tormod!' said Ishbel. 'You will not use such words.'

'But Donald Mòr—'

'Donald Mòr is a . . .' She looked at Iain and stopped.

Iain was struggling not to laugh. 'There's nothing you could say of Donald that would be news to me or that he himself would argue with.' He turned again to the child. 'But I need to know, Tormod, if you found a key that night as well, the one to my shop. I lost it at the same time.'

Ishbel wrinkled her brow. 'But that was the night that man was . . .'

'Murdered in my shop,' Iain finished for her.

She began to shake her head, a look of terror on her face. 'But Tormod is not yet six years old. Tormod! Tell him you never found a key.'

The boy looked from her to Iain and back to her again. It was clear he was confused by her panic. 'There wasn't a key. There was just the button. Can I keep it?'

'No,' said the woman, her voice trembling, 'you cannot.' She took him by the shoulders and turned him firmly back through the door to their dwelling before saying to Iain, 'He knows nothing of your key. You have your button. Much joy may it bring you.' Then she followed the boy into the house before slamming the door shut behind her.

Iain stood, looking uselessly at the door. Little more than twelve hours beforehand, she had been seated opposite him, drinking whisky by candlelight in his shop, and now he had as good as accused her boy of theft and he was standing halfway up her forestairs, holding a button. He didn't entirely understand how it was that he had not managed the thing better, but he knew that he had made some grave mistake. As he put the rogue button in his pocket, a heavy purring from the top of a nearby wall made him look up. There was Donald Mòr's cat, observing all with a malevolent eye. 'Not now, Morag,' he said as he began his trudge back to the bookshop, 'not now.'

Once through the door, he was greeted anxiously by Richard Dempster.

'Has something happened?'

'Eppy was down, with a message. I couldn't understand her properly, so sent her through to Donald.'

Iain went through to the bindery, where Donald Mòr warned him to come nowhere near his gluepot.

'Richard tells me Eppy was here.'

'Aye, with a message for you,' Donald lowered his voice, 'from Hector. He needs to see you at your grandmother's house. You are to lose no time.'

Iain could almost sense the presence of the Grandes Dames before he heard them. He knocked on the door of his grandmother's room and went in, but there was no sign of Hector there, only the four old women. The mischief and delight that had enlivened their faces the previous day was utterly gone. His grandmother looked weary to her bones, and Janet Grant in particular seemed to have aged ten years. It was clear Mairi had told them not only of her brother Kenneth's death, but also of his treachery.

'Has there been any more word – from Dochfour?' he asked.

'I have heard all I will ever need to hear from Dochfour,' said his grandmother. 'Your father is in your room – he's anxious to speak to you.'

Hector had been pacing the floor and whipped around as he opened the door.

'There you are. You've been a good while coming.'

'I had someone to see,' said Iain. 'What's happened? Have you got the code?'

Hector nodded. 'I have. And I've got the next name.'

When his father told him, Iain couldn't comprehend it.

'Do you know him?' Hector asked.

'Yes,' said Iain.

'Will he not still be in Perth then?'

'Not any more,' said Iain, throwing on the jacket he had just put off.

'Take someone with you.'

'I'll be quicker on my own,' said Iain.

'Aye, and – if you're found amongst trouble, you'll be needing a witness there ready to swear you didn't cause it. If he's still alive, bring him back here. I need to question him.'

Iain had no doubt that his father would know methods of questioning that few could stand up to.

'All right,' he said.

He ran up Baron Taylor's lane and burst into Arch MacPhee's workshop, to find the cobbler sitting at his last, demonstrating some technique to his apprentice. Arch put down his hammer and came towards Iain.

'Iain Bàn. I was sorry as can be to hear of the death of your great-uncle. A terrible thing. To think—'

'I have no time for that now, Arch. I need you to come with me.'

Arch was a little taken aback and looked back to the job he had left his apprentice at. 'What is it? Can it not wait?'

Iain looked over to the apprentice who instantly looked away. 'No, Arch. It's Watch business. I need you to come right this minute.'

Arch took off his apron and handed it to his apprentice with a few hasty instructions. Hurriedly, he wrestled on his jacket and found his 'town hat'. It was only once they were safely back out onto the lane that he said, 'So, what is it? Is it to do with Kenneth Farquharson's murder?'

'No,' said Iain, setting the pace. 'Well, perhaps. I need you to come with me to Hugh Sinclair's house.'

'Hugh Sinclair?'

'Barbara Sinclair the milliner's father.'

'Him? That man never said boo to a goose. What can he have to do with your uncle's death?'

'Maybe nothing, but . . . there are things I can't tell you, Arch. You must trust me.'

Arch's brow clouded. 'Is this to do with Hector?'

They were crossing Church Street towards the old school vennel that would take them down to the river. Iain made no response to the constable's question other than to give him a look.

'I knew it,' said Arch. 'I knew when that body turned up in your shop and the next thing I heard was that Hector MacGillivray was back in town, I knew it was only the start of the trouble.'

Iain spoke very low as they strode down the vennel. 'The trouble is nothing to do with my father.'

Arch snorted. 'That would be a first. Hector MacGillivray is like an omen. Every time he shows his face in this town, some calamity is not long in following.'

Iain felt himself bristle. Arch had stopped for breath outside Provost Hossack's new house at the bottom of the vennel. 'You're talking of the risings in the name of King James?'

Arch pointed up towards the ruin of the castle. 'Well, you can hardly say the town did well out of them, can you? And your own people – Hector for ever a fugitive and your mother goodness knows where.'

'My mother?' Iain was astonished at the turn of Arch's conversation.

'Well,' said the cobbler, looking somewhat abashed, 'I just mean, she'd have done better to marry Aeneas Farquharson, like everyone thought she was going to, than an adventurer like your father.'

Iain turned and started to walk briskly again, in the direction of Forbes of Culloden's town house and the narrow wynd that would take them to the bridge. 'If you'll recall, Arch, she didn't marry my father either!'

The day was warm and the breeze was coming up the glen from the west. The smell of the channel taking refuse to the river from the nearby tanyard turned his stomach. Further upriver, in avoidance of the noxious waste of the skinners' and tanners' trade, housewives and maids pounded their laundry. On a day like today, he envied those women — their bare legs stamping in the cool rushing water, their skirts tucked in at their waists and the breeze rifling their hair. It was different in the wintertime — he didn't envy them then when, regardless of the ice floes and the melted snow carried along the river, they stamped their linens, legs and feet as bare as the day they were born, skin red and mottled with the cold. As Iain drew nearer to the gatehouse on the town side of the bridge, he discerned Eppy's voice amongst those of the women singing and pounding their laundry. She had a fine voice and was much in demand amongst his grandmother's friends and acquaintances when they were having their entertainments. He hadn't thought this to be Eppy's day for doing the household washing, but once they were through the gatehouse and onto the bridge there she was, stamping her feet at the sodden material in time to the battle song she was singing, the other women taking up the refrain. By the time they'd crossed to reach the western gatehouse, the song was thoroughly embedded in his head.

Barbara Sinclair lived with her father in a house on the western approaches to the town. Bisset's Close was tucked down off the street, its houses were thatched but well built, of rubble rather than wood. Only now did it occur to Iain that while he was an irregular and clandestine visitor to the milliner's working premises on the High Street, he had never been to her house, and didn't know which one it was. They asked a woman out tending to her hens and she pointed to a solid house of two storeys, at the far end of the row. The place appeared well kept, with glazed windows, and fruit trees and herbs growing in a small front garden. All looked more or less as it should do as they approached, but then Iain noticed that all the shutters, above and below, were still closed – an odd thing for this hour of the day and in this weather.

Arch noticed it too. 'Did you send anyone to her shop, to see if she was there?'

Iain shook his head. He had considered it, but only for a moment. If his father was right, better that Barbara was safe in her shop than witness to what they might be about to find. Only now did it dawn on him that she might be in danger herself.

There was no sign of the milliner's father in the yard, nor of anyone else besides the now curious neighbour. As they approached the door, they saw that it was slightly ajar; there was a creak and it opened in the breeze. A hen wandered out into the yard and the door continued to swing slightly behind it. The neighbour informed them that she hadn't seen Hugh Sinclair or his daughter that morning, but there was nothing unusual in that – the daughter left early for the town and the old man rarely left the house.

They thanked her and approached nearer to the cottage. 'I'll go in first,' said Arch. 'If there is anything amiss, it's better that I come upon it than you.'

Iain waited outside. All was quiet save the usual sounds of the river in the distance and of the bees at work amongst the flowers. But then the harmony of the summer's afternoon was broken by a harsh shout from Arch MacPhee. 'Iain! Come, come, for God's sake.'

Iain ran, stooping beneath the low lintel into the house. The place was so dark he could hardly see. He flung open the nearest shutters and then saw that Arch MacPhee was bending over something on the floor behind a kitchen bench. He went around the table and stopped. They were too late. Hugh Sinclair was lying on his side on the floor, a cooking pot knocked over behind him, and his eyes staring ahead of him. From the side of his neck protruded a dirk identical to the one that had killed Davie Campbell, down to the last detail of the white cockade on its hilt.

Arch was leaning forward then held up a finger that had been dipped in the blood trickling along the floor. He looked up at Iain. 'He's not long dead. As well you took me with you, or the magistrates would have had you up for this.'

Iain thought of his father's warning. It felt as if iron bands were tightening around his head. 'Arch, you don't think I . . .'

Arch stood up and wiped his hands on his breeches. 'No, I don't think you did it. But do you not wonder if there might be someone trying to make it look as if you did? Davie Campbell dead in your shop, your uncle killed when he was out with his dogs that should have protected him and not a sound did the brutes make, and now you here and the breath hardly left Hughie Sinclair's body? Whatever darkness is going on in this town, Iain, it's swirling around you. How is it you knew to come here?'

Iain stepped back, as if closeness to the old man's corpse might somehow incriminate him further. 'It's . . . I can't tell you, Arch. It's something I don't rightly understand myself. Someone is carrying out a work of revenge.'

Arch picked a spoon from the table and carefully hooked the handle through a loop of the blood-spattered cockade. 'And has it something to do with this?'

'I think so. Can you take it off?'

'Aye,' said Arch, removing it and handing it to Iain. 'Get you back into town. Tell them at the tolbooth that I've just found Hughie Sinclair dead. Tell them we were coming to see about – God knows – something to do with Friday, anything.'

'Friday?' said Iain stupidly.

'The assembly. We are playing, had you forgotten?'

'No.' He shook his head. The night of the dance, when Hector was to make his escape. 'I hadn't forgotten.'

Arch followed him out to the Sinclairs' yard in search of water from the butt to wash his hands. The neighbour that'd been observing them was now standing at the back door and threatening to come in.

'God in Heaven!' She put a hand to her chest when she saw the blood on Arch's hands. 'What has happened?'

'Someone's killed Hugh Sinclair.' Now her hand went in horror to her mouth and she was about to set up a mourning when Arch spoke to stop her. 'Wait, now think: who has been here this morning?'

The woman thought. 'I've seen no one but if anyone had come by the back way, I wouldn't have seen them.'

Arch looked at the house. 'Is there a back door?'

'No, but see, here.' She led them round the side of the woodshed, to where there was an opening in the back wall of the close. 'We use this to go in and out to the green.' She was pointing to the square of laundresses' cottages edging a wide flat green a few hundred yards away, where much of the good linen of the town was laid out to dry. The women took it in turns to watch the green, day and night.

The neighbour turned to go back down the path. 'I had only just come out to the hens when you appeared. If anyone came into the close by this way, I wouldn't have seen them.'

*

Iain's report of the murder of Hugh Sinclair was received with deep shock but the involvement of Arch in the discovery released him from any further role in the matter as far as the authorities were concerned, and they wasted little time in hearing his version of events before sending a further contingent of the burgh officers across the bridge to Bisset Close.

But one thing they had done before releasing him was to send a messenger to the milliner's shop on the High Street.

Iain hadn't seen Barbara since the day after Davie Campbell's murder, when she had taken more than a passing interest in Hector in his clergyman's guise. The tinkle of the small bell above the shop door brought not Barbara but her assistant through from the back workshop. The girl's eyes were red and swollen and her face suffused with confusion. Iain's heart sank. He should have come here first.

'Where's your mistress?'

The girl tried to speak but her words disintegrated into unintelligible sobbing. It took three further attempts but eventually the girl managed to get out that Barbara had gone to the old Greyfriars' kirkyard.

The old churchyard of the abandoned Greyfriars lay at the far end of Church Street, beyond the High Kirk and covering a wide extent of land from above the river to the edges of the desolate area known as the Longman. While the church and houses of the friary had been plundered time and time again in the two centuries since the Franciscan brothers had abandoned them, the dead of Inverness slept peaceful in their graves. Not like in the nearby High Kirk, where the blood of executed Jacobite prisoners mingled amongst the soil and bones, and headstones and walls were marked by musket shot from Cumberland's firing squads. Iain set his face straight ahead and was soon passing through the gates into Greyfriars.

He stopped. The place was vast and the trees growing amongst the graves in full leaf. There were so many places where a person might conceal themselves. Iain recalled childhood games of hide-and-seek that had ended in the terror of being unfound and alone, behind a tomb in the Greyfriars' yard.

He started picking his way round by the wall, scanning the whole graveyard. The afternoon was warm, and bees and butterflies flitted amongst purple blooms of shrubs that no human hand had planted, or danced from head to head of dandelion, daisy and clover. The names of people he had known leapt out at him from stone tablets set into the wall, the bare details of their lives carved below memento mori, lest any passer-by forget where they were and where they too were headed. Birds flew down from the trees to peck worms from the rich soil, and a family of rabbits scampered from bush to gravestone, oblivious to the danger of a hundred housewives' cooking pots.

Then he saw her. She was seated about fifty yards away from him, on a raised grave slab beneath two wild cherries. She was sitting very straight, her back to him, unmoving. He walked carefully across the grass and around the graves between them, saying her name quietly so as not to startle her.

She made no response or movement and he quickened his pace, saying her name again. Still there was no response. He reached the grave slab on which she was sitting and rounded it with caution. Barbara was staring ahead, her eyes red as if from weeping, but she wasn't weeping now.

He sat down beside her, but she made no acknowledgement of his presence. 'Barbara,' he began. It occurred to him to put an arm around her, but she shrugged it away.

'I have come here to grieve,' she said.

He felt suddenly very aware of the lack of any real feeling between them. 'I'm sorry,' he said. 'I'm sorry about what has happened, to your father.'

'It was not supposed to happen.'

'It was a terrible thing . . .' he continued.

She stood up. 'It was not supposed to happen, and you are not sorry.'

'What? Barbara,' he also stood, 'what are you taking about? Of course I'm sorry!'

'You are not sorry. It was your father, that walked the street with you dressed as an English clergyman, that killed him, and you are not sorry.'

She brushed a dead leaf from the skirt of her gown. As she walked away, she added, 'But you will be.'

FIFTEEN

An Innkeeper of Perth

Aeneas was in the kitchen, astride a low stool, sleeves rolled up and polishing his boots when Iain returned. His customary expression of displeasure deepened when he saw Iain's face. 'What now?'

'Hugh Sinclair is dead.'

Aeneas thought for a moment. 'The milliner's father? He would have been a good age, I suppose.' He returned to his boots.

'He was killed,' said Iain. 'Murdered.' He spoke freely since Flossie and the scullery maid were out in the yard, plucking hens, and Eppy was still down pounding linens at the river. He pulled from his pocket the bloodstained ribbon that had been a white cockade and held it up for Aeneas to see.

'Good God,' said Aeneas. 'Another cockade?'

Iain thrust the ribbon into the fire beneath the cauldron of broth perennially hung over it. 'Yes. I've to go up and tell my father.'

Iain was hardly through the door to his own bedchamber

when Aeneas came in behind him, sleeves rolled down, boots and jacket back on.

'Sheesh, you're a man can creep about, Aeneas.' Over thirty years, and still he was not used to his grandmother's servant and kinsman suddenly materialising behind him.

'Hmmph,' was all the response. 'Have you told him?'

'I'm only in the door.'

Hector was standing at the edge of the brown velvet window drapes, watching the street for any sign of a further deputation from the garrison. 'Well?' he said to Iain.

'Already dead when I got there. A dirk with a white cockade in his neck.'

'Damn.' Hector turned away from the window and sat down, rubbing a hand over the stubble on his chin. 'I should have realised. I was sure I had seen him before, when we saw him out in that street with that courtesan.'

'I told you, that was his daughter, and she's a milliner, not a courtesan.'

'Not far off it,' murmured Aeneas, picking up a sheaf of Hector's notes, frowning and putting it back down.

Iain ignored the barb and spoke again to his father. 'Well, whatever she is, she thinks it was you who killed him.'

Aeneas's eyebrows shot up and he looked from Iain to Hector, waiting. Hector himself showed no surprise at the declaration.

'No doubt.'

'Would you care to enlighten us as to why?' Iain demanded. But when Hector spoke, it was to Aeneas.

'You remember in the '15, when we were on the way home from Preston, and we stopped a night at Perth?'

'Of course,' said Aeneas.

'You recall we were billeted in an inn near the North Port in Perth? The innkeeper would have been, oh, around forty years of age at the time. His wife was younger. There was a baby too, as I recall.'

Iain knew what was coming next. The remnants of the Jacobite army had marched north from Perth to Ruthven, on the orders of King James, but as Hanoverian strength gathered, the king had lost heart, and slipped quietly back to France, leaving his supporters to their own devices. Retribution had been thorough, the lesson exemplary. But not all Jacobite leaders could be caught, nor evidence found against them. Until the 'evidences' were brought into play. The evidences were often common men and women, taken prisoner for their support, one way or the other, for King James's cause, and who were able to purchase their own freedom by swearing oaths as to the involvement of others. Hector, Aeneas, Iain's Uncle Willie and his grandfather Neil Farquharson had all been arrested and imprisoned on the testimony of such an 'evidence', and Iain's grandfather had been put to death on the strength of it.

Iain sat down on his bed, his voice strangely hoarse. 'It was Hugh Sinclair. Hugh Sinclair was the evidence that betrayed my grandfather.'

Hector leaned forwards. 'Did you not tell me yourself that he kept an inn at Perth in the '15 and was taken prisoner

to London? I should have known it. I should have recognised him, for he sure as Hell recognised me!'

'Did he?' asked Aeneas, surprised.

Hector nodded, his jaw working in anger at himself. 'He
sent the woman, his daughter, down to the shop just after
we passed them in the street. Don't you remember it, Iain?'

'I remember.'

'Sinclair gave his interrogators our names,' Hector went
on, 'as people who had definitely been out for the king.
By the time they got their prisoners to court, even the
British government would not execute them without some
evidence against them. Just like after the '45 – men not
taken on the field or on the run but condemned out of the
mouths of innkeepers under whose roof they had slept or
supped. Women – your own grandmother amongst them –
thrown into prisons on the word of informants such as
Hugh Sinclair.'

But Aeneas's face was very dark and he shook his head.
'It may have been Hugh Sinclair who gave them our
names, but it wasn't him who betrayed the escape plan
in London all those years ago, for he cannot have known
of it.'

The room grew colder as the sun made its way westwards.
Aeneas went to see to his duties in the rest of the household
while Eppy brought ale and cold beef as they had missed
their dinner. Then Hector continued working at his deci-
phering of the book as Iain paced the room, furious that
he had become entangled with the daughter of a man who

had betrayed his family so long ago. Suddenly, Hector's voice broke into his thoughts.

'When did they come here?'

Iain stopped pacing. 'Who?'

'Hugh Sinclair and his daughter. When did they appear in Inverness?'

Iain thought back. It had been at an assembly, a year or so after he'd got back from Virginia. He'd been amongst the musicians hired to play. Barbara had watched him all night, approached him at the end. They had 'seen' each other after further assemblies and other nights when he'd taken too much drink — perhaps half a dozen times a year since.

'It was about three years ago,' he said.

'Why did they come?'

Iain frowned. 'She said there was an opportunity. The town needed a milliner. Her father's health was not good and she thought the Highland air would strengthen him. I don't think anyone really questioned them much further.'

'And,' said his father, 'I take it you have a history of sorts with the woman.'

'I'm not a monk, Father.'

'I wouldn't expect you to be, but a woman like that — does she ask you things, about the cause?'

Iain looked at his father. 'You think she's a spy too?'

'I think it possible. It's plain she knows what her father's activities were, and given your relationship to me, and our family's involvement in every Stuart rising since the start, it would hardly be a surprise if you were a target for a Hanoverian intelligencer.'

Iain stood up and went to splash water over his face at the bowl on his washstand. He looked in the glass above it. As always, his eyes lit on the damaged part of his face. 'I doubt she had an interest in me for anything else.'

'I'm sorry,' said his father softly.

'Don't be. She meant no more to me than I to her. And much good did it do her because I didn't tell her anything.'

'You're certain?'

Iain stood up. 'What could I have told her? I don't even know why you're here. I couldn't have told her a damned thing!' He went out of the room, not troubling to close the door behind him.

He spent the first hours of the evening reading in the bookshop, the only place, he told himself, where he could get peace. Donald Mòr and Richard Dempster, the one happily ensconced in his bindery and the other already sleeping soundly in his garret above the shop, did nothing to disturb him, and yet he couldn't settle. Time and again, he saw the upper door to the confectioner's house slam shut. The emptiness of the chair where she had been sitting last night seemed to fill the room, defeating his attempts to think of anything else. As the clock struck nine, he gave up on his attempt at his book, locked up the shop and crossed the street to Bow Court.

No light showed from the garret room of the confectioner's

home, but there was a glow from beneath the door to the cookhouse and sweet sugared smells lingered on the air. The sound of singing came down the close from Bessie Stewart's tavern, and a man appeared at the other end, relieving himself in the shadows. Iain lifted his hand to knock at the cookhouse door, but let it drop again. This was foolish. The confectioner would dislike him or not – there was nothing he could do about that. He let his hand drop but had not yet turned away when the door opened in front of him and left him looking into the face of Ishbel MacLeod. 'Oh,' she said. Her face was flushed and some hair had escaped from beneath her white cap. Unthinkingly, Iain pushed back his own hair just as she did hers.

'I'm sorry to disturb you so late in the evening,' he began.

She nodded, waiting.

'I wanted to say sorry.'

'Oh,' she said again. 'What for?'

'For whatever it was I said or did before that so upset you.' He had started now, so there was nothing for it but to blunder on. 'I mean, when I spoke about the button, you seemed to think I was speaking about something else, and I haven't the first notion what that was, but whatever it was, it seemed to upset you greatly. So, I'm sorry.'

She looked down. 'Really, there was nothing at all.' She made to turn away, back into her cookhouse.

Iain steeled himself. 'I think there was. I had not meant . . . to upset you. About whatever it was about.'

She stopped when he spoke and turned back to face him.

More noise came from Bessie Stewart's tavern and then a soldier and a woman of little repute came swaying out of it into the close. 'Can I come in?' he asked.

'I was about to take Tormod up to his bed,' she said, indicating the child sleeping on some sacks in the corner of the small cookhouse.

Iain stepped past her into the room and bent down. 'Let me carry him up for you then.'

Ishbel made no argument and once she had taken a lit candle from the cookhouse and snuffed out or covered over all other sources of flame there, she slipped past Iain to lead the way up the outer stairs to the room in which they lived.

Iain followed her and, having stooped to get through the door of the garret, laid Tormod down on the box bed Ishbel showed him. She settled the child beneath his blankets and sat down on the bed herself, indicating that Iain should take one of the two stools set at a small deal table. She lit no other candle, and there was no fire in this upper room beneath the wooden rafters and the thatch, where he could hear the mice running. The place smelled of straw and peat and warm wood. It reminded him of the smell of Lachlan's house in Strathnairn, although Ishbel MacLeod's home did not also smell of cattle and hens and sheep. He could see clothes hanging off pegs, a chest or two, and on the table a child's letter book and tablet. She was obviously teaching the boy to read.

'He is your son, isn't he?' he said at last. This was not

what he had come to say, but it was what had come into his mind.

Ishbel looked away. 'He's just a child and he prefers to call me mother but of course he's not . . .'

'Ishbel,' said Iain.

She was staring down at her own hands, one grasped in the other, and the tears started to roll down her cheeks.

He groaned inside. How had he done this? He got up and knelt in front of her, took her hands in his.

Her voice was almost inaudible. 'How long have you known?'

'Since whenever you arrived in Inverness with him in tow.'

She stared at him and began to look about her for a handkerchief. Iain let go her hands and rummaged in his pocket to produce one. He took one of the stools and sat closer to her. 'It was in about '48 or '49, wasn't it?' he continued. 'You arrived here, saying you were Hamish MacLeod's widow and letting everyone think Tormod was a slave child you had brought back with you from Virginia.'

'It was in '49,' she said, her voice hollow. 'I am Hamish MacLeod's widow.'

Iain's voice was low, and he looked directly into her eyes. 'I knew Hamish MacLeod. Poor soft Hamish who never a woman would look at.'

'He was a good man.'

'Transported off to Virginia at the end of '46. Dead of a fever in '47.'

'I nursed him in that fever.'

'I know,' said Iain. 'I was also in Virginia in '47. Off one of the transport ships.'

'So how is it that you were back in Inverness a year later?'

'I was fortunate.'

'I've never heard anyone come off a transport ship and call themselves "fortunate". To be alive, perhaps.'

'I had friends there, kinsmen who'd gone before. They bought my indenture from the captain of the ship and released me from it. After the indemnity was declared in July of '47 I started to make my way home. I travelled north, to Boston. I met in with plenty folk from home as I made my way.'

'Hamish was dead before July of '47,' she said.

'Yes, but there were others from Inverness who weren't. And they told me that Hamish had got married before he died, and that his wife had been with child, but had left as soon as he was buried.' He paused for a moment, wanting to give her time to understand that he wasn't threatening her. 'What would you have done if the child had been born before Hamish died? What would you have told him?'

'I didn't need to tell him anything. He knew.'

'That you were carrying the child of a slave?'

She nodded. 'He needed a nurse and I needed a husband. I knew if I had a husband or at least a minister's line saying I had been lawfully married, I might have a chance. I might get back here with my child, pass him off as an orphan slave child I had bought, have a chance.'

Iain looked at his hands, his feet. None of this was any of his business. Normally, he would have said so, and walked away.

'What were you transported for?'

'What was I . . .?' She got up and began to pace the small, darkened room. He couldn't see her face any more, but he could feel the anger emanating from her. 'I was transported because I couldn't run fast enough. I was transported because I had gone down to the shore at Glenelg to gather kelp and didn't know that our chief had sold us to freebooters waiting to grab us off the beaches. There was a man, Bremner, I will never forget his face . . . That was all my crime, Mr MacGillivray, for which I was put on a boat and carried to America and set to work for seven years.'

Iain had heard rumours of it before, what MacLeod of MacLeod and Macdonald of Sleat had done – sold away their own people to pay off their debts. Aeneas had always claimed that this was what had kept them from joining the prince's army as they had promised to do – because the Hanoverians had got wind of their crimes and blackmailed them with them. They had avoided prosecution, but it was a point understood amongst his grandmother and all her friends that there wasn't a pit in Hell hot enough for Norman MacLeod of MacLeod.

Ishbel was still talking. 'I was lucky too, I suppose. I was bought into seven years' service by a "good Christian man" with a wife and large family. I was put to work in their kitchen and soon showed a turn for making pastries and cakes and all sorts of confections. The mistress and her daughters made great play of my facility with preserves and caramels and barley sugars, and I was a favourite dancing monkey for them when they had their soirées and their tea parties. When I finished my seven years and had worked my way to my freedom, they asked me to stay. Promised me a decent wage, better accommodation, further away from the slave quarters. They had a large plantation where they grew tobacco.'

'And what did you say?' asked Iain.

She laughed, a laugh like a breath, extended her hand as if for the better display of her tiny apartment. 'What do you think I said? I had nothing else. I would hardly go back to Glenelg for Norman MacLeod to sell me again and I had known nowhere else in my life. Glenelg. The ship. Virginia.'

'So you stayed there and worked as a free woman.'

'Yes,' she said, 'as a free woman. And then I found that I was carrying Tormod.'

Again, Iain waited.

'His father's name was Matthew. He was – he was a very fine man. He looked fine – the men of the master's family, the overseers, the freed labourers – they were like goblins by comparison. Such small, ugly goblins. Matthew could read and write, which the family thought a great mark of their own civility, and they liked to have him in the house, to open doors in front of them and to serve at their friends' table. They thought it reflected very well upon them that they were not able to open their own doors.' She smiled, and Iain saw again a glimpse of the great anger she carried.

'So Tormod's father was their slave.'

'Oh yes.' The bitterness in Ishbel's voice was rising all the time. 'Matthew could not earn his way; he could not work his way to freedom as I had. When I found I was carrying Tormod, I knew I had to leave.'

'If you had stayed?' asked Iain.

'If I had stayed, and my pregnancy been discovered, I would have had to pay fifteen pounds, which I could not have produced, to the church wardens of the parish, or be sold on their behalf to work for another five years. What would have happened to Matthew does not bear thinking about.'

'And the child?'

'Tormod would have been taken from me and bound to service until he was thirty-one years of age.'

Iain thought of the little boy whom he had grown used to seeing scamper about the street and his shop and who lit up the humanity in Donald Mòr. He thought of the brightness of the boy, the curiosity, the potential. Ishbel hadn't finished though.

'I took what little money I'd saved, and I left in the night. I didn't tell Matthew. I didn't even leave him a note, for fear it would be found and he suffer for it. I travelled through Virginia to a place where I knew some others from Glenelg were settled. Hamish MacLeod was there, already ill, but he remembered me and was kind to me. I told him my story.

He offered to marry me and I to nurse him in return. I took his name and he left me the money he had managed to save. After his death I bought a passage back to London. A respectable widow expecting a child, rather than a harlot and her bastard. In London, I found a room in a house where no one would care, and a midwife who cared only that she would be paid. As soon as Tormod was safely weaned, and I would not be seen feeding him myself, we started to travel north.' She swallowed. 'I told people I had bought him.'

His own voice was hoarse as he spoke. 'No one can take him from you, then.'

She nodded, wiping her eye with the side of her hand. 'When I have the money, when I'm sure he will be safe, I'll see a lawyer, have papers made up. And he'll have his freedom here, Mr MacGillivray. He'll have his life. In Virginia he would have been bound in service. But if you accuse him of stealing your button or your key . . .' She was turning her hands over each other, almost gripping them, her knuckles taut.

He leaned towards her, took her hands in his again. 'Ishbel, I'm sorry. I would never have mentioned button or key to you if I had thought.' He heaved a long sigh. 'But I always think too late.' There was hardly room for the two of them and the child in this little room, the life she had made for herself and her son. He made her look at him, to be sure she understood. 'Don't be afraid. You have friends. In the bookshop. Donald, Richard. Me. No one will take Tormod from you.'

'Thank you,' she said.

Of all the bad things, the darkness that had attended this day, at last there was something good. He bade good night to the confectioner and her sleeping child and went home.

The house was in complete darkness by the time he returned. He crept through the kitchen, anxious not to waken Eppy or the scullery maid asleep in their box beds, and went as silently as possible past the door to Aeneas's chamber. The man had had ears like a bat when Iain had been a young man and trying to sneak into the house after some late-night escapade, and he was in no humour for whatever homily the steward might have ready for him tonight. To his relief, there was no light beneath Aeneas's door, and he passed without incident. His father had been given the use of a bedchamber, now that the soldiers had already made their searches of the house, and there was no light beneath his door either. Even Hector had to sleep sometimes, although Iain wondered if perhaps he would find his father in his own room, still studying the *Book of Forbidden Names* and scratching out his formulae with his pen, but his own room was also in silence when he reached it, and no one there.

SIXTEEN

The Third Cockade

He felt he had hardly laid his head on the pillow when he was awoken by the sound of his door being thrust open and the shutters being pulled wide to admit the morning light. Hector was already dressed and had the book in his hand as he sat himself down on the end of Iain's bed. Iain rubbed a hand across a bleary eye as his father started talking as if there had been no difficulty between them the previous night.

'So there are two cockades left, two names,' Hector said, 'and I have one of them.'

Iain sat up, wide awake now.

'Evan Inkster of Balblair. Do you know him?'

Iain shook his head. 'I don't think so.'

'Would Aeneas?'

'If he doesn't, he would find someone who does within the hour.'

They went down to the kitchen.

'The breakfast isn't ready,' Flossie told them. 'You know fine well the porridge isn't made, nor your draught either until the mistress has finished her devotions.' Iain's grand-mother had held to her Episcopalian faith throughout the destruction of their meeting houses and chapels, and the harrying of their ministers.

'We're not looking for our breakfast. Where's Aeneas?' It was rare that Iain was up before him.

At that moment, Aeneas came through from his own bed-chamber and office, his chin tilted upwards as he finished tying the stock at his neck. 'Aeneas is here and he's looking for his breakfast, even if you are not. What do you want of me?'

Hector glanced towards Flossie and Eppy and jerked his head in the direction of the stairs. Aeneas sighed and put his foot on the bottom step. 'You'll have my morning draught ready when I come down, Eppy.'

'Yes, Mr Farquharson,' said the girl as he started to mount the stairs.

'Well, what is it?' he said, once they were safely behind the closed door of Iain's room.

'My father has found the next name. Do you know an Evan Inkster?'

Aeneas frowned. 'I know of one, but there may be others. Have you nothing more?'

'From Balblair. Or at least he was when the book was put together.'

'On the Black Isle? I know of an Evan Inkster who lives across the firth at Charleston, but I believe that many years ago he did live at Balblair, yes. Are you telling me he is the next traitor named in the book?'

Hector nodded. 'Have you any notion what he might have done?'

Aeneas got up and walked over to the window, looking down the street as Hector had been doing. It struck Iain that the old man, a fearsome figure for almost all of his life, looked tired. 'If he's in the book, it must be something, I suppose.' He thought a bit longer then turned and came to the table where they were both seated. 'There was talk, a long time ago, of guns for the cause, to be landed on the Black Isle, but when our people went to collect them, they found a detachment of Munros waiting for them on the government's behalf. The government got the guns and our men were arrested, tried and transported. Evan Inkster held the tack of the ferry at Balblair at the time. He'd have been back and forth between the Black Isle and the Munros' country a dozen times a day. It must have been him who told them of the arms landing.'

'It sounds likely enough,' said Hector.

Aeneas glanced at the book. 'That being so, what do you propose to do about it? You'll not be warning him, I hope?'

Hector took a breath. 'It can't be helped, Aeneas. If he spied for the government then, he may still be at it, or know who else is. The matter that brought me here, what I came to see Bailie John Steuart about, may have been compromised. If I could get to even *one* of these traitors from the '15 before they are all dead, I might learn something of value to us now.'

Aeneas looked unconvinced. 'And you expect him just to tell you?'

'There are ways of being persuasive,' said Hector.

'Well, you can't send him,' said Aeneas, jabbing a thumb towards Iain. 'The army's eye is too much on him already. And you can't risk going over the firth to Charleston yourself.'

'You could do it,' Hector said. 'No one would suspect a thing of you, and if memory serves you have some persuasive techniques of your own when required.'

Aeneas rested his chin on clenched hands. 'I would question him, all right, but I have no desire to forewarn him of the retribution coming his way.'

'Nor I,' said Hector, 'but if that's the price of us learning more about a threat to Prince Charles that Bailie Steuart has warned me of, then so be it.'

The older man sniffed and cleared his throat, signs Iain knew to be preparatory to one of his rare concessions. 'Well, if it is in the prince's interest . . .'

'And the king's,' said Hector.

Aeneas nodded. 'I'll set out for Charleston directly.' He turned to Iain. 'And you'll be good enough to tell the mistress I'll be back before suppertime.'

When the door had closed behind him, Iain looked at it, a degree of admiration on his face. 'He didn't even ask.'

'Didn't ask what?' said Hector.

'What threat to the prince it is that has brought you here. What Bailie Steuart told you. He's near enough seventy and looks all done in, but he's off to the Black Isle and back in an open boat on your say-so, a man whose name he can barely tolerate, just on the slimmest chance that he might obtain information of use to Prince Charlie.'

Hector shrugged. 'Aeneas has given his entire life to the king's cause. Why would he abandon it now?' He looked at the miniature of Iain's mother, painted in Edinburgh when she'd been sixteen. 'Oh, I know he loved your mother, but he knows well enough Charlotte would never have married him. If it hadn't been me that took her away it would have been some other rogue. Aeneas Farquharson was always far too dependable for Charlotte. He loves her, but he loves the prince more. By God, we all loved him. How could you not? Although . . .'

'What?'

Hector glanced over at the brandy bottle on the chest in Iain's room. 'The medication he is at, it doesn't help.'

Iain also looked at the bottle. 'The rumours are true then – of the drinking and the rages?'

'Oh, they're true, all right. His father is in despair and his brother the Duke of York fled Paris in disgust. God, Charles is better than that.'

Iain gave a deep sigh. 'You can hardly blame him, though. God, we are all in despair. I go in the morning to my book-shop, I come home at night. I listen to my grandmother dream the same dreams and tell the same stories. I drink with her a toast to my dead grandfather, to a king I've never seen and a prince I would happily have died following. But

I didn't die. Instead I go to bed and shut my eyes and I can hear the screaming and the weeping, and I can feel Lachlan going to sleep on the moor beside me. A thousand miles we marched together, a thousand miles for him to die back here, on Drummossie Moor, in sight of home.'

Hector reached a hand towards him. 'I know, I—'

But Iain hardly noticed him. 'I can feel the flesh of dead and dying men next to me, lying crammed without food or water in the Gaelic church. I smell it. Sometimes I wake up gasping for air, thinking I'm back in the hold of that Virginia trader, crossing the ocean. When the daylight finally comes, I get up and dress and go to my shop and live another day of a life I do not know the point of.'

Waiting for the ferry at Kessock, Aeneas's reluctance for his mission grew. He had no desire to waste the next few hours traipsing over the firth to Charleston and back on the whim of Hector MacGillivray – there would be nothing to be had of Evan Inkster, but there would be no peace if he didn't go. The salt of the water was already on his lips, in his hair, the dank seaweed, warming in the sun, in his nostrils.

Aeneas watched with distaste as the ferrymen brought to shore the boat with its complement of Black Isle housewives and hawkers, ministers and gentlemen. It was his preference to travel on smaller craft, without half the population of the Highlands asking his business, but time was pressing and it was the public ferry that suited present purposes.

As the passengers trooped off the boat onto the jetty, his heart sank. A garrulous woman, known to him as an acquaintance of Mairi Farquharson's cook, disembarked amongst the rest. He lowered his head and affected to be looking at a small brown dog that was wandering the shore, but still she noticed him. 'And where are you making for at this early hour of the day, Aeneas Farquharson?'

'I have business at Charleston.' He nodded to the strip of cottages across the water.

'Charleston, is it? What business have you at Charleston?'

'None of yours,' he said, waiting to pass her.

'Well, I hope it's not with Evan Inkster.'

Aeneas abandoned his interest in the dog. 'And why would that be?'

She leaned a little closer to him. 'Because Evan Inkster was found lying dead in his own house this very morning, a knife in his throat.' She glanced to the side and waited for another passenger to move past before whispering, 'There was a white cockade on it.'

Julia Rose had not been sorry to get out of the Horns hotel that morning and away from her mother. The atmosphere between them had scarcely thawed in the last two days, since Elizabeth had gone to the garrison to inform on Hector MacGillivray. The sense of unease between them seemed to have permeated to the breakfast parlour of the Horns, and indeed spread into the streets outside. But the unease out in the town, she realised, had more to do with the murder of the milliner's father, in his own home across the river. The parlourmaid had told them of it as she brought them their breakfast. Julia's mother said it was a pity, because his daughter made good hats.

Julia had murmured the first excuse she could think of to get out into town by herself. From the moment she stepped onto the street, she was aware of an even greater military presence than usual. There were always soldiers in Inverness, either going back and forth to the fort works at Ardersier or concerned in the matters of the Military Survey, but today there was a heightened sense of purpose in their movements, a greater focus on the town itself. She had heard in the Horns that Captain Dunne was still over in Ross, gathering rents in the Mackenzie lands. Perhaps he would not be back in town until after the assembly, after she was gone back to Kilravock.

All around, preparations for the next night's gathering were under way. Windows on the first floor of the town house had been opened to give the place a good airing, and porters and tradespeople were already going in and out at the side door, carrying chairs and trestles and dishes. She noticed Barbara Sinclair emerge from her own premises with a letter in her hand, and cross with it towards Castle Wynd. No doubt she was on her way to the coffee house, where it would be picked up by the post carriers. She wondered if the woman would stay in the town now that her father was dead. The milliner wore a black hood and a gown of muted grey. Julia had no wish to catch her eye and looked away. All around her people were going about their day with purpose, for good or ill it didn't matter, and she had none.

She felt drawn to the bookshop, despite everything, despite what her mother had done. She could hardly blame Iain MacGillivray for thinking she was no more to be trusted than her mother, but the short time she had spent there the previous day, helping Richard Dempster, working with Ishbel MacLeod to start putting the place to rights, had been the only time for a long while that she could remember feeling she belonged anywhere. She would go back down there. She would try again to talk to the bookseller.

As she turned onto Church Street, she saw the confectioner's boy who'd come dancing out of the ground-floor shop of Bailie John Steuart's town house as Ishbel herself struggled through the door after him, carrying a heavy lump of sugar loaf. Ishbel was calling after the child, telling him to be careful, to watch where he was going, but he paid her no heed as he twirled away down the street ahead of her. Julia quickened her pace to try to catch up with them.

The confectioner looked startled when she first heard her name being called from behind but smiled and slowed her pace a little when she saw who it was.

'I have never seen a child so free or joyful,' said Julia.

Ishbel pursed her lips. 'He will go to the school at Martinmas, and that will put a stop to the nonsense.'

Julia laughed and said she hoped it would not. They carried on down the street together in a companionable silence, although Julia wished she could think of something more to say. Suddenly, there was a commotion at the corner of the Queensgate, a small dog being chased for its life by some larger creature that snarled and spat after it. Tormod let out a yell and set off in pursuit of the animals. There was a great deal of shouting from people passing down the bridlepath of Queensgate, and by the time Julia and Ishbel reached the corner, a stand-off had ensued. The session clerk of the High Kirk was standing at the top of his forestairs, the terrified white terrier in his arms, whilst Tormod, on the ground, struggled with a squirming, spitting burden.

'And what's more,' the man was saying, 'you will tell Donald Mòr that if that cat comes after my dog again, I'll have its gizzards strung for my fiddle!'

Tormod, his dark eyes huge with the seriousness of the situation, swore that Morag would trouble the dog no longer.

Julia might have laughed, had she not been concerned for what the creature, at best feral and at worst wildcat, might do to the child, yet Ishbel seemed unconcerned. 'Morag will not hurt him,' she said.

The cat was released back down Church Street with the admonishment from Tormod to 'keep away from the elders'. They soon reached Bow Court and the boy looked up to her and said, 'Are you going to the bookshop?'

Julia grasped at the suggestion. 'Yes, I thought I would see how Richard is doing, after the troubles of the other day.'

There was no sign of the bookseller or anyone else when

Julia stepped into the bookshop a few minutes later. The sun was coming in at the windows, the shutters all being opened, and motes of dust danced in the air. She stood there a moment, content, then she saw Richard Dempster moving above in the gallery.

The young man's head appeared over the banister, and he gave her a broad smile. 'Miss Rose! How lovely.'

She was a little relieved that Iain MacGillivray himself didn't appear to be there.

'Is all . . . well?' she asked at last.

'Everything appears to be as it should be,' he said, straightening up and coming down the stairs.

'And your eye?'

He winced. The eye was still swollen and thoroughly purple. 'A little tender yet. Thank you for your help yesterday.'

'It was nothing,' she said. 'I – I wondered if the binder's cat had come safely home.'

It was like watching a cloud descend on Richard Dempster. 'Oh dear. What has happened?'

Julia told him of the incident between the cat and the session clerk's dog.

'And Morag was unharmed?' he asked, as if enquiring after an elderly relative involved in a coaching accident.

'Utterly,' she said. 'She – I believe it is a *she*?'

He nodded enthusiastically.

'She was the aggressor.'

Richard let out a long sigh of relief. 'Thank goodness.

Should anything happen to her, you cannot conceive how terrible it would be.'

'Is the binder very attached to her?'

'They snarl at one another from morning till night, but he would kill the man who harmed a hair on her head.'

'Morag is an unusual name for a cat,' she observed.

'I understand she is named for his late mother-in-law.'

'He has a *wife*?'

Richard shrugged. 'Whether he has a wife or not, I couldn't tell you. But he most certainly had a mother-in-law and he believes her spirit inhabits that cat. Out of spite.'

Just then the door to the shop burst open under an onslaught of boys running in from the school in Dunbar's Hospital across the street, their master roaring after them. Julia took this as her opportunity to slip away, but her attempt at departure was brought to a halt by the arrival of Major Philip Thornlie. The major looked as unsettled by their unexpected encounter as she was. He didn't immediately move aside, but just stood there, looking at her. Then he cleared his throat.

'Miss Rose.'

'Major,' she said, inclining her head slightly and looking to go past him.

'Oh, oh, yes, forgive me,' he said, stepping aside.

Julia smiled and made herself small as she passed. She was through the doorway and already on the street when she heard her name being called. She turned around.

'Forgive me,' said the major again. 'But I wondered – will

you be attending the assembly in the town house tomorrow night?'

'Yes,' she said, startled by the question.

'Ah.' He gave a small smile. 'Good. Good. Thank you.' He touched the brim of his tricorn hat and retreated, not meeting her eye, back into the darkness of the shop.

There had been an inevitability, almost, about the news brought by Aeneas on his unexpectedly early return from the Kessock ferry.

'So that's it,' said Hector after the door had closed behind Aeneas and his news of the death of Evan Inkster.

'There's still one name,' said Iain. 'Six black cockades. Two of them dead and crossed out years ago, my great-uncle in Dochfour, Barbara Sinclair's father, and now Evan Inkster in Charleston.'

'There's one cockade left,' said Hector, 'but no name. When your Captain Dunne tore the last pages from this book in Castle Leod, he must have destroyed the page with the markings giving away the last name on it. We won't know it till we hear of their death.'

He punched his fist into the wall. 'Too late, always too late. God!' He sat down with his head in his hands. 'Was there ever anything in this cause that was not too late?'

There was silence between them for a few moments then Iain spoke. 'I have spent the last six years believing it was too late, paying little more than lip-service to the hopes of my grandmother, and Aeneas and all the rest, but the fact that you are sitting here in front of me says it is not too late.'

Hector turned to him, a glimmer of hope in his eyes. 'Is it so, Iain?'

Iain gave a low laugh of disbelief at himself and said, 'Yes, it is so, God help me. The town may be occupied and buzzing with redcoats, and you'll have seen what they're doing at Ardersier? The size of their new Fort George?'

'Yes,' said Hector.

'And I have spent the last six years in the knowledge that the chiefs who supported the prince are broken, executed, exiled. I've seen those who might have led their clan are putting on red coats and taking King George's coin. We're not even allowed to carry a weapon, wear the kilt, play the pipes, and yet . . . I see you here now and I somehow believe that it might not be too late after all . . .'

Hector's face was alight and he gripped Iain by the shoulders. Iain could see the old conviction burning again in his father's eyes. 'It's not too late. There are officers enough in the service of France with as much Highland blood as you or I. And there is money – some, at least. What I am about to tell you must not pass your lips to another living soul. Not yet.'

Iain felt his heart beat faster. 'Is he coming back? Is he on his way?'

'Sit down,' said Hector, and went on. 'Charles has given up on France. He's given up on Catholic Europe. His hopes lie in Frederick of Prussia and in Sweden. The king fears that Frederick will only use him as a pawn to annoy his Uncle George of Hanover, and that Sweden will find itself distracted.'

'But?' said Iain.

'The prince will heed no counsel but his own. There are plans afoot for a new rising. Lord Elibank's brother in Boulogne is at the heart of it. Arms have been sent for. Young Glengarry claims to have three hundred men that will help him in laying hold of the usurper's family in Westminster. The London Jacobites are then to rise and take the city. By that time the clans will be on the march southwards, all the way to London this time.'

Iain stared at his father. 'The clans march?"

'Numbers are already promised.'

Iain looked up at the portraits on the wall. Those who had gone before him, those who had given their lives for the cause. He spoke, very quietly, as if to himself rather than to his father. 'There is truly a new rising afoot?'

Hector was hesitant. 'Not afoot, but in preparation. The arms have been ordered and there is still at least some of the Arkaig Treasure left. The king sent me here in response to a letter from the bailie informing him of the bones of the affair, and of his fears of a spy at the heart of it. On the grounds of an intercepted letter he is of the firm view that the Hanoverians have a spy in place, but he has no inkling as to the real name of that person. I was to try to discover if the plans have indeed been compromised. If they have, I must get to the prince and warn him.'

Iain felt a sudden chill go through him. 'There *is* a traitor.'

Hector looked at him. 'How do you know?'

'It was at Castle Leod. Calum Mackay was there with orders for Captain Dunne and his detachment. I was sent from the room while they conducted the meat of their business, but just before he left, Calum told Dunne to look for evidence of any stirring amongst the clans and some matter concerning Elibank.'

Hector gave a deep sigh and he looked suddenly old and very tired. 'What the bailie fears is true then.'

Silence hung in the room a moment, then Iain pointed to the copy of Blind Hary's *Wallace* his father had been working on. 'Do you think the final one of the forbidden names in this book could be this traitor mentioned by the bailie?'

'It's possible, though I doubt it – those accorded a black cockade in this book were all active in some way in the '15 rising, and their treachery refers to that time. But as I said before, I fear the name corresponding to the last of the black cockades is no longer in this book – that it was amongst the pages you told me of, torn out and burned at Castle Leod. I am almost out of time – I must take my leave of Inverness tomorrow night, or risk not getting away at all.'

SEVENTEEN

The Dance

In his first few years with the Military Survey in the Highlands, the terrain had been utterly alien to Philip Thornlie. In those days he had longed for the winter, when their small team of surveyors and engineers would decamp to the drawing room in Edinburgh Castle and work up the traverses they had sketched in the spring and summer into a projection for their great map. Their work of surveying, blasting and building was a continuance of General Wade's work of carving open the Highlands so that they might prove profitable to Britain, rather than being an eternal breeding ground for rebels. The winters spent south of the Forth had been a respite from the constant vigilance required here – the town of Edinburgh might be filled with its own dirt and rogues and danger, and yet it had its graces. He would not have said that, at first, of Inverness. But at some time in the last five years, a change had come, not in the town but in himself, and now it was the winter in the capital he dreaded, and the months of light in the Highlands that he longed for.

He looked at his reflection in the glass and considered what he saw. Was it a fool? He was forty-three years of age and blind in one eye. He had feared that that loss in sight might cost him his career, but it hadn't. He could measure, gauge and calculate better with that one eye than almost anyone else on the survey could with two. And his leg – not a problem on horseback, but the damp Edinburgh winters affected it more with every year. His gaze travelled from the image in the looking glass to the letter from the Royal Military Academy at Woolwich. It lay on the dresser, where he had left it since yesterday, alongside a previous letter with the same offer. He had a decision to make, for he knew they would not ask a third time.

He looked again in the glass. His gaiters were the same pure white as his breeches. There was not a speck of dust on his shoes, the light danced off the gold braid of cuffs, collar and shoulder, and glinted in his regimental breastplate. His shirt and breeches gleamed white against the scarlet of his coat and the blue of its facings. A black velvet ribbon tied the dark queue of his own hair – he needed no wig beneath his tricorn hat. Finally, he buckled on his sword. The whole was not so bad – the man looking back at him was trim, not gone to fat like others of his age and rank, and stood erect, for all the bad leg. His face was not red or raddled with sun or drink, the one blue eye clear amongst the dark lashes. The man looking back at Philip Thornlie from the glass was not a fool, and there was time yet to ask something more of life.

★

Upstairs in Mairi Farquharson's house, all was quiet, although, below, Flossie and the scullery maid were busy preparing a late supper for their mistress and her friends when they returned from the ball at the town house. Flossie had worked forty years for this Jacobite family and would be loyal to them to her dying day, but their enjoyment of dancing and revelry scandalised her afresh every time. And that her mistress should attend such an entertainment when she should have been mourning her brother was altogether beyond her comprehension. As for Eppy – the girl had nothing in her head but the dresses of all the ladies and had been allowed to go with Aeneas as he escorted the mistress to the town house. Iain was long gone, to meet with Arch MacPhee and go over their tunes, and so all that were left in the house were the old cook, fussing the scullery maid over the dainties, and the wanted Jacobite agent, the excepted skulker, upstairs in his son's room, preparing for his escape.

Aeneas had laid out on Iain's bed the clothes Hector was to wear on his way out of the town and across the firth to the Black Isle. There, he was to join Bailie Steuart's son-in-law's boat as it departed for London from Cromarty. Hector examined the clothes – coarse woollen breeches the colour of old tea, a darker jacket of the same stuff, worn at the elbows and somewhat frayed about the edges. A light buff waistcoat and a shirt and neckerchief that looked as though they had been washed in peat water and dried by an open fire. The clothes were so dull and dun – no one at the Palazzo del Re in Rome would believe that Hector

MacGillivray would ever be seen in such items. But that was the point, he supposed: it would not be Hector MacGillivray that people saw. He would just be some poor, honest fellow, going about his business. Hector picked up one of the thin grey woollen stockings laid out beside the workaday leather shoes. Aeneas had chosen well.

And yet, the costume would not do. Hector lifted the items and rolled them up in the plain brown plaid Aeneas had also provided. Tying the bundle, he set it at the door. Then he crossed to the heavy oak chest that must have come from the time of Mairi's grandfather at least. It was not locked. Hector lifted the lid and carefully set aside the first few items he came upon. And there it was – not much out of fashion and hardly, if ever, worn. Hector took out the deep grey silk suit Iain's mother had sent from Milan for her son's thirtieth birthday. The embroidery on collar and cuffs, a pattern of songbirds and luscious flowers, was exquisite and beyond anything a bookseller in the town of Inverness would have occasion to wear. Iain would not have got much use out of it in any case. It was a little too neatly made, the breeches perhaps a fraction too short in the leg, as the jacket would be in the arms. Poor Charlotte – she had not known the build and dimensions of her own son, and so had guessed them to be the same as those of his father. Hector knew on sight that the grey silk suit with its silver thread *passementerie* buttons and oyster satin waistcoat would fit him like a well-made glove.

★

Arch MacPhee grimaced and held out his hand. 'Is that thing in tune at all, Iain? Here, give it to me.'

Iain smiled and handed over his fiddle. The instrument had been perfectly tuned, but it was a point of pride in Arch that none but he in the whole of Inverness could tune a fiddle, and Iain was happy to indulge that one vanity in him. Had it not been for Arch's friendship, he was certain he would now be in the tolbooth, awaiting trial for not one, but two murders. There was no sign yet of Robert Edwards, the town's music master, who always led their performances. His best pupil though, a lad of twelve, had already appeared, labouring through the crowd carrying his own clarinet as well as his master's flute and bearing the expression of one arriving to have a tooth pulled.

'And where's himself?' demanded Arch, indicating with a peremptory flourish the empty stool behind the spinet.

The boy let down his instruments and pointed over the growing crowd to where his teacher was making his way to the punch table. Arch and Iain had long ago learned that if Edwards could only make it to the interval, the rest of the assembly-goers would themselves be too far gone to notice the lost and sliding notes.

Iain had a flask in his pocket. He offered it to Arch but not to the boy. Whisky from his grandmother's people in Glenlivet.

'A good drop,' said Arch, wiping his mouth and returning the flask. 'Steadies the nerves.'

And Iain needed his nerves steadied. He looked over at

the long-case clock on the far side of the assembly room, and then at his own pinchbeck pocket watch, whose minute hand moved relentlessly forwards. He could feel his stomach tighten with its every progress. The assembly-goers had been arriving for some time. They were to start playing at eight and the thing would be in full swing by nine. The interval would be called at ten and they would play again at eleven. That hour before the interval had been lighted upon as his father's best chance of slipping out of his grandmother's house. He would get down to the river by the passageway from the cellar, whilst the redcoat guards watched the front and side doors to the house. From the riverbank, a small rowboat would be waiting to get him clear of the town and over to the Black Isle. A walk along the high moor atop the peninsula would take him to Cromarty before morning. There the bailie's son-in-law's ship waited to depart on the next evening's tide.

They had already said their goodbyes, with promises to meet again soon, God willing, should Elibank's plot come to fruition and a new rising come out of the Highlands. Iain's heart had been heavy as he'd left the house. His father's presence had somehow filled it, and by the time they had finished playing here tonight, Hector would be gone. For now, his fingers could hardly hold the bow for nerves, fearing that something in his father's escape attempt would go wrong.

The assembly room was getting busier. The smaller side room was set with card tables, whilst the supper table and punch bowls were laid out on trestles in the hall. Ishbel MacLeod was there, arranging platters of cake and trays of sweetmeats. She was not in her usual workaday woollen gown and apron, but instead in a simple pale sprigged cotton gown and yellow petticoat.

'She's a bonnie lassie, that,' said Arch casually, watching him.

'Like a wildflower amongst the forced beauties of the hothouse.'

'Oh?' said Arch, raising an eyebrow. 'It's like that, is it?'

Iain laughed, 'Ach, no. Not at all,' but it was clear from the look Arch gave him that his friend was not convinced.

The doors of the cardroom, by day used for guildry business, opened on to the dance hall. It was no surprise to Iain that the table nearest the door, with the best view of the dancing, was already occupied by the Grandes Dames. His grandmother and her friends knew with justified confidence that no one arriving before them would risk taking possession of Mairi Farquharson's preferred table. The fact that the Grandes Dames were all accounted inveterate rebels by the soldiery who had ordered and were paying for this gathering was a thing of little consequence to the inhabitants of Inverness. Iain found himself smiling: the old ladies were magnificent, and they required that all should know it. He was glad to see Janet Grant there, for she had not looked well of late, but the others glowed with anticipation of the evening ahead. He wondered how long it would be before Eilidh Cameron had them all up dancing.

Chairs had been set around the sides of the main room, and had filled up already, mainly with matrons requiring a good view of events. Most of the young women, the daughters of middling and landed families, Jacobite and Hanoverian both, evidently preferred to stand, where they might be seen. There were plenty of men to do the looking. Burgesses, sons of burgesses, farmers and gentlemen, but most of all, soldiers.

It was because of the soldiers, the redcoats, that any of them were here at all. The occupying forces had sought to alleviate their own boredom in this godforsaken outpost by instituting public entertainments. Iain wouldn't have deigned to scrape as much as a note on his fiddle for them, were it not for the fact that he knew Arch and the music school master, whose assistant already eyed his post, needed the money. And for their ensemble, they needed him.

The officers stood in groups, talking amongst themselves. One or two conversed with the burgesses – merchants and craftsmen whose businesses flourished under their occupation. There was a wariness, though, always a wariness, even in those who had never supported the Jacobite cause. In the aftermath of the battle, there had been plenty amongst the government forces who had never stopped to ask whose side a Highlander might be on.

Iain saw that Philip Thornlie had come in, along with the eager young draughtsmen and engineers of the Military Survey. The major stood a little back from the younger men, as if fearing his presence made them ill at ease. The loathed Captain Dunne was nowhere in evidence. Not back yet from Castle Leod, then. On any other night, Iain would ten times rather have known that Dunne was out patrolling the streets of Inverness than swaggering drunkenly around the assembly room in front of him. On any other night.

The gleaming buckles and glinting brocade of the officers' uniforms met their match in the finery displayed by the citizenry. The Hanoverian ladies wore their wealth by the inch, but the Jacobite women carried their greater poverty in style. Julia Rose was here, he saw, with her mother. Arch's eyes lighted on them just as Iain's did. 'It's a pity the mother didn't stay at home, give the lassie a chance.'

'What do you mean, Arch?' he asked.

'What do I mean? That girl might not appear so plain if the mother wasn't beside her, so bonny.' Then Arch cocked his head. 'Her figure's fine enough though.'

The sight of the young woman that everyone, even his grandmother, dismissed as 'plain' gave Iain a wave of regret. He'd known for as long as they'd been coming into his shop that Julia was different from her mother, and yet he had treated her as if she were exactly the same. And he did not see the plainness others saw. The ivory silk mantua she wore tonight, with its ruffled sleeves, trimmed in salmon pink and fresh green bobbin lace, framed delicate forearms and picked out the hint of rose in her lips and cheeks, and the pale green of her eyes. The hoop in her gown was less extravagant than in many, and her dress had not the sack-back that had become so fashionable. Altogether, he thought she had grace.

Arch looked at him. 'Not her as well, surely . . .'

Iain laughed. 'Arch, you're worse than Eilidh Cameron for trying to marry me off, as if anyone would have me. Call Julia Rose plain if you must, but she has the merit at least of conversation.'

'Conversation?' Arch stared at him, then roared, slapping him on the back with such vigour that the schoolboy took a step sideways, almost toppling off the platform. From nowhere, it seemed, the music master appeared and, in tones still closer to sobriety than to drunkenness, bade them all behave. The provost gave a speech — from experience he kept it short, then nodded to the music master. Robert Edwards fluffed out the skirt of his coat and sat with some importance at his spinet. He raised a hand, Arch gave a look to Iain, and Iain lifted his bow for a minuet. The gentlemen took their ladies to the floor, and the dance began. Julia Rose had stood up with one of the Munros, a relative of Culcairn. Perhaps Arch was right — away from her mother her aspect did change, she became at one with the music. Iain felt he was drawing her along with his bow. He saw that Ishbel MacLeod had stopped for a moment to watch Julia Rose and her partner too, and that she was smiling.

The dancers were not half through their steps when he realised that someone else was also watching Julia Rose. Philip Thornlie was standing alone now; the younger officers of the Military Survey all having taken to the floor with the prettiest young women they could find. Iain had never seen Thornlie dance. The man came rarely enough to the assemblies at all, and always had the look of one who has come to 'show face' and leave at the earliest opportunity. Tonight, though, there was something different. Every part of him was fully here, fully present at the assembly, in the dance, even though he appeared only to stand and watch. But it was not really the dance he was watching.

Iain looked from officer to girl: she was completely unaware of him, still pulled along, it seemed, by Iain's bow. And all the while Thornlie looked on her as a man might when confronted with the answer to a problem that he didn't know he had.

The set finished, Julia curtsied to her partner who led her back to her enraptured mother. But after the necessary pleasantries were exchanged, young Munro left the Rose women and returned to his own friends. The mother looked bereft.

Iain and the other players took a drink of the ale that had been set out for them and prepared to take up their instruments again. The men who had not kept their partners from the previous set made haste to secure someone amenable for the next dance. None were making their way towards where Julia Rose sat, apparently indifferent, by her mother. None until a resolution appeared to take hold in Philip Thornlie's mind and he peeled himself away from the back wall and began to move towards her. As he watched, Iain found himself willing Thornlie through the crowd. He was about to turn to Arch, having considered what they would best play for them. But the major was too slow, too polite: he waited while younger and more eager officers and girls flitted past him; he waited while elderly matrons exchanged their seats for others that suited them better, and portly merchants squeezed past on their way to the punch table. Philip Thornlie had not got three quarters of the way towards Julia Rose when Iain saw the scarlet back of another officer obscure her from his view. Captain Edward Dunne.

'No, thank you. I prefer to sit.'

Dunne looked none taken aback by her refusal. He seemed, in fact, to have expected it, and to be encouraged.

'Ah, Miss Rose, but I saw you dance there with such vigour, it can hardly be all used up. I am sure you will take pity on a poor officer, so far from home.'

'Pity?' asked Julia. 'I did not think pity formed part of your lexicon.'

He smiled, pleased it seemed at the challenge. 'It is simply a question of discipline, Miss Rose. It is important to distinguish between a cause that requires pity, and one that requires discipline.'

'It is equally important,' she said, 'to distinguish between a woman who wants to dance with you and one who does not.'

'Julia!' Her mother looked at her, appalled. 'Your pardon,

Captain Dunne,' and then she turned back to her daughter and muttered, almost through gritted teeth, 'You will dance with the captain and stop making an exhibition of yourself.'

Dunne's smile had disappeared in an instant and his face turned scarlet. A hint of contempt manifested on his lips. Julia thought that now he must turn away and save what face he might. Past him, she caught sight of Major Thornlie watching them, and hoped desperately for a moment that the major might save her from the captain's odious attentions, even ask her to dance himself. But people were up on the floor. Instead of turning away, Captain Dunne leant forward and forcibly took hold of her hand. Simultaneously, her mother gave a push to her lower back. Julia's choice was now between enduring the dance with Captain Dunne or engaging in an unseemly tussle. Major Thornlie had now started to force a way through the couples already up and assembled, but Julia could only carry on going forward under Dunne's surprising force, to the dance floor. She found herself now on public display, aligned with all the others on the floor, facing Dunne and unable to do a thing about it. She flinched at the touch of his hand as they waited for the music of the allemande to begin. The reels would come later in the night, when the inhibitions were dying. At the first few bars of Bach she steeled herself for the touch of Dunne's hands on her, but then something went wrong. The music, instead of progressing, became discordant and died away, a few notes from the spinet being the last to trail to nothing.

Julia, like the rest of the assembly, turned her eyes to the musicians on the dais.

Arch lowered his own bow and fiddle. 'What are you about, Iain? Have you a string broke or something?'

'We're not playing that.'

'What?'

'The Bach. We're not playing it.'

'Did we not practise it this very afternoon?' He looked from Iain to the astonished Edwards. 'Did we not say we would have that first and the Scarlatti later?'

'We're not playing Scarlatti either.' Iain set down his fiddle and lifted his bodhran. It had been a piquet of the Irish Brigade that had taught him to play the Irish drum. In his other hand he took the double-headed beater and as beater struck taut skin, he began to stamp his foot. Then, into the breathless room, he started to sing.

> Cope sent a challenge frae Dunbar,
> Charlie meet me an' ye daur . . .

Arch's mouth fell open. On the dance floor there were shocked intakes of breath and faces stared, aghast, as the notes of the notorious Jacobite song carried through a room filled with government soldiers. The only face Iain was looking at though, was Julia Rose's, and hers was not aghast. In her eyes he read surprise as she stared back at him, then the light of amusement which soon travelled from her eyes to her lips. Her foot started to tap in time to his beat. His gaze went beyond her, to where his grandmother and her friends sat, their feet also tapping. The old ladies, too, began to sing. To his side, Arch was on his fiddle and behind him, Robert Edwards had caught them with his flute, the boy scrambling now for his whistle.

Julia Rose, her eyes shining and never leaving Iain's, began to move the rest of her body in time to the music at her feet, then, to a roar of approval from half the hall – the Jacobite half – she curtsied and set to the speechless Captain Dunne, and she began to dance. By the time Iain reached for a second time the refrain, 'Hie, Johnnie Cope, are ye wauken yet?', a hundred voices had joined him, and feet that hadn't danced in years had taken to the floor, swirling and whooping around their mortified Hanoverian neighbours and the astonished redcoat officers. Iain felt utterly alive. It was a wonder the beater didn't go through the skin of the drum. By the time the song at last came to its end, the sweat was pouring from all four musicians, and the whole room was in uproar. Julia Rose sank to the floor in the deepest of curtsies, her skirts a lake of silk, and the furious Captain Dunne, scarlet with rage and humiliation, stalked from the room.

Iain only just caught the look Ishbel MacLeod was giving him, the warmth of it going through him like honey. As the provost, his eyes popping, marched up to the dais to call a short break, Arch turned to Iain and shook his head. 'By God, boy. We'll have the devil of an encore.'

★

Julia's heart was racing, her bosom heaving behind the low, tight stomacher her mother had insisted upon. Her mother was surely collapsed behind her somewhere, with someone calling for brandy to revive her. Julia did not dare turn around. Neither did she dare look up. She'd thought Dunne had left. She'd been certain, in her exultation, that she'd seen him take up his hat and stride out of the room, but now in front of her were the silver-buckled shoes and bright white gaiters of an officer. A hand reached out to her from the richly embroidered cuff on a scarlet sleeve. Then she heard the voice.

'Miss Rose?'

Not Captain Dunne, but Major Thornlie.

The other dancers were drifting off, laughing and out of breath. Julia felt the blood rising in her cheeks and knew her hair must be dishevelled. She put her hand in the major's and felt an unexpected strength in it as he raised her up.

'Thank you,' she said.

He smiled. 'You . . . dance with great joy.'

'Perhaps I had been better not to dance at all. I don't think Captain Dunne will have appreciated it.'

'The captain would have done better to accept your refusal the first time.'

He was still holding her hand, although she had fully regained her feet now, and he really did not need to. Julia made no move to take it away. She glanced over to where her mother sat in the company of a gleefully scandalised

THE BOOKSELLER OF INVERNESS

aunt. 'I think I'm in need of a diversion to the supper room, before I must face my mother.'

The major clicked his heels and offered her his arm in the direction of the supper room. 'She doesn't share your sympathies?'

'My sympathies?'

His smile was a little awkward. 'I think you must know the story of the song the bookseller just sang. That "Johnnie Cope" was commander of King George's forces in Scotland at the outset of the late rebellion?'

She laughed. 'And ran as fast as his legs would carry him from his defeat at Prestonpans? Seven years ago, and the shock of it has not long stopped resounding. I know all about General Cope, but that's not why I danced as I did.'

'Oh?'

'I did refuse Captain Dunne the first time he asked me, and the second, but still I found myself forced to dance with him. I felt,' she looked away, wondering if she should really go on, 'I felt the bookseller saw it and that his song was a defiance of Captain Dunne, and all his cruelties.'

She saw an awkwardness flit across his face, as if she had accused him of complicity, and she was sorry for it. 'I'm probably mistaken. He no doubt wished to amuse his grandmother. Sometimes I take too much upon myself.'

Iain's heart was still thumping with exhilaration when they had finished their jug of ale at the end of the short break ordered by the provost, who had told the music master in no uncertain terms that he would be out on his ear – from his post in the town as well as his engagement at the assembly – if there was any repeat of the outrage occasioned by 'Johnnie Cope'.

He'd glared at Iain too, but Iain had simply cocked his head to the side and winked at the self-important old magistrate. Poor 'Provost Muck', that had rung the bells of Inverness to welcome Cumberland into the town, only for the Fat Duke to order him up from his dinner table to muck out his own stables for the duke's horses.

The music master looked at Iain as if he might kill him and almost spat to his pupil, 'Handel. Flute sonata. E minor.' The child took up his instrument as the master attacked the keyboard of the spinet. Should all else fail, the work of their favoured German composer would surely soothe the tempers of King George's officers. As Iain started to play, he looked over to where Ishbel MacLeod was watching from the doors to the supper room. She smiled at him and inclined her head a little. He had made amends to Julia Rose.

Julia had emerged from the supper room, still escorted by Major Thornlie, and after some tentative waiting at the edges through one dance and then another, they finally advanced to the floor together. Iain wondered how the major might manage the dance. 'Easy,' he murmured to his companions, 'go easy.' And so they played a simple minuet. Iain could see that Thornlie felt some pain and moved a little stiffly, but he saw that Julia Rose noticed it too, and she took the burden of it somehow on herself and made it lighter.

The evening went on. The drinking went on. The dancers grew bolder. They'd started on the reels and Iain had stopped looking at the clock. His father would be long gone by now. Aeneas had a couple of young lads of trusted family posted in the town who were to report to him immediately on any trouble. The old steward had been standing stony-faced behind Iain's grandmother all night, although Iain could see beyond her chair to where his pewter-buckled foot tapped to the music. Hector was again becoming a memory in Inverness.

There were calls for the windows to be opened as the heat and the odour of human bodies rose. Arch MacPhee's face was puce and his jacket long removed; the schoolboy was flagging and something not far off pure whisky was making its way from the music master's pores. Iain visualised his father, on the water or even crossed over to the Black Isle by now, and he played on the more determinedly. Julia Rose and Major Thornlie were no longer dancing but standing in a group with other officers and their partners, talking and sometimes laughing.

They were coming to the end of a jig and making ready for a more stately allemande to precede the final reel of the night when Iain saw him – a figure emerging from the top of the town house stairs and making his way carefully through the throng. The new arrival was more finely dressed than anyone else in the room. He

wore a deep grey Italian silk suit with an embroidered
oyster satin waistcoat, not a thread of fabric too much
or too little. Iain felt sick. The sudden shock of it almost
took his breath away. He dropped his bow and only just
held onto his fiddle. Hector wore a neat white peruke,
tied at the back with a cream velvet bow. The stubble he
had cultivated for the last few days as part of his disguise
while hiding in Mairi Farquharson's house was gone and
he was clean shaven. Heads had started to turn and people
to whisper to one another as he paused very briefly at
Mairi Farquharson's table and bent low to say something
into the ear of Janet Grant. The shock on Janet's face
was mirrored by the other Grandes Dames and Iain's
grandmother was clearly rendered speechless. Then the
newcomer cast his eye about the place a minute until it
lighted on Elizabeth Rose. He began to walk towards
her. It was Hector MacGillivray, by some distance the
most handsome man in the room.

The jig came to its end and Iain almost held his breath.
Hector had come to a halt somewhere near where some
women were seated. Behind Iain, the waning schoolboy
and his inebriated master had already struck the opening
notes of the allemande. Arch, who had looked from Iain's
face to the new arrival, was a little slower. Iain watched
in astonishment as his father bent low to say something to
Elizabeth Rose. He watched as the look on her face changed
from shock to one of profound emotion. Hector nodded as
if in reassurance then extended his hand. To Iain's disbelief

Elizabeth Rose, a little hesitant, reached out and took it. Then he saw his father lead Elizabeth to the floor before turning to look directly at him. There was nothing else to be done – Iain lifted his bow and began to play.

EIGHTEEN

The Pit

Philip Thornlie had lowered his head and leaned in to say
something to her, but Julia couldn't catch the words. The
music had calmed and was not so loud as it had been, and
yet she could not hear anything but the rush of confusion
in her head, like a storm that had come from a great distance. Her mother was dancing. Her mother had not danced
for as long as Julia could remember – she would not even
dance with Julia's father – and yet she was dancing here at a
public assembly with this man, this newly arrived stranger.
But he was not a stranger. Julia knew it, and she saw in her
face that her mother knew it too. This was the same man
who had played the part of a Yorkshire clergyman in the
parlour of the Horns Hotel only a few days ago. The man
whom her mother had then reported to the authorities at
the garrison – the excepted skulker, Hector MacGillivray.
Julia's glance shot to the bookseller where he played on the
dais, and she knew immediately that she was right – the
man in the grey silk suit with the gleaming white wig was
his father. But her mother – she couldn't understand it.

Hector MacGillivray was talking to her mother. And her mother was watching his face, watching his lips as they moved, taking in every word as he held her hand high for her to twirl underneath and as they passed and repassed each other like the elegant hands of a clock.

'Julia, is something wrong?' Philip Thornlie had noted her abstraction.

She tried to shake her head, to say something, but she could not take her eyes off her mother and the man in the grey silk suit. The major's glance followed hers. She heard the low exclamation that escaped him, and then, 'Excuse me,' and he was moving through the crowd, through the dancers.

Julia felt her stomach tightening. As Major Thornlie made his determined way across the room, she counted the remaining steps and turns of the dance in her mind. Still her mother appeared completely in thrall to her partner. Then, at about eight feet from the couple, Thornlie stopped and turned slightly to one side and then the other, signalling to the junior officers whom she only now noticed were waiting there.

'Please,' she said, not knowing why as the music entered its last bars, 'please.' But it was too late, the music finally stopped, the dancers came to a halt, and the men bowed to their partners. At the head of the set, Hector MacGillivray lifted her mother's hand to his lips and brushed it with a kiss. He had hardly straightened himself when the advancing red of the officers' coats caught his eye. With a last look to

Elizabeth Rose, he swung himself around and ran not for
the assembly room door but the large window that looked
out over the Exchange. Women started to scream and men,
burgesses of the town, moved quickly out of the redcoats'
way as they pursued the fleeing stranger. Julia's mother,
alone it seemed of everyone in the room, did not move.

Iain had crashed down off the players' platform the moment
the music had finished, the same moment that he had realised that Thornlie had recognised his father too. There
were women screaming and men shouting, and bodies and
noise everywhere. His father was a grey silken streak disappearing and briefly re-emerging into his vision. And there
was Aeneas, no longer behind his grandmother but moving
quickly across the back of the room and towards the town
house window, Aeneas, unnoticed by anyone else, working
at the sash of the great window and flinging it open just
as Hector reached him and set a foot on a chair beneath it.
    Iain felt sick – he would surely break his neck. He charged
past those in his way as he tried to get to the window.
Hector was on the chair while Aeneas melted away. Iain
still had half a dozen yards to go, when two young redcoat
soldiers, coming at Hector from different directions, pulled
him down from the chair. Out of the corner of his eye,
Iain saw the tip of a rifle rise, to be levelled at his father's
back. With all his might he launched himself towards it, his
leading arm just catching the barrel as the redcoat pulled
on the trigger, forcing the man's aim upwards. The bullet

exploded into the ceiling and sent crumbling plaster and powder down on the stupefied revellers below. Iain hadn't time to wait. The rifle dispensed with he tried to power on, to reach his father, but suddenly found his own arms pinned back behind him in an unshakeable grip. 'Don't be a fool, MacGillivray, or you'll go down with him.' He continued to struggle but do what he would he couldn't release himself from Philip Thornlie's hold. It was over.

There was light, coming from somewhere. Iain turned over on the filthy straw. His bones were aching, and he had no idea if he had really slept at all – the night had been a haze of sudden startings, imaginings that he was back with hundreds of others amongst the agonies and degradation of the Gaelic kirk. He could hear the sounds of early traders arriving on the Exchange and the calling of gulls on the river, made more discordant by the snoring rising from a few feet away, and the groans and complaints coming from the next cell. There was rarely an empty cell in the tolbooth on the morning after a fair or an assembly, and the stench in the place suggested the revels of the night before had had the usual consequences. The Justice of the Peace loft, where he judged himself to be, was the worst part of the building, miserably cold in winter and overwhelmed by flies in summer.

Iain felt a pressing thirst. Stepping over a protesting neighbour, he inspected the jug of water in the corner. It looked as foul as he had expected, and not worth risking.

He sat back down against a wall and let out a long sigh. How had it come to this, again?

When the soldiers had handed him over to the gaolers at the tolbooth, Iain had asked a dozen times where his father was, but the soldiers had ignored him and the gaolers didn't know. All he could do was wait.

It was already light and the clock above the tolbooth tolling seven when there came a hammering on the outer door and the clanking of bolts. A minute later Iain heard the sound of the guards' weary trudge up the stairs. He went back to the grille and saw behind the guards the red of the soldiers' coats. As the gaoler worked at the locks to his cell door, they readied their muskets, bayonets already fixed. Bayonets? He had not as much as a *sgian-dubh* or any other knife on him – what did they think he was going to do? The gaoler opened the door to his cell and told him to come out whilst warning the other prisoners to stay where they were. Iain wondered if his last view of Inverness would be today, from the gibbet on the Haugh.

'Where am I going?' he asked the soldiers.

'House arrest, Major Thornlie's orders.'

Iain was bemused to find himself being marched down Church Street and presented at his own front door between the two redcoats, who then banged on it.

Aeneas answered in his regulation time and looked the soldiers and their cargo up and down in a manner to suggest a mighty degree of offence.

Iain made to step into the house but one of the soldiers

barked an order to wait, while the other produced a paper from which he proceeded to read.

'By order of Major Thornlie, the inhabitants of this house are to remain in this house until advised otherwise. No one but the servants is to leave this house until advised otherwise, and they only with permission of the guards who will remain posted outside.' With that, he snapped away his order and stepped to one side of the door while his companion stepped to the other. Only now did Iain notice that a further two men, who'd been coming down the street behind them, had peeled off down the alleyway to the side of the house in order to take up position at the gate in the back wall.

'Well,' said Aeneas, as he stepped back to allow Iain through before closing the door with a firm slam, 'it appears we are to behave ourselves.'

Upstairs, his grandmother was waiting. A wave of relief crossed her face when she saw him.

'Thank God. I feared the worst.'

Iain smiled and bent to be embraced. 'The worst we have known already, Grandmother. Last night was just a stooshie at a dance.'

She pressed his hand to her shoulder. 'A stooshie that might have seen you on a transport ship once again.'

'Or worse,' observed Aeneas. 'Had not Thornlie held you back, you would have got right in about matters, and who knows where that might have ended? Your father was well-taken by then, and all you might have done was to get yourself into more trouble.'

'I could have . . .' But no, Iain had known at the time that it was hopeless. 'Where is he? Do you know? What have they done with him?'

Aeneas glanced at Mairi Farquharson, his lips tight, and then said, 'They've put him in the pit.'

Iain held onto a nearby seat. The pit. The one gaol in Inverness from which there could be no escape, whereas the tolbooth was infamous for its escapees. The place was in such a decayed condition and, in the years prior to the rising at least, a gaoler's first loyalty was to his clan, and many an escape was 'arranged' before the magistrates had finished pronouncing sentence. Nowadays, the liberal application of whisky or brandy to the gaolers would usually do it. But the pit was a different order of prison entirely, a cramped stone vault hanging over the river, built between two arches of the bridge and reached only by a stairway descending through a trapdoor from the road above. One small, high, barred window allowed in light and whatever meagre foodstuff might be lowered down from outside to the unfortunate prisoner. For comfort inside, two wooden benches and a flagon on a rope that might be lowered through a small hole in the stone floor for water from the river below, the same hole serving for ridding the place of noxious waste. Men had died in that pit, of hunger, of exposure, even, it was said, eaten by rats. No one had ever escaped from it.

Iain sat down. How many times had he thought he'd lost his father, only to find that Hector had cheated death —

laughed in its face and gone on to more adventures in the service of the king? A man who had run through the blinding smoke of musket shot towards a hundred Hanoverian bayonets and yet survived, who had skulked in the heather for months avoiding the death squads after Culloden, could not end his days in a pit under the bridge over the river Ness.

'Thornlie would have had him under guard at the garrison, but there were rumblings from Dunne and others that he might never see the morning. He was put into the pit as much as to keep them out as to keep him in, until Lord Bury returns from the west to give advisement.'

'I know what advisement Bury will give,' said Mairi with some bitterness. It was just a matter of months since George Keppel, Lord Bury, had returned to the town to resume his regimental command a few days before the anniversary of the battle of Culloden, and he'd insisted the people of Inverness celebrate that day of carnage with fireworks and all the rest. Lord Bury was unlikely to show leniency.

Aeneas looked at Iain. 'And no doubt but he'd have had you up in front of him too, if Thornlie hadn't got you out of the way double-quick.'

Iain walked to the window. 'We can't leave him there. We have to do something.' He turned to his grandmother. 'Surely, there is something?'

His grandmother's face, for once, registered defeat. No one had learned better than Mairi Farquharson that there

S. G. MACLEAN

are some prisons, some fates, men cannot cheat, and on this occasion, she said nothing.

An hour later, after much grumbling from Eppy about the work of fetching and heating the water, Iain had washed off the stench of his night's imprisonment and was pacing the upper floor of the house, looking for answers that would not present themselves. Aeneas appeared at his door.

'You are wanted below. We have visitors.'

Whoever he might have been expecting to see, it wasn't Richard Dempster from the bookshop, nor Ishbel MacLeod's boy, Tormod. Richard was standing in front of Mairi Farquharson, hands behind his back, twisting his hat. The child was over by the hearth, giving close scrutiny to the portrait of Iain's grandfather that hung over it.

'Richard,' said Iain. 'How did you get in past the guards?'

'I – I told them I was your assistant and needed to consult you on a matter relating to the shop.'

'The shop?' How could Richard think he had time to worry about the shop just now?

'It seemed the best way of getting past them. Donald Mòr thought it more likely they would let me in than him. As an Englishman and not quite so . . . well known a person . . .'

'Donald Mòr?'

Aeneas grinned, a thing rarely seen. 'Donald Mòr has a plan.'

NINETEEN

The Escape

The reason for Richard bringing Tormod along with him soon became clear. Neither Donald's idiosyncratic spoken English nor Richard's comprehension of the binder's Gaelic having been equal to the task of making them fully understand each other over so important a matter, it had been necessary for Tormod to translate one or two essential words in the binder's plan to Richard, and Richard had taken him to Mairi Farquharson's house lest he was required to perform the same task there.

'Could it work?' said Iain after they had finished listening to the pair.

Aeneas threw out a hand. 'Well, for lack of a whole battalion of MacGillivrays coming down from Dunlichity to blast him out, it must be our best hope.'

Mairi Farquharson was more emphatic. 'Of course it will work! Did you listen at all? They have the whole thing worked out. It can hardly fail.'

'But if it does fail, and they are caught . . .'

Mairi looked at the small boy, his face alive with belief, and turned back to Iain. 'It won't fail.'

Lord Bury was expected back at any day from his visit to inspect the repaired barracks at Bernera in Glenelg. The elements had to be put in place that afternoon, if there was to be any hope of the escape being executed that night.

The first difficulty Donald Mòr had to attend to was the boy's mother. It was his own view that a boy, be he never so young, should not be always about his mother's skirts, and the boy himself shared that view most vehemently. However, Ishbel MacLeod had a tremendous terror of Tormod disappearing. That he was permitted to attend Donald in the bindery 'where he might begin to learn a man's trade', had in itself been a great concession, but to wander the town in Donald's company was something else. Donald claimed to know little of women, and he was near to certain they didn't understand a thing about him, but mothers he understood. 'I had a mother myself,' he'd assured Iain when Iain had raised the objection of Ishbel MacLeod. 'I know what works with them.'

And he had been proven right. A visit to the little house on Bow Court had seen Donald granted the confectioner's permission to take her child to the riverside for the day, where Donald would teach him to draw. 'The child has an eye, Mistress, and there's no one knows better than myself what to look for. Was it not myself first saw it in Allan Ramsay's boy, when I was working at the fellow's bindery? Who knows to what workaday trade his father might otherwise have put him?' Wary though she might be, there had been nothing in Ishbel MacLeod's armoury to be ranged against the suggestion that her son might prove an artist to rival Allan Ramsay, son and namesake of the bookseller from whom Iain had learned his trade.

Next, he and the child gathered what they would need from the supplies in the shop – offcuts of paper for drawing, pencils, charcoals – for Iain kept a decent stock and made a good profit from the requirements of Major Thornlie and the Military Survey. Everything went into Donald's old saddlebag, along with the drawing board he liked to take with him whenever he was out at work on sketches for the engravings Iain sold from the shop. The final two items were a flask of Mairi Farquharson's best whisky and the lump of clay Donald had been up before first light to get from his friend the potter out past the Longman. This last was well wrapped in a damp cloth.

At either end of the bridge was a gatehouse. The western entryway to the bridge was the toll house for anyone wishing to cross over into the town. At times of low tide, those who chose not to or were unable to pay the toll would wade across into town from the west side. As well as the guards at each gatehouse, a local man, Johnnie Brown, stood guard at the trapdoor on the section between the second and third arches over the river, at the entrance to the pit.

They sat a while on the banks beneath the castle, Donald

showing Tormod how to sketch Ben Wyvis, the great mountain that dominated the skyline to the north. And then it was time for them to move onto the bridge. They had little difficulty in gaining access to the bridge, Donald having explained at the gatehouse on the town side that he required to take the child along the bridge to view the Ben from a different perspective. He brought out one of his sketches to further explain. The gatehouse-keeper, being well used to seeing Donald about the town with pencil and paper, made no objection.

After they had been at their sketching a while, Donald took out the flask of Mairi Farquharson's whisky, took a dram himself and waved the bottle at Johnnie Brown who crossed over from his post at the trapdoor to join him. At the same time, a cart that had been waiting on the west bank of the river started to trundle slowly across the bridge. Before it drew level, the carter called to Donald, complaining of a bill he said had not been paid. Donald denied it, and soon, with the application of another dram from the flask, had Johnnie Brown drawn into the row. Things came to such a pitch that no one but the boy Tormod noticed Donald quickly slip his hand into Johnnie's coat pocket, and then into his own, that had the lump of clay in it, before returning whatever he had taken from Johnnie's pocket to its unsuspecting owner. And no one but Donald noticed the boy scamper around the cart and across to the trapdoor to the pit, where he bent down, his mouth close to the lock.

★

Darkness eventually fell. Hector MacGillivray had watched through the small barred window of the pit as the sky had changed from hour to hour until in the evening an almost never-ending flow of colours unfolded itself across the sky. It felt to him as if it must be June rather than August, so long had the light seemed to linger, but at last, the sun had gone down, and now the heavens were pitch. There was not as much as a single star to be seen, nor the hint of a moon. The moon had often been Hector's friend, as he'd travelled his way north-westwards then south again in the summer of '46, in the wake of the prince, but tonight he was glad of the clouds.

The sounds were different now too. All day he had listened, to the call of the fishermen hauling their nets on the river, the squawking of the gulls wanting their share, snatches of Gaelic song from the laundrywomen and girls as they'd stamped the cold waters of the Ness through shirts and petticoats. Closer at hand, there had been the sounds of men, women, animals and their cargoes crossing the bridge into town or away. The world continued regardless as he sat in this dark, damp, stone box, only a few feet above the flowing river. At one point, he thought that he caught the voice of an old, half-forgotten love, and then sometime later, of an enemy.

The old loves had not been as many as Hector liked to let people believe, but the enemies were legion, and not all had worn the uniform of King George's army. There had been plenty of those, of course, but there were others –

in King James's very court in Rome and amongst those who hovered around Prince Charlie in France, Germany, Switzerland. There was always someone whose goals and loyalties didn't accord with those of Hector MacGillivray. And in that, the town of Inverness was really no different from anywhere else. Nonetheless, Hector knew he was in here, incarcerated in this dreadful, seemingly unbreachable place, not because of any of those enemies, but because of himself. The dance with Elizabeth Rose could only ever have ended this way, and yet if given the choice again, he would have done it again. What was the point in a life without honour, and where the honour in a promise that is not kept?

He stood up and began to pace the small space. 'Aye, Hector,' he said to himself, 'all well and good for honour then, but what do you do now?' Whatever else he might be, the government army of occupation would see him as only one thing: a Jacobite spy. Hector knew what treatment the redcoats were wont to mete out to Jacobite spies. They would hardly bother going all the way out to the Haugh to hang him: they would string him up from the apple tree on the Exchange. But there were important things that Hector still had to do, and he was not quite ready to make himself available for a length of Hanoverian rope.

But how was he to get out of this place? Another man might have considered praying, but that notion did not detain Hector long. There were items on his account that it would probably do better not to draw the Almighty's attention to. Similarly, any practical solutions that suggested themselves were few and, after short examination, discounted. Greater adepts than he must have tried and failed to pick the lock from the underside of the trapdoor. The soldiers had lost no time in stripping him of Iain's grey Italian silk suit and had left him almost naked save a nightshirt and an old blanket, which he had fashioned into a plain brown kilt that did him well enough, but they had left him no implement whatsoever that he might use to pick the lock. There was nothing to be done with the hinges either. That the soldiers who'd guarded him by night seemed to have been replaced in the daylight hours by a stout townsman might promise something, though Hector did not know what. He would just have to trust to the ingenuity of his friends, and his own wits.

Nothing of note had occurred until around noon, when a cart trundling across the bridge above him had stopped and then voices risen to the point of argument. It was the usual stuff of small men in small towns – an unpaid bill. Hector's pulse quickened when he recognised the voice of Donald Mòr amongst the antagonists. The guard's voice reached him too – the fellow had evidently been drawn into the matter. Hector crept up the stone stairs and listened more closely at the trapdoor. As the argument rose there came, so soft Hector almost missed it at first, another sound – secretive, unexpected, quiet – a child's voice, hailing him in Gaelic, 'Hector MacGillivray, are you there?'

Cautious but intrigued, Hector set his mouth close to the trapdoor. 'I am here,' he said.

The small voice came again, urgent. 'You must listen tonight, after dark. Listen *below* for Donald Mòr and lower your jug when you hear him.'

'Donald Mòr? But how will . . .' Hector never finished his question. Suddenly all he could sense above the trapdoor was the flow of air, the circling of the gulls, but the child was gone.

Hours and hours ago that had been, and now it was truly dark. So dark, Hector could hardly distinguish the walls of his cell from the window and the night sky. The gulls had been long silent, the bridge gatehouses closed, his lazy town guard replaced again by two soldiers, who complained of their posting in this miserable northern town, surrounded by savages.

Hector paid only the necessary attention to the grumbling of the soldiers though. It was the sound of the river as it flowed beneath the stone floor of the pit that filled his ears and coursed through his body. 'Listen below,' that strange, childish voice had said, and Hector was listening. A rat ran across his foot. Hector had heard the stories of those who'd been in here before, those who'd died in here, of their wounds and starvation, eaten by rats. He was certain now, as he listened on in the darkness, that his fate would be different.

Richard Dempster preferred it when Tormod was here, to mediate between himself and Donald Mòr. The binder terrified him at the best of times. Richard had made a great deal of progress with the Gaelic tongue since those first, exhilarating days in 1745 when he had signed up along with his brothers for the new Jacobite force that would become 'the Manchester Regiment'. Now he could understand much of the Highlanders' language, but the binder made no concession to him that it was not his native tongue, and spoke in a thick, fast, perpetually animated flow replete with oaths and curses. And while Donald Mòr could read English perfectly well, it was almost beyond him to speak it. Tormod having long been returned to his mother, their communication was beset by difficulties.

The requisite black clothing had been got together and Donald Mòr had been about to change into it when Richard had put out an arm to stop him.

Donald glared at him.

'I'm going,' said Richard.

'Indeed, you are not!' replied Donald, fury building.

But Richard didn't let go his arm. 'You cannot swim.'

Donald's face was quickly scarlet. Richard's nation was condemned, his manhood insulted, and the morals of his parents questioned for daring to throw at his betters such an insult, but Richard held firm. 'You cannot swim. Iain told me what happened at the crossing of the Esk.'

Donald stared, then spluttered, 'The Ness is running low tonight, I'll hardly wet my toes.'

'It's not running low enough, and the current is always faster under the pit.'

Donald looked for a moment again as if he would argue, but then Richard saw that his words had had their impact. The binder looked at him with a degree of curiosity.

'You have studied the river?'

'I like to watch it, try to understand its flow, where the best fishing places are, where best to avoid.'

Donald nodded slowly, acknowledging the wisdom of such study. 'And yourself – as to swimming?'

'Like a seal,' said Richard.

And so it was Richard Dempster who, as darkness fell, donned dark clothes and went down by quiet ways towards the river. It was Richard who, ignoring the stench, crept into the skinners' yard and, keeping close to the walls, arrived unseen at the riverbank, still a good long way from the bridge. He was on the wrong side for the flow, west to east, of the water. But the other approach was much too exposed, and far too easily seen by guards on the bridge or the remaining ramparts of the semi-ruined castle. Looking carefully about him, Richard lowered himself to the ground and then slipped silently into the cold black water and began to swim.

He had just about reached the bridge when he heard voices somewhere over to his left – two drunks ignoring curfew and setting themselves up for a fight. Then there was another shout, from the direction of the bridge this time, and the last thing he saw before he sank his head below the Ness was the tip of a musket pointed from the parapet towards the source of the disturbance, held by an arm encased in red.

Richard moved as swiftly as he could against the current, keeping as much as possible below the surface of the water. At last he reached the bridge. He lifted his head and gulped for air. He had swum under the fourth arch. He took a moment to settle his breathing and to listen. The soldier was calling threats out to the drunks, the drunks calling curses back. Richard moved up against the stone pier of the archway and swam back out the other side, sinking his head once more under the water as he emerged. He kept under water until he'd moved under the third arch before coming up again for air. His heart was thumping with the cold and the fear, but he had known so much worse and there was only one more to go. He dipped his head under once more, swam again and then he was there, in the channel running under the pit. The soldiers and the drunks were still trading insults. He would have no better chance. 'Hector,' he called.

Nothing.

Then again, louder. 'Hector! I come from Donald Mòr. Lower your flagon.'

A rasped voice. 'Donald?'

'Donald Mòr sent me. Lower your flagon.'

And then there was a clanking of metal against stone and in the few inches between the bottom of the pit floor and the waters of the Ness, the jug began to appear. Richard took hold of it with one hand and, treading water, with the other pulled the newly modelled key from around his neck and dropped it into the flagon.

'Now pull it up.'

There seemed to be a moment's hesitation and then, to his immense relief, there was a tug and the jug began to disappear back up into the floor of the pit. Richard let out a long breath. There was nothing more to do, his part was done. He turned, ready to swim again and heard the words, 'Tell Iain . . . Dunlichity . . . the book.' He called up, 'What?' but there was nothing else. He began to swim again, arch by arch until he had reached the far end of the bridge, away from town, and hauled himself quietly up on the other side. As he did so, he was certain he heard, through the commotion now coming from the town side of the river, a splash, as of a large object entering the water far behind him, from the bridge.

TWENTY

Dunlichity

It wasn't long past dawn when the hammering came at the door. By the time Iain was out of bed and halfway down the stairs, still in his nightshirt, Aeneas had already emerged, clear-eyed and fully dressed, from his small room by the kitchen.

'Go up to your grandmother,' he said to Iain. 'I'll deal with whatever this is.'

Mairi Farquharson was by this time standing at the head of the stairs. The shouting and banging had grown more urgent and more threatening. 'Go, Iain, see what those oafs want now.'

'All right, all right, stop your din,' Aeneas said as he unlocked the door and drew back the bolt. The four redcoats who'd been guarding the house through the night had been joined by ten more, fully armed and headed by Captain Edward Dunne, who all but exploded into the house. 'Where is he?'

'Where is who?' said Iain, holding his ground.

The captain brought his puce face within an inch of Iain's.

S. G. MACLEAN

He hadn't shaved since before the assembly and his breath reeked. 'That damned spy, the dog your mother claimed was your father.'

Iain was opening his mouth to answer when he was cut short by Aeneas. 'Insult my mistress's daughter once more in this house, Captain, and you will need your wits about you when you walk the streets of Inverness.'

Dunne glared at Aeneas but was already too angry to respond to the steward's threat. He reserved his words for Iain. 'Where is he?'

A surge of excitement was building through Iain. Donald Mòr's plan had worked. 'What do you mean, where is he? You know fine well you have him in the pit.'

Such was the rage manifested in the bulging veins of Dunne's temples that Iain wondered for a moment if the man might have a fit.

'And you,' spat Dunne, prodding him in the chest in a futile attempt to push him backwards into the wall, 'know damned fine well that we do not.'

'You do not?' enquired Mairi Farquharson. 'Then where, pray, have you put him?' The amusement in her eyes was too much for Dunne. He swung round to the soldiers behind him. 'Search the house and everyone in it. Start with the hag. Spare her nothing.'

Images from the aftermath of Culloden flashed through Iain's mind, stories told of women, young, old, or with child, butchered and dishonoured. A fury took hold of him and before Dunne had quarter-turned away he had the English redcoat captain slammed up against the wall. 'They'll go nowhere near her, Dunne, or you'll leave here with your brains down the front of your shirt.'

The captain's men, initially too stunned to move, had in the next moment Iain's arms wrenched behind his back and a set of bayonets pointed at his neck. Something flared in Dunne's face that told Iain he might be dead before another minute was out, but before any further order could be issued, a voice barked from the door, 'Captain Dunne! What in God's name is going on in this house?'

Dunne spun around, ready to lash out again, but recognition of his superior officer just stopped him. 'Major Thornlie.'

'Well, Captain?'

'The Jacobite spy and excepted skulker Hector MacGillivray has escaped from the pit.'

Thornlie was stunned. Clearly, he had no knowledge of this. He stared at Dunne. 'That is impossible.'

'And yet it has been done,' said Dunne. 'The men guarding the pit last night ascertained that the prisoner was there when they took up their watch, but when they looked again prior to handing over to the next watch the prisoner was gone.'

'Gone?' said Thornlie. 'But how can that be?'

'Damned if I know. *Sir*,' responded Dunne through clenched teeth. 'But Lord Bury is returned from Bernera and has ordered this house searched for the prisoner.'

'But has there not been a guard, front and back, on

this house all night?' Then Thornlie directed his attention beyond Dunne. 'Lower your bayonets, men! This is the British Army! Are you afraid of a man in his nightshirt?'

For a fleeting moment, the refrain of 'Johnnie Cope' came back into Iain's head, but he managed to silence it. The men lowered their bayonets and took a step back.

'The men guarding this house have been questioned, I take it, Captain?'

'Yes,' said Dunne, sullen. 'They claim no one entered or left the place all night.'

'Then I think it unlikely you will find the person you seek in here. Nonetheless, if the general is of a different view, you must continue, but you will treat the household with respect, or you will answer for it.'

As soon as the search party had left, Iain, Aeneas and Mairi Farquharson sat around the table in her parlour while Eppy brought them breakfast.

'Well,' said Mairi, the gleam of satisfaction in her eyes, 'Donald Mòr said he would do it.'

'Donald Mòr is in the tolbooth,' remarked Eppy as she set down the butter, 'for fighting and carousing down by the river last night, shouting at the soldiers on the bridge.'

'A fine distraction for them,' said Aeneas, with approval. 'You'll take him up some food and ale, Eppy.'

'As soon as I can get in there,' she said.

'And Richard?' asked Iain. 'What have you heard of him?'

'The Englishman you have in your shop? Nothing.'

'Get down there as soon as you are able then.'

'Hmmph,' said Eppy as she made her way out. 'A fine thing then that I have nothing else to do with my time.'

It was not much more than an hour later that she returned.

'Well?' demanded Iain. 'Was he there? In the shop?'

'Wrapped in a blanket and like to die of cold if I hadn't lit that stove for him, clothes in a puddle on the floor, half the Ness dripping out of them!'

'I hope you took them away with you,' said Mairi.

'Aye, Mistress, I did.'

'Never mind his clothes,' said Iain, 'what did he say of last night?'

'Last night? I cannot tell. The fellow can hardly string three words of decent Gaelic together. But he was very concerned I would bring you a message.'

'What message?' said Iain, as his grandmother and Aeneas both leaned forwards.

Eppy pronounced the words very distinctly. '*Hector*,' she said, '*Dunlichity*, and *book*.'

The day had been interminable, the lack of any news the best thing about it, for if Hector had been caught, the very birds in the air would have been telling it. Everything had been got ready – a bundle of clothes, money, his forged papers and some food – everything Hector would need to get him out of the Highlands and back on a boat to the continent. And finally, the book. Iain had reasoned this could only be their damaged copy of the Blind Hary's *Wallace*, in which was encompassed Lovat's *Book of Forbidden Names*. What the point was in his father having it now, he didn't know. Aeneas had wanted to be the one to take everything to Hector, and Mairi Farquharson keen that he should do so, but Iain refused to give in to them.

'He's my father.'

'But think if you were caught . . .'

'They would serve Aeneas no better.'

'I am a servant,' said Aeneas. 'You are the last of Neil Farquharson's line. It would go the worse for you, and the loss of you would be a matter of greater importance than me.'

But Iain had refused to cede their point and so it was that at almost midnight, a good two hours after the bellman had gone through the town, he was in the vaulted cellars of his grandmother's house, Aeneas holding up a lantern and repeating his last instructions.

'I *know* the way to Dunlichity, Aeneas. Good God, I spent half my life there.'

'They'll have patrols out everywhere looking for Hector,' he said. 'If they catch you, neither of you will escape the rope.'

'I know, Aeneas. Now, time is getting on. I must go or chance getting caught by daylight. I'll be back as soon as I can manage.' And then, taking the bundle for Hector, he pulled the rough bonnet down over his head and crouched to go through the opening into the long tunnel leading from his grandmother's cellar to where it came out near the river.

Once he had crept past the castle and gone over the Haugh, he started to climb, tracing Wade's Essich road towards Dunlichity. He went familiar ways, past old cairns and tumbledown stone huts where he and Lachlan had played and learned to hunt, lochans where they had fished. At last, as a tinge of light threatened in the east, he was going down the little pass between Creag a Clachain and Creag Shoillier, and by the time the first true ray of the sun was hitting off the stones of the old kirk, he was in Dunlichity.

Iain rested for the first time since leaving Inverness and took in the scene. Little had changed and everything had changed. The kirk and kirkyard were somehow still there, grey stone amongst all the grey stones, scattered rocks and abandoned boulders left from an age of gods and heroes. Running just below the kirkyard was the burn carrying water from the loch into the Nairn, where Lachlan's mother had washed their clothes and sent them for a dooking whenever they came home filthy. Further up the hill was the way to Dunmaglass, the seat of their chieftain, where many good times had been had.

The black cattle stirring now to begin their day's grazing were not Lachlan's father's cattle though, nor the few sheep his either. It didn't matter where Iain looked – there was not a house within sight that had not suffered irreplaceable loss. Cautiously, he made his way down, finding what cover he could amongst boulders and bracken and the occasional whin as the cattle observed him, wary but unmoved. Where would Hector have gone? Iain looked out over the little glen and considered the possibilities amongst those he knew still to be there – old women, fatherless children, one or two lamed men, women waiting for men put on transportation ships six years ago to somehow find their way home again. At last he settled on the possibility of a cousin of Lachlan's father, a club-footed cobbler who had not been out in the '45 and who still lived across the burn in a small house a little way up towards Creag Buidhe.

Just at that moment came a sound that stopped him in his tracks. It came through the sounds of the other bird calls: a moorhen, but not quite a moorhen – Hector never had been able to get it right. Iain stood stock-still, and there it came again. He turned his head a little to the right. It was coming from the kirkyard. There was scant cover between where he now was and the kirkyard wall. If it wasn't Hector making the bird call, he could be walking straight into a redcoat's musket fire. But there was no option. The hillside behind the kirk was beginning to glow as the sun rose on, regardless of his situation. He went quickly, and as he drew closer to the kirkyard wall, the bird call ceased. Still some way away, he stopped in the shadow of a huge rock and picked up a stone which he threw in the direction of the moorhen call. There was an exclamation of annoyance and the same stone came whizzing back past his left ear, accompanied by a round of cursing in Italian.

Iain breathed out a huge sigh of relief. 'They'll hang you twice, for a spy and an Italian papist, moorhen or not.'

Hector stepped out from behind a tombstone. 'If you haven't brained me first.' In place of the grey silk suit was a too-big, yellowed woollen shirt and an old brown plaid, wrapped round to make a kilt. The periwig was gone and the hair bedraggled, the arms and legs bruised where he'd been beaten, but across Hector's face was the broad handsome grin and in his eyes a sparkle at having once more outwitted the best efforts of George of Hanover's army.

Laughing, Iain went forward and gripped hold of his father's arms. 'You got out.'

'Did you doubt it? It required nothing more than that Donald Mòr set his mind to it. And such a show he put on for those guards on the bridge, I nearly stayed to see it play out.'

'And they didn't even get a sight of you?'

Hector raised his eyebrows and grinned again. 'A close-run thing it was. When I got that trapdoor unlocked and lifted it up a crack the devils were no more than eight feet away. I thought I'd never do it without them hearing and seeing me. But Donald, good Christian that he is, summoned almost the only English he knew – he got out his best and favourite insults, and there wasn't a matter relating to those two redcoats and all that appertained to them that he did not set his talents to. The only wonder is that it wasn't them that were over the side of the bridge and down to get to him the quicker. I took my chance and slipped out of that trapdoor, quiet as you like.' He lifted a key, the one Donald had had fashioned from the imprint

in his lump of clay, on a cord from around his neck. 'I
even took a moment to lock it up again, to disorder them
the more, and I was down into the water like a rat with a
terrier on his tail.'

Iain was almost sorry he hadn't seen it. 'But if they had
turned at the wrong time . . .'

Hector made a gesture that suggested such worries had
never crossed his mind. 'But they did not turn, Iain, that's
the thing.'

Iain looked about him. The birds were still singing. Bees
were at their work from one pink clump of heather to the
next and the butterflies were already flitting amongst the
harebells. It might have been a paradise.

Hector ran his fingers over a scored stone in the corner
of the kirk's outer wall, and Iain knew he was remembering the days before the battle. 'Perhaps the Almighty
thought it a sacrilege, when we gathered here to sharpen
our broadswords.'

'Well, he had his revenge, did he not?' The arms of Clan
Chattan might be carved in stone over the tombs of the kirkyard, but more men of the confederation – Mackintoshes,
MacGillivrays, Farquharsons and others – lay beneath the
heather on Drummossie Moor than would ever lie here.

'Aye,' said Hector. 'He had his revenge. But perhaps we
shall yet have ours. First though, we must be away before
the whole of Strathnairn is up. Now, have you clothes for
me?'

Hector changed quickly and put the clothes borrowed

from his lame kinsman Calum MacGillivray behind an old, marked headstone. 'He'll know where to find them, poor Calum. Literally the shirt off his back, he gave me. He would have given me every bit of grain in his girnel too if I'd have taken it.'

Taking what cover they could find, and keeping low, they left the kirkyard. The sun grew stronger as they skirted Loch a' Chlachain. There was not another human soul to be seen, but the whole world brimmed with life. Heather, broom, bracken and bramble jostled one another for space and the hum of small winged creatures was everywhere. Iain could feel Hector relax beside him, and time unpeel itself.

'That's where Lachlan taught me to swim,' Iain said, pointing to a rock like a huge toad that jutted out into the loch.

'Did he now?'

'Aye. By dint of giving me a dunt in the back and shoving me in.'

Hector laughed. 'His father did me the same service.'

They were quiet then, for there would be none of Lachlan's line to one day teach any child of Iain's to swim.

Within half an hour of leaving the kirkyard they had reached the south side of Loch Duntelchaig and were looking past the mass of tumbled boulders to the clefts and crevices in the rock high above the loch. Iain knew where his father was headed. 'You still remember? You can't have been there in over forty years.'

'Aye, but I remember,' said Hector. 'I was there often enough when my mother had the birch out. That was a hard woman, indeed, and it wouldn't be the first time I was glad of a skinned knee in place of a tanned hide!'

Iain had had a few skinned knees himself clambering up these rocks, taking handholds between trees and shrubs, looking for caves and hidden passages between the massive tumbled stones.

At last, after some slips and false turns, they found the place Hector was looking for, and crawled between two rocks into a sort of cave in which they might shelter in safety until dusk. From there they could see for miles over Loch Duntelchaig towards where General Wade's road ran, and any redcoat hunting party that might be coming for them.

Iain brought out some of the food Eppy had prepared while Hector threw Aeneas's old plaid down on the cave floor and stretched out upon it. He let out a long sigh. 'I'm getting too old for these capers, Iain.'

'You don't lurk in graveyards and scramble up rocks in Rome then, Father, nor Paris?'

Hector looked up to the roof of the cave and smiled. 'Those cities have other dangers. Which I am also probably getting too old for.'

Iain passed him the whisky, along with a bannock and a hunk of cheese. He raised the subject that was seldom spoken of between them. 'Do you ever hear from my mother?'

'Charlotte?' said Hector. 'I hear *of* her from time to time, but not from her. I believe she is well enough.' There was a pause. 'And you yourself, does she ever write or . . .'

Iain made a dismissive noise and took a swig of the whisky. 'Once in a blue moon. I doubt she would know me if she saw me in the street. But tell me, the other night — why didn't you leave?'

'The night of the assembly, you mean?'

'Yes.'

'I had some unfinished business to attend to.'

'Elizabeth Rose?'

Hector nodded.

'How is it that you know her?'

Hector sat up, held the whisky bottle between his knees. 'I didn't — at least I hadn't met her until I came back to Inverness and walked into the Horns. But I knew of her, had known of her a long time.'

Iain waited.

'It was because of Henry Rose, who was her husband's cousin. I knew Henry when we were young men — the MacGillivrays traded with the Roses from time to time and fell out over it from time to time too. Henry was as bold as anyone; he was a glowing young man and every good thing was in him. All the women were after him, both young and those who should have known better, but he told me there was no one for him but a girl called Elizabeth. Anyway, Henry was a student at the college in Edinburgh when the '15 rising began. The Roses, of course, were on the Hanoverian side, and while his uncles and brothers

were busy trying to wrest Inverness from our hands, Henry
headed south to join the government forces on their way
to Preston. As you know, at Preston we threw away what
should have been a victory, but not before I came across
Henry Rose lying dying in the street. God, what a mess he
was. His arm had been blown right off, and his face that
all the women had been in love with . . . Well, anyway,
I held him as he died. Other men speak of their mothers,
but all Henry spoke of was Elizabeth, and how would he
dance with her without his arm? He made me promise
that I would dance with her for him. I'm ashamed to say
I forgot about it until I walked into the Horns that night
and realised who she was.' Hector looked up at the roof
of their cave. 'I didn't leave Inverness on the night of the
assembly because I had a promise to keep for Henry Rose.
I danced with her because he could not. It was a debt of
honour and that assembly my only chance to pay it. What
point is there in a life without honour?'

It was growing cold in their narrow shelter, the sun
having moved so that its rays fell well beyond the fissure
in the rocks. There were a good few hours yet until dusk,
when they must leave their hiding place. To wait for complete darkness would mean to attempt their descent of the
rock without seeing where to put hand or foot, and would
likely be fatal, so they must leave whilst there was still
sufficient light. Hector had arranged with Calum MacGillivray that Calum's son should be at the promontory known
as Preas Dubh with a boat to take them right down Loch

Duntelchaig. From the other end of the loch they might walk in darkness into Stratherrick. Hector's plan was to head westwards, for Morar, and there to find a passing boat that might take him back to France. He had to find Prince Charles as soon as possible, to warn him of the threat to Elibank's plot and the planned new rising. There was no hope now of getting Bailie John Steuart's son-in-law's ship which had sailed from Cromarty the night before without him, and so he must head westwards. The bailie, who knew fine and well that Hector was *not* on his son-in-law's boat, had nonetheless been dropping hints whenever in earshot of a redcoat that he was certain Hector MacGillivray was headed for that ship or another leaving after it. The Black Isle was swarming with soldiers looking for signs that Hector had passed through.

Hector laughed when Iain told him of it. 'The bailie has always been fit for them. He'll make his shilling out of them and they think him their friend, a servile Highlander eager to turn a penny. Well, indeed his penny will perhaps have bought me a day or a day and a half, which is all I need.'

'You'll make straight for Morar?'

Hector took a swig of the whisky. 'As fast as my feet will carry me. I'd have one last look at that book though. You did bring it, didn't you?'

'Blind Hary's *Wallace* with the *Book of Forbidden Names*? Yes, I've brought it.' He had *Peregrine Pickle* with him too, the illiterate Eppy having assumed it would be the book that had been lying by Iain's bed that his father was so anxious for him to bring. He was grateful that it was only the first volume the girl had encumbered him with.

'Good. But I'm dog-tired and you look worse. Let us take a few hours' sleep while we can – we have another long night ahead of us.'

The cave, or shelter made by the assortment of boulders that had landed one upon the other some unimaginably long time ago, was cramped and cold, the floor hard and uneven, yet there was room for Iain to stretch out by his father. Bone-tired, he did so, and soon fell into a very deep and dreamless sleep.

When he awoke, the air around him felt a good deal colder, and the light coming through the gaps in the rocks was just a dim grey. He stretched his limbs and muscles and looked to see if his father was still asleep, but beside him was only empty space and rock. Hector was gone, and all his belongings with him.

TWENTY-ONE

Into Stratherrick

Iain felt a dread begin to creep into him. He pushed himself through the cave opening, but there was no sign of Hector anywhere outside. Back in the cave he searched quickly through the remains of what he'd brought with him from Inverness – most of the food had been taken, along with the whisky and all the money. The books, both Blind Hary's *Wallace* with *The Book of Forbidden Names* and Smollett's *Peregrine Pickle* were gone too. All that was left was enough food to give him a decent breakfast.

Iain had been to go with him as far as Fort Augustus and they had been to part company there, Hector for France and Iain back to Inverness. He couldn't for the life of him think what could have happened while he'd been sleeping to change Hector's mind, but there was no more time to be wasted in this cave. He took a bite of the food, gathered up the rest of his meagre bundle, and slid himself out of the narrow opening back onto the hillside.

There was enough light, still, to pick his way back down through the boulders and outcrops of Stac an Fhithich, with only a few slips and scrambles. On the Duntelchaig shore he began to lope over grit, root, moss and rock. Dusk was giving way quickly to darkness, and the night creatures were out and not pleased with his company. An owl screeched; some other airborne thing almost flew into his face. The darker it became, the more difficult it was to negotiate the tentacles of roots waiting to trip him. Still, a clear sky would have been worse: he had seen the moon shine unencumbered over the loch often enough, and on those nights, nothing could be hidden.

At last he came within sight of Preas Dubh where the remains of an old kiln offered shelter. He quickened his pace, and as he did so, a mass appeared to move in the water, the dark shape of a small boat, nosing its way out onto the loch from behind the promontory. Iain shouted after it. With a muttered curse, Hector told Calum MacGillivray's son, also Calum, to row back towards the shore. As the boat turned, there was a splash as if something had been dropped into the water. After a few strokes they were within reach of him and then, as Calum MacGillivray weighted the other side for balance, Hector reached out and hauled him into the boat.

Iain could hardly speak for anger. When at last he got his breath back he said, 'What the Hell is going on?'

Hector glanced towards Calum MacGillivray. The boy's mother tongue was Gaelic, but there was always the chance that he would understand English too. Iain took the hint and addressed his father in French. 'Why did you leave? And what was that you dropped in the water?'

'There is too much to explain.'

Iain gestured across the water. 'It's a while yet till we'll be over the loch. You could start with why you crept away like a thief from that cave as I slept.'

Hector looked away. 'It was something I read in that book, after you went to sleep.'

'That you couldn't tell me?'

Hector's reply was emphatic. 'I don't want you to be involved in what I have to do now.'

'Involved? I have been involved in this business since the start. A man was murdered in my shop over that book!'

'It's not the *Book of Forbidden Names* that I'm talking about,' said Hector. 'It's this one.'

Now Iain could see that his father was in fact holding a book in his hand. It was the book mistakenly packed by Eppy. The first volume of *Peregrine Pickle*. 'What on earth are you talking about?'

And so, his voice low, Hector went over again the details of the planned Elibank rising: the kidnapping in London of the Hanoverian royal family on their way home from a visit to the theatre, the taking of the city by Jacobites already there, ships from Sweden, soldiers from Prussia, the clans to march down into England and carry Prince Charlie to his father's rightful throne. All as if Culloden had never been.

Even in the darkness, Iain could see his father's eyes glowing. 'The prince might be in Flanders already, and there he is to be met by Young Glengarry, whom the bailie tells me has been back and forth here, taking names and numbers of the clans that could yet rise.'

'Young Glengarry?' Alasdair Ruadh Macdonell, son of the chief of the Macdonells of Glengarry and a man designed to cut a swathe in the world. 'Yes,' said Iain. 'I told you. He was here a few months since. I couldn't believe it when he just walked into the shop one day, bold as brass. He had on a disguise, but if anyone from the garrison had spotted him, they wouldn't have wasted any time putting him in the pit, they'd have hanged him on the Haugh before dinnertime. I don't think Richard realised who it was when he came in. Donald Mòr knew him the minute he saw him, of course, and nearly passed out for joy. Young Glengarry was keen to pay his respects to my grandmother so I took him up to the house, and of course she would have nothing but that the Grandes Dames would be gathered to look upon the wonder. But Janet Grant wasn't there – she was at home in Corrimony.'

Hector sat back a little. 'So she didn't see him?'

'Oh, she saw him all right. He was asking after her and my grandmother insisted that I escort him there myself.'

'And did you?'

'What do you think? There'd have been no peace if I'd said no.'

'And what then?'

Iain shrugged. 'I left him there, at Corrimony. Janet pressed me to stay, but I had business to get back for. When I think of it, I'm not sure she was best pleased at her visitor, and I don't think he was there long before he was off over the hills to Glengarry. He said nothing to me of taking numbers for some new rising, only of going home to see what was left. He'd have found precious little.' Glengarry's castle had been blown up and the Macdonell clanlands laid waste, for that the chief, although surrendering on Cumberland's terms, had been late in handing in his weapons.

Hector shook his head. 'He was gathering numbers of clansmen able to rise again. It's Young Glengarry himself who is to lead the London Jacobites in the seizing of the usurper's family and the securing of the English capital. He told you none of this?'

'Not a word. Why would he have done? I am but a bookseller with a ravaged face and diminishing social graces. It is my father who is adept of the passages and secret stairways of the courts of Europe.'

Hector ignored the barb. 'So what *did* you talk of?'

'The usual things – friends we had, who was dead, who was in France, who in the Caribbean, who in Virginia. The state of the Highlands now, the prince, books . . .'

It was here his father interrupted him by holding up the book in his hand. 'When I came into your shop that first day, you told me you had spoken of this book.'

Iain peered at the volume to be certain. 'Peregrine Pickle? Yes, I'd not long got it in, and he was talking of it. He'd enjoyed it greatly, as I recall. Why? What is the significance of that book?'

'As you slept, I took the book and I went out and laid

myself down flat in the heather under Aeneas's plaid and
I began to flick back and forth, reading a little here, a
little there. A deal of nonsense, of course, but entertaining
enough, and I recognised a chancer or two in its pages that
I've met myself on my travels. But it was the tale of our
hero's Oxford days that brought me up short. He got in with
a great crowd for a while, it seems, young Peregrine Pickle,
but then they discovered Peregrine had been blabbing about
their activities. The words struck me very forcibly: "he
was considered as a spy, who had intruded himself into
their society, with a view of betraying it; or, at best, as an
apostate and renegado from the faith and principles which
he had professed." Pickle the Spy.'

Iain knew they had come to the nub of the thing now.

Hector continued. 'For some time, there have been fears
of a spy in the prince's circle. The government expends
vast amounts of money on trying to pin down the where-
abouts of the prince, but with little success. In recent
months though, their information seems much improved
and the betrayal of Elibank's plot suggests they have indeed
infiltrated Prince Charles's circle. Our sources in Whitehall tell us the spy goes by the pseudonym of "Pickle".
The circle of trust around the prince is small, and those
entrusted with the details of Elibank's plot smaller still.
Young Glengarry is one of the few admitted to both. I
think it likely that he is the spy I seek, and that being
the case, the prince must be warned not to embark for
England and the plan stopped, or he and all who take part

in it will end their days on a scaffold on Tower Hill or Kennington Common.'

'If Prince Charlie ever makes it that far. They'll murder him before he ever gets near a court. They'd never risk putting him on trial. Can you imagine it? He'd have the whole of London at his feet.'

It was true. Gnarly old men, wily chiefs who'd thought from the start that the '45 had no hope, had been helpless in the face of the charm of Prince Charlie. Daughters of the most ardent Whigs or fervent Presbyterian ministers the length of Scotland had ruined their eyes, sewing him cockades. The government in London could never risk the people of that city clapping eyes on Charles Edward Stuart. Much safer to deliver him a corpse – a bullet in the back, saying he was running from arrest, a knife in the neck, saying he was in a drunken fight, or an ambush on the road, blaming common highwaymen. They had tried to do it abroad often enough.

'If Young Glengarry betrays the prince, he betrays all those who already suffered and died for him.'

Hector nodded. 'That's why I need to know, one way or the other. If there has been treachery, then the plan must be called off. But if there has been none, the day may soon be at hand that we will put right the wrongs of my entire life. When I realised Young Glengarry might be the spy, I knew I had to get down to Glengarry myself and find out what he had been telling people when last he was there. There isn't much time. The attempt on the Hanover family is set for November.'

Iain leaned forward. 'Then let me come with you.'

Hector gave a great sigh. 'I travel quicker and I travel safer when I am alone, but what you have told me complicates matters somewhat. If Young Glengarry was so keen to get to see Janet Grant when last he was here, I think I must find out from Janet what he said to her.'

'What on earth would he have said to her that would be worth your while to hear? Compliments and nonsense that he made my grandmother and the others in Inverness.'

Hector looked into the darkness. 'Even so, I think I must see her. She will have gone home to Corrimony by now. Before I go into Glengarry, I must first go to Glen Urquhart, and Corrimony.'

Iain's heart sank, for they were on the wrong side of the Great Glen – they were on the south side of Loch Ness, and Glen Urquhart was on the north. Hector clearly saw what was going through his mind. 'Never worry, I have a plan.' He indicated Calum again. 'I will tell it to you later.'

No more was said then of plots, or of Young Glengarry, or of the *Book of Forbidden Names*, which now seemed little more than an indulgence, an old folly. Instead, Hector switched back from French to Gaelic, and drew the stoical young Calum MacGillivray into their conversation. He asked the boy about his kin and friends and tested his loyalties. The boy had only one loyalty and told them that all he looked for was the chance to run Cumberland through, should that fat butcher ever show his face in the Highlands again.

When Hector attempted to give the boy a shilling from

the money Iain had brought him, Calum shrank away. 'My father would make himself new brogues of my hide,' he said, 'should I take as much as a boddle.' So they relented, and Calum brought his boat about and commenced the lonely row back down Loch Duntelchaig. 'There's hope,' Hector said, watching him. 'There's always hope.' When the boat had at last been enfolded in the darkness, they turned and started to walk into Stratherrick.

TWENTY-TWO

Across Loch Ness

They passed into Stratherrick and by the south side of Loch Mhor, the water at their feet, the mountains at their shoulder. It occurred to Iain that in his thirty-six years, he had never spent as much time alone with his father as he was now. In the early years of his childhood in France they had rarely been alone – a stream of visitors coming and going, and one of them taking Iain's mother with him, his father perpetually required to go between one court and another, to cross the Channel again and again.

And as for the eight months of the campaign of the '45, from when the prince had raised his standard at Glenfinnan to that bloody afternoon on Drummossie Moor, they had hardly seen one another. Iain and Lachlan had not waited on their chief but joined with the prince's forces as soon as they could. In battle, Iain had always been with Lachlan and rarely beside his father, more often behind or searching for him. Hector had always been in the van, leading the charge. While Iain had been taken after Culloden, Hector had not. All Iain knew was that his father had skulked for months, taken messages back and forth between those sheltering the prince and those trying to arrange his escape. At last he had made away to Holland and thence to Rome, some months after the prince had finally been got away to France. All those years, all that absence. Iain knew this time with his father might well be the last.

They were a good way down the side of Loch Mhor by the time the sun began to rise behind them. Tints of dusky rose appeared upon the black surface of the loch and light was creeping onto the hills all around, trailing new shades onto the hillside. They had almost reached the safety of the ancient stone huts clustered at the end of the loch when, without a word, Hector stopped and turned around. Iain also looked eastwards. They watched the sky between the mountains change from red to pink to a pale orange, that suffused the brown hillsides until the heather flowers began to show against the bleakness, and inexorably to turn the land purple.

'The sun is up. We should get on, Father. We're nearly at the huts.'

But Hector didn't move. 'A minute yet, Iain. Just a minute.'

Iain's nerves were pulled tight as the strings of a fiddle. The sun was fully up, and they risked being seen by any keen-eyed traveller that might pass by on the other side of the loch. But the look on Hector's face spoke of an old longing and so he forced himself to be patient. Finally, Hector turned and gave his son a reluctant smile as he started to walk again.

They gained the shelter of the stone huts and lay themselves down on the fresh heather, already beginning to be
warmed by the sun. The bees were up and buzzing, and
the birds communicating who knew what. Iain stared up
at the expanse of blue above him and let his weary body
sink into its rest. There was little to disturb them save
the occasional querulous bleat of some far-off sheep. They
would wait out the daylight hours here. Hector insisted on
taking the first watch, keeping a lookout for any parties of
soldiers that might be taking Wade's road by Whitebridge,
to or from Fort Augustus.

As for them, they would not be going any further along
the way to Fort Augustus, but hacking down from here to
Loch Ness, through the old friendly territory of Gorthleck.
A boat would be got, or stolen if need be, to take them
across the loch from Foyers, but they would have to wait
here until darkness fell.

As Iain drifted off to sleep, Hector told him stories of the
old place of Gorthleck, where the prince himself had been
brought the night after the battle, and where he had finally
met the Old Fox, Lord Lovat, for the first and only time.

'After Charles had been got off the field at Culloden he
was brought across from Strathnairn here to Stratherrick.
Lovat tried to persuade him to take to the hills, to harry
Cumberland in raids, wait till the clans could gather in
strength again. He was desperate that Charles shouldn't
abandon the Highlands to what he knew would be coming.'

'But he did,' said Iain. The prince had gone, and he'd left

them, and told the leaders who would have fought on to disband their men. *Sauve qui peut*. Every man for himself.

'No.' Iain could see that old certainty in his father's eyes. 'He truly believed that if he could get back to France, he would rally enough support and he would return. And he will, if this traitor can be outed and Elibank's plan brought off somehow . . .' The cause was Hector's faith and all his philosophy. He would either see it triumph or die in it. There was no point in going over again what had already been lost, and whatever lay in the future could not be changed. Iain closed his eyes.

At some point, he felt the pressure of his father's hand on his back, keeping him down, and then came the sounds of feet. The sun had already passed its height. He opened his eyes and saw that his father was flat on his belly, but with his eye to a gap in the stone wall. Iain squinted through a gap in his own eyeline. Redcoats – a corporal and six men. Iain recognised some of them from the 20th Foot that were at Inverness. It was clear from the way they scanned the hilltops and horizons that they were not a regular patrol out of Inverness or Fort Augustus. They were searching for someone. Iain hardly dared breathe. His father was as still as a hare, listening.

Suddenly, there was a call from the back and the party came to a halt. One of the men was clutching at his guts, and there was a laugh and some groaning from the others before he peeled off the road and started running towards the huts. The corporal at the head of the party swore copiously about the delay but he nonetheless ordered another of the men to go with him.

'And see you make a search of those huts!' shouted the corporal, marching the rest of the men off.

There was a muttered response from the infantryman sent to keep his comrade company and as the rest of the party passed out of earshot a sound of flint being struck. The soldier settled himself against the outside wall of the hut Iain and Hector were sheltering in and lit his pipe. He called to his distressed companion, groaning in one of the other huts. 'Take your time there, George. The bugger can do without us a while.'

Iain's whole body tensed. Beside him, Hector clutched the knife Aeneas had furnished them with. To be found with forbidden arms would be death, but if they were found here now it would be death in any case. The time was interminable, the suffering infantryman taken by new pains while the first were scarcely over. His companion, lighting a second pipe, reassured him that all would be well and that there was no hurry. A bee landed on Hector, attracted either by the heather on which they lay or the traces of pomade which he somehow still carried about his hair, and crawled over his nose and eye, making each twitch. The smoke from the soldier's pipe was finding its way through gaps in the stone and beginning to catch in Iain's throat. At last, when it seemed they could lie silently no longer, the first soldier emerged from his hut, praising the Lord for his relief. 'Have you checked them other ones?' he asked.

'Oh aye,' said the pipe man, his knees creaking as he slowly got to his feet. 'Nothing in 'em.'

They moved off, muttering about the corporal, muttering about the cost of drink at Fort Augustus, and muttering about bloody Hector MacGillivray. As their voices receded to nothing, Iain and his father sank their faces into the heather and thanked God for the Englishman's sloth.

As dusk at last started to fall they set out again, listening all the while for the sounds of more search parties. They heard little but the occasional bleat of a sheep somehow separated from its flock, or the posturing bellows of stags on the high tops and ridges, readying themselves for the rut. Steering clear of the military roads, their descent to the loch shore was by rough moor and woodland. The worst would come at the very end, at the thunderous Falls of Foyers, where the waters of the river Foyers tumbled from dizzying heights over treacherous rock before meandering sedately into Loch Ness.

Hector set a brisk pace and not for the first time, Iain wondered at his father's stamina. As they travelled through scraps of wood, over bog and rock, the ominous, unseen presence of Loch Ness beyond only seemed to grow. At last they came within sound of the falls thundering into the never-ending black. There could be no hope of negotiating them in the dark. Neither, though, could they emerge at the bottom in daylight, ready to cross the loch for all to see. 'We'll have to wait until dusk, tomorrow night,' said Hector. They scrambled back up the hillside to take shelter on Carn Dearg, from where they might watch the road until the next night.

As the hours passed, when they were both awake Hector told Iain of the Palazzo del Re in Rome, and the palace of St Germain in Paris, of the courts of the Elector of Brandenburg and the King of Prussia. He told him of the painters he had met, the poets and the philosophers whose writings filled the books Iain sold in his shop. The sun rose and then fell, and the hills remained around them, still in their ever-changing colours. At last the light started to fade and they made their way down the hill, trees and rocks secluding them from view. Soon they could hear the roar of the Falls of Foyers.

Iain felt himself grow cold as they drew closer. The noise of the water, furious as it rushed over the edge of the rocks to crash into pools far below, was like the guns. Eas na Smuide – the Smoking Falls people called them. He felt they were walking, not running this time, right towards the guns. He took a deep breath, steeled himself, and went on.

The path down past the falls was steep and twisting, and the noise more terrible the closer they got. At times, they found themselves lashed with spray as water thundered down upon water. They said little, both anxious not to make a mistake, not to slide on a rock, or trip on a root, or step where there was nothing underneath. Bats came out and owls started to screech as the last of the daylight faded to grey and then to nothing, but by the time darkness had fully fallen they were well down past the falls and tracing the river as it meandered the final part of its way to the great loch. Near the shore they found a boat, moored at the riverbank. Iain cut the rope and soon they were pulling away across the water, towards Glen Urquhart.

They rowed in silence for a while but then, as their oars cut as quietly as possible through the water, Iain recalled something from their previous boat journey across a loch.

'Going across Loch Duntelchaig . . .' he began.

'Yes?'

'As Calum MacGillivray's boy turned the boat around, I heard something hit the water, there was a splashing sound.'

Hector snorted. 'Do you wonder – the size of that lad? He could have thrown the boat from one end of the loch to the other. That's not a boy that could put an oar through water without making a splash.'

'I'm not in jest, Father. It wasn't the oars.'

'Well, maybe it was a fish jumping.'

'It wasn't a fish either. Where's the book?'

'What book?' said Hector, looking over his shoulder to the far shore.

'*The Book of Forbidden Names*. I know you took it from the cave above Loch Duntelchaig, but it's not in the pack and I haven't seen it since. I think you dropped it into the loch.'

Hector's mouth was tight and he pulled determinedly on the oars a few more times. Then he spoke. 'It was of no more use, with the last few pages being missing. I had all the information that was to be had from it.'

'We already knew that, though. We knew it before the

night of the assembly, before you were ever put into the pit. Why did you send word by Richard Dempster when you escaped from there that I should bring it?'

'Because . . . if it had been known or discovered that you had it, it might have proved dangerous to you. Some things are better lost.'

It was clear he was going to say no more about it, and Iain knew he had no option but to hope for a better answer before they parted once more in Glen Urquhart. He glanced up the loch towards Dochgarroch, where his great-uncle Kenny Farquharson had kept his inn and his secrets for so many years, before those secrets had been found out and he had been murdered because of them. But if you could not hide a secret here, then where? The loch was so long, and so deep and so dark that a man might go in and the waters pass over him so that it was as if he had never been. Who would see? The mountains looking down from either side were silent, immovable, and the glens and peoples they hid might almost be unguessed at. For a moment Iain had the mad thought that they would get to the other side of the loch and discover that nothing of the past years had ever been − no rising, no marching, no battles, no vengeance, no loss. But then a sudden breeze blew his hair across his eyes. He put a hand up to push it back and felt the scarring beneath his fingers. A stronger gust of wind sent ripples over the flat surface of the water, and he set to his work at the oars.

Over Hector's shoulder, looming ever closer, was the

spectral silhouette of Urquhart Castle. Sixty years a ruin and yet still somehow commanding the loch and the entrance to Glen Urquhart. From time to time, a cantonment of government troops would be found there, pitching camp for a week, or a month, sending out patrols to keep an eye on the populace or to attempt to gather rents, before gratefully moving on. Tonight though, only mice and bats watched from the ramparts or cracks amongst the walls as the two fugitives pulled their stolen boat onto the shore beneath.

Keeping very close to the walls, they made the steep ascent up past the castle. It seemed impossible that, abandoned though the place was, there were not some ghostly guards watching their every movement. Hector looked as glad as Iain felt to get the place behind them. Resting a short while to eat and drink at the ancient fort of Craig Mony, they set out again, deeper into Glen Urquhart, feeling their way carefully in the darkness, disturbing only foxes and other creatures accustomed to having the place to themselves at that hour. The white lumps of sheep on the hillside did not trouble themselves to stir at their approach, and the deer on the tops were fleeting grey silhouettes.

They should have made it to Janet Grant's place at Corrimony before dawn, but a glow of torches appearing on the road below revealed itself to be another scouting party. They lay low, and by the time the party had passed on down towards Urquhart Bay, it was already light. They were within sight of friends at Shewglie, not far from Corrimony, and yet they could not risk going down there by daylight. And so they waited out another day, with only the last of the oatmeal Iain had brought from home mixed with some burn water, and a few berries to eat.

At last it was dusk again and they began to move. Very soon, what remained of the house and outbuildings at Shewglie emerged from a cluster of trees below them. An offshoot of Clan Grant, the old chieftain of Shewglie had been shipped to London after the '45 and died there of gaol fever, one of his sons already dead at Culloden and another escaped. Many of the men had been transported, with their kinsmen of Glenmoriston, to the sugar canes of Barbados. But there were still some friends to the king's cause left here. As Hector and Iain drew closer, they could see smoke rising from several fires, and a good deal more torch light than they would have expected.

'There's something going on,' said Hector, his hand again readying the knife Aeneas had given them. They crept closer. There was noise, that was the most notable thing after the light, a great babble of noise. And they realised it at the same moment, Hector turning to Iain with a great grin on his face. A ceilidh. They were having a ceilidh at Shewglie.

They quickened their pace, their feet settling into the rhythm set by the bodhran, flutes and fiddles. Hector was laughing and Iain had begun to hum the notes of an old song. And then, not twenty yards from the byre from which the sounds were coming, they were brought up short, their arms pulled behind their backs and the points of knives applied to their necks.

'Your names and your business,' said a voice from the darkness, 'or those'll be the last steps you take.'

TWENTY-THREE

Corrimony

Iain felt the tip of the knife at his throat. Everything around him was suddenly still and the music was momentarily lost to him. All he could hear as he waited for what his father would say was the crackling of a fire somewhere close by, and the breathing of the man standing pointing a pistol at them, alongside that of his two knife-wielding companions.

After longer than can have been comfortable for any of them came Hector's reply, low and slow to begin with. 'God in heaven, Archie Grant. A man would be hard put to say if you were blind or drunk.'

Iain couldn't arrange the words in his head for the roar that came from the man with the pistol, and then the knives were gone and he was being charged aside by the huge, unkempt figure of Archie Grant on his way to throw his arms about Iain's father.

'Hector MacGillivray! Are you not dead yet?'

The two greeted one another like stags at the rut and there was such a wrestling and slapping of backs that Iain thought one of them must surely fall over. Then Grant, his face shining where it could be seen between knots of hair and straggling beard, held Hector away from him to get a better look. 'By God, man, it's true. When the news came from Inverness, everyone else said it couldn't be right, that no one could escape from the pit. But I told them, Hector MacGillivray was that very man.' He broke off to seek confirmation from his attendants. 'Did I not say it, now?'

'You did, Archie, you did,' their eyes wide at the legend that was Hector MacGillivray.

Hector the Hero. Again. Iain only just managed to refrain from telling them that Hector had not actually sprouted wings and flown from his prison, but he knew these men would have no interest in the unsung individuals who had planned and executed his father's escape.

Then Grant became serious.

'You know there are parties out looking for you? They're coming down from Bury in Inverness and up the loch from Wolfe at Fort Augustus. There's been a cantonment at Glenmoriston for a few weeks, and they were out scouring the hills before dawn, and another at Glen Strathfarrar that can't be long in hearing of your escape and being sent out for you.'

'I know it.' Hector glanced towards Iain. 'Are they looking for both of us?'

'No, there was no word of Iain, only of yourself.'

'Thank God.'

'I've had a watch out on the road ever since we heard you got out of the pit. But I had the guards looking out there for a man on his own, rather than two. You'll excuse them their caution, I hope.'

Iain nodded, nevertheless rubbing at his neck and breathing out with relief.

'The soldiers will be back down the glen tomorrow at first light, I'd say,' said Grant. 'But you can rest assured they'll not find you. Come away in though, I never saw two men so fit to die of thirst.'

Archie Grant took them to a quiet part of the byre, having sent two more men out to keep watch on the road and given orders for food and drink to be brought for the travellers. They were provided with slabs of the pig that was roasting over a spit outside, and good measures of ale and whisky.

Hector looked about him. 'Is Janet Grant here tonight, Archie? I was wanting to see her.' A near neighbour, and widow to Archie's father's cousin, it would be natural for Janet to be at any gathering at Shewglie.

Archie shook his head. 'She was here earlier to welcome Duncan home but would hardly wait at all before she was off back to Corrimony.' The ceilidh was in honour of a cousin of Archie's who'd found his way home at last. He'd been transported out of Liverpool, on a ship bound for Antigua that had been taken by a French captain off Martinique. The Frenchman had refused to hand over the Jacobite men, women and children to the British authorities and so, seven years after leaving Glen Urquhart to fight for Prince Charlie, the cousin was finally home. 'I'll tell you Hector,

Janet's not well. She came back from the town only two days ago and the look of death is on her. She told us about Kenneth Farquharson' – here he nodded his condolences to Iain over the demise of his great-uncle – 'and she's taken it awful hard. I'm not sure what sense you'll get out of her.'

'I'd see her all the same, Archie, and then I need to get into Glengarry, and away west as soon as possible.'

'Black Peter will take you,' said Archie. 'There's no one knows the way over the hills better than him, and no one who knows the redcoats' lurking places better, either.'

Black Peter – Patrick Grant of Craskie – was a legend to any who had fought in the Jacobite cause. He had kept Prince Charlie safe as he skulked in the hills above Glen-moriston and would have drawn his own entrails before he'd have dirtied his fingers on one of the thirty thousand English pounds the Duke of Cumberland had put up for any Highlander willing to give up the prince. Five months Charles Stuart had been on the run after Culloden, amongst people who had barely a blanket on their backs, and not a ha'penny of Cumberland's blood money had been claimed.

'Black Peter could guide you past the search parties in his sleep. He's up at the shieling. I'll send my boy Davie up for him now – he runs like the wind. Peter will take you to see Janet and then get you off – you'll get a decent start.'

There was nothing to do then but to wait and to enjoy the ceilidh, with no need for the musicians here to worry about Hanoverian sensibilities. All the old favourites, and a few new ones that Iain was only hearing for the first time, spun out into the night. Iain found himself thinking of Ishbel MacLeod in her pale sprigged cotton gown with the yellow petticoat. Ishbel who had had to stand in the shadows at the Town House assembly. He could picture her here, dancing though he had never seen her dance, laughing though he hardly knew if he'd heard her laugh. He himself hadn't danced in almost seven years, hadn't wanted to, but he would have asked Ishbel to dance, tonight.

Hector was in his element, up for every reel, quietly echoing the words of the laments, and paying court to every woman between sixteen and seventy. Iain wondered how he managed in the mannered courts of Italy and France, with their proprieties and petty intrigues. The returned cousin, emaciated and looking at least ten years older than he was, was pledged so often he was soon too drunk to stand and so was set in a place of honour at the top of the byre to enjoy proceedings in his sleep. There were Grants from Glenmoriston and Frasers from Glen Cannich and Chisholms from Strathglass. The players seemed to drink as much as anyone, but kept their feet, the sweat lashing off them as they worked the dancers to near exhaustion.

'You play the fiddle yourself, do you not, Iain?' said Archie Grant, as the musicians at last stopped to rest.

Iain smile. 'I can scrape the odd tune.'

'Scrape it!' his father said. 'The finest fiddler in Inverness.'

Archie Grant's dark eyes danced. 'Would you take a wager, Hector?'

Hector leaned forward, interested. 'What sort of wager?'

Archie nodded over to where the musicians had laid down their instruments and were refreshing themselves. 'That fellow there, the tall one – the best fiddler in Strathglass and all the Aird. If your boy can keep up with him, I'll stand you a drink in every tavern in Edinburgh, the next time the prince comes home.'

Hector slapped his thigh. 'You're on! Iain . . .'

Iain had no desire to be made a spectacle. 'It seems that on the run from Inverness, I somehow neglected to bring my fiddle.'

But word of the challenge had got around and a crowd was gathering. A fiddle was found and handed to Iain, and he was left with no option but to tune it. When he was satisfied with the tension of each string, calls were made for the Strathglass fiddler. Grinning as he passed through the parted crowd, the man came. He was tall and spare, with a lively eye and amusement written on his face. He nodded to a man with a flute who raised his instrument to his lips and began a tune. The fiddler then made a bow to Iain before putting his fiddle to his chin. Iain did likewise, and waited, there was not a breath of sound in the place, and then the Strathglass fiddler started to play.

He pulled his bow long and slow across the strings, and then he was off – a hind across the mountain tops, stopping occasionally to sniff the air, survey her surroundings, before setting off again. Iain listened for a few bars. Sometimes the hind's herd would keep up with her, sometimes she ran free. Iain started to move his head in time to the other man's music. His foot was moving, he realised he was tapping his bow against his leg. The Strathglass fiddler looked at him, a question in his eyes, played the question on his strings. Iain gave the merest of nods, played his own bow across his fiddle in assured response, then the other man smiled again and they were off. Iain was a hind too, keeping pace with the one in the lead, bounding, flying almost, until the others were far in their wake and there were only the two of them left, the mountain tops to themselves. A hunter appeared, they flew on, from ridge to ridge, disdaining him, past shielings and crofts and great houses where the people came out to wonder and to dance. And on the two hinds went, faster and faster. Iain didn't know when he had last felt such freedom, known such joy. They raced along ridges he had never seen, through straths lost to memory and man, all the time leaving the herd and the people here, in this byre, far, far behind them. But then Iain began to falter and to tire. Notes were missed as the Strathglass fiddler went on, oblivious. At last Iain could keep up no more. The flautist had taken his leave long ago. Iain's bow went loose in his hand and he watched in wonder as the other man spun on, faster and more urgent, to arrive at last, alone, at its end. The Strathglass fiddler played his final note, let down his fiddle and made Iain the most profound of bows.

The place erupted. Iain found himself lifted onto the shoulders of two of the Glen Urquhart men, and paraded around the floor in the wake of his conqueror, who rode high on the shoulders of two Chisholms. Archie Grant was clapping Hector round the arm. 'Never, never was there such a flyting of fiddlers as this night at Shewglie. Men will speak of it, Hector. They will speak of it.'

The fiddlers were at last set down and the best of whisky insisted upon for each of them and not to be refused. Iain felt the warmth of his father sitting beside him, the infection of his laugh, the glow of pride in his eyes as the flames of the fire lit his face. He thought this was the happiest night of his life.

The company became reflective and a woman of around Iain's age, a Chisholm, sang a lament for her lost husband, standard-bearer of their clan at Culloden. Not long after the last notes had died away, the sound of running feet broke into the quiet.

Archie Grant stood up at the arrival of one of his watchmen. 'Jamie, what is it?'

'Ranald has run over from Delshangie. There's a party of redcoats headed this way.'

Everything then happened very quickly. Parcels of food and flasks of drink were brought, instructions given. 'I'll send Black Peter to you when it's safe. And never worry about the soldiers, I'll lead them such a dance, their heads'll be spinning off their necks.'

'Don't bring trouble on yourself, Archie.'

'Ach, I'm not daft, Hector. But one of these days . . .'

'Soon, God willing,' said Hector.

'Aye,' said Archie, 'soon.' Then he turned to the messenger. 'Jamie, take them to the cairn.'

And then they were on their way again, trotting behind their guide as he led them into Corrimony. Iain knew which cairn they were going to. It was nothing like the piles of rocks that Major Thornlie and the Military Survey put at staging posts on the hill routes. Instead, the cairn at Corrimony was a huge, low drystone dome, its capstone perhaps only six feet from the ground, and the whole taking up as much ground space as a small house. He had played near there often, as a child, with Janet Grant's son, Alasdair. They'd been born only weeks apart, in the months after the ending of the '15 rising, Iain the inconvenient bastard grandchild of Mairi Farquharson, Alasdair the longed-for only child born late to her best friend. Neither of them would ever have dared to try to enter the cairn, but on one occasion Alasdair had gone as far as to dance round it, threading himself like a ribbon through the circle of its guardian standing stones. Janet Grant had beaten him black and blue when she had heard of it and taken the time to give Iain a tongue-lashing for not stopping him. As if anyone could have stopped Alasdair doing anything. But Alasdair was dead now, and his mother alone.

The moon was bright, and the jagged stones of the circle came into view, sentinels guarding access to the dead. Their guide slowed his pace and they walked the last hundred or so yards. Once they were within six yards of the outermost stone, it became clear from the look on the young man's face that he was reluctant to go any further. A flash of something across Hector's eyes told the same story. It was a sacred place, and no good could come of violating it.

And yet, they had no choice. Hector looked at Iain and said, 'We are here to claim sanctuary,' then he uttered an old blessing under his breath. The guide appeared a little encouraged.

'There's a stone at the mouth of the entrance,' he said. 'It's not as heavy as it looks. I'll push it away, to let you in, and back again enough to cover it. I'll leave enough of a gap though that you can get purchase to move it away again, if you need to, but otherwise you're to wait until Black Peter comes for you.'

Thinking of the ghost of the dancing Alasdair beside him as he passed through the ring of stones, Iain got down on his hands and knees and crawled the few feet of the passageway into the chamber of the cairn. Hector was a minute or two after him. 'It'll take a good hard effort to shift that stone,' he said as he finally emerged into the almost pitch blackness of the chamber. Such was the density of the packed stones and rubble around them, only the tiniest of chinks of moonlight found their way in. The thin shafts of illumination served only to heighten the tension in the tomb, the precariousness of their situation and their consciousness of the third presence there with them, the soul for whom it had been built.

Suddenly, Hector sat bolt upright. Then Iain heard it too – a party on horseback. As the party came closer there was the sound of the horses' hooves on the turf and the clanking of metal stirrups, of swords against flanks.

Hector went to move through the passageway. Iain waited. There wasn't space enough for them both to see out through the gap at the entrance at the same time. The sound of the horses came closer, so close that Iain began to brace himself for the thundering of hooves over the cairn, because they were so near that they must surely ride over it. He sensed his father tense in front of him, and then they both held their breath as the command went out to halt.

There was the sound of men dismounting, guns being cocked and spurs rattling on boots. 'Two to the left and two to the right.' Iain felt himself go cold as he recognised Captain Dunne's voice. 'Burt, check the entry.'

They pressed themselves back against the walls of the chamber. Indistinct sounds of metal striking stone, men's voices, a whinnying of horses found their way through the walls, and all the time they listened for movement at the entrance. They heard the creak of boots as the man Burt squatted down, heard a puff of breath as he placed his face to the gap between sealing stone and the passageway wall, a slight grunt as he pushed ineffectually at the stone before uttering an oath. 'Nothing here, sir.'

'Come on then, the horses are nervous. They don't like it here.'

There were mutterings of agreement as the men returned to their mounts. 'Barbarism,' they heard one of them comment. 'You could build a decent wall with that lot.'

Iain and Hector waited until the sounds of Dunne's search party had faded into the distance.

'They didn't turn around,' said Hector.

'What do you mean?'

'They haven't turned to go back the way they came.'

Iain felt himself go cold. 'Oh God, Janet.'

Hector sat back on his heels and cursed, but then he shook his head. 'It's all right, she won't know we're here yet.'

'What?' said Iain. 'It doesn't matter if she knows or not. She's hardly out of my grandmother's company when she's in the town. The redcoats'll be through that house like a swarm of rats, looking for us. And lucky if they don't frighten the old woman half to death while they're at it.' He was gathering his things, preparing to leave the cairn, but his father didn't move.

'She'll be fine.'

Iain was incredulous. 'What? You *know* how they treated the women here, and in Glenmoriston after the battle. They have no respect for age or anything else.'

But Hector shook his head. 'I'm telling you, Iain, they won't harm her. All that will happen if you go charging in there is that you'll get a musket ball through the chest.'

'If *I* go charging in? You will not come with me?'

'No. I will not. But more than that, I will not let you go.'

Iain swore, and went to go past his father. 'You won't stop me.'

But Hector clamped a strong hand round his wrist. 'Listen to me. I have served the king since the day I could hold a sword, I have travelled Europe in his cause and I have encountered more enemy soldiers than there are cattle still on these hills, and I am *telling* you, they will not harm Janet Grant. More, if you raise the alarm by appearing at that house just now, there is a much greater risk that they will find me. I have to get away to France to warn the prince that Elibank's plot has been compromised. His safety is of greater importance than the property and dignity of an old woman.' His grip held firm, but his voice became softer. 'Trust me on this one thing, Iain, and I'll never ask you to do anything for me again.'

Iain was stunned with shock. 'How do you know they won't hurt her?'

'I just do,' said Hector. 'You must trust me.'

Again. Trust. Trust. Trust.

'All right,' said Iain, and Hector at last loosened his grip, 'I'll trust you.'

It was one of the longest hours of his life. And that was somehow strange in itself, that it was only an hour. There had been none of the terrible noise, no hint of the flames that Iain had been fearing. He was still listening for it, still looking through the gap in the entrance to the cairn, when instead he saw the party of riders coming back. They would hardly have had time to search Janet Grant's house and properties at Corrimony, never mind actually ransack the place and do the old woman harm. Certainly, there was no sign of her with them as they passed. Iain was almost sick with relief.

'Well?' said Hector, as he moved back into the chamber of the cairn.

Iain let out a heavy breath. 'They don't have her with them, nor anyone else, and they didn't look to be in any particular hurry. I think they've given up for the night.'

'May it be so,' said Hector. 'We'll just wait a little longer to be sure. We have perhaps two hours before Black Peter comes to guide me over into Glenmoriston and then Glengarry. That'll be more than time enough for me to speak to Janet.'

They waited almost in silence, until they could be sure the party of soldiers was far enough away but then, as they were making ready to leave the safety of the cairn, there came again the sound of hooves. These hooves however were softer, lighter than before, not a soldier's mount, and there was only one set of them. 'Black Peter?' whispered Iain.

Hector shook his head. 'Black Peter would hardly come on horseback.'

Iain moved to the gap at the entrance. The horse was moving more slowly than the soldiers' horses had, but it didn't stop, and only when it was a good bit past the cairn did horse and rider finally come into his line of vision.

Iain caught his breath and only just managed to stop himself from calling out.

'What is it?' breathed his father.

'It . . . there must be something wrong.'

'Who is it?'

But Iain already had his fingers round the edge of the sealing stone and had started to tug. 'We need to go after him. There's something wrong.'

TWENTY-FOUR

The Last Cockade

The old house was white against the darkness. It had suffered in the aftermath of the '45, and Janet had not had the means to put it right, nor the son to help her do it. Mairi Farquharson said she had not the will, either. Since she had lost Alasdair, Janet had seen nothing in the future and had increasingly taken refuge in the past.

Most of the trees Iain had known from his childhood visits were long gone, the army of occupation having taken almost everything for its never-ending building of roads and bridges and barracks. The hut Alasdair had had high up in an old elm, his sanctuary from his ever-fussing mother he'd said, had been cut down not long after its young master, who'd been taken and shot against a wall in the act of trying to get home to her after Culloden.

There were no lights showing in the house, which was strange. The household might have had time to settle after the visit of Captain Dunne and his men but would surely have wakened again at the arrival of its latest visitor.

'Where can he be?'

'Perhaps he didn't want to disturb them at this hour.'

They went to check the stable; the horse was there but not its rider.

They had gone next to the kennel block, empty now that all but one of Alasdair's beloved hunting dogs were gone, the last having been brought into the house to keep Janet company. All was silent. They were about to go around the back and check first with a servant, as some would surely have been awoken by the arrival, but Hector put a hand on Iain's arm.

'Wait,' he whispered.

'What is it?'

'The door.'

Iain looked across. On first sight the main entrance door, set into the small corner turret that linked the two wings of the house, had appeared to be shut, but now he saw that it was just a little ajar, as if someone had not wished to fully close it. No door had ever been locked at Corrimony, but they had always been shut at night.

Hector took his knife from its sheath. 'Come on.'

They approached the door in silence and, with great caution, Hector began to open it. Iain's heart thumped waiting for a creak but none came. His father was expert at moving around in silence and at night. Hector slipped into the house and Iain followed him.

They came first into the main hall, but nothing stirred, an elderly cat sleeping by the ashes of the fire merely opening an eye to watch them. There was no sound but their own breathing and the creaking of the old house.

The ashes were dead and all candles out, but while little of the moonlight made its way through the small windows of the lower floor, Iain remembered his way. Often, he and Alasdair had crept about the place in the dark, pursuing night-time adventures. He was about to lead his father through the little door and down the steps to the kitchen when they heard a low growl. They stopped. 'Bracken,' whispered Iain. Alasdair's dog.

The dog was not in the room with them though, the noise of the growl was faint and travelling down to them from above. 'This way.' Iain went as quickly as possible to the turret stairs. The growl became a snarl and then a bark, and they gave up any attempt at silence, Iain taking the stairs three at a time and shouting Janet's name.

They could hear cries of distress from the old lady and then a crash and a furious barking of the dog. Iain burst through the open door of the bedchamber, half-expecting to find the hound attacking its mistress, but his mind could make no sense of what he saw. Janet was sitting tight up against her pillows begging with the dog to stop. But the animal in its frenzy was at the throat of a man sprawled face-down on the floor, a dagger with a white cockade on its hilt in his hand. It was Aeneas.

Iain tried to call the dog off as Hector went to ensure Janet was not hurt, but it was only when the servants appeared and the housekeeper's young lad threw a hood over the beast's head that they managed to pull the animal off and force it out of the room.

Then they were alone: Iain, Hector, Janet and Aeneas. The old woman did not move from her bed, but continued to sit up, her shawl clutched in bony knuckles, staring at the man on the floor. 'Is he dead?' she managed to say at last.

Iain was on his knees beside Aeneas, a piece of torn bed-linen in his hand, desperately trying to staunch the bleeding from the older man's throat. Aeneas had him pinioned in his dark gaze, the lights not yet faded from the unrepentant eyes. He said something. Iain could not make it out and leaned in closer. The dying man made a supreme effort. 'For your grandfather,' he said. 'Finish it.' And then those black lights went out.

No one spoke. Time rolled back to the ticking of the clock on the wall. Decades passed before Iain's eyes. The dirk had fallen from Aeneas's hand, its white cockade spattered with his own blood. Janet Grant sat, her knees under their blankets bunched almost to her chin, the knot of her shawl clutched in her palms. She was watching Iain and she was terrified. Iain looked again to the fallen dirk and then to his father. Hector's face was filled with regret.

The realisation hit Iain. 'You knew,' he said.

Hector let out a deep sigh. 'Let us deal with the body first, and then I'll tell you.'

They sent the housekeeper's lad to Shewglie, and he was soon back with Archie Grant and two of his strongest men. They took the body of the dead man and tied it to his horse, then led it away. 'They'll take it over Strathglass into

Strathfarrar, then unbind him and let the animal loose. By the time anyone finds him, if anyone ever does, the eagles and ravens will have done their work. There'll be not much more than bones left of Aeneas Farquharson.'

At the last moment, before they tied the body to the horse, Hector remembered. He slipped his hand in underneath the breast of Aeneas's black coat and drew out the book.

Janet's cook and housemaid had got their distraught mistress into a different bedchamber and it took all of Hector's persuasive talents to prevent the cook from administering some soporific cordial to the old woman. There were things he needed to know that only she could tell him. He called instead for brandy then dismissed the servants. Hector waited for Janet to down her measure, and for her trembling to lessen. She was looking at them in terror, as if they were malignant strangers, rather than men she had known her whole life.

When he was certain the servants were back downstairs, Hector drew his chair closer to Janet's bed and said, 'Was it you who hired Davie Campbell to find *The Book of Forbidden Names*?'

Her eyes never leaving his, she nodded.

'How did you learn of it?'

She opened her mouth to try to speak but nothing came but a half-croak. She tried again. 'I had always known there was supposed to be such a book. I hoped it had died with the man who made it.'

'Lord Lovat?'

A slight nod, her eyes still fixed on theirs. 'I doubt he would have scrupled to use what he knew against me, if he'd thought there was some benefit to be had for himself. I thought I would not have to worry about it again, when he was executed.' She stared past them, old, old in her nightcap, and thin, her eyes reddened. 'But then came word that one of Lovat's old servants had died in Paris and spoken of the book.'

'Who told you of this?' asked Hector.

'Captain Dunne. The news had reached the garrison commander in Inverness, and he sent Dunne out to warn me.'

'But how . . .' began Iain.

Hector knew though. Lord Bury, regimental commander at Inverness, was the son of Lord Albemarle, King George's ambassador in Paris. 'Albemarle must have heard of it and told his son.'

Janet nodded, her mouth bitter. 'What pleasure he took in telling me of it.' She looked up. 'You remember, Iain? You came with your grandmother and found Dunne here that day? You had words and I thought you might come to blows.'

'I remember,' said Iain, regretting that he had not taken the chance there and then to deal with the captain as he deserved.

But Hector's interest was not in Captain Dunne. 'And Young Glengarry?'

Janet's voice was toneless. 'What about him?'

'Did he know, when he visited you here the last time he was in the Highlands, when Iain brought him – did he know your name was in the book?'

She looked down at her hands and whispered, 'Yes.'

Iain understood now why his father had insisted on seeing Janet.

Hector continued. 'What did he want of you when he came here? Did he speak of plots, risings?'

Janet nodded.

'Did he mention the name Elibank?'

Again, a nod.

'And what then? Why was he telling you this?'

She raised her head, her tired eyes looking straight at Hector. 'He wanted me to let him know if you ever appeared back here in the Highlands, looking for him. I was to send him a letter by means of Barbara Sinclair, the milliner.'

'And under what name was the letter to be addressed?'

Janet had little strength left. 'It was to be addressed to "Mr Pickle",' she murmured.

Black Peter was out in the yard, hopping from foot to foot, saying he wouldn't be responsible if they didn't get away before dawn, and that he for one would not be waiting for the redcoats to put him in a boat for Jamaica.

Hector had begged a half-hour more, and assured Peter he would fly like the wind and not tarry a moment thereafter. The fine German clock on the wall of Janet's house told them there was an hour yet till dawn. A half-hour more could be nothing to a man of Black Peter's hill craft.

The half-hour and not a minute more was conceded, and so, as Janet Grant slumbered in her bed, her cook finally having been allowed to administer the sleeping syrup, Iain and Hector sat below in the hall of her house, Aeneas's copy of *The Book of Forbidden Names* on the table between them. There was no doubt that it was the one so lately stolen from Iain's shop.

Iain laid a finger on the spine of the book, as if scared to find out what it contained. But he knew already, if not yet fully what it meant. 'It was Aeneas all along, then, exacting revenge upon the names, and Janet's name the last of them.'

Hector nodded.

'And that was why you dropped your copy in Loch Ness.'

Again, Hector nodded.

'When did you find out it was him?'

'I only knew for certain when I saw him sprawled upstairs on the floor with that hound on top of him, but I had suspected for a while. Ever since I discovered that Janet Grant's was the last remaining name in the book. The last of the black cockades.'

'You *found her name*?' said Iain, incredulous. 'But the last pages in our book were missing.'

'They were,' conceded Hector, 'but the coded markings spelling out Janet's name were not on the last pages, they came only a few pages after those giving the name of Evan Inkster, who was murdered in Charleston.'

'I don't understand.'

Hector picked up the book, flicking through to the end. 'The last pages of the book *we* had – the ones burned by Dunne at Castle Leod – must correspond to these pages here, which are simply the last pages of the book, without the coded markings that are on earlier pages. Perhaps Lord Lovat was leaving them free in case he uncovered the names of more traitors. I don't know. But there are six black cockades on the front inside board, and hers is the sixth name.'

'But how did you know, and why Janet? And why didn't you say anything? And Aeneas?'

Hector was choosing his words carefully. 'I only worked out Janet's name on the night of the assembly. I had some time to kill between changing into your Italian finery and leaving your grandmother's house to make my grand entrance at the Town House. I took another look at the book, and then I saw it – something my eye must have passed over before. The code markings were very faint but once I'd seen them, I'd seen them, and it didn't take me long to realise they spelled out the name of Janet Grant as the last of the six black cockades.'

Now Iain was following. 'You spoke to her that night, I remember it. When you came into the assembly room. You went over to my grandmother's table and you said something to Janet before you went on to dance with Elizabeth Rose.' He could see it all again in his mind's eye. The shock of seeing Hector there at all had outweighed any curiosity as to what his father might have said to Janet Grant.

'I told her to leave,' said Hector. 'I told her Aeneas knew, and that she should leave, straight away.'

Iain's mind raced. He had been so busy wondering what on earth Hector was thinking of, asking Elizabeth Rose to dance, that he hadn't noticed what Janet Grant had done after he'd spoken to her. But then, it hadn't been so long after that that all the commotion had started.

'But Janet's name – how can Janet's name be in the book?' Even as he said it though, Aeneas's last words came back into his mind. 'My grandfather,' he said at last. 'It was to do with my grandfather.'

Hector nodded. 'I'd wondered, once or twice, over the years, if it might have been Janet who betrayed him, but I couldn't say anything, because I knew there were people who thought it was me.'

So Iain heard once again a tale he'd thought he'd known his whole life, but this time it was as if it were being played on some far away stage, and he was watching the players from a different place than he had before.

'It was after the '15 rising, as you know. We'd all been together under Old Borlum at Preston – me with the MacGillivrays, your grandfather, your mother's brother Willie and Aeneas with the Farquharsons, and Colin Grant, Janet's husband, with the Grants of Glenmoriston. We'd been ordered south to bolster the English Jacobites. But that drunken coward Forster brought us to disgrace at Preston and forced the surrender. Your grandfather was hard put not to shoot him himself. Nonetheless, we made our escape, and might have won home, had we not stopped at Perth on the way and been betrayed by your "friend" Barbara Sinclair's father, after we had billeted at that damned inn of his. It was on his evidence that we were arrested and transported down to Tilbury fort for trial in London.'

'I know all this,' said Iain.

Hector put up a placatory hand. 'Patience though. Once they offloaded us in London, they put us into different prisons. I was sent to Newgate along with your grandfather, Aeneas, and Willie, who was little more than a boy. Others were sent to the Marshalsea, and some to the Tower, Colin Grant amongst them. It wasn't long before your grandmother and Janet arrived down in London along with many other Jacobite women. The day before those of us at Newgate were to be tried, we were permitted out for exercise in the prison yard, and our shackles removed. Our captors thought we were too starved and exhausted to give them any trouble, but they soon knew better.

'A good lot of us got away and went our separate ways to help evade our pursuers. Willie, Aeneas, your grandfather and I stayed together. Your grandmother had arranged a hideout for us to make for, and a boat to take us down to Gravesend where we were to get a sloop for France, but your grandfather utterly refused to go without Colin Grant. Again, your grandmother had a plan for getting Colin out of his prison. She had everything arranged, and the night we were to leave London, she sent Janet to Colin's prison to effect the escape.'

'And Colin did escape but my grandfather was recaptured.'

'Exactly that,' said Hector. 'We should have been away but had to delay because it took Mairi so long to persuade Janet to do what she had to do. To tell the truth, I thought the plan was madness – it's one thing to escape from Newgate, quite another from the Tower. The boatman we had settled with to take us to Gravesend tried to cheat us. When night came, he claimed to have agreed for six passengers, not seven. We hadn't a single shilling more to give him. I slipped away just as your grandmother arrived, so that there would be places enough for your grandparents, your uncle William, Aeneas, Janet and Colin Grant. It wasn't long after I left that soldiers arrived at the hiding place. They didn't get your uncle Willie,' Hector shook his head with a smile on his face, 'your grandfather pushed him into the river and told him to swim for it, but they got your grandparents and Aeneas. They contented themselves with jailing Aeneas. As you know, they executed your grandfather with their preferred barbarities, and it was only when he was dead that they let your grandmother go. Janet and Colin Grant, on the other hand, achieved the near impossible in getting out of the Tower. They somehow melted into the night and were not heard of again until they appeared in Paris, at King James's court at St Germain.'

Iain sat very still, his hand resting on the cover of the *Book of Forbidden Names*. 'They exchanged my grandfather's life for Colin's.'

Hector was uneasy. 'I doubt Colin Grant knew anything about it. He was an honourable man, as honourable and courageous as his boy Alasdair grew up to be. Janet – I don't think she could see past the child she was at last carrying, her fear that his father would never see him.'

There was turmoil going through Iain; grief for the grandfather he had never met, for the grandmother who had been too young and too long a widow, for the unborn child who had grown up to be his friend and whose mother had betrayed them all. There was grief, too, for Aeneas, the devoted old steward whom he had always thought an adversary. At last he managed to speak.

'And did no one suspect her?'

Hector shook his head. 'They were all too busy suspecting me, who'd slipped away just before the soldiers came to our hiding place.'

'Did they accuse you?'

Hector shrugged. 'There were – exchanges – in the early years. But I had found favour in the king's service, and of course, there was you. While your mother had no intention of staying very long with me after she had delivered herself of you, she always defended me to your grandmother. Your grandmother would have done almost anything to get you into her care and brought up in the Highlands. I think, perhaps, that Aeneas believed for a long time that it was me who betrayed your grandfather. But you must believe me, Iain: I loved Neil Farquharson as if he had been my own father.' He looked away at the cold hearth, vacated now by the cat. 'You know, when I first began to suspect that it was Aeneas who had stolen the book from your shop, I was glad, because he would finally know for certain that I was not the one who had betrayed his master.'

Iain realised then what a burden his father must have carried all these years, what had truly been at the root of Aeneas's dislike of his father, and of himself, and why it was that the old steward had finally seemed to unbend a little. 'What made you suspect him?'

Hector swirled the last of his brandy round in his glass. 'It's not so difficult really. There were only two keys to your shop. One of them went to Perth and back in the pocket of Richard Dempster. Now, I don't doubt Richard's courage, and I'll never forget that I owe him my freedom from the pit, but whatever that boy might have done when he marched with his brothers in our army, he's no killer now. Even supposing him the most murderous creature in Christendom though, he couldn't have been cutting Davie Campbell's throat in your shop when he was not halfway back to Inverness from Perth.'

Hector looked to see if Iain was following him, then continued. 'That left your own key.'

'The one that I lost when you were hurled out of Bessie Stewart's tavern and fell into me.'

'I don't think that's when you lost it, Iain. Think. What exactly happened after you fell?'

Iain cast his mind back to the night all of this had begun,

the night Davie Campbell had been murdered in his shop. It might have been a time from someone else's life. 'I recall dropping my coat as I threw my arms out to break my fall. A button came off it and rolled away. The confectioner, Ishbel MacLeod, was there, and her child. She picked up my coat and gave it to me.' He looked up at his father. 'It was the child who found the button – I got it from him a few days later.'

'Never mind a few days later,' said Hector. 'What happened then, that night?'

Iain shrugged. 'I went home. Wait, no. I met in by chance with Barbara Sinclair. She took hold of the jacket and tried to brush it down for me, before I got to the house. The Grandes Dames were there, and I was to play for them. She didn't make much of a job of cleaning the coat. Aeneas made me change it, because of the condition it was in after my fall. He insisted I give it to Eppy for a proper brushing and mending there and then.'

'And did you give it directly to Eppy?'

'Yes, of course,' said Iain. But then he saw again the jacket as he'd wrestled it off in his grandmother's kitchen, Aeneas standing between him and the harassed housemaid who was clutching a good green velvet jacket for him to put on instead. Aeneas with his hand out to take the dirty jacket and pass it to the girl. 'No,' he said at last, leaning forward in his eagerness. 'No. I handed it first to Aeneas.'

'And before Aeneas passed it to the girl, he must have slipped his hand into the pocket and taken out the key.'

It had all been so simple. Iain couldn't understand how it was that he hadn't seen it. 'He came into the shop,' he said, remembering now. 'When Davie Campbell was in there, to remind me that I was to be home in good time to play for the Grandes Dames. He must have spotted him up in the gallery and recognised him.'

'Well,' said Hector, 'he'll have known that whatever Campbell was up to it was no good. He probably went looking for him to find out what it was.'

Iain nodded slowly. 'There were parts of the evening when Aeneas wasn't around. It was a little strange at the time, for he rarely left my grandmother's side when there was company in the house.' He gave a small half-laugh. 'I remember, Eilidh Cameron was almost constrained to pour her own drink. He must have gone looking for him.'

'He must have found him,' said Hector. 'And then when he discovered why Campbell was in Inverness decided to take matters into his own hands. He always had a sharp mind for the mathematics, Aeneas. He would have deciphered the book more quickly than I did.'

'And started on the killings,' said Iain, who could still hardly believe it of the old man. Though not so old, really. Only a few years older than his father and fit enough to do what he had done. Often, over the past days and weeks, Iain had been away or too preoccupied with his father's business to notice whether Aeneas was around the house or not. Little wonder the man had begun to look tired.

Time was getting on. Black Peter would soon be at the

door, demanding Hector come away if he was to have any hope of getting off safely. But Hector was making no move yet to get up. He spoke now with a degree of hesitation. 'There's no easy way to say this, Iain, but I think you would come to realise it yourself anyway – Aeneas could not have done what he did without your grandmother's knowledge, and he would certainly never have dared do it without her approval.'

'You're saying she's responsible for the murder of these people? Her own brother, even? And that she would countenance the murder of her oldest friend . . .'

Hector continued to look at him levelly. 'I would say she must certainly have known of the substance, if not the detail, the actual names. Perhaps she would just have trusted that to Aeneas, like she did everything else. Her grief for her brother was real enough, until Dod Fraser confirmed how he died, and then she didn't question that he had been a traitor.'

As the sense of what Hector was saying began to sink in, Black Peter came in the door, behind him the fiddler, who was to guide Iain down Strathglass and into the Aird. It was time.

Hector stood up. 'I must go now, Iain. I don't know when I will see you again. Soon, God willing, and in better days.'

Iain felt a sense of panic. He wasn't ready. He had never been ready, any of the times they'd had to part.

All he knew, each time, was that he might never see his father again.

'Forgive your grandmother, Iain. She has been in mourning your whole life.' And then he was gone.

TWENTY-FIVE

Tormod Delivers a Message

Two Months Later: October 1752

It was a grey, dreich day, chill, even for October. 'You'll not be sorry to leave our cold northern climate,' said Iain.

Thornlie smiled. 'I doubt you would believe me if I told you how much I had dreaded leaving.'

'Not now, though,' said Iain. Over in the library corner, Julia Rose was deep in conversation with young Tormod MacLeod about the voyage she was about to undertake.

'Do you think she will like it?' said Thornlie. 'Do you think she'll be happy?'

Iain raised an eyebrow. 'You're asking me about women?' Then he smiled. 'Well, I think your wife has looked happier this past while than I ever saw her before. She'll be a great ornament to Greenwich.' He wondered what he himself could offer any woman – nothing but this shop and a house full of secrets.

The major was turning over in his hands the volumes of the journal he had kept throughout his five years with the Military Survey in the Highlands. Donald Mòr had bound the notebooks for him. The tooling was perfect, the image of a theodolite intricately worked into the wheel binding, all on blue morocco over Russian leather lining. The endpapers were gilt-embossed, with the most delicate pattern of native wildflowers. Thornlie was transfixed. 'I have never seen anything like it,' he said.

'Nor I,' said Iain. 'It's the finest work he ever did.'

'I must go and thank him, but first, I will pay you.'

Iain closed his account book and moved it out of the way. 'There's no charge.'

Thornlie frowned, the brow above his eyepatch furrowed. 'How can that be? I know I haven't paid for it. Has Julia . . . .?'

'She hasn't paid for it either and if either of you were to try, there is no one in this shop who would take your money.'

'I don't understand.'

Iain drew a deep breath. 'I saw you. On the battlefield, after the fighting was over . . .'

There was silence for a moment. Thornlie did not move. 'Culloden,' he said eventually. They had never spoken of it.

Iain wetted his lips. 'It was sometime late on in the day – I don't know really. I was injured and lying with my cousin amongst the dead.' His voice became flat. 'I was pretending to be dead myself, but I saw you.'

Thornlie waited.

'You were with Cumberland,' Iain went on.

All the lightness had gone from the major's face.

Iain carried on. 'Your party came upon a young clansman lying injured – Young Inverallochy. He was a gentleman. He was badly injured, but not like to die. Cumberland ordered you to shoot him. You refused.'

Thornlie's face was like a stone. 'They shot him anyway,' he said.

'I know it. It was a common soldier he got to do it. But *you* had refused. You stood up to that butcher, son of a king or not, for decency, and for humanity, and you have been honoured amongst us for it ever since. No one here will take your money, Major Thornlie.'

As Donald returned to his bindery after bidding the Thornlies a long and perplexing farewell, in which admonitions in Gaelic had been mixed with attempted English politenesses, he murmured, 'Well, Morag, let us hope he does not regret it.' Donald's distrust of even the best of women was not to be easily overcome. He had very much approved the information that Iain would be having nothing more to do with Barbara Sinclair.

Iain knew he had let himself be taken for a fool, even before Janet Grant's revelation that it had been through the milliner that she had communicated to Young Glengarry the news that Hector was back in the Highlands and looking for him. Janet's avoidance of Barbara and her shop became more understandable now. She had betrayed her friends to secure her husband's life, but in agreeing that bargain she had delivered herself into her enemies' hands for ever, and she could hardly bear it.

Not long after the departure of the Thornlies, Donald appeared through from the bindery, dressed in his travelling clothes. He had in recent days completed a commission for the Countess of Sutherland, and such was his particularity that he would entrust the delivery of the books to no one but himself. Iain knew it was more likely that Donald wanted a good look at the library at Dunrobin, and that his return journey from the castle would take him past many of his favourite and most infamous watering holes. It was understood that Donald should not be expected back from Sutherland for several days.

Donald gone and the bindery locked up, Iain was nevertheless in no hurry to shut up the shop and go home. He could never have imagined that he would miss Aeneas's dark presence around the house, but he found himself always expecting to see the steward as he rounded a corner or entered the kitchen, always momentarily startled, wondering at the space at his grandmother's shoulder. Mairi Farquharson was braving the loss as well as she could, but he could see how hard his death had hit her. She had lost, too, a lifelong friend in Janet, whom word from Corrimony told them was failing by the day. Mairi had no sympathy for her, though, and would not allow that Catriona Lamont or Eilidh Cameron should either. The Grandes Dames could never again be what they had been, but still those who were left gathered and made their toasts – and hoped.

The authorities had made little progress in the matters of the deaths of Davie Campbell in Iain's shop, Kenneth Farquharson at Dochfour, Hugh Sinclair the milliner's father, or Evan Inkster across the firth at Charleston. They had not even gone so far as to make a connection between them, other than that there would always be tinkers, travellers and strangers to be blamed. In the case of Barbara Sinclair's father, the laundrywomen who watched over the drying green across the river had seen no one suspicious near Bisset Close on the morning of his death, only respectable burgesses going about their business, like Mairi Farquharson's steward, Aeneas.

Mairi, it transpired, had known what her kinsman had been about from the time Aeneas had recognised Davie Campbell in Iain's bookshop. She it was who had ordered him to find out what Davie was doing in Inverness, and then to find the *Book of Forbidden Names*. The only point on which Aeneas had demurred was that she should know the names he found in the book. 'He would not tell me until afterwards, after he had exacted justice upon them. He said I could not be punished for what I had no fore-knowledge of. The worst though, was when he found my brother Kenny's name. Aeneas told me that when Dod Fraser came later to tell us of Kenny's murder, he still feared that he might have made a terrible mistake. But then Hector managed to drag the truth out of Dod, about what had happened at the time of Glen Shiel.' So she hadn't known of the treachery of her own brother, or of her best friend, until after Aeneas had attempted his retribution. He had been determined that, even in death, he would protect her.

They had spoken of it only on the night of Iain's return from Corrimony with the grim news of Aeneas's death. Since then, night after night, their conversation turned to wondering about Hector, and the progress of Elibank's plot. There had been no word from Iain's father, other than that Black Peter had seen him safe over into Glengarry. There was nothing they could do but wait.

This afternoon though, after the departure of Donald Mòr, the shop was very quiet, which was just as well, as Richard Dempster had come down the stairs ill that morning and spent much of the day shivering and swathed in blankets in a chair by the stove. Iain was on the point of persuading him to return to his bed when the street door suddenly burst open and Tormod came running in, almost bursting with news of some sort.

'What is it, Tormod?' asked Richard, raising himself a little from his cocoon.

The boy was beside himself with importance. 'It's a message, for Iain Bàn. A man told me on the street and gave me a penny to bring it to him.'

Iain leaned over from behind his desk and held out his hand in expectation of a note. 'What man?'

'You're not getting my penny!' said Tormod, clamping shut his fist.

'I'm not wanting your penny, but you must give me the

note,' said Iain, summoning all his patience. The child was far too much in Donald Mòr's company.

Regarding him with deep suspicion, Tormod said, 'There's no note. I've just to tell you.'

'Who was this man?' asked Richard.

'I don't know. A dirty-looking wee man.'

'Hmm, a dirty-looking wee man with a penny,' said Iain. 'Well, you better give me his message then.'

Tormod nodded. 'The man said he was passing on a message from a friend, that,' here he took a deep breath, concentrating, '"A man seeking Pickle is waiting for you at Clava Cairns."'

'What?' said Iain.

Tormod began to repeat his message, but Iain didn't stay to hear it. He picked up his coat. 'I need to go out, Richard. You'll have to shut the shop tonight.'

'But what does it mean?' called Richard, his voice feeble. His question was lost in the sound of the banging door as Iain disappeared out onto the street.

Ishbel had just been up to the garrison with the confections that had been ordered for the dinner in Major Thornlie's honour before he and his young wife took ship for Green-wich. The Military Survey had finished its work here and the major was to take up a new appointment at the Royal Military Academy at Woolwich, where he was to have charge of the training and instruction of future engineers. Ishbel could scarcely envisage the world her friend – for

Julia had become a friend – was going to, but it was a good marriage, and the major a good man. She had no wish to be elsewhere herself. She was paying little attention to her surroundings as she made her way back to Bow Court, but a sudden chill wind coming up the old school vennel caused her to snap out of her reverie, and she almost cried out at what she saw. Barbara Sinclair was standing in the street about twenty yards up on the other side from Iain's bookshop. She was talking to a man, a small, dirty-looking man that held a scrawny nag by its halter. They were both looking down towards the door of the shop. Then Tormod came out of the door. Barbara motioned with her hand towards him and handed the man what looked like a purse of coins. The man nodded and the milliner walked away.

Ishbel was for a moment frozen with horror, but then she started to run. She ran faster than she had ever run in her life before, faster even than that day on the shore at Glenelg, trying to run away from the men off the boats who'd come to spirit them off the beach onto their ships and across the ocean. Her shawl fell from her shoulders, her lungs burned fit to tear open her chest, but still she ran. She hardly noticed anyone as she sped past, not even Iain Bàn who was striding up the street in the other direction. All she could see was Tormod, and the man who'd been watching him.

But before Ishbel reached her son, the dirty-looking man had mounted his poor horse and begun to ride up the street. Ishbel didn't slow her pace. Tormod had crossed the road and was turning into Bow Court when she at last lunged at him, calling his name and almost knocking them both over.

'Mother!' he cried out, startled and afraid at her behaviour.

She clung to him so tightly he began to squirm in protest. Gradually, she loosened her hold on him, to swamp him instead with kisses. He wiped his sleeve across his cheek in disgust.

'Oh, Tormod,' she said.

'What is it, Mammy?'

'I was scared. So scared.'

He screwed up his face. 'What were you scared of? It's not even dark.'

'It was that man.'

'What man?'

'The man who was with the milliner.' She took him by the shoulders and turned him around to look up the street. She pointed to the man who'd been watching the bookshop door as he'd come out of it.

'That fellow on the horse?' said Tormod. 'Why would you be scared of him?'

'I thought he might try to take you away.'

Tormod looked a little hesitant for a moment, and she saw that his small fist was clenched tight, but then he smiled. 'Don't be silly, Mother.'

She hugged him to her again and they went up the forestairs into their home under the rafters.

It was only as she was setting out their supper a little later that Ishbel noticed Tormod's fist was still clenched. She put down the dish of butter and crossed over to him. 'What have you in your hand?'

'Nothing,' he said, clenching it all the tighter.

'Show me,' she said.

His eyes became huge and his mouth turned down as he uncurled his fingers to reveal a worn penny.

Ishbel thought again of the time he had kept the book-seller's button. 'Where did you get it, Tormod? You did not take it from somewhere?'

'No, I did not! The man gave it to me.' Instantly, he bit his lip and looked down, but it was too late.

'What man?'

'The man on the horse,' he mumbled, refusing to look at her.

'The man . . .' She was on her knees in front of him now, gripping him by the shoulders. 'You told me that man didn't speak to you!'

'No, I didn't,' he shouted in frustration. 'You didn't even ask me that, you just said you thought he had tried to take me away but he didn't. He was a nice man and he gave me a penny.'

Ishbel could hardly get the sound past her throat. 'Why? Why did he give you a penny? What was it for?'

His bottom lip was out and the tears were coming now. 'To take a message to Iain Bàn.'

'What message?' she asked. 'What was it?'

'I don't know, Mammy,' and he dissolved into huge sobs. 'It was just nonsense – about looking for pickle at Clava Cairns. But I told Iain Bàn anyway and he let me keep my penny.'

Without further thought of supper, Ishbel scooped the boy up and ran down the stairs and across the street to start hammering on the door of the bookshop. It was a good while before Richard Dempster, hunched in on himself and gripping a blanket to his shoulders, answered.

'Ishbel, what's wrong?'

'Where's Iain Bàn?' she said, looking past him into the darkened shop.

'He left an hour ago, after Tormod brought him the message.'

'Donald Mòr, then – where is Donald?'

Richard leaned into the door, his face contorted with effort. 'He set off two hours since for Dunrobin. Whatever's the matter?'

Tormod let go his mother's skirt and tugged at Richard's blanket. 'It's the message I gave to Iain Bàn. She said it was from a bad man, and now she is very frightened. But I did not know he was a bad man!'

Ishbel moved her son aside and followed Richard into the shop, where he slumped down onto a stool.

'Can you remember exactly what this message was? What Tormod says makes no sense,' she asked.

'I don't know.' Richard's head was in his hands. 'Something about Clava Cairns, Iain was in too much of a rush to tell me any more. Who is this man that gave Tormod the message?'

'Gavin Bremner,' said Ishbel.

'Gavin Bremner?' echoed Richard. The name meant nothing to him.

Ishbel nodded, shaking. 'He is a wicked man who would betray his own mother for a shilling. He was one of MacLeod's men, who took us off the beaches to the transportation ships when MacLeod sold us into servitude. Me and my brother he lifted, as we were gathering kelp.' Her mouth was twisted. 'I will never forget his face. I have watched for him every day since I came back to Inverness. I had heard tell that he was keeping the door at Castle Leod now, taking the Hanoverian coin. Whatever he wants with Iain Bàn, it cannot be good.'

Richard stood up. 'I must get to Clava Cairns.' He swayed and put out a hand to steady himself, knocking papers off Iain's desk. 'I must get Iain's grandmother's horse.' He took a step forwards before collapsing to the floor in front of her.

Iain was on foot. A horse at Clava Cairns would draw attention that his father did not need. There would be too many people keen to know his business as he went up past the King's Mills and out towards the moor. It was over four years since he had returned from Virginia and made his way from Liverpool to Glasgow and then home, and only once in all that time had he set foot on Drummossie Moor. He had gone alone to the Well of the Dead where so many of their clan had fallen and he had sat there for hours, until long after darkness had fallen, wishing the ground would just take him as it had so many others at Culloden.

But the ground hadn't taken him. Wouldn't. Iain had a life to live while those others had not. He had often thought in those years that the life he had lived had done little to merit itself, but if Hector was back, now, it surely meant Elibank's rising was to go ahead. Perhaps something worthy might yet be done after all for all those who had lost their lives in the Stuart cause.

By the time he reached the edge of the moor, the light had begun to fade. The dull sky of the afternoon was now obscured by low cloud and drizzle. The dun brown of the spent heather and the pools of water amongst the peat bogs were turning to grey and black. A wind was whipping up from the firth below and the mountains to the south were disappearing beneath the mist. And as Iain stepped out onto the moor, he saw them everywhere – the ghosts. He felt them, passing in the whispers of the wind. He steeled himself but still, to his left and to his right, and up ahead of him they marched, starving, exhausted, but not yet broken. He might have put his hand out to touch their shades, but they did not look at him and they did not acknowledge him. He closed his eyes, as if that might somehow still the sound of the battle that played out eternally on the moor and in his head. The pipes, never-ending, never quite fading away as they led the generations to oblivion in the face of the oncoming drums. A moor bird cried and he shivered, coming back to himself. It would be dark soon. He turned his eyes from the ghosts and recommenced walking, leaving their silences behind him.

Across the moor, he went by cottages and byres down the steep decline towards the river Nairn. God, if they had known, he and Lachlan, when Strathnairn had been their playground, what atrocities one day awaited them there. They had gone sometimes to the cairns and scared themselves half witless, playing with the boys from the manse and listening to the stories of the minister's son, of terrible things that must have happened at Clava Cairns, long before memory or man could lift a pen to record them. But those boys were all gone now and Iain was here alone.

Hurried though his pace from the shop had been, he felt himself slow as he approached the cairns. He couldn't see them yet, through the mirk, but he sensed them. The three cairns were huge, almost perfectly circular stone and rubble structures, much larger than that he and Hector had hidden in at Corrimony, and each was guarded by its ring of sentinel stones. They had thrilled all those years ago to tales of burials of long-dead warriors, tragic princesses and dark murmurings of druids and human sacrifice at Clava. Whatever the truth of any of it, Iain was in no doubt as he approached them through the dusk that he was entering upon sacred ground, the realm of the dead.

Somewhere, across the strath, a cow lowed and from some lonely tree an owl hooted in response. Iain began to wonder if he should have come alone, but then chided himself for his foolishness. He approached the first of the cairns and then stopped within about twelve feet of it. Hector might be concealing himself anywhere. He put his hands to his mouth and gave out the moorhen call. For a moment there was complete silence, and then the call was returned. Perfectly.

Iain's heart was thumping, its beat loud as drums in his ears. Whoever had returned his call of the moorhen could not be his father, for Hector had never once got it right. He looked about him but could not discern any human form amongst the grey mounds of the burial chambers and the standing stones, some a good deal taller than he was himself. He gave the call again. Nothing. He cast about for some stick he might improvise as a weapon. There was nothing but scattered twigs and pebbles. He scooped up a handful of the stones for want of anything better. His childhood aim had not been bad.

Now he heard a movement and a low sound of laughter. 'Much good may those do you, Iain Bàn MacGillivray.'

He didn't know the voice, but when he peered in the direction it had come from, he saw the outline of a man sitting atop the nearest cairn. Whoever it was, it certainly wasn't his father. Iain narrowed his eyes, trying to see the man better through the dusk. And then there was a familiarity. It took him a moment, but then he had it – it was the surly doorkeeper from Castle Leod, that both himself and Donald Mòr had thought they knew from

somewhere. But there was something else about the man
sitting atop the cairn with an arm extended and his pistol
trained at Iain's head. He knew this man from something
further back than his visit to Castle Leod. A face, a glance
of a face, a pistol pointing and then being retracted. Iain
was back on the moor, lying with Lachlan, playing dead,
when a party led by the loathed Henry Hawley, Cumberland's lieutenant general, hove into view. A stricken
Highlander was prodded with a bayonet and cried out.
One of Hawley's men was going to shoot him when the
lieutenant general had looked at the man and drawled,
'Not that one,' and the stricken Highlander, thus spared,
scuttled away like a rat.

'You,' said Iain. Gavin Bremner, the doorkeeper from
Castle Leod.

'Me indeed,' the fellow answered. 'I am a message for
you, from Barbara Sinclair, a debt she owes you for the
death of her father.' From somewhere near the small settlement up the brae a horse whinnied and a dog barked.
Their warning was too late for Iain. But he didn't care.
He didn't care what Barbara Sinclair might mean by this
either. His mind was elsewhere, a mile or two up on the
moor, over six years ago.

'Hawley let you go, after Culloden. I remember it.
Hawley let you go.' It hadn't been an act of mercy, like
that of Philip Thornlie towards Young Inverallochy. It had
been something else. Iain recalled Hawley's smile, the sneer
in the voice – return for a bargain struck. 'Why did he

let you go? What did you do?' And then he remembered. Donald Mòr had said it as they'd snuck away from Castle Leod. "That shiftless fellow from the Nairn march . . ." And Iain saw that it was. On the night before the battle of Culloden, it had been this man, this same doorkeeper, who was supposed to be guiding the prince's column that got lost in woods and bogs long before it could ever join up with Lord George Murray's.

'You were in Hawley's pay all along. If it hadn't been for you, it might all have been a different story.' The hurt and the rage came storming through Iain. He hardly cared what he did any more. He started to run towards the cairn.

Gavin Bremner lifted his gun. 'Too late, Mr Bookseller. Your story's done.' He cocked his pistol and the hammer drew back, there was a creak, a flash and a noise of gunpowder ignited. Iain was braced for the bullet, but instead he saw Bremner's arm swing as the gun went off. Behind him, a voice cried out.

Iain hurled himself round. She was a spectre, so pale, so insubstantial, collapsed to the ground. One hand was held to the spreading stain at her left shoulder and fallen from the other was Donald Mòr's pistol. There was no time to think. Gavin Bremner had leaped from the cairn, a dirk in his outstretched hand. Iain dived in front of Ishbel, picking up the pistol as he did so. Bremner was above them, the glint of his blade momentary. The flash from Donald's pistol briefly obscured all, then Gavin Bremner was on the ground, staring Iain in the face, a bullet hole in the centre of his forehead.

Iain dropped the pistol onto the heather. 'And may Hell mend you,' he said.

Epilogue

Iain had torn strips from Ishbel's own apron to bind the wound at her shoulder, then he had dragged Bremner's body into the chamber of the nearest cairn and left it there, to be found, or not, as the gods decreed. Ishbel had been fading in and out of consciousness as he'd got her up onto the horse and held her to him by the waist as he urged the horse on as quickly as could safely be managed on the road back to Inverness. She had been lifted, insensible, from the horse by Catriona Lamont's servant, before Iain had slid from the saddle, to almost collapse at his grandmother's feet.

Time and again in his dreams Iain had gone through the moment of that flash, that noise and thinking that it was over and knowing suddenly that he did not want it to be over. When he awoke his first realisation was that he had escaped only thanks to the ghostly young woman who had for the last few months been more and more present in his world; his second that his father had not come back after all. No word had come in those two short days from Bailie John Steuart or any of the other conduits of information from the continent as to whether Hector had got safe back to France, or whether Elibank's rising was still in preparation. There was nothing to be done, his grandmother said, but be in readiness, and go on with their lives as before.

But their lives were not as they had been before. Aeneas was gone. For all that he felt his absence, Iain more and more walked his own house free of his shadow. The bookshop was not quite what it had been, for Tormod was less often there, a great point of contention between Donald Mòr and Iain's grandmother, who was beyond entranced with the child. 'Who else,' she would say, as she paraded him before the Grandes Dames, 'who else would have known to find Donald Mòr's pistol? Who else would have thought of making his mother take it? My husband's line would be dead, ended, were it not for this child. Great things he will do one day. Great things.'

And Ishbel. In those first days, Mairi had scarcely left her side. The best physicians were brought, the most trusted of apothecaries consulted, the most efficacious remedies applied to the wound. Ishbel recovered, only to refuse, with a force that surprised everyone, Mairi's suggestion that she and the boy should move permanently into her house on Church Street. Mairi had protested that the little place on Bow Court was not suitable for a child of such promise, and Ishbel had protested that she would never again be a servant in anyone's house, no matter how humble her own. Iain was back and forth between the two houses often, escorting the boy from one place to another, taking small gifts to Ishbel from Mairi, good new gowns that his grandmother claimed to have had made for herself and would not fit, cuts of the best meat that she said would go off for it would never all get eaten in the Farquharson house. Shoes and a new coat, that Tormod might go respectable to school.

In return, Iain would travel the other way with pots of jam and dishes of sugared fruits and nuts, and soon Ishbel was following him, because she wasn't certain that Flossie and Eppy were looking after the old lady quite right.

December came. One dark night close to the beginning of that month, the bailie arrived in the kitchen of the house on Church Street to inform Iain and Mairi that word had come of the postponement of Elibank's plot. They would try again in the spring.

A letter came from Julia Thornlie in Greenwich, that Ishbel took to the bookshop, so that Richard and Iain and Donald Mòr could hear the news of the major and of London. In fact, Ishbel was almost as often in the bookshop now as Tormod was himself. She fitted in, somehow, as she moved about the place, from bindery, to library, to the chair by his own near the stove. And each day Iain felt more hopeless, more desperate, surrounded as he was by words, page upon page, book upon book, of words, when the words he needed eluded him completely. One evening, as Tormod was in the bindery practising his letters with Donald, and Richard was cataloguing new books for the circulating library, Ishbel was going about the shelves, dusting where books had been taken out, replacing volumes that had got disordered. Iain had been sitting at his desk, attempting to tally his takings and calculate his expenses, but at last with a curse of frustration he put down his pen and got up from his chair. Richard looked up from his work and swiftly looked down again.

Iain went to the end of the shelf Ishbel had been working on and cleared his throat. She looked round. 'Is something the matter?'

'No,' he said, irate, 'there is nothing the matter.'

She carried on with her work and he cleared his throat again.

'What is it?' she said. 'Are you needing a syrup for that?'

He frowned in annoyance. 'Syrup? No.' He pushed his hair off his face, his hand passing over the scar, and she began to turn away again.

'Good God, woman! Will you put down that book? This is intolerable!'

'Intolerable?' She stood there, book in hand. 'What in the world is intolerable to you now?'

He flung up his hands. 'This! Everything! You have walked into my life and wander about it as if it were a thing of no greater interest to you than the price of sugar or Donald Mòr's cat.'

'Although I did save your life,' she said, affecting only to look at the book.

'Exactly! And so I was just thinking. About Tormod, and my grandmother, and you and the house. And well, I am thirty-six years of age and have nothing but this.' He waved his hand around the shop. 'But surely, well, it would just be easier, do you not think?'

'What would be easier?'

'Everything,' he said, taking a step closer to her, the frustration going out of him at last. He lifted his fingers to touch her face and kept them there a moment. 'Everything would be easier. If we were married, don't you think?'

All around them, the life of the shop seemed to stop. Richard held his pen suspended over his catalogue. From the bindery came only silence. By the stove, Morag regarded them with a critical eye. Slowly, Ishbel put down the book she was holding.

'*Easier.*' She pursed her lips as if in displeasure but then relented, smiling as she lifted her hand to push back the swathe of hair that had fallen again over his face. She traced her own fingers gently down the scarred cheek to rest within a breath of his lips. 'Yes,' she said at last as he closed his eyes, 'it would definitely be easier.'

Author's Note

Today, anyone who knows Inverness and loves books will know that at the very bottom of Church Street, on the site of the old Gaelic church, is a vast second-hand bookshop. It was over ten years ago, in the then coffee-shop in the gallery of Leakey's, as I read of the Jacobite soldiers imprisoned in the Gaelic church before being shot outside in the graveyard of the Old High Kirk, that I first got the germ of an idea for what would become *The Bookseller of Inverness*. The earliest definite notice I can find of a bookseller in Inverness is of William Shap in 1762 (William Simpson, *Old Inverness Booksellers*, 1931, p.3), but print culture in eighteenth-century Scotland, as exemplified by the career of Allan Ramsay, publisher father of the artist of the same name, and founder in 1725 of one of the first circulating libraries, was vibrant. My own fictional bookshop is to be imagined a little way up from Leakey's, and in a smaller building.

The events portrayed in this book are set in the wake of the fundamental event of Highland history – the battle of Culloden that brought to an end the last great Jacobite rising. The bibliography of the Jacobites and of that particular battle is huge, constantly growing, and diverse in intent. For instance, of recently published histories, Desmond Seward's *The King Over the Water* is a fascinating read with a decided Jacobite slant, Jacqueline Riding's *Jacobites* is an excellent and even-handed account of the lead-up to and history of the '45 rising, and Trevor Royle's *Culloden: Scotland's Last Battle and the Forging of the British Empire* is rather mistitled, having decidedly more to say of the latter than it does of Culloden or Scotland. Paul O'Keeffe's *Culloden, Battle & Aftermath* will prove a more satisfying read for those interested in how events of the rising affected those on the ground and were reported further afield, and in general looks at well- and lesser-known issues from a very fresh perspective.

A figure hovering in the shadows of my story without actually making an appearance, principally because he was executed in 1747 at the age of seventy-seven, is that of the Old Fox – Simon Fraser, 11th Lord Lovat. If the Old Fox's life had been a work of fiction, it would scarcely be believed, but the actual story of his life and of his world has been told in Sarah Fraser's immensely readable biography, *The Last Highlander.* It was my starting point in reading for this book, and I found its portrayal of the world of the Jacobites in exile and of the complex loyalties of Highland society at the time, invaluable.

Anyone wishing to understand more about the clan

system and the fundamentals of Highland geography would be advised to begin with Bruce Lenman's *The Jacobite Clans of the Great Glen*. The complex loyalties of the Highland clans in each Jacobite rising are laid out very clearly in Allan I. MacInnes's *Clanship, Commerce and the House of Stuart 1603–1788*. Professor MacInnes it is who, with characteristic verve, branded the Lowland Scottish redcoat officers Captain Caroline Frederick Scott and Major William Lockhart, 'psychotic'.

As to Inverness itself, James Miller's *Inverness, a History*, Leonella Longmore's *Inverness in the 18th Century*, and Norman S. Newton's *Lost Inverness*, have been invaluable in helping me build up a picture of the town in the period. Carolyn Anderson and Christopher Fleet's *Scotland, Defending the Nation: Mapping the Military Landscape* is a beautifully illustrated and indispensable resource for anyone wishing to grasp the almost incredible engineering achievements of the British military in the Highlands in the eighteenth century, or indeed the origins of the Ordnance Survey. A first-hand account of the early stages of that work, and of life in Inverness in the 1730s, can be read in the fascinating *Letters from the North of Scotland* of Captain Edmund Burt, whose experience informed that of my character Major Philip Thornlie.

The roads, the bridges, the fortresses – they can be seen as the history of the victors written in stone, but it is not always true that history is written by the winners, and in the history of the '45 in particular, this is not the case. The greatest resource for anyone wishing to understand the Jacobite experience in the '45 rising and its aftermath must be *The Lyon in Mourning*, the astonishing, one thousand page, three volume life's work of Bishop Robert Forbes. Relentlessly, indefatigably, remorselessly, Bishop Forbes sought out and interrogated those who, like himself, had first-hand experience of the rising and what followed, and he wrote down their testimony. Not only did he write down their testimony, he sought corroboration from others and the same stories appear time and again, from different witnesses and perspectives, throughout the pages of his monumental work as he seeks to make as accurate a record of events as he can. An avowedly Jacobite work, *the* avowedly Jacobite work, *The Lyon in Mourning* relates in grim detail the many accounts of atrocities perpetrated by Cumberland's forces in the aftermath of Culloden, but nevertheless takes pains to tell tales of courage, honour and decency on the part of the Hanoverian government soldiers and supporters who showed them. The experiences Iain recalls in this book and the atrocities his family and neighbours underwent are all to be found in the pages of Bishop Forbes's monumental work, but so too are acts of mercy such as that attributed in my book to Major Thornlie, which is adapted from the true tale of the two anonymous officers who refused Cumberland's order to shoot the injured Young Inverallochy on the field after Culloden, the job eventually being done by a common soldier. It was a lucky (if expensive), day for me when I found Henry Paton's three-volume Scottish Academic Press edition of *The Lyon in Mourning* on the shelves of Leakey's while I was looking for something else.

Another key document for anyone seeking to understand the Highlands in the eighteenth century is *The Letter-Book of Bailie John Steuart of Inverness, 1715–1752*. The *Letter-Book* is available in a 1915 printed edition by the Scottish History Society, but due to the idiosyncrasies of research life in the pandemic of 2020, while I was unable to access the printed edition in the reference section of Inverness public library, I was able to study it in its manuscript original at the Highland Archive Centre in Inverness. Ostensibly a book of letters of family and business interest, this is a magnificent document of a life lived as history evolves and plays out around it, and the inimitable bailie emerges, querulous, suspicious, crafty and witty, from its pages. It is known that the bailie was a Jacobite who had indeed travelled to Boulogne in 1751 in a fruitless attempt to obtain a pension from the French, and while it is possible to take his letters at face value as containing only family and business concerns, they can also be read in quite another way which suggests to me that, as far as preparations for a rising in the 1750s were concerned, Bailie John Steuart was up to his neck in it.

That rising, the Elibank rising, did not take place. The plans were indeed betrayed to the British government by a spy named Pickle, embedded in Prince Charles Edward Stuart's circle. The principal victim of this betrayal was Dr Archibald Cameron, brother of Cameron of Lochiel. Dr Cameron was arrested in the spring of 1753 on his way to raise the clans for the rising that had been postponed from November of 1752. Imprisoned and tried for treason, he was put to death at Tyburn on 7 June, 1753, the last Jacobite to be executed for the cause. Historians are still not utterly certain as to the identity of this 'Pickle', but the arguments of Andrew Lang in his 1897 work, *Pickle the Spy*, that he was Alasdair Ruadh Macdonell, Young Glengarry, are persuasive.

The story of Richard Dempster, Iain's assistant in this book, is based on the true story of Charles Deacon, son of a Manchester physician and divine who, along with his two older brothers, joined the Jacobite army's 'Manchester Regiment'. All three were taken prisoner at Carlisle; Robert died in Kendal gaol while Thomas, the eldest, and Charles, the youngest, were shipped to London for trial. Thomas was condemned to be hanged, drawn and quartered, and his head to be put on public display in Manchester. Charles, spared execution because of his youth, was ordered to watch the savagery. The experience provoked a breakdown. Sadly, he did not recover to find some sort of peace as my fictional Richard Dempster does; rather he was sentenced to two years' imprisonment in an English gaol then transportation for life. He died two days after reaching Jamaica in April of 1749.

At every turn in the Jacobite story, you will find tales of the courage and agency of women. The Grandes Dames are products of my imagination, but their lives and experiences are based on those of the many real women who feature in the history of the Jacobite cause. These women's voices can be heard in the pages of *The Lyon in Mourning* and their stories are told with warmth and verve in Maggie Craig's *Damn' Rebel Bitches: The Women of the '45*, the book's main title taken from what Cumberland had to say about them. Amongst other stories told is that of Lady Anne Mackintosh, née Farquharson, who raised Clan Chattan in support of Prince Charles Edward Stuart and in defiance of her husband, chief of the Mackintoshes, who held a commission in the Black Watch of the government's army. Years after Culloden, Lady Anne found herself partnered with the Duke of Cumberland on the dance floor. She would only dance with him on condition of being allowed to pick one of the tunes, and the tune she picked was the Jacobite favourite, 'Auld Stuart's Back Again'. This provided the germ of the idea for the scene in my book in which Julia Rose dances with Captain Dunne to 'Johnnie Cope'. Many recordings of Johnnie Cope are available, but my favourite, and the one to which the scene was written, is by Ceolbeg. Despite the best efforts of the Duke of Cumberland, Highland culture remains vibrant, and the 'Flyting of the Fiddlers' scene in this book was inspired by and written to the accompaniment of the tune 'Dizzy Blue', composed and played by 21st-century Highland fiddler, Duncan Chisholm. Father Mel Langille, Episcopalian priest and bagpiper extraordinaire, kindly checked over my Gaelic - any remaining errors or inconsistencies are my own.

The story of Ishbel MacLeod is again fictional, but it

is rooted in the fact that MacLeod of MacLeod and Mac-Donald of Sleat in the 1740s connived in the kidnap of their own people off beaches and hillsides and the selling of women and children into indentured servitude in North America. The involvement of Scots and Highlanders in the North American and Caribbean trade, increasingly as agents rather than victims, would greatly accelerate in the years following Culloden. This involvement, and the impact on the Highlands of profits generated by slave-ownership have begun to be publicly acknowledged in recent years and form the subject of several ongoing studies. As I write, Dr David Alston's *Slaves and Highlanders: Silenced Histories of Scotland and the Caribbean* has just been published. The character of Ishbel's son Tormod anticipates the children of mixed race who begin to appear, if fleetingly, in memoirs of Highland life in the late eighteenth and early nineteenth century. Documents studied by Lorna Steele of the Highland Archive Centre, and discussed in her lockdown YouTube talk of 17 September 2020, show that these tended to be the children of white male planters and enslaved or previously enslaved women of colour, the children being brought home and acknowledged, the mothers being left in the Caribbean. The Statutes of Virginia of November 1753 make clear what would have been the fate of any white woman servant becoming pregnant by a black slave, and of her child. The fate of the father is not specified.

I finally made the decision to write this book in June of 2020, as the world was beginning to open up a little, before it shut down again. Writing a book so close to home had its advantages – I could do much of my research on foot, or by bike. My friend, historical biographer Jennifer Morag Henderson, came with me up Tomnahurich, around Craig Phadrig and to the old Greyfriars kirkyard in Inverness, and told me stories. Professor David Worthington of the University of the Highlands and Islands joined us in search of a particular cave in the hills above Loch Ness. We didn't find the cave, but had good conversation and a very enjoyable day regardless. I was fortunate that by the summer of 2021, restrictions had lifted sufficiently for me to be able to visit Castle Leod, seat of the Clan Mackenzie. I'm very grateful to the Earl and Countess of Cromartie for being so welcoming to me – for the Mackenzies did get back their castle, and they have kept it – and to Dr Jonathan MacCall for explaining the castle's many interesting features with his accustomed enthusiasm and gusto.

In spite of all that, though, I have found this the hardest of my books to write. It had its origins in the idea that the ghosts of those who suffered so badly after the battle still haunt the site where Leakey's bookshop now stands, but working on it recalled to me again and again the loss of those who'd seemed somehow more than a generation closer to Culloden, and who were no longer here for me to ask things. Most of all there was my father, a native Gaelic-speaker born close to Drummossie Moor, who had first taken me to Culloden and to Clava Cairns. He grew up with his brothers, those 'boys from the manse', in Strathnairn.

Inside Dunlichity church is a memorial panel to my grandfather, who was minister there in the 1920s and 30s. My uncle Lachlan died tragically young, but the other three boys grew up to go through their own war. This book will come out in 2022, the centenary of the birth of my father's brother Alistair, 'the minister's son who was always telling stories', and who, despite going on to tell stories that entertained millions the world over, remained, essentially, a Highlander. And then there was Angus Cameron of Roy Bridge, 'Uncle Angie', shopkeeper, coalman, Gael, and Lovat scout, who knew the hills of Lochaber like the back of his hand and who could tell you stories of Prince Charlie's wanderings as if they had happened last week. They were all gone by the time I started to write this book, but I felt them with me and regretted their loss all through it.

Shona MacLean, Conon Bridge, October 2021.

Acknowledgements

I would like to thank everyone at my publisher, Quercus, for their continuing hard work and support throughout all the difficulties of the pandemic, and for the magnificent way they and the printers, distributors and booksellers have risen to what must have been a huge logistical challenge. Thank you to Liz Hatherell for her eagle-eyed, light-touch copyedit, thank you to Nicola Howell Hawley for the careful proofread, to Ella Patel in publicity for somehow still getting me places either virtually or in person, to Lipfon Tang in marketing for keeping a bewildered author straight on matters technological, and especially to my editor Jane Wood, and her assistant, Florence Hare. Flo has done confidence and morale no end of good with a kind word here and an efficient 'dealing with' of things there. Jane has guided me through ten books now, and with patience, tact, and a degree of determination, made them much better books than they would otherwise have been. Thank you all.